VALHALLA MAD

Image Comics, Berkeley, CA

www.manofaction.tv

Valhalla Mad

First printing. February 2016.

ISBN: 978-1-63215-602-0

For international licensing inquiries, write to:
foreignlicensing@imagecomics.com

Printed in the USA.

For information regarding the CPSIA on this
printed material call: 203-595-3636 and provide
reference #RICH-667096.

Joe Casey
writer

Paul Maybury
artist & colorist

Sonia Harris
graphic designer
logo, covers, interstitial pages

Rus Wooton
letterer

flats
Chuck Knigge & Yesflats

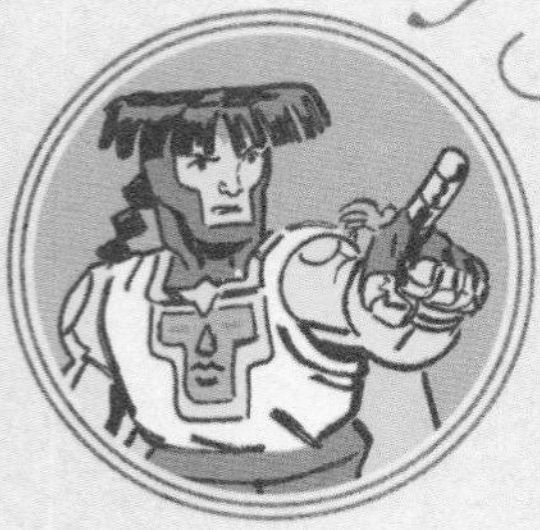

GREGHORN
THE BATTLEBJÖRN!

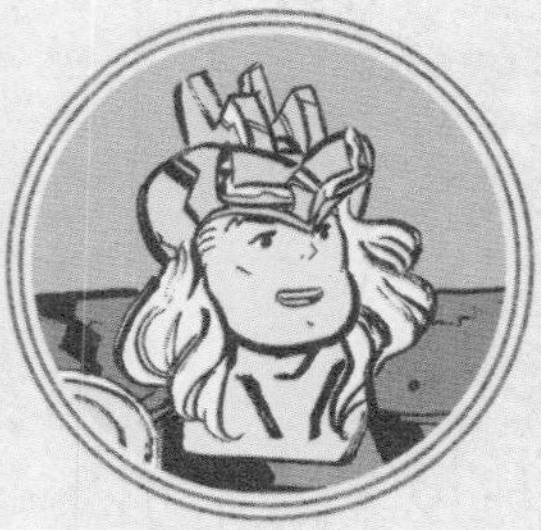

THE GLORIOUS
KNOX!

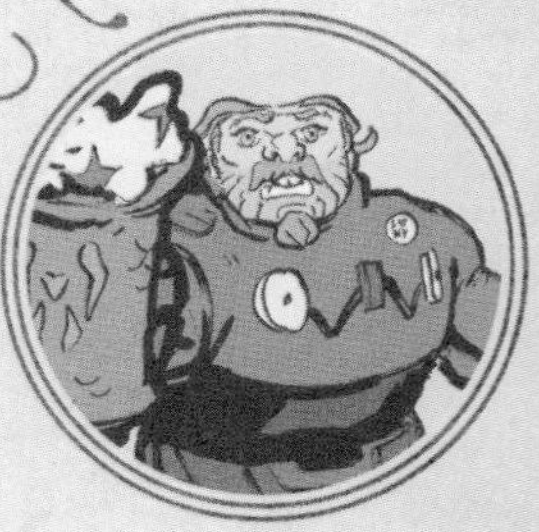

JHAGO
THE IRRITATOR!

JOE CASEY & PAUL MAYBURY

ISSUE NUMBER ONE
THREE DOLLARS AND FIFTY CENTS

CHAPTER

1

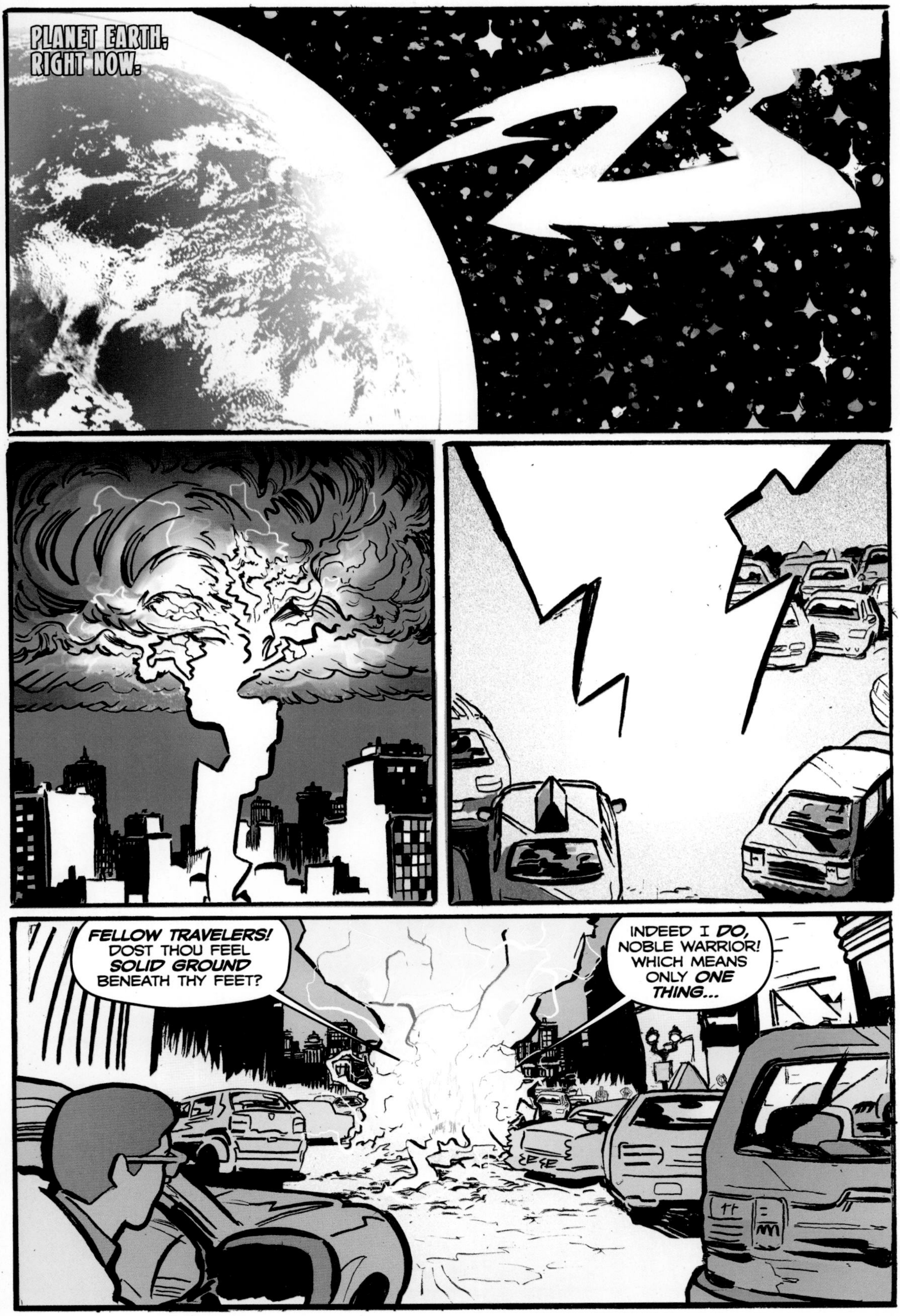
PLANET EARTH;
RIGHT NOW:
FELLOW TRAVELERS! DOST THOU FEEL SOLID GROUND BENEATH THY FEET?
INDEED I DO, NOBLE WARRIOR! WHICH MEANS ONLY ONE THING...

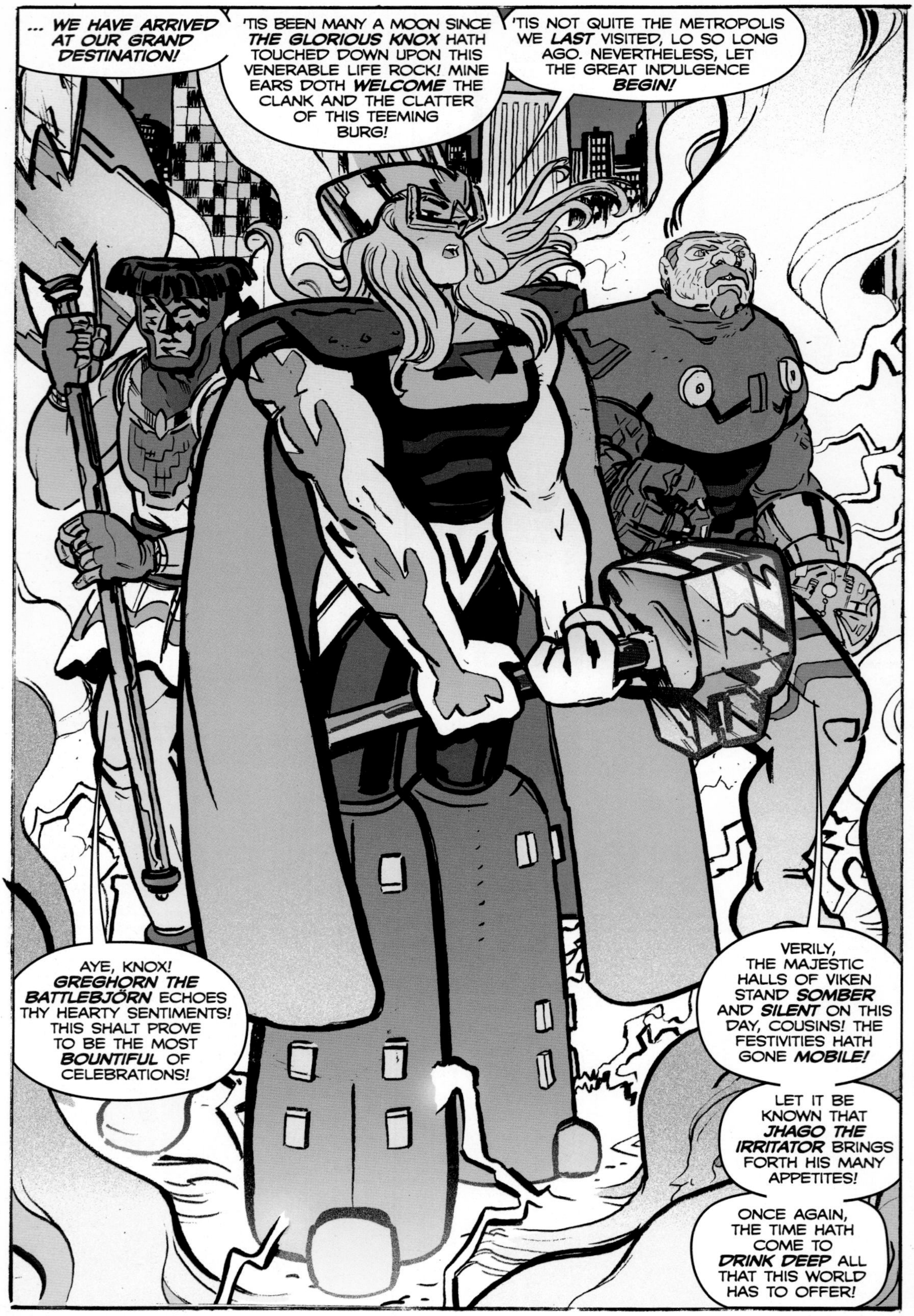
... WE HAVE ARRIVED AT OUR GRAND DESTINATION!
'TIS BEEN MANY A MOON SINCE THE GLORIOUS KNOX HATH TOUCHED DOWN UPON THIS VENERABLE LIFE ROCK! MINE EARS DOTH WELCOME THE CLANK AND THE CLATTER OF THIS TEEMING BURG!
'TIS NOT QUITE THE METROPOLIS WE LAST VISITED, LO SO LONG AGO. NEVERTHELESS, LET THE GREAT INDULGENCE BEGIN!
AYE, KNOX! GREGHORN THE BATTLEBJÖRN ECHOES THY HEARTY SENTIMENTS! THIS SHALT PROVE TO BE THE MOST BOUNTIFUL OF CELEBRATIONS!
VERILY, THE MAJESTIC HALLS OF VIKEN STAND SOMBER AND SILENT ON THIS DAY, COUSINS! THE FESTIVITIES HATH GONE MOBILE!
LET IT BE KNOWN THAT JHAGO THE IRRITATOR BRINGS FORTH HIS MANY APPETITES!
ONCE AGAIN, THE TIME HATH COME TO DRINK DEEP ALL THAT THIS WORLD HAS TO OFFER!

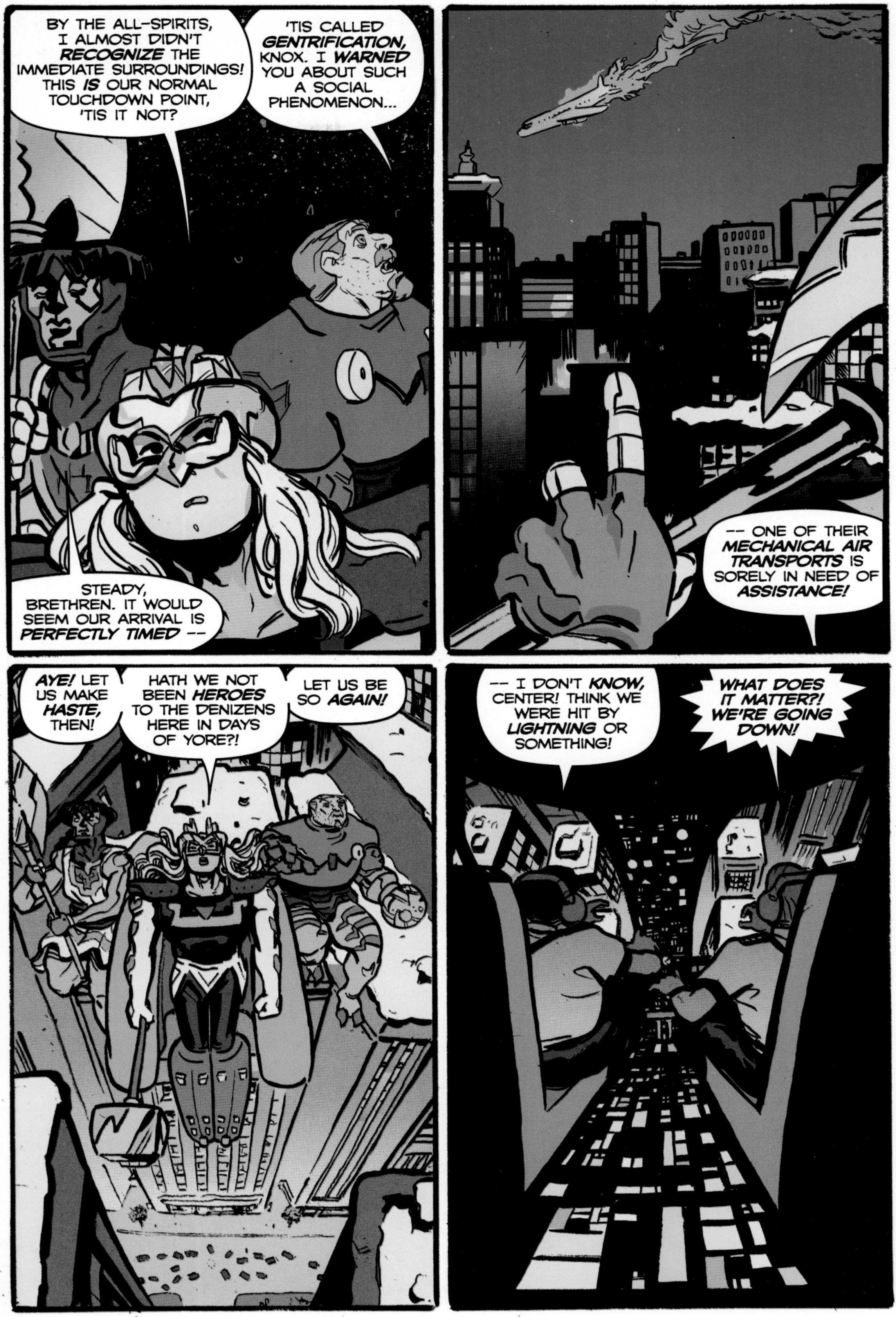
BY THE ALL-SPIRITS, I ALMOST DIDN'T RECOGNIZE THE IMMEDIATE SURROUNDINGS! THIS IS OUR NORMAL TOUCHDOWN POINT, 'TIS IT NOT?
'TIS CALLED GENTRIFICATION, KNOX. I WARNED YOU ABOUT SUCH A SOCIAL PHENOMENON...
STEADY, BRETHREN. IT WOULD SEEM OUR ARRIVAL IS PERFECTLY TIMED --
-- ONE OF THEIR MECHANICAL AIR TRANSPORTS IS SORELY IN NEED OF ASSISTANCE!
AYE! LET US MAKE HASTE, THEN!
HATH WE NOT BEEN HEROES TO THE DENIZENS HERE IN DAYS OF YORE?!
LET US BE SO AGAIN!
-- I DON'T KNOW, CENTER! THINK WE WERE HIT BY LIGHTNING OR SOMETHING!
WHAT DOES IT MATTER?! WE'RE GOING DOWN!

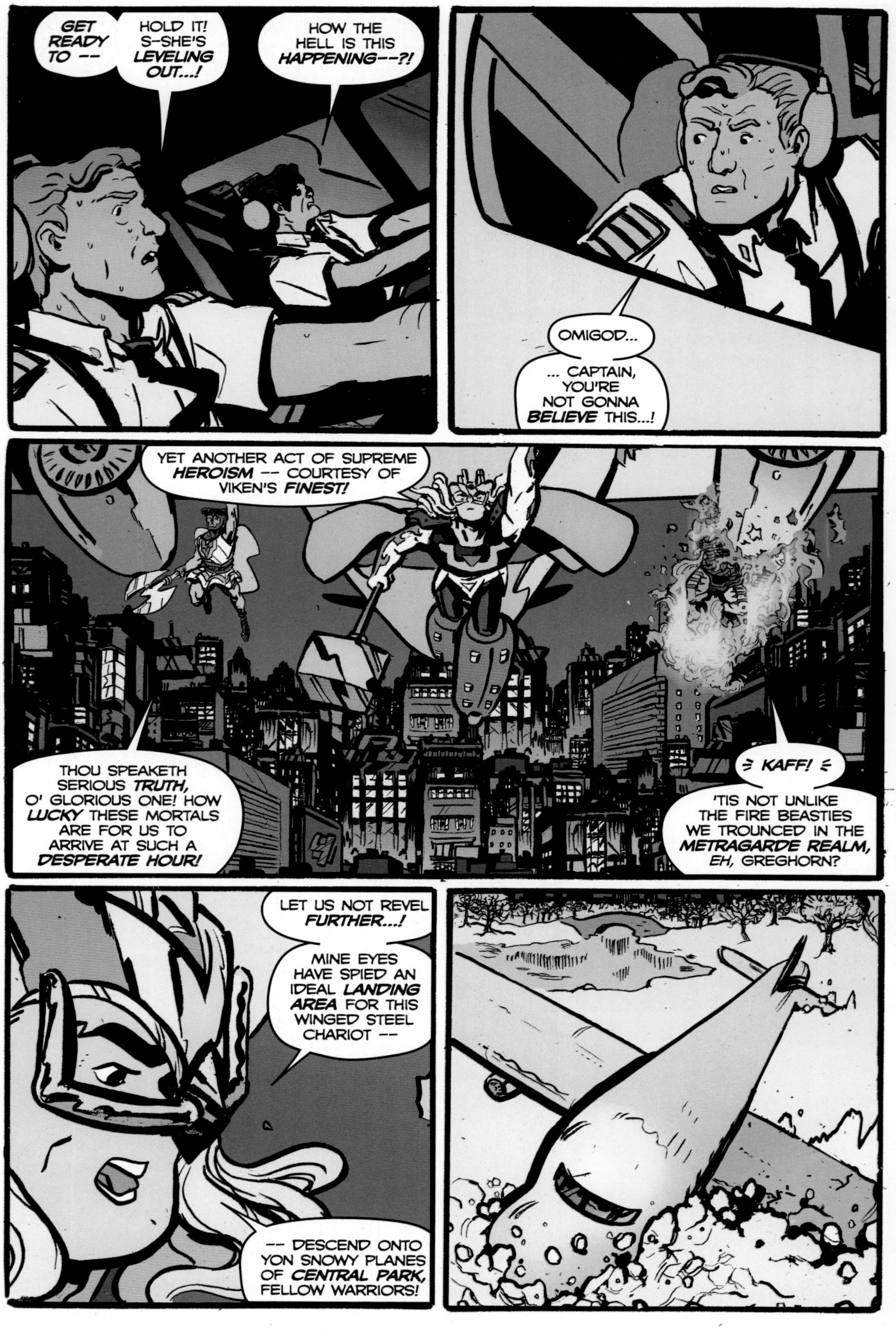
GET READY TO --
HOLD IT! S-SHE'S LEVELING OUT...!
HOW THE HELL IS THIS HAPPENING--?!
OMIGOD...
... CAPTAIN, YOU'RE NOT GONNA BELIEVE THIS...!
YET ANOTHER ACT OF SUPREME HEROISM -- COURTESY OF VIKEN'S FINEST!
THOU SPEAKETH SERIOUS TRUTH, O' GLORIOUS ONE! HOW LUCKY THESE MORTALS ARE FOR US TO ARRIVE AT SUCH A DESPERATE HOUR!
KAFF!
'TIS NOT UNLIKE THE FIRE BEASTIES WE TROUNCED IN THE METRAGARDE REALM, EH, GREGHORN?
LET US NOT REVEL FURTHER...!
MINE EYES HAVE SPIED AN IDEAL LANDING AREA FOR THIS WINGED STEEL CHARIOT --
-- DESCEND ONTO YON SNOWY PLANES OF CENTRAL PARK, FELLOW WARRIORS!

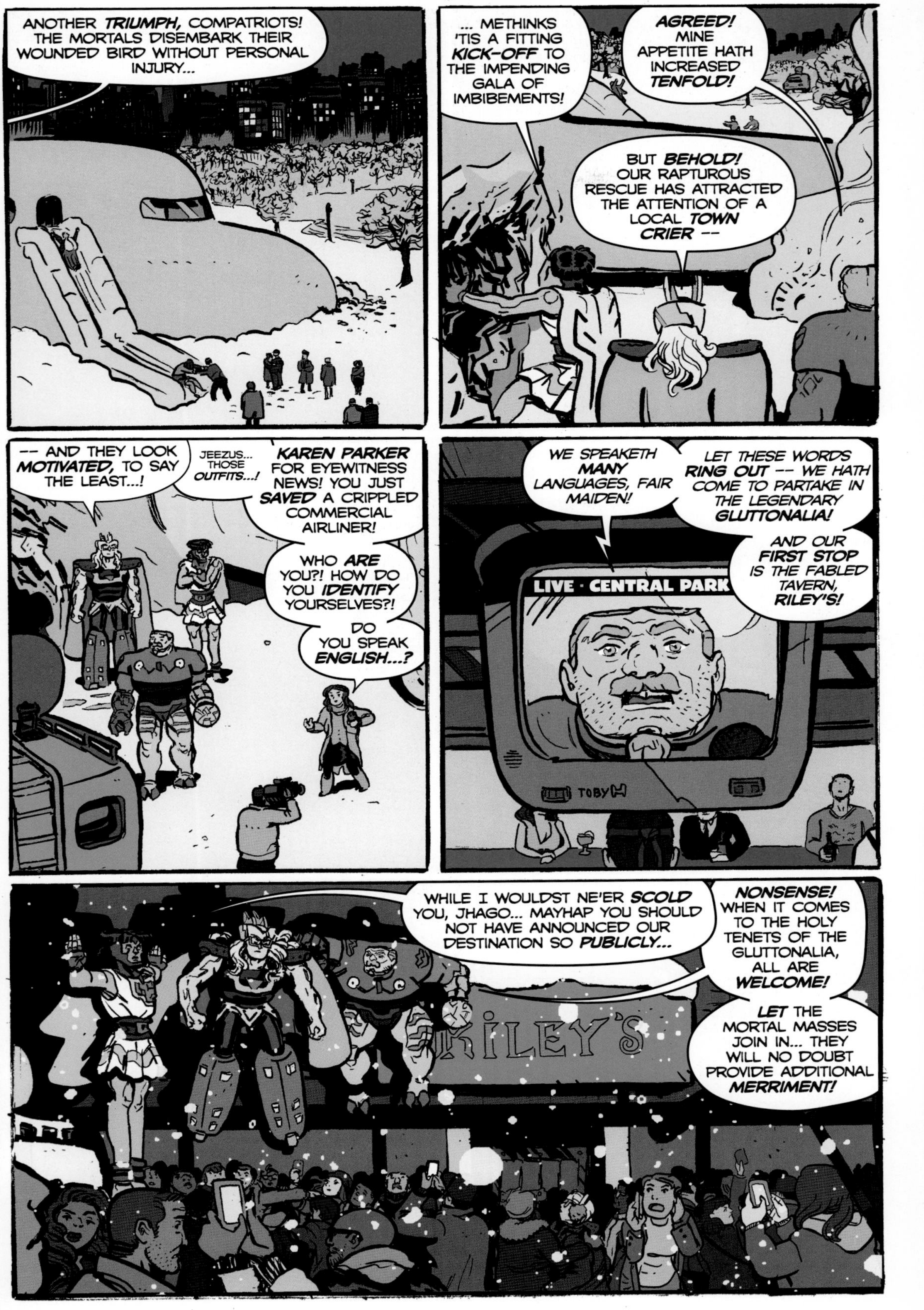
ANOTHER TRIUMPH, COMPATRIOTS! THE MORTALS DISEMBARK THEIR WOUNDED BIRD WITHOUT PERSONAL INJURY...
... METHINKS 'TIS A FITTING KICK-OFF TO THE IMPENDING GALA OF IMBIBEMENTS!
AGREED! MINE APPETITE HATH INCREASED TENFOLD!
BUT BEHOLD! OUR RAPTUROUS RESCUE HAS ATTRACTED THE ATTENTION OF A LOCAL TOWN CRIER --
-- AND THEY LOOK MOTIVATED, TO SAY THE LEAST...!
JEEZUS... THOSE OUTFITS...!
KAREN PARKER FOR EYEWITNESS NEWS! YOU JUST SAVED A CRIPPLED COMMERCIAL AIRLINER!
WHO ARE YOU?! HOW DO YOU IDENTIFY YOURSELVES?!
DO YOU SPEAK ENGLISH...?
WE SPEAKETH MANY LANGUAGES, FAIR MAIDEN!
LET THESE WORDS RING OUT -- WE HATH COME TO PARTAKE IN THE LEGENDARY GLUTTONALIA!
AND OUR FIRST STOP IS THE FABLED TAVERN, RILEY'S!
LIVE · CENTRAL PARK
TOBY
WHILE I WOULDST NE'ER SCOLD YOU, JHAGO... MAYHAP YOU SHOULD NOT HAVE ANNOUNCED OUR DESTINATION SO PUBLICLY...
NONSENSE! WHEN IT COMES TO THE HOLY TENETS OF THE GLUTTONALIA, ALL ARE WELCOME!
LET THE MORTAL MASSES JOIN IN... THEY WILL NO DOUBT PROVIDE ADDITIONAL MERRIMENT!
RILEY'S

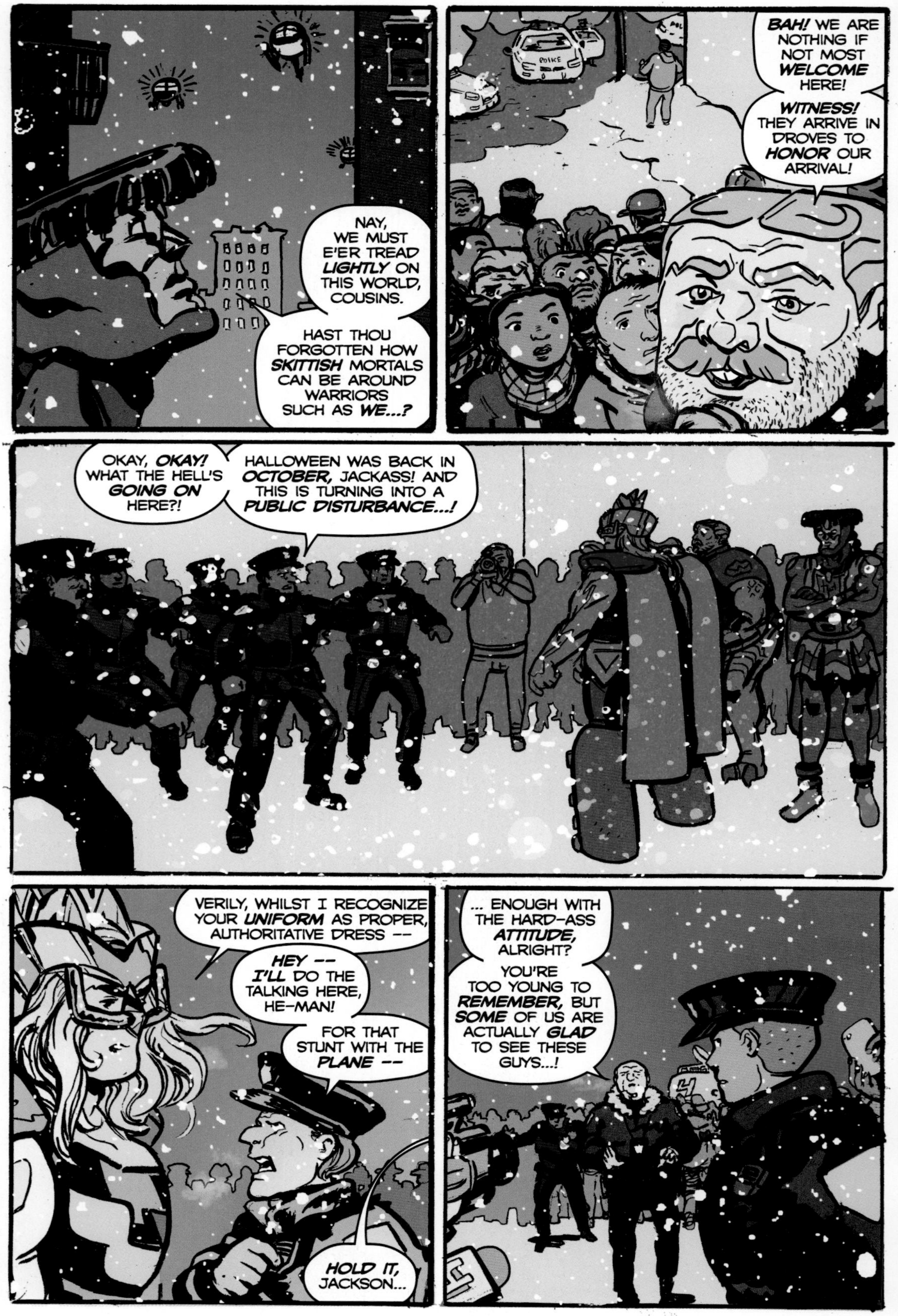
NAY, WE MUST E'ER TREAD LIGHTLY ON THIS WORLD, COUSINS.
HAST THOU FORGOTTEN HOW SKITTISH MORTALS CAN BE AROUND WARRIORS SUCH AS WE...?
POLICE
BAH! WE ARE NOTHING IF NOT MOST WELCOME HERE!
WITNESS! THEY ARRIVE IN DROVES TO HONOR OUR ARRIVAL!
OKAY, OKAY! WHAT THE HELL'S GOING ON HERE?!
HALLOWEEN WAS BACK IN OCTOBER, JACKASS! AND THIS IS TURNING INTO A PUBLIC DISTURBANCE...!
VERILY, WHILST I RECOGNIZE YOUR UNIFORM AS PROPER, AUTHORITATIVE DRESS --
HEY -- I'LL DO THE TALKING HERE, HE-MAN!
FOR THAT STUNT WITH THE PLANE --
HOLD IT, JACKSON...
... ENOUGH WITH THE HARD-ASS ATTITUDE, ALRIGHT?
YOU'RE TOO YOUNG TO REMEMBER, BUT SOME OF US ARE ACTUALLY GLAD TO SEE THESE GUYS...!

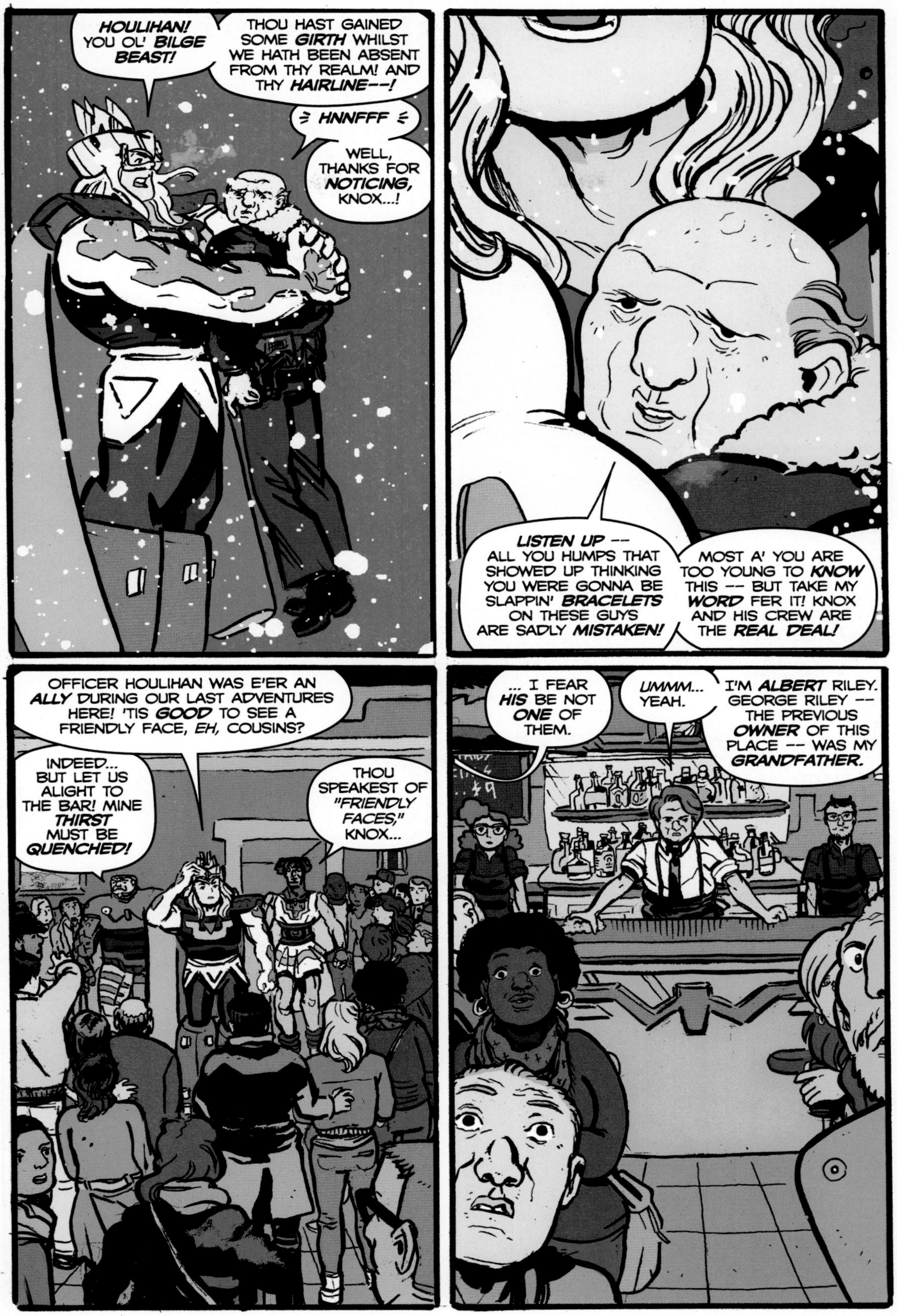
HOULIHAN! YOU OL' BILGE BEAST!
THOU HAST GAINED SOME GIRTH WHILST WE HATH BEEN ABSENT FROM THY REALM! AND THY HAIRLINE--!
HNNFFF
WELL, THANKS FOR NOTICING, KNOX...!
LISTEN UP -- ALL YOU HUMPS THAT SHOWED UP THINKING YOU WERE GONNA BE SLAPPIN' BRACELETS ON THESE GUYS ARE SADLY MISTAKEN!
MOST A' YOU ARE TOO YOUNG TO KNOW THIS -- BUT TAKE MY WORD FER IT! KNOX AND HIS CREW ARE THE REAL DEAL!
OFFICER HOULIHAN WAS E'ER AN ALLY DURING OUR LAST ADVENTURES HERE! 'TIS GOOD TO SEE A FRIENDLY FACE, EH, COUSINS?
INDEED... BUT LET US ALIGHT TO THE BAR! MINE THIRST MUST BE QUENCHED!
THOU SPEAKEST OF "FRIENDLY FACES," KNOX...
... I FEAR HIS BE NOT ONE OF THEM.
UMMM... YEAH.
I'M ALBERT RILEY. GEORGE RILEY -- THE PREVIOUS OWNER OF THIS PLACE -- WAS MY GRANDFATHER.

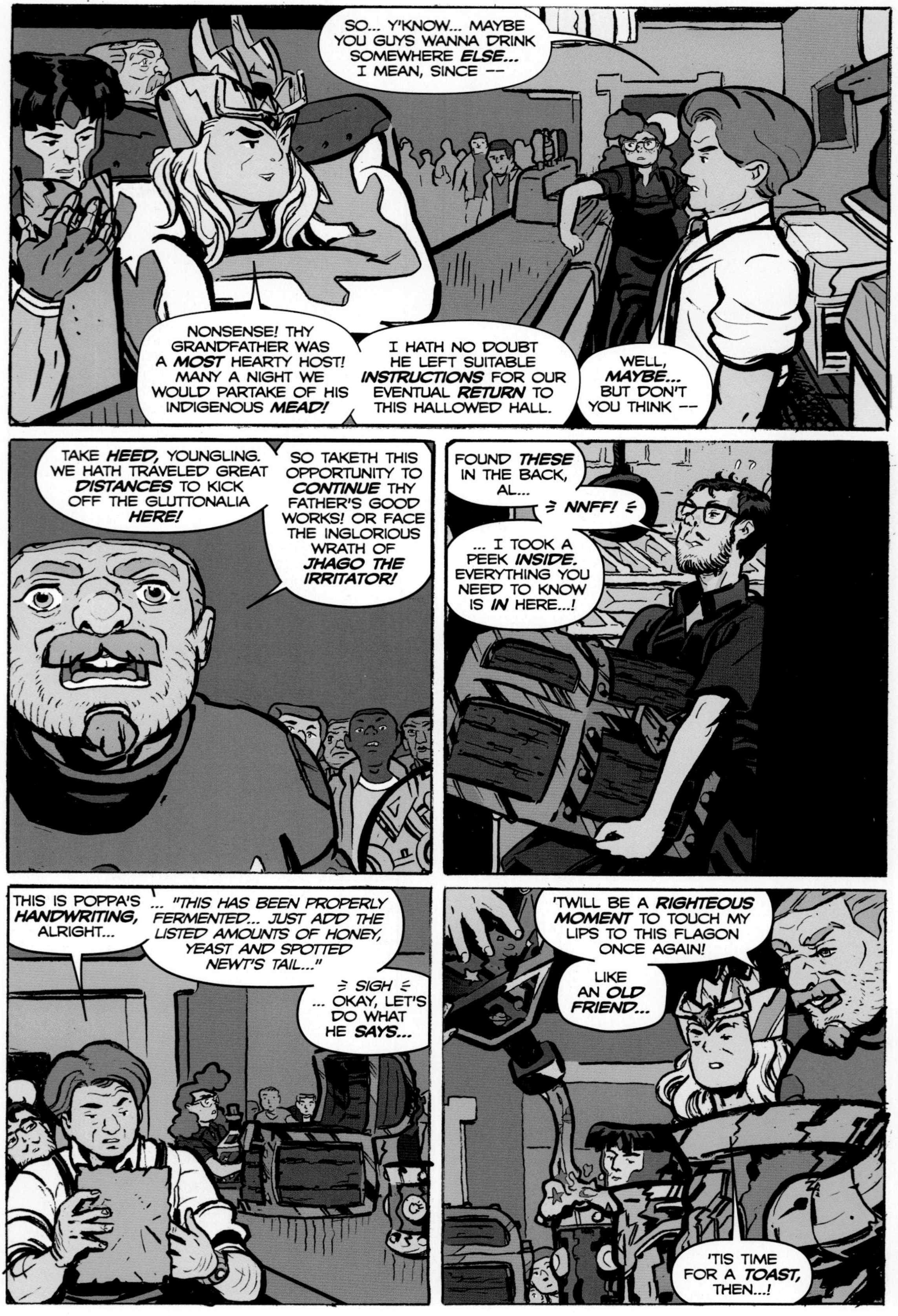
SO... Y'KNOW... MAYBE YOU GUYS WANNA DRINK SOMEWHERE ELSE... I MEAN, SINCE --
NONSENSE! THY GRANDFATHER WAS A MOST HEARTY HOST! MANY A NIGHT WE WOULD PARTAKE OF HIS INDIGENOUS MEAD!
I HATH NO DOUBT HE LEFT SUITABLE INSTRUCTIONS FOR OUR EVENTUAL RETURN TO THIS HALLOWED HALL.
WELL, MAYBE... BUT DON'T YOU THINK --
TAKE HEED, YOUNGLING. WE HATH TRAVELED GREAT DISTANCES TO KICK OFF THE GLUTTONALIA HERE!
SO TAKETH THIS OPPORTUNITY TO CONTINUE THY FATHER'S GOOD WORKS! OR FACE THE INGLORIOUS WRATH OF JHAGO THE IRRITATOR!
FOUND THESE IN THE BACK, AL...
NNFF!
... I TOOK A PEEK INSIDE. EVERYTHING YOU NEED TO KNOW IS IN HERE...!
THIS IS POPPA'S HANDWRITING, ALRIGHT...
... "THIS HAS BEEN PROPERLY FERMENTED... JUST ADD THE LISTED AMOUNTS OF HONEY, YEAST AND SPOTTED NEWT'S TAIL..."
SIGH
... OKAY, LET'S DO WHAT HE SAYS...
'TWILL BE A RIGHTEOUS MOMENT TO TOUCH MY LIPS TO THIS FLAGON ONCE AGAIN!
LIKE AN OLD FRIEND...
'TIS TIME FOR A TOAST, THEN...!

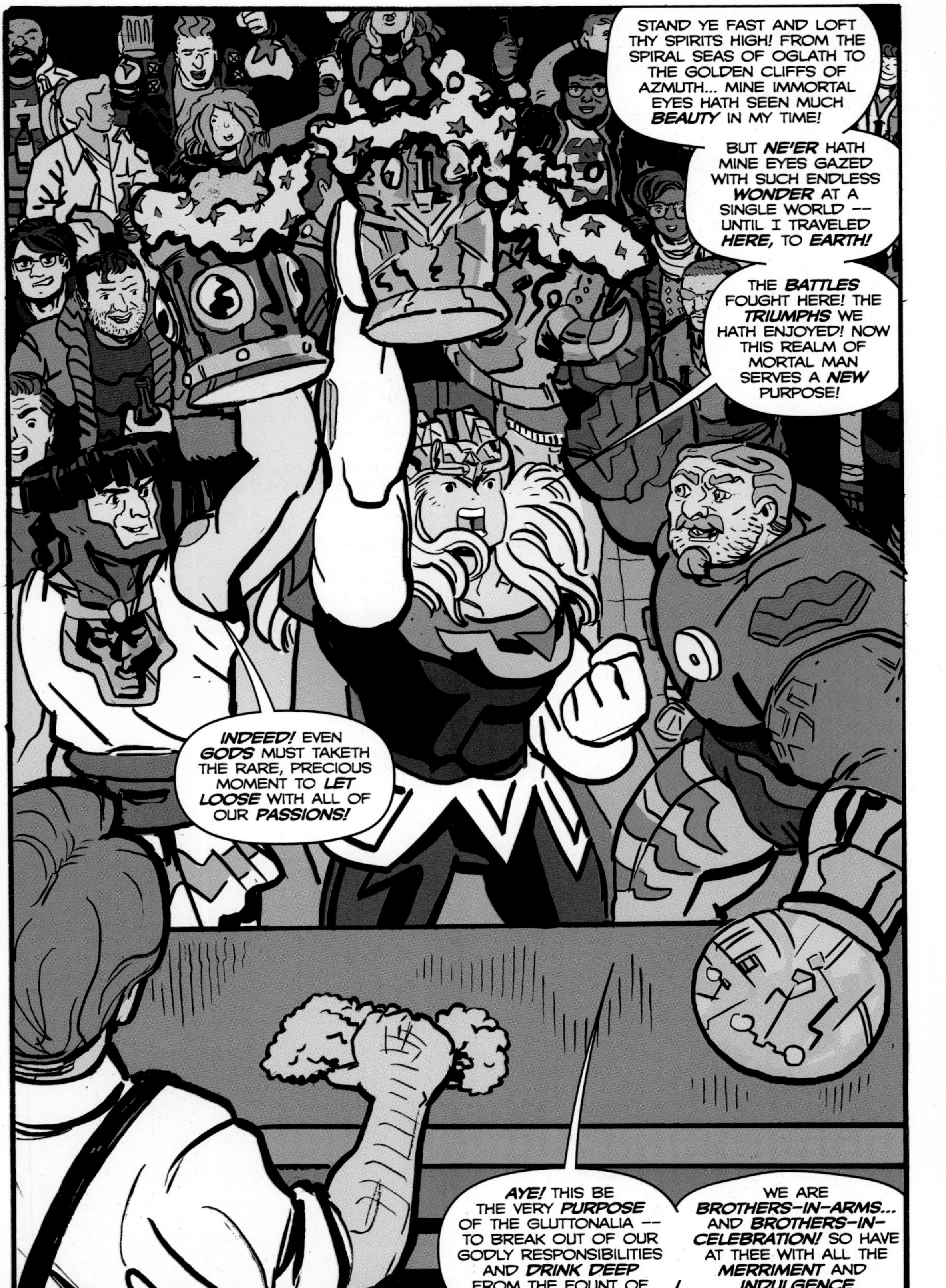

STAND YE FAST AND LOFT THY SPIRITS HIGH! FROM THE SPIRAL SEAS OF OGLATH TO THE GOLDEN CLIFFS OF AZMUTH... MINE IMMORTAL EYES HATH SEEN MUCH BEAUTY IN MY TIME!
BUT NE'ER HATH MINE EYES GAZED WITH SUCH ENDLESS WONDER AT A SINGLE WORLD -- UNTIL I TRAVELED HERE, TO EARTH!
THE BATTLES FOUGHT HERE! THE TRIUMPHS WE HATH ENJOYED! NOW THIS REALM OF MORTAL MAN SERVES A NEW PURPOSE!
INDEED! EVEN GODS MUST TAKETH THE RARE, PRECIOUS MOMENT TO LET LOOSE WITH ALL OF OUR PASSIONS!
AYE! THIS BE THE VERY PURPOSE OF THE GLUTTONALIA -- TO BREAK OUT OF OUR GODLY RESPONSIBILITIES AND DRINK DEEP FROM THE FOUNT OF LIFE ITSELF!
WE ARE BROTHERS-IN-ARMS... AND BROTHERS-IN-CELEBRATION! SO HAVE AT THEE WITH ALL THE MERRIMENT AND INDULGENCE THOU CAN MUSTER!

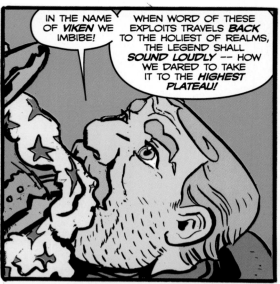

IN THE NAME OF *VIKEN* WE IMBIBE!

WHEN WORD OF THESE EXPLOITS TRAVELS *BACK* TO THE HOLIEST OF REALMS, THE LEGEND SHALL *SOUND LOUDLY* -- HOW WE DARED TO TAKE IT TO THE *HIGHEST PLATEAU!*

'TIS AN ART FORM ALL ITS *OWN* TO EMBRACE SUCH MIGHTY HEDONISM!

I'LL GLADLY DRINK TO *THAT*, O' GLORIOUS ONE!

YOU GUYS... I THINK ONE OF MY GREAT *UNCLES* TOLD ME ABOUT YOU...!

BUT THE THINGS HE *SAID*... I JUST THOUGHT HE WAS *SENILE* OR SOMETHING...!

HA!

SAFE TO SAY YOU'RE NOT *FROM* AROUND HERE, ARE YOU...?

SUCH AN *UNDERSTATEMENT!* THOU HAST NO *IDEA*, YOUNG SQUIRE!

WHERE *WE* HAIL FROM... THOU HAST NOT THE *PERCEPTIONS* TO EVEN CONCEIVE E'EN AN *IOTA* OF ITS GRANDEUR!

FORGIVE JHAGO'S *BLUSTER*, MORTALS. HE *LIVES* FOR THE GLUTTONALIA... PERHAPS TO A *FAULT*.

BUT ALLOW *ME* TO *ENLIGHTEN* YOU WHILST I ATTEMPT TO *DESCRIBE* WHAT IS MAYHAP *INDESCRIBABLE!* FOR NOW...

... CLEAR YOUR MINDS OF ANYTHING THAT EARTHLY *SCIENCE* HAS PROVEN, FOR THERE EXISTS AN ETERNAL REALM *BEYOND* ALL IMAGINATION!

'TIS A REALM OF *IMMORTAL MAGIC!* 'TIS A PLACE WHERE *GODS* ARE SPAWNED!

IT HAS A NAME *REVERED* THROUGHOUT ALL OF COSMIC REALITY --

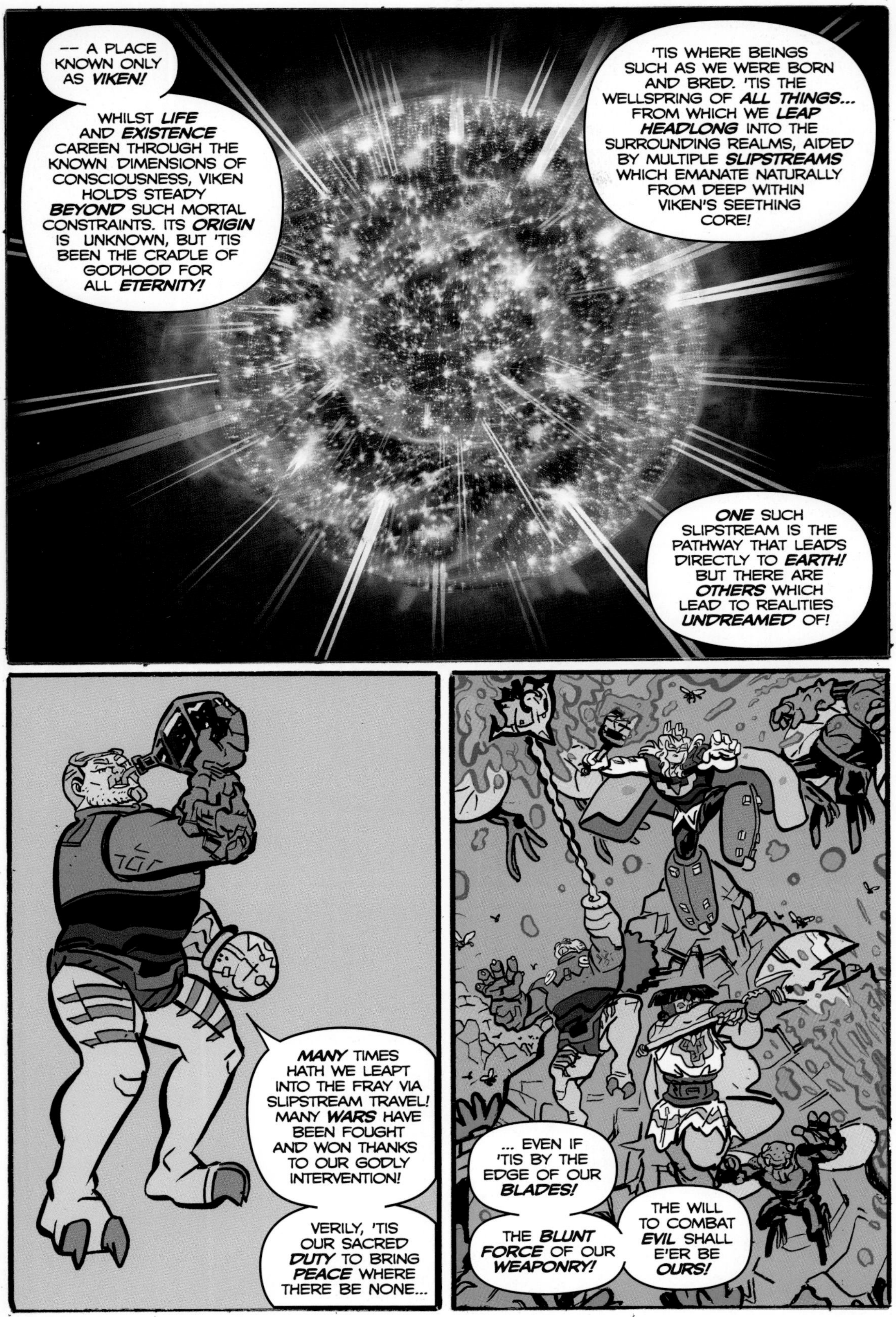
-- A PLACE KNOWN ONLY AS VIKEN!
WHILST LIFE AND EXISTENCE CAREEN THROUGH THE KNOWN DIMENSIONS OF CONSCIOUSNESS, VIKEN HOLDS STEADY BEYOND SUCH MORTAL CONSTRAINTS. ITS ORIGIN IS UNKNOWN, BUT 'TIS BEEN THE CRADLE OF GODHOOD FOR ALL ETERNITY!
'TIS WHERE BEINGS SUCH AS WE WERE BORN AND BRED. 'TIS THE WELLSPRING OF ALL THINGS... FROM WHICH WE LEAP HEADLONG INTO THE SURROUNDING REALMS, AIDED BY MULTIPLE SLIPSTREAMS WHICH EMANATE NATURALLY FROM DEEP WITHIN VIKEN'S SEETHING CORE!
ONE SUCH SLIPSTREAM IS THE PATHWAY THAT LEADS DIRECTLY TO EARTH! BUT THERE ARE OTHERS WHICH LEAD TO REALITIES UNDREAMED OF!
MANY TIMES HATH WE LEAPT INTO THE FRAY VIA SLIPSTREAM TRAVEL! MANY WARS HAVE BEEN FOUGHT AND WON THANKS TO OUR GODLY INTERVENTION!
VERILY, 'TIS OUR SACRED DUTY TO BRING PEACE WHERE THERE BE NONE...
... EVEN IF 'TIS BY THE EDGE OF OUR BLADES!
THE BLUNT FORCE OF OUR WEAPONRY!
THE WILL TO COMBAT EVIL SHALL E'ER BE OURS!

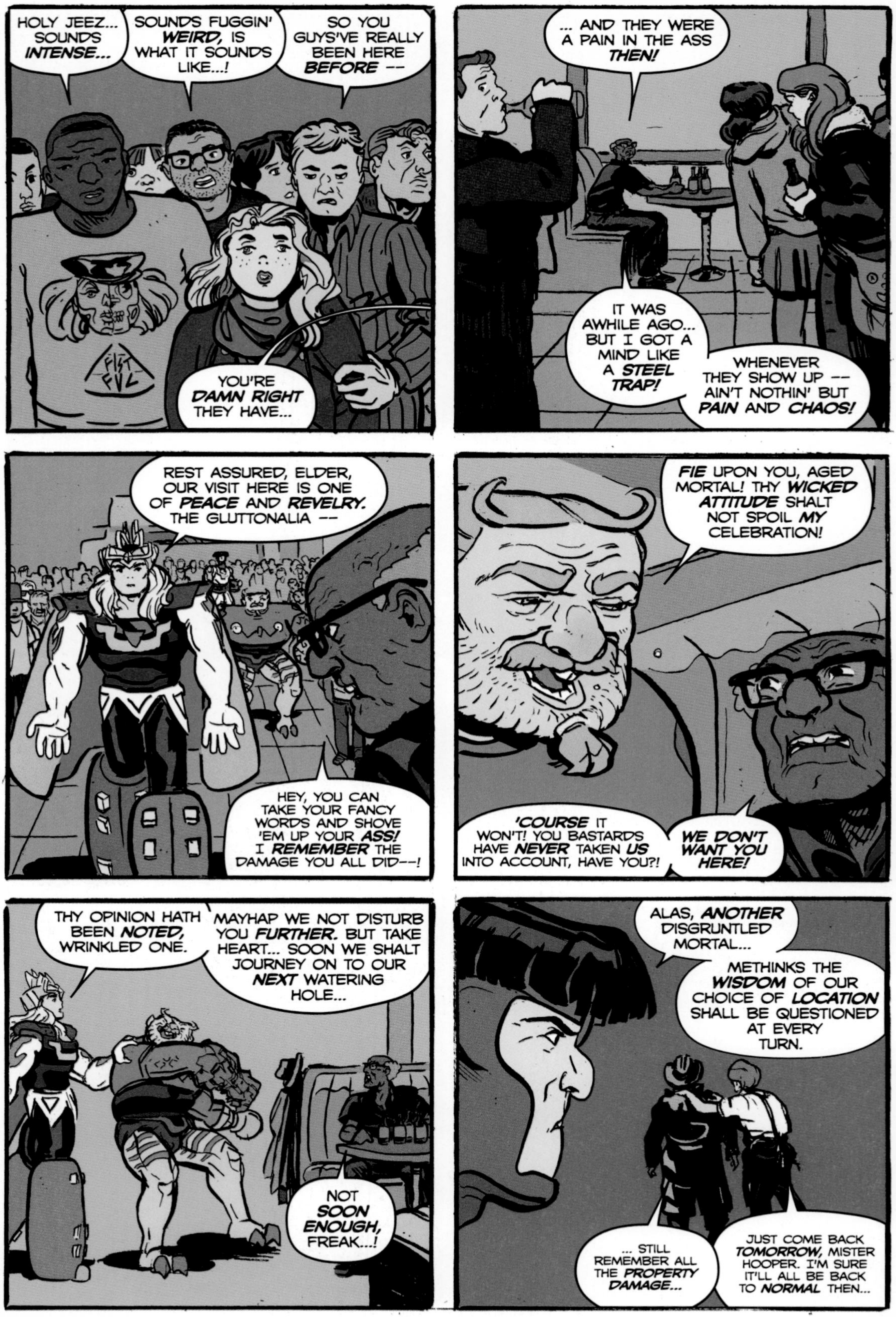
HOLY JEEZ... SOUNDS INTENSE...
SOUNDS FUGGIN' WEIRD, IS WHAT IT SOUNDS LIKE...!
SO YOU GUYS'VE REALLY BEEN HERE BEFORE --
FIST FVL
YOU'RE DAMN RIGHT THEY HAVE...
... AND THEY WERE A PAIN IN THE ASS THEN!
IT WAS AWHILE AGO... BUT I GOT A MIND LIKE A STEEL TRAP!
WHENEVER THEY SHOW UP -- AIN'T NOTHIN' BUT PAIN AND CHAOS!
REST ASSURED, ELDER, OUR VISIT HERE IS ONE OF PEACE AND REVELRY. THE GLUTTONALIA --
HEY, YOU CAN TAKE YOUR FANCY WORDS AND SHOVE 'EM UP YOUR ASS! I REMEMBER THE DAMAGE YOU ALL DID--!
FIE UPON YOU, AGED MORTAL! THY WICKED ATTITUDE SHALT NOT SPOIL MY CELEBRATION!
'COURSE IT WON'T! YOU BASTARDS HAVE NEVER TAKEN US INTO ACCOUNT, HAVE YOU?!
WE DON'T WANT YOU HERE!
THY OPINION HATH BEEN NOTED, WRINKLED ONE.
MAYHAP WE NOT DISTURB YOU FURTHER. BUT TAKE HEART... SOON WE SHALT JOURNEY ON TO OUR NEXT WATERING HOLE...
NOT SOON ENOUGH, FREAK...!
ALAS, ANOTHER DISGRUNTLED MORTAL...
METHINKS THE WISDOM OF OUR CHOICE OF LOCATION SHALL BE QUESTIONED AT EVERY TURN.
... STILL REMEMBER ALL THE PROPERTY DAMAGE...
JUST COME BACK TOMORROW, MISTER HOOPER. I'M SURE IT'LL ALL BE BACK TO NORMAL THEN...

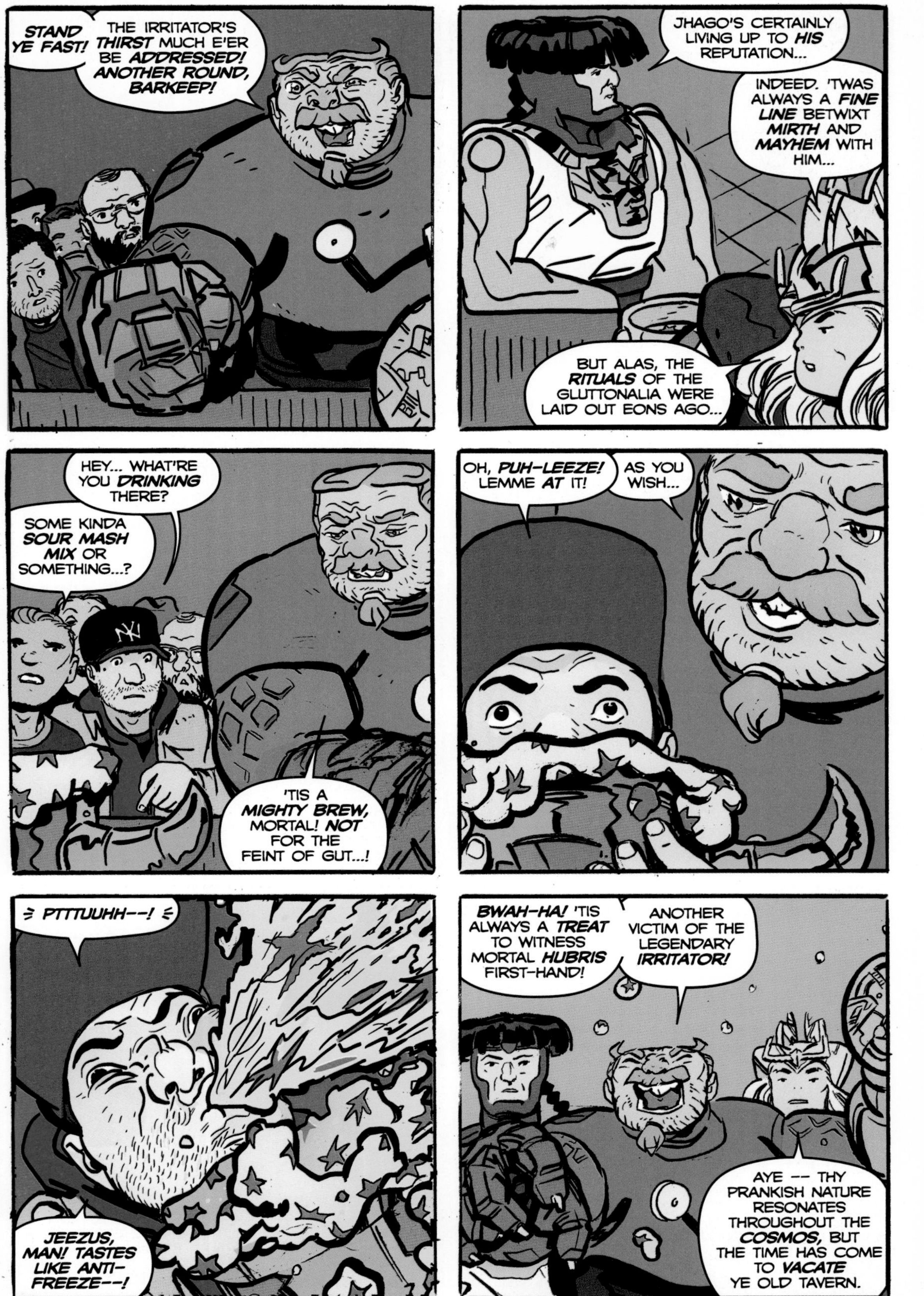
STAND YE FAST!
THE IRRITATOR'S THIRST MUCH E'ER BE ADDRESSED! ANOTHER ROUND, BARKEEP!
JHAGO'S CERTAINLY LIVING UP TO HIS REPUTATION...
INDEED. 'TWAS ALWAYS A FINE LINE BETWIXT MIRTH AND MAYHEM WITH HIM...
BUT ALAS, THE RITUALS OF THE GLUTTONALIA WERE LAID OUT EONS AGO...
HEY... WHAT'RE YOU DRINKING THERE?
SOME KINDA SOUR MASH MIX OR SOMETHING...?
'TIS A MIGHTY BREW, MORTAL! NOT FOR THE FEINT OF GUT...!
OH, PUH-LEEZE! LEMME AT IT!
AS YOU WISH...
PTTTUUHH--!
JEEZUS, MAN! TASTES LIKE ANTI-FREEZE--!
BWAH-HA! 'TIS ALWAYS A TREAT TO WITNESS MORTAL HUBRIS FIRST-HAND!
ANOTHER VICTIM OF THE LEGENDARY IRRITATOR!
AYE -- THY PRANKISH NATURE RESONATES THROUGHOUT THE COSMOS, BUT THE TIME HAS COME TO VACATE YE OLD TAVERN.

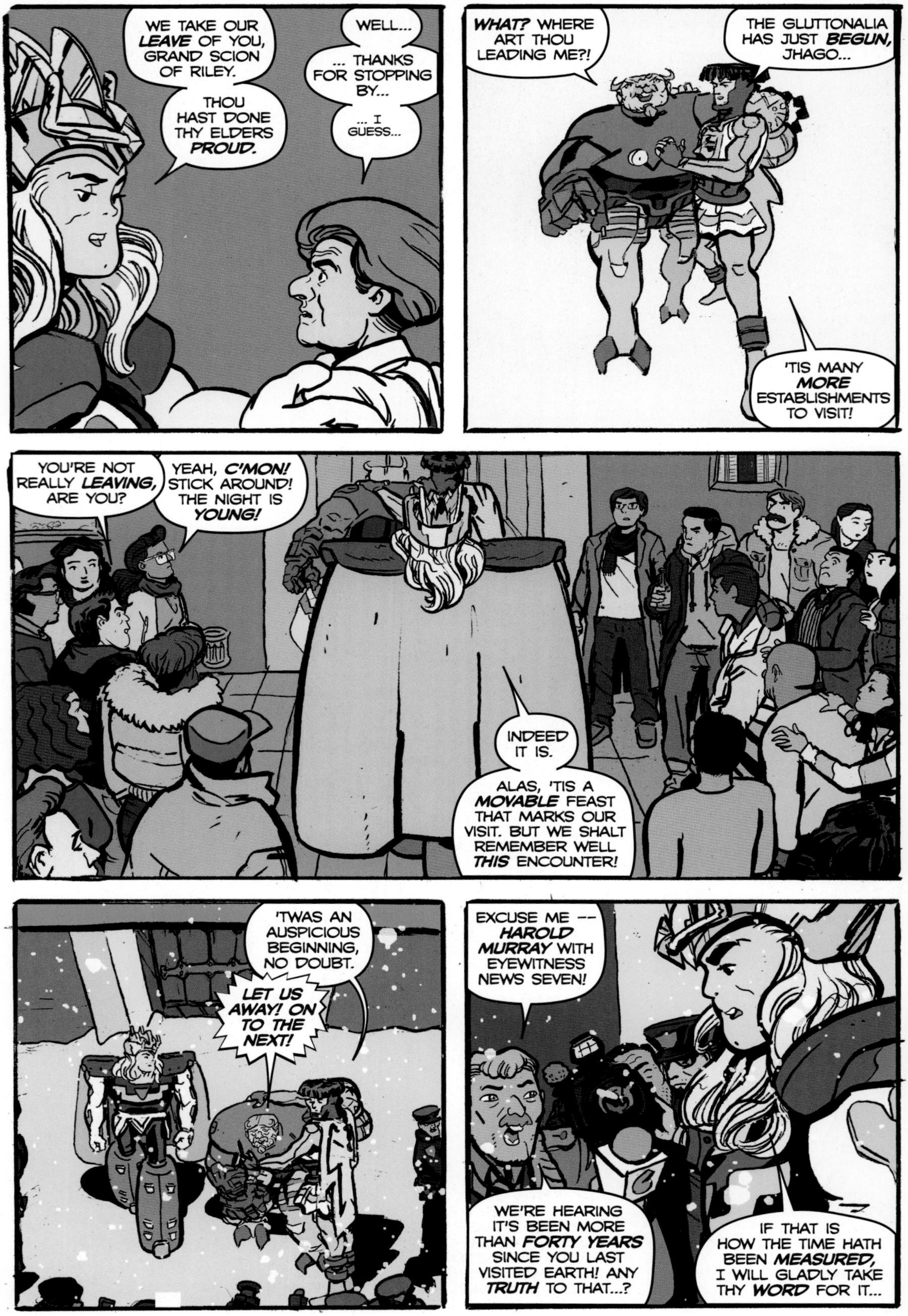
WE TAKE OUR LEAVE OF YOU, GRAND SCION OF RILEY.
THOU HAST DONE THY ELDERS PROUD.
WELL...
... THANKS FOR STOPPING BY...
... I GUESS...
WHAT? WHERE ART THOU LEADING ME?!
THE GLUTTONALIA HAS JUST BEGUN, JHAGO...
'TIS MANY MORE ESTABLISHMENTS TO VISIT!
YOU'RE NOT REALLY LEAVING, ARE YOU?
YEAH, C'MON! STICK AROUND! THE NIGHT IS YOUNG!
INDEED IT IS.
ALAS, 'TIS A MOVABLE FEAST THAT MARKS OUR VISIT. BUT WE SHALT REMEMBER WELL THIS ENCOUNTER!
'TWAS AN AUSPICIOUS BEGINNING, NO DOUBT.
LET US AWAY! ON TO THE NEXT!
EXCUSE ME -- HAROLD MURRAY WITH EYEWITNESS NEWS SEVEN!
WE'RE HEARING IT'S BEEN MORE THAN FORTY YEARS SINCE YOU LAST VISITED EARTH! ANY TRUTH TO THAT...?
IF THAT IS HOW THE TIME HATH BEEN MEASURED, I WILL GLADLY TAKE THY WORD FOR IT...

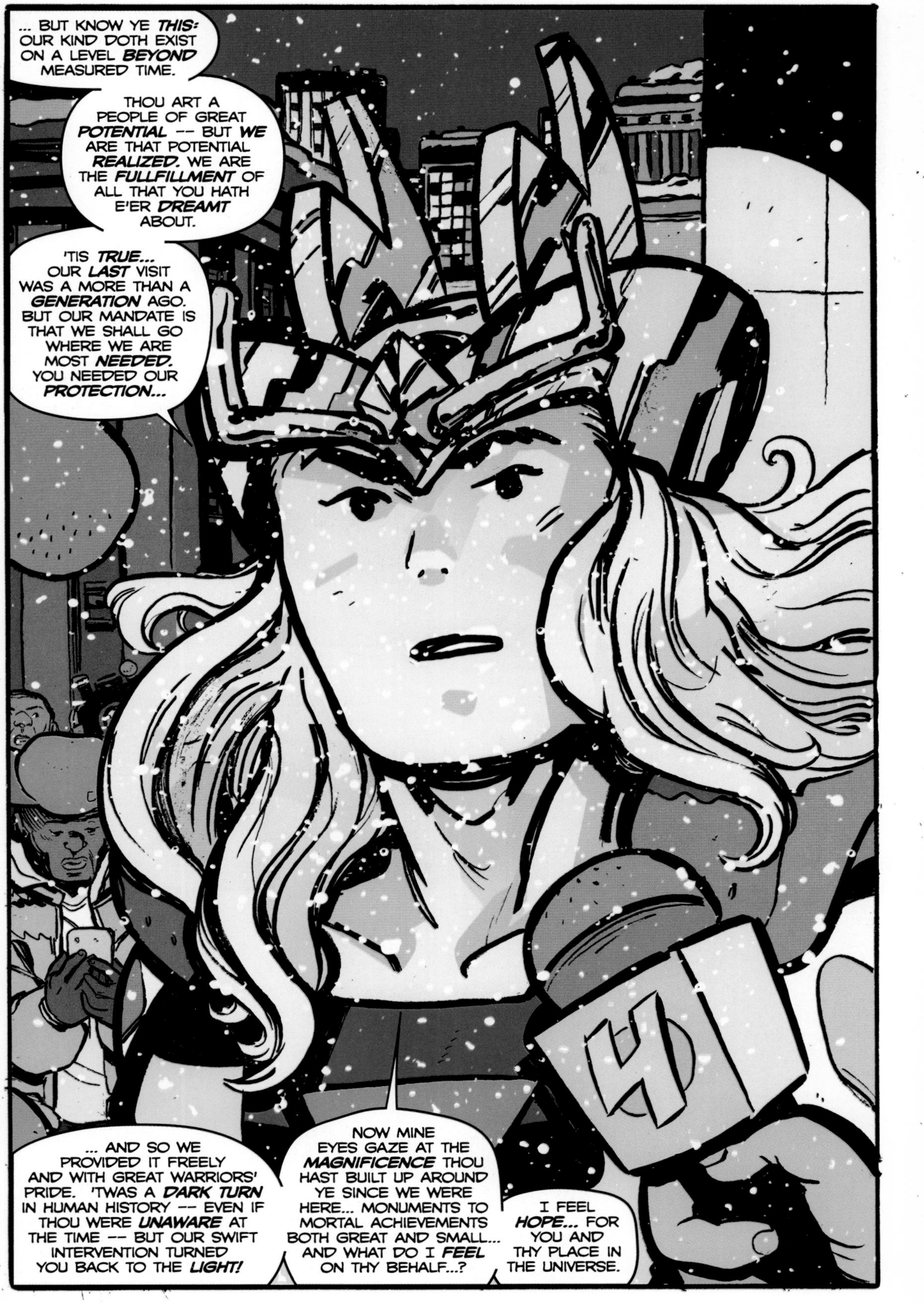
... BUT KNOW YE THIS: OUR KIND DOTH EXIST ON A LEVEL BEYOND MEASURED TIME.
THOU ART A PEOPLE OF GREAT POTENTIAL -- BUT WE ARE THAT POTENTIAL REALIZED. WE ARE THE FULLFILLMENT OF ALL THAT YOU HATH E'ER DREAMT ABOUT.
'TIS TRUE... OUR LAST VISIT WAS A MORE THAN A GENERATION AGO. BUT OUR MANDATE IS THAT WE SHALL GO WHERE WE ARE MOST NEEDED. YOU NEEDED OUR PROTECTION...
... AND SO WE PROVIDED IT FREELY AND WITH GREAT WARRIORS' PRIDE. 'TWAS A DARK TURN IN HUMAN HISTORY -- EVEN IF THOU WERE UNAWARE AT THE TIME -- BUT OUR SWIFT INTERVENTION TURNED YOU BACK TO THE LIGHT!
NOW MINE EYES GAZE AT THE MAGNIFICENCE THOU HAST BUILT UP AROUND YE SINCE WE WERE HERE... MONUMENTS TO MORTAL ACHIEVEMENTS BOTH GREAT AND SMALL... AND WHAT DO I FEEL ON THY BEHALF...?
I FEEL HOPE... FOR YOU AND THY PLACE IN THE UNIVERSE.

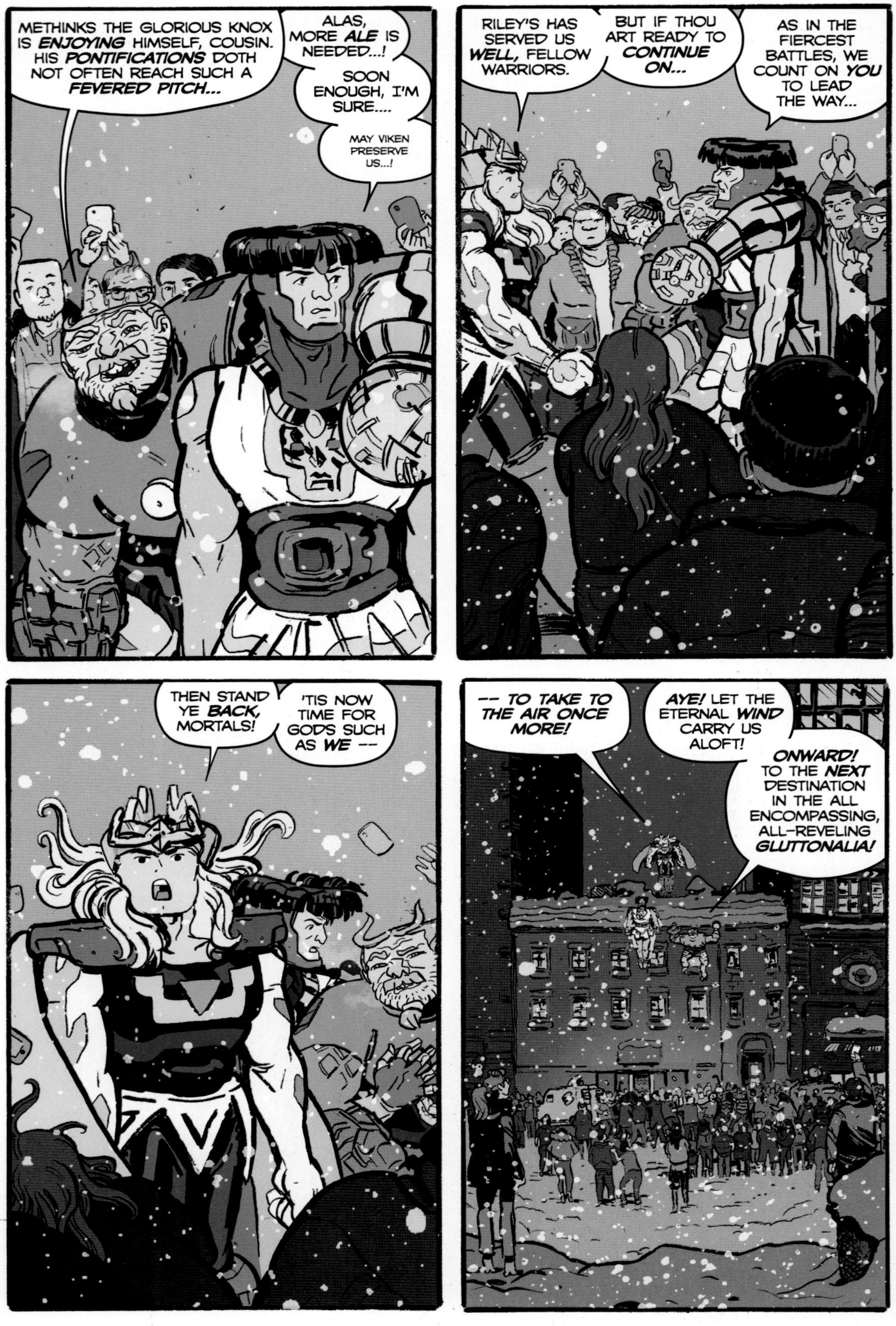
METHINKS THE GLORIOUS KNOX IS ENJOYING HIMSELF, COUSIN. HIS PONTIFICATIONS DOTH NOT OFTEN REACH SUCH A FEVERED PITCH...
ALAS, MORE ALE IS NEEDED...!
SOON ENOUGH, I'M SURE....
MAY VIKEN PRESERVE US...!
RILEY'S HAS SERVED US WELL, FELLOW WARRIORS.
BUT IF THOU ART READY TO CONTINUE ON...
AS IN THE FIERCEST BATTLES, WE COUNT ON YOU TO LEAD THE WAY...
THEN STAND YE BACK, MORTALS!
'TIS NOW TIME FOR GODS SUCH AS WE --
-- TO TAKE TO THE AIR ONCE MORE!
AYE! LET THE ETERNAL WIND CARRY US ALOFT!
ONWARD! TO THE NEXT DESTINATION IN THE ALL ENCOMPASSING, ALL-REVELING GLUTTONALIA!

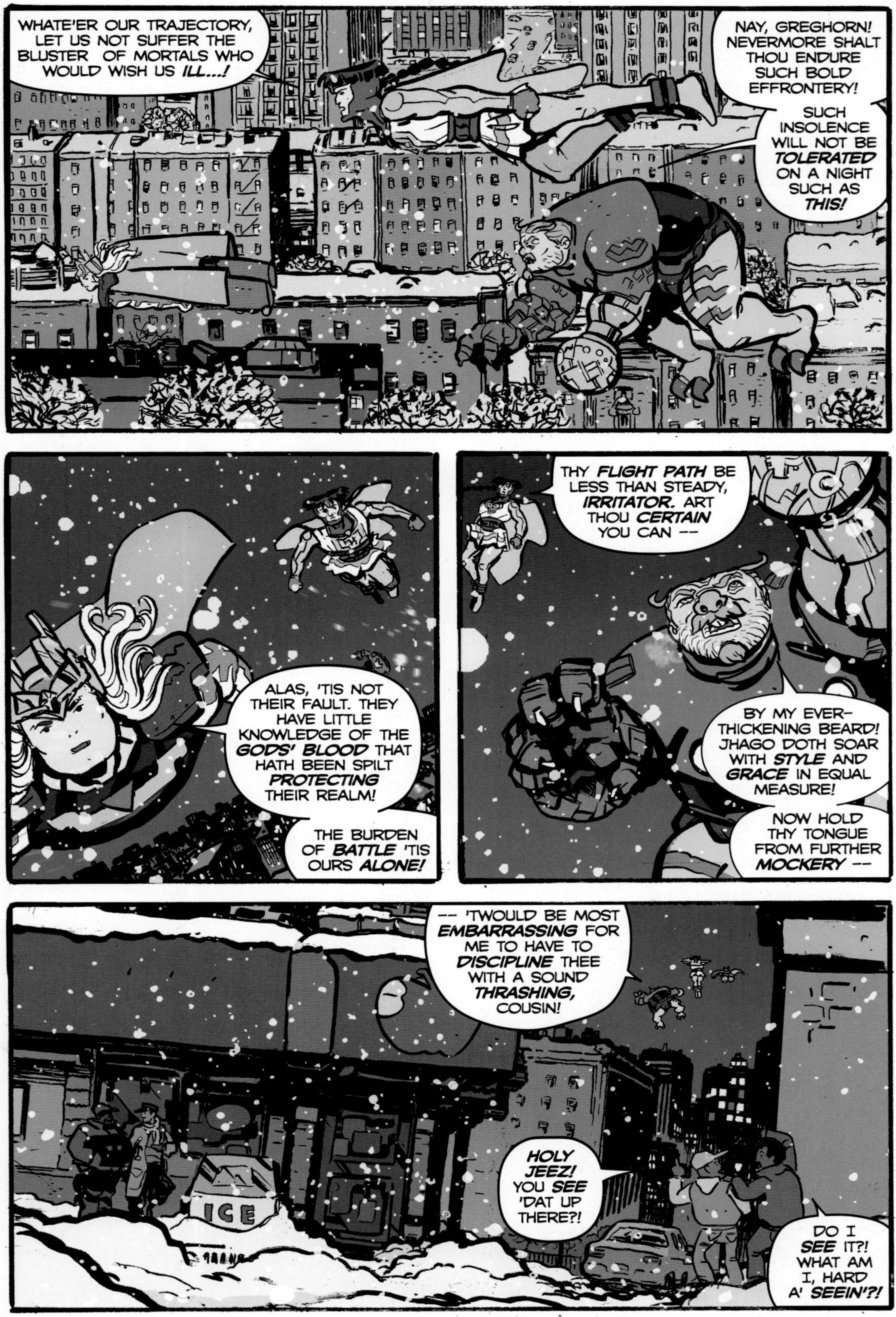
WHATE'ER OUR TRAJECTORY, LET US NOT SUFFER THE BLUSTER OF MORTALS WHO WOULD WISH US ILL...!
NAY, GREGHORN! NEVERMORE SHALT THOU ENDURE SUCH BOLD EFFRONTERY!
SUCH INSOLENCE WILL NOT BE TOLERATED ON A NIGHT SUCH AS THIS!
ALAS, 'TIS NOT THEIR FAULT. THEY HAVE LITTLE KNOWLEDGE OF THE GODS' BLOOD THAT HATH BEEN SPILT PROTECTING THEIR REALM!
THE BURDEN OF BATTLE 'TIS OURS ALONE!
THY FLIGHT PATH BE LESS THAN STEADY, IRRITATOR. ART THOU CERTAIN YOU CAN --
BY MY EVER-THICKENING BEARD! JHAGO DOTH SOAR WITH STYLE AND GRACE IN EQUAL MEASURE!
NOW HOLD THY TONGUE FROM FURTHER MOCKERY --
-- 'TWOULD BE MOST EMBARRASSING FOR ME TO HAVE TO DISCIPLINE THEE WITH A SOUND THRASHING, COUSIN!
ICE
HOLY JEEZ! YOU SEE 'DAT UP THERE?!
DO I SEE IT?! WHAT AM I, HARD A' SEEIN'?!

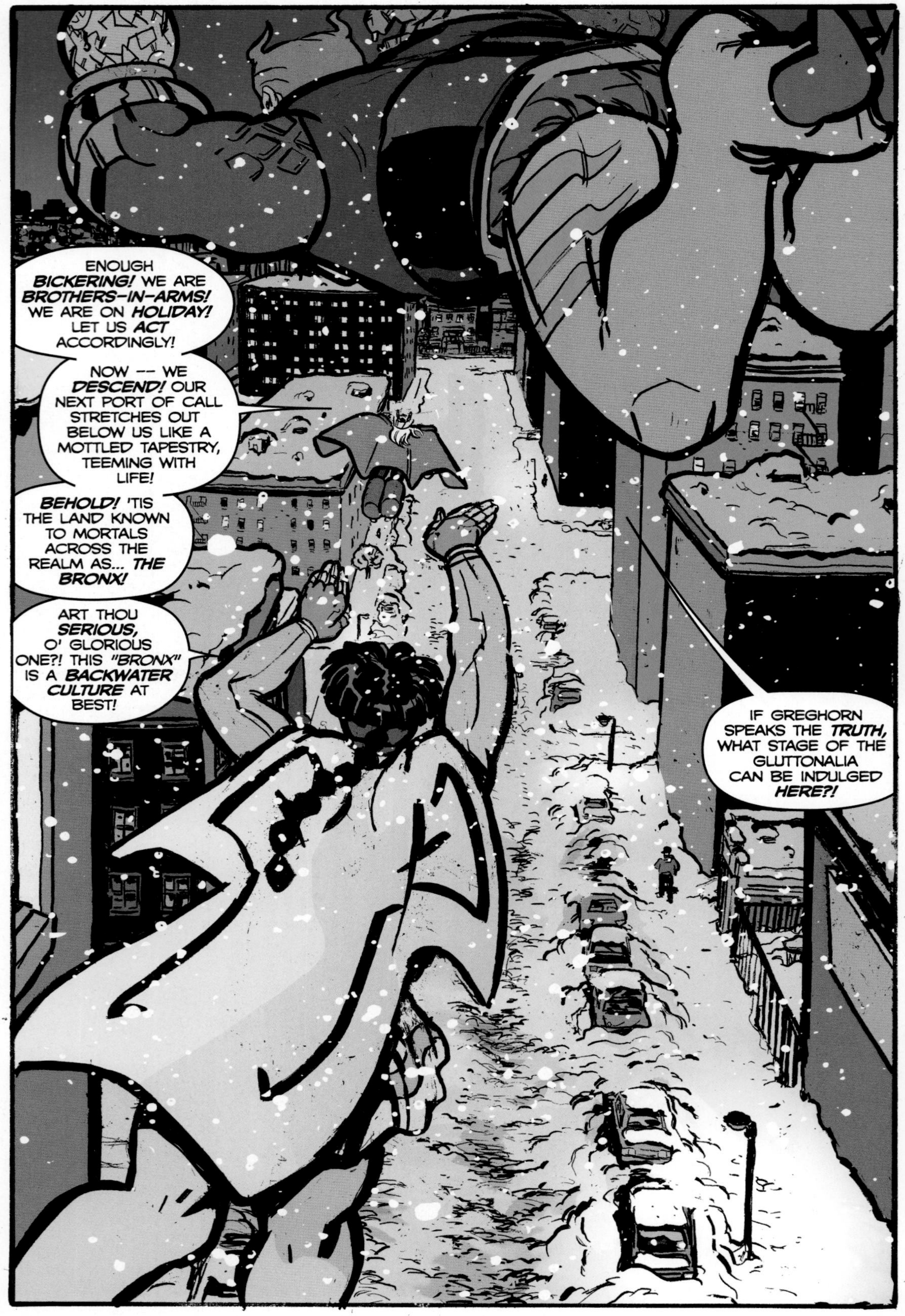
ENOUGH BICKERING! WE ARE BROTHERS-IN-ARMS! WE ARE ON HOLIDAY! LET US ACT ACCORDINGLY!
NOW -- WE DESCEND! OUR NEXT PORT OF CALL STRETCHES OUT BELOW US LIKE A MOTTLED TAPESTRY, TEEMING WITH LIFE!
BEHOLD! 'TIS THE LAND KNOWN TO MORTALS ACROSS THE REALM AS... THE BRONX!
ART THOU SERIOUS, O' GLORIOUS ONE?! THIS "BRONX" IS A BACKWATER CULTURE AT BEST!
IF GREGHORN SPEAKS THE TRUTH, WHAT STAGE OF THE GLUTTONALIA CAN BE INDULGED HERE?!

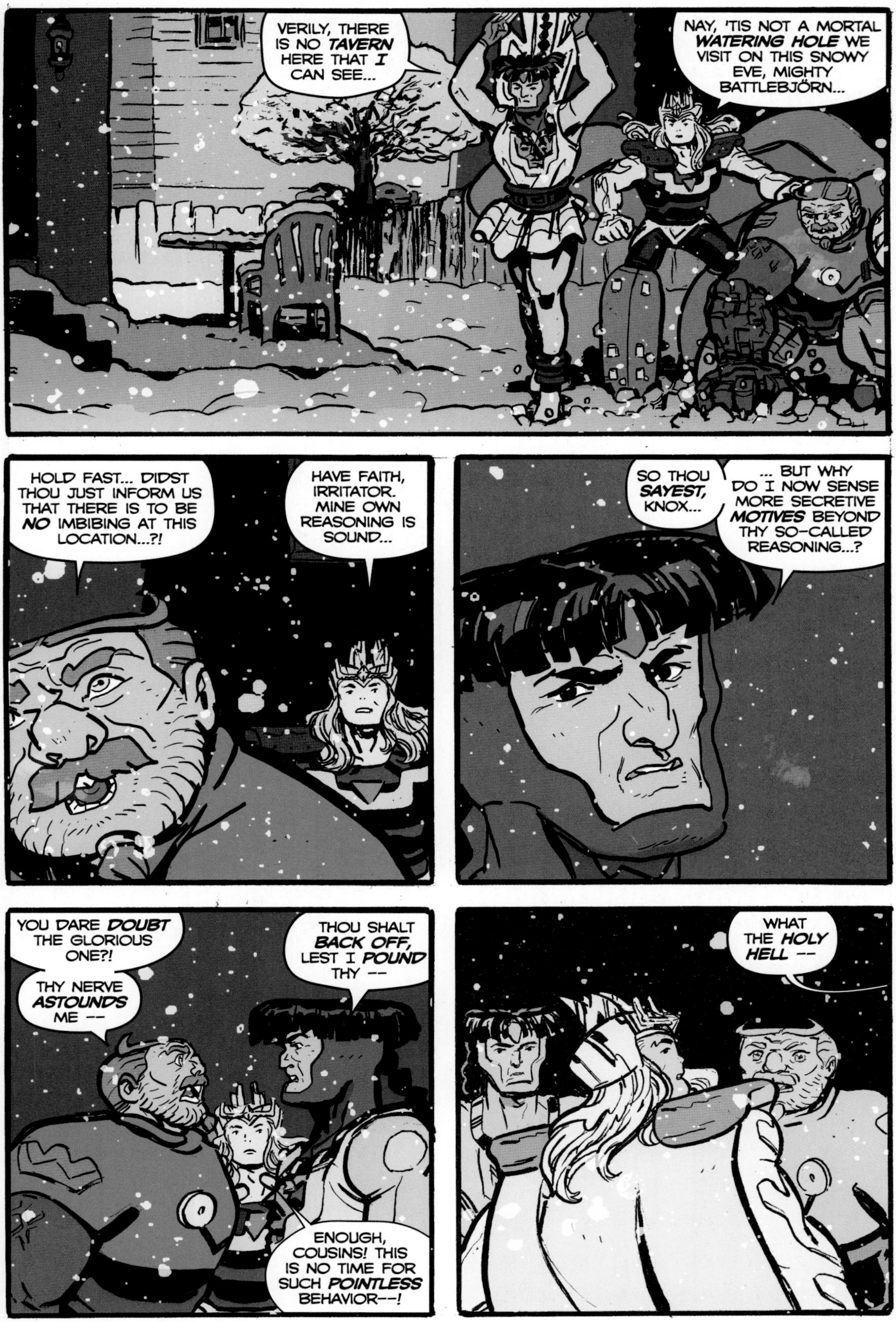
VERILY, THERE IS NO TAVERN HERE THAT I CAN SEE...
NAY, 'TIS NOT A MORTAL WATERING HOLE WE VISIT ON THIS SNOWY EVE, MIGHTY BATTLEBJÖRN...
HOLD FAST... DIDST THOU JUST INFORM US THAT THERE IS TO BE NO IMBIBING AT THIS LOCATION...?!
HAVE FAITH, IRRITATOR. MINE OWN REASONING IS SOUND...
SO THOU SAYEST, KNOX...
... BUT WHY DO I NOW SENSE MORE SECRETIVE MOTIVES BEYOND THY SO-CALLED REASONING...?
YOU DARE DOUBT THE GLORIOUS ONE?!
THY NERVE ASTOUNDS ME --
THOU SHALT BACK OFF, LEST I POUND THY --
ENOUGH, COUSINS! THIS IS NO TIME FOR SUCH POINTLESS BEHAVIOR--!
WHAT THE HOLY HELL --

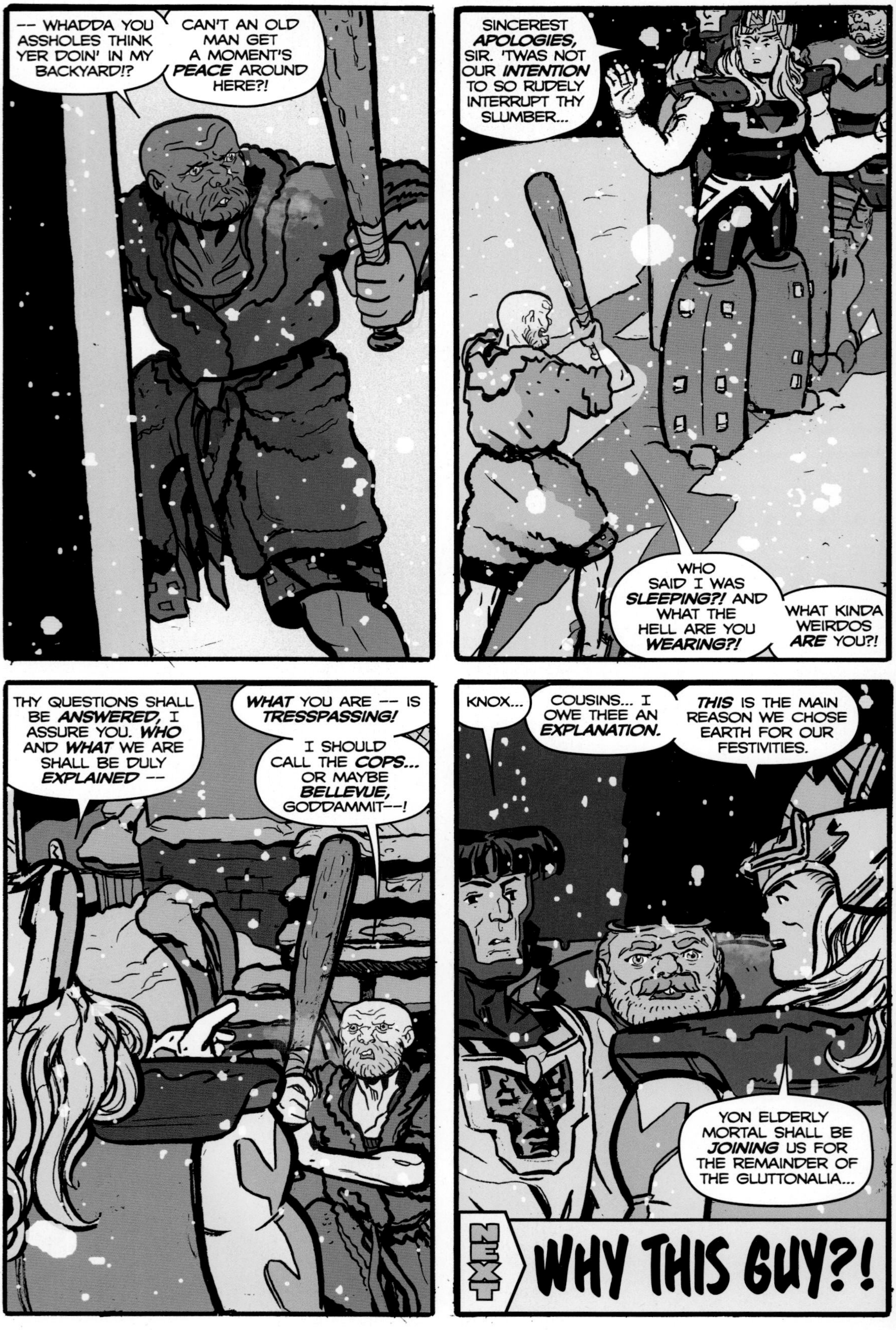
-- WHADDA YOU ASSHOLES THINK YER DOIN' IN MY BACKYARD!?
CAN'T AN OLD MAN GET A MOMENT'S PEACE AROUND HERE?!
SINCEREST APOLOGIES, SIR. 'TWAS NOT OUR INTENTION TO SO RUDELY INTERRUPT THY SLUMBER...
WHO SAID I WAS SLEEPING?! AND WHAT THE HELL ARE YOU WEARING?!
WHAT KINDA WEIRDOS ARE YOU?!
THY QUESTIONS SHALL BE ANSWERED, I ASSURE YOU. WHO AND WHAT WE ARE SHALL BE DULY EXPLAINED --
WHAT YOU ARE -- IS TRESSPASSING!
I SHOULD CALL THE COPS... OR MAYBE BELLEVUE, GODDAMMIT--!
KNOX...
COUSINS... I OWE THEE AN EXPLANATION.
THIS IS THE MAIN REASON WE CHOSE EARTH FOR OUR FESTIVITIES.
YON ELDERLY MORTAL SHALL BE JOINING US FOR THE REMAINDER OF THE GLUTTONALIA...
NEXT
WHY THIS GUY?!

JOE CASEY & PAUL MAYBURY

ISSUE NUMBER TWO

THREE DOLLARS AND FIFTY CENTS

CHAPTER

2

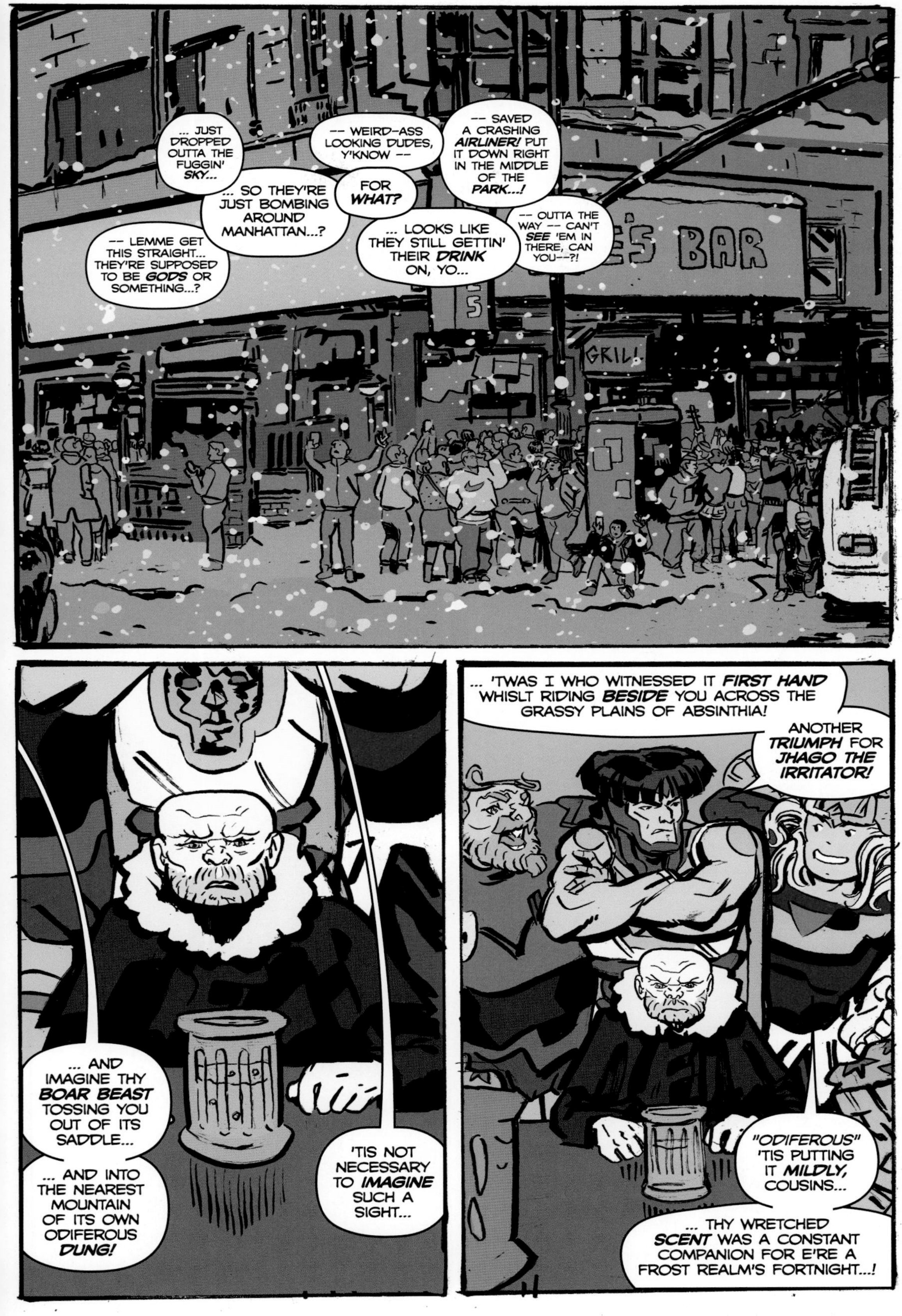
... JUST DROPPED OUTTA THE FUGGIN' SKY...
-- WEIRD-ASS LOOKING DUDES, Y'KNOW --
-- SAVED A CRASHING AIRLINER! PUT IT DOWN RIGHT IN THE MIDDLE OF THE PARK...!
... SO THEY'RE JUST BOMBING AROUND MANHATTAN...?
FOR WHAT?
-- LEMME GET THIS STRAIGHT... THEY'RE SUPPOSED TO BE GODS OR SOMETHING...?
... LOOKS LIKE THEY STILL GETTIN' THEIR DRINK ON, YO...
-- OUTTA THE WAY -- CAN'T SEE 'EM IN THERE, CAN YOU--?!
ES BAR
GRILL
... AND IMAGINE THY BOAR BEAST TOSSING YOU OUT OF ITS SADDLE...
... AND INTO THE NEAREST MOUNTAIN OF ITS OWN ODIFEROUS DUNG!
'TIS NOT NECESSARY TO IMAGINE SUCH A SIGHT...
... 'TWAS I WHO WITNESSED IT FIRST HAND WHISLT RIDING BESIDE YOU ACROSS THE GRASSY PLAINS OF ABSINTHIA!
ANOTHER TRIUMPH FOR JHAGO THE IRRITATOR!
"ODIFEROUS" 'TIS PUTTING IT MILDLY, COUSINS...
... THY WRETCHED SCENT WAS A CONSTANT COMPANION FOR E'RE A FROST REALM'S FORTNIGHT...!

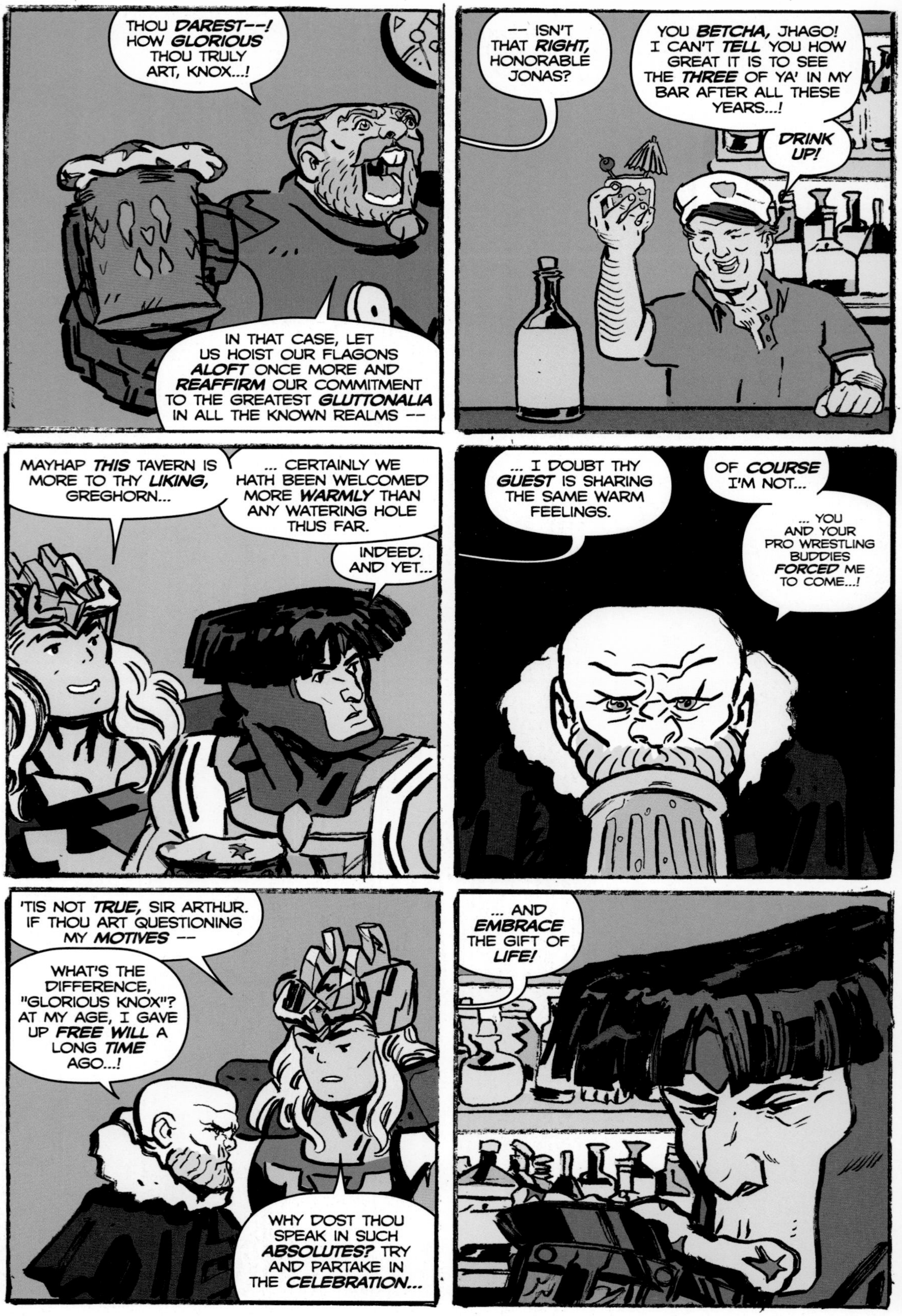
THOU DARREST--! HOW GLORIOUS THOU TRULY ART, KNOX...!
IN THAT CASE, LET US HOIST OUR FLAGONS ALOFT ONCE MORE AND REAFFIRM OUR COMMITMENT TO THE GREATEST GLUTTONALIA IN ALL THE KNOWN REALMS --
-- ISN'T THAT RIGHT, HONORABLE JONAS?
YOU BETCHA, JHAGO! I CAN'T TELL YOU HOW GREAT IT IS TO SEE THE THREE OF YA' IN MY BAR AFTER ALL THESE YEARS...!
DRINK UP!
MAYHAP THIS TAVERN IS MORE TO THY LIKING, GREGHORN...
... CERTAINLY WE HATH BEEN WELCOMED MORE WARMLY THAN ANY WATERING HOLE THUS FAR.
INDEED. AND YET...
... I DOUBT THY GUEST IS SHARING THE SAME WARM FEELINGS.
OF COURSE I'M NOT...
... YOU AND YOUR PRO WRESTLING BUDDIES FORCED ME TO COME...!
'TIS NOT TRUE, SIR ARTHUR. IF THOU ART QUESTIONING MY MOTIVES --
WHAT'S THE DIFFERENCE, "GLORIOUS KNOX"? AT MY AGE, I GAVE UP FREE WILL A LONG TIME AGO...!
WHY DOST THOU SPEAK IN SUCH ABSOLUTES? TRY AND PARTAKE IN THE CELEBRATION...
... AND EMBRACE THE GIFT OF LIFE!

THE GLORIOUS KNOX SPEAKS A NOBLE *TRUTH!* THOU HAST BEEN INVITED TO JOIN IN A SACRED WARRIOR *TRADITION!*

DO I LOOK LIKE ANY KIND OF WARRIOR TO *YOU?!*

ARE YOU SO *DRUNK* THAT YOU'RE BLIND TO THE *OBVIOUS...?*

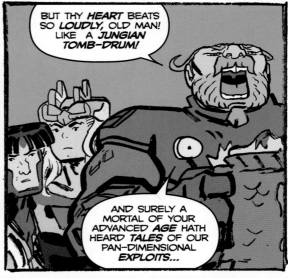

BUT THY *HEART* BEATS SO *LOUDLY,* OLD MAN! LIKE A *JUNGIAN TOMB-DRUM!*

AND SURELY A MORTAL OF YOUR ADVANCED *AGE* HATH HEARD *TALES* OF OUR PAN-DIMENSIONAL *EXPLOITS...*

"... VERILY, THEY ARE THE STUFF OF *LEGEND,* AFTER ALL! TO WIT -- THE FABLED *FENRIS HORDES* THAT WOULD SWARM WHENE'ER THE LUNAR BEACONS SHONE THEIR BRIGHTEST --

"-- CLAWING THEIR WAY THROUGH SPACE-TIME BARRIERS ALL IN THE NAME OF WANTON *CONQUEST* -- E'EN *VIKEN ITSELF* WAS A TARGET! BUT, NAY, THESE VICIOUS DOGS WERE SOUNDLY BEATEN *BACK* BY THE MOST *STALWART* AND *CUNNING* OF WARRIORS!

"'TIS BUT *ONE* EXAMPLE OF OUR LUST TO PROTECT! SO MANY *FATEFUL DAYS* N'ER RECORDED IN THE ANNALS OF MYTHIC COMBAT! TOO MANY *VICTORIES* TO COUNT!

"THUS SPAKE *JHAGO!*"

AYE. 'TIS OUR *MANDATE* TO BRING *WAR* TO THOSE WHO WOULD ENDANGER THE PRECEPTS OF *PEACE.*

AN IRONY NOT LOST ON *SOME* OF US.

BUT THOU HATH LIVED THINE *OWN* LIFE, ARTHUR. 'TIS *THAT* WHICH IS ONE OF *MANY* THINGS WE HONOR HERE TONIGHT...

... A MORTAL LIFE THAT I HOPE HAS *FULFILLED* YOU.

WE DOTH BELIEVE THAT *EVERY* SENTIENT CREATURE SHOULD STRIVE TO FIND THE PEACE THAT THEY ARE *ENTITLED* TO.

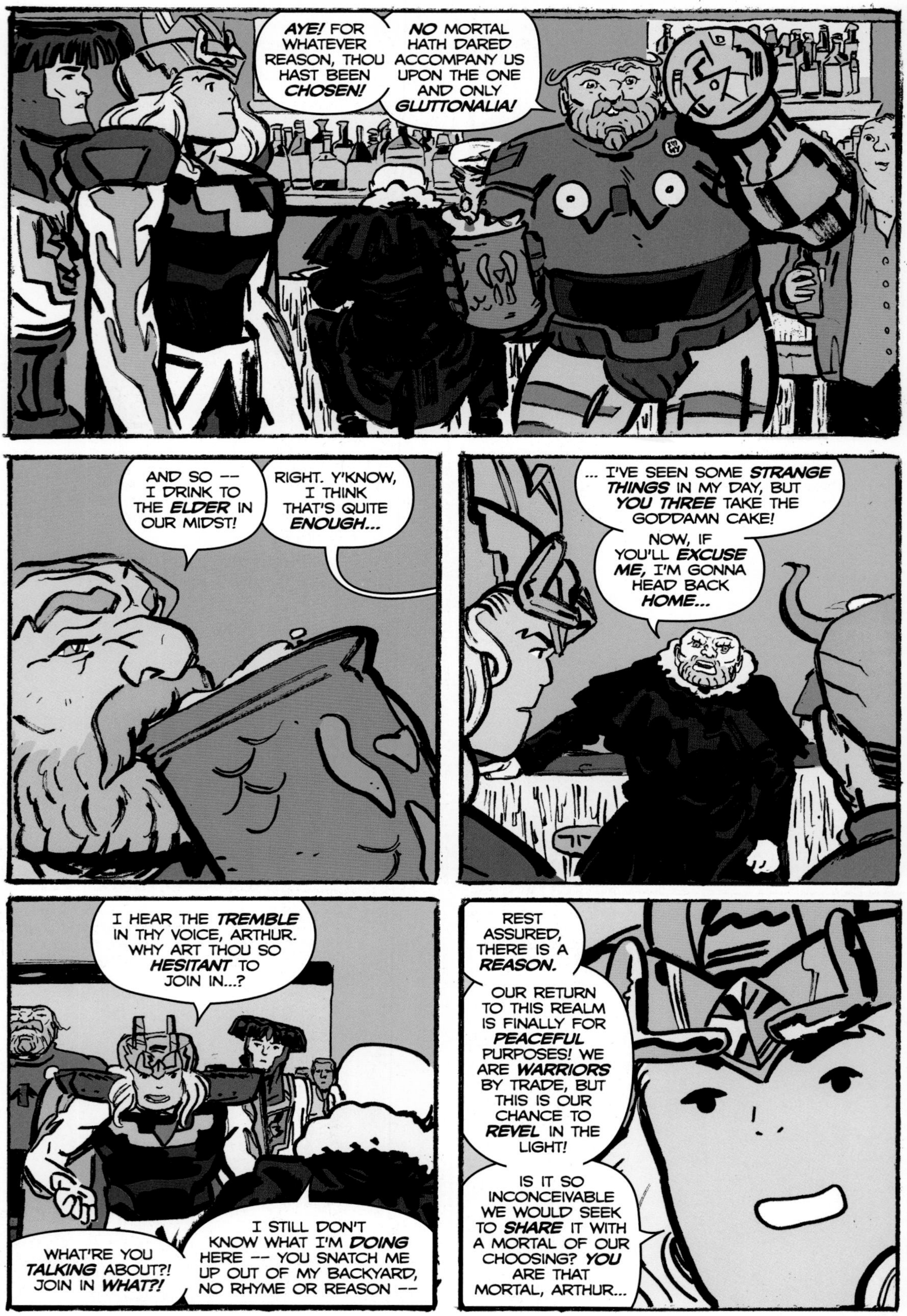
AYE! FOR WHATEVER REASON, THOU HAST BEEN CHOSEN!
NO MORTAL HATH DARED ACCOMPANY US UPON THE ONE AND ONLY GLUTTONALIA!
AND SO -- I DRINK TO THE ELDER IN OUR MIDST!
RIGHT. Y'KNOW, I THINK THAT'S QUITE ENOUGH...
... I'VE SEEN SOME STRANGE THINGS IN MY DAY, BUT YOU THREE TAKE THE GODDAMN CAKE!
NOW, IF YOU'LL EXCUSE ME, I'M GONNA HEAD BACK HOME...
I HEAR THE TREMBLE IN THY VOICE, ARTHUR. WHY ART THOU SO HESITANT TO JOIN IN...?
WHAT'RE YOU TALKING ABOUT?! JOIN IN WHAT?!
I STILL DON'T KNOW WHAT I'M DOING HERE -- YOU SNATCH ME UP OUT OF MY BACKYARD, NO RHYME OR REASON --
REST ASSURED, THERE IS A REASON.
OUR RETURN TO THIS REALM IS FINALLY FOR PEACEFUL PURPOSES! WE ARE WARRIORS BY TRADE, BUT THIS IS OUR CHANCE TO REVEL IN THE LIGHT!
IS IT SO INCONCEIVABLE WE WOULD SEEK TO SHARE IT WITH A MORTAL OF OUR CHOOSING? YOU ARE THAT MORTAL, ARTHUR...

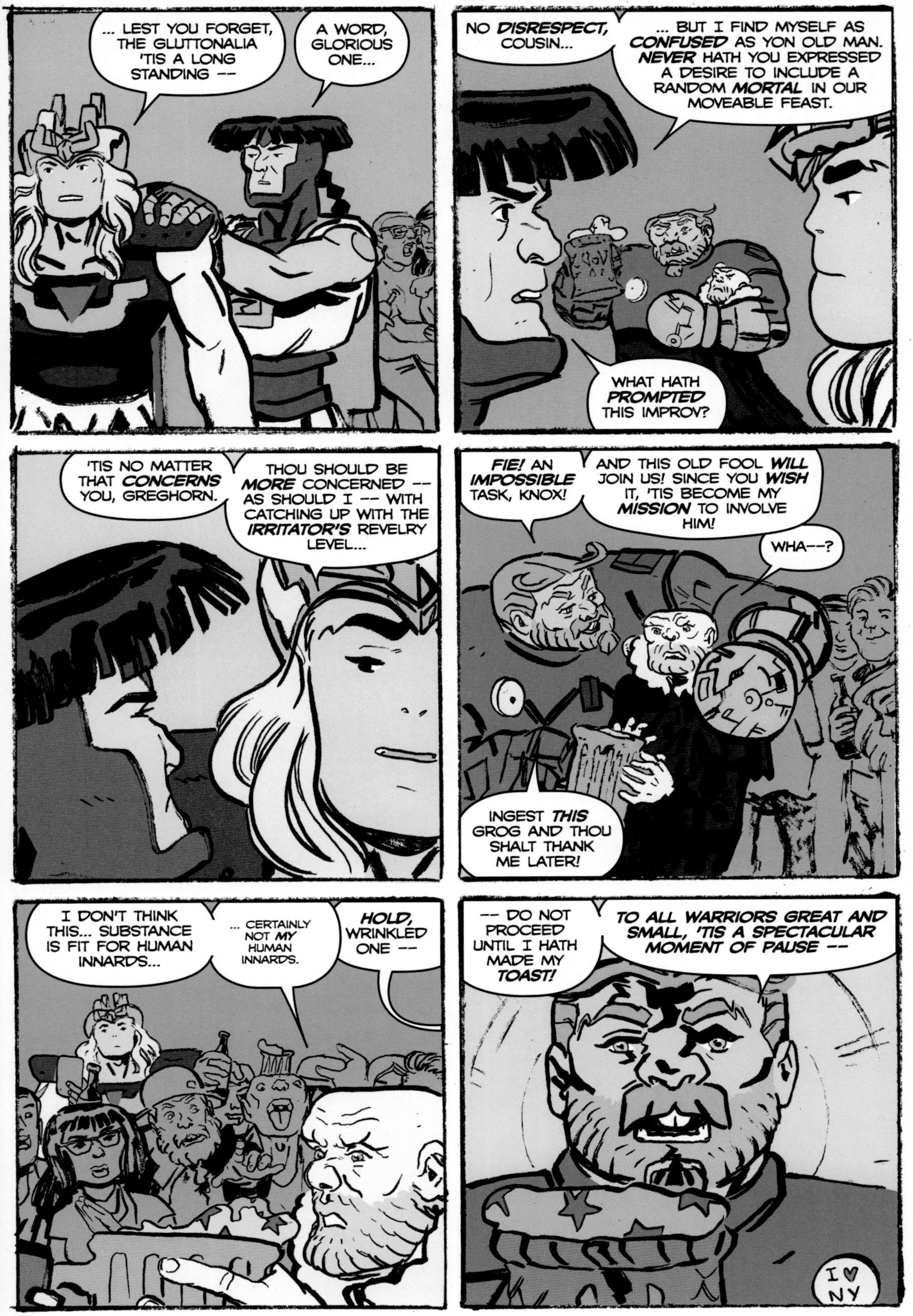
... LEST YOU FORGET, THE GLUTTONALIA 'TIS A LONG STANDING --
A WORD, GLORIOUS ONE...
NO DISRESPECT, COUSIN...
... BUT I FIND MYSELF AS CONFUSED AS YON OLD MAN. NEVER HATH YOU EXPRESSED A DESIRE TO INCLUDE A RANDOM MORTAL IN OUR MOVEABLE FEAST.
WHAT HATH PROMPTED THIS IMPROV?
'TIS NO MATTER THAT CONCERNS YOU, GREGHORN.
THOU SHOULD BE MORE CONCERNED -- AS SHOULD I -- WITH CATCHING UP WITH THE IRRITATOR'S REVELRY LEVEL...
FIE! AN IMPOSSIBLE TASK, KNOX!
AND THIS OLD FOOL WILL JOIN US! SINCE YOU WISH IT, 'TIS BECOME MY MISSION TO INVOLVE HIM!
WHA--?
INGEST THIS GROG AND THOU SHALT THANK ME LATER!
I DON'T THINK THIS... SUBSTANCE IS FIT FOR HUMAN INNARDS...
... CERTAINLY NOT MY HUMAN INNARDS.
HOLD, WRINKLED ONE --
-- DO NOT PROCEED UNTIL I HATH MADE MY TOAST!
TO ALL WARRIORS GREAT AND SMALL, 'TIS A SPECTACULAR MOMENT OF PAUSE --
I ♥ NY

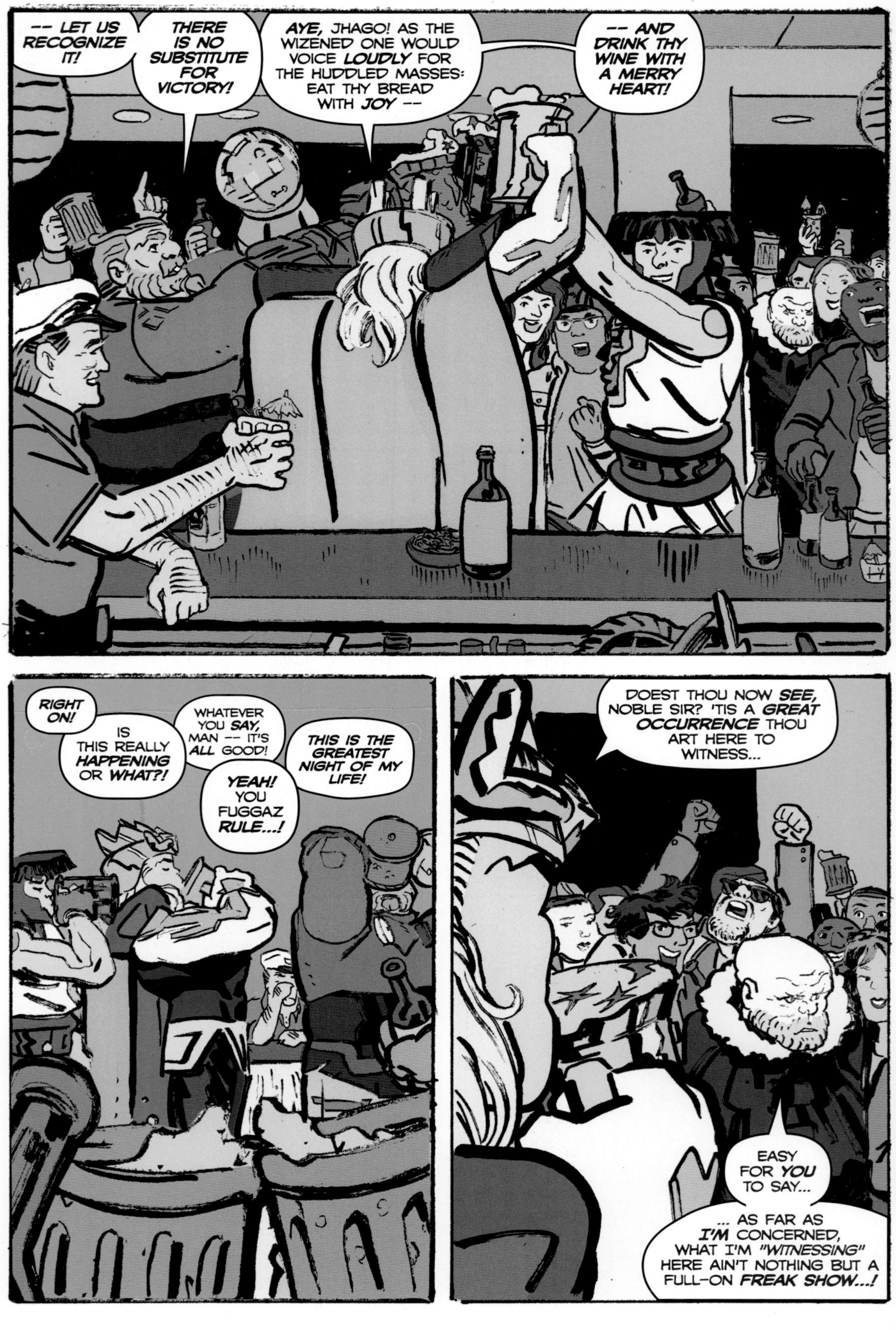
-- LET US RECOGNIZE IT!
THERE IS NO SUBSTITUTE FOR VICTORY!
AYE, JHAGO! AS THE WIZENED ONE WOULD VOICE LOUDLY FOR THE HUDDLED MASSES: EAT THY BREAD WITH JOY --
-- AND DRINK THY WINE WITH A MERRY HEART!
RIGHT ON!
IS THIS REALLY HAPPENING OR WHAT?!
WHATEVER YOU SAY, MAN -- IT'S ALL GOOD!
YEAH! YOU FUGGAZ RULE...!
THIS IS THE GREATEST NIGHT OF MY LIFE!
DOEST THOU NOW SEE, NOBLE SIR? 'TIS A GREAT OCCURRENCE THOU ART HERE TO WITNESS...
EASY FOR YOU TO SAY...
... AS FAR AS I'M CONCERNED, WHAT I'M "WITNESSING" HERE AIN'T NOTHING BUT A FULL-ON FREAK SHOW...!

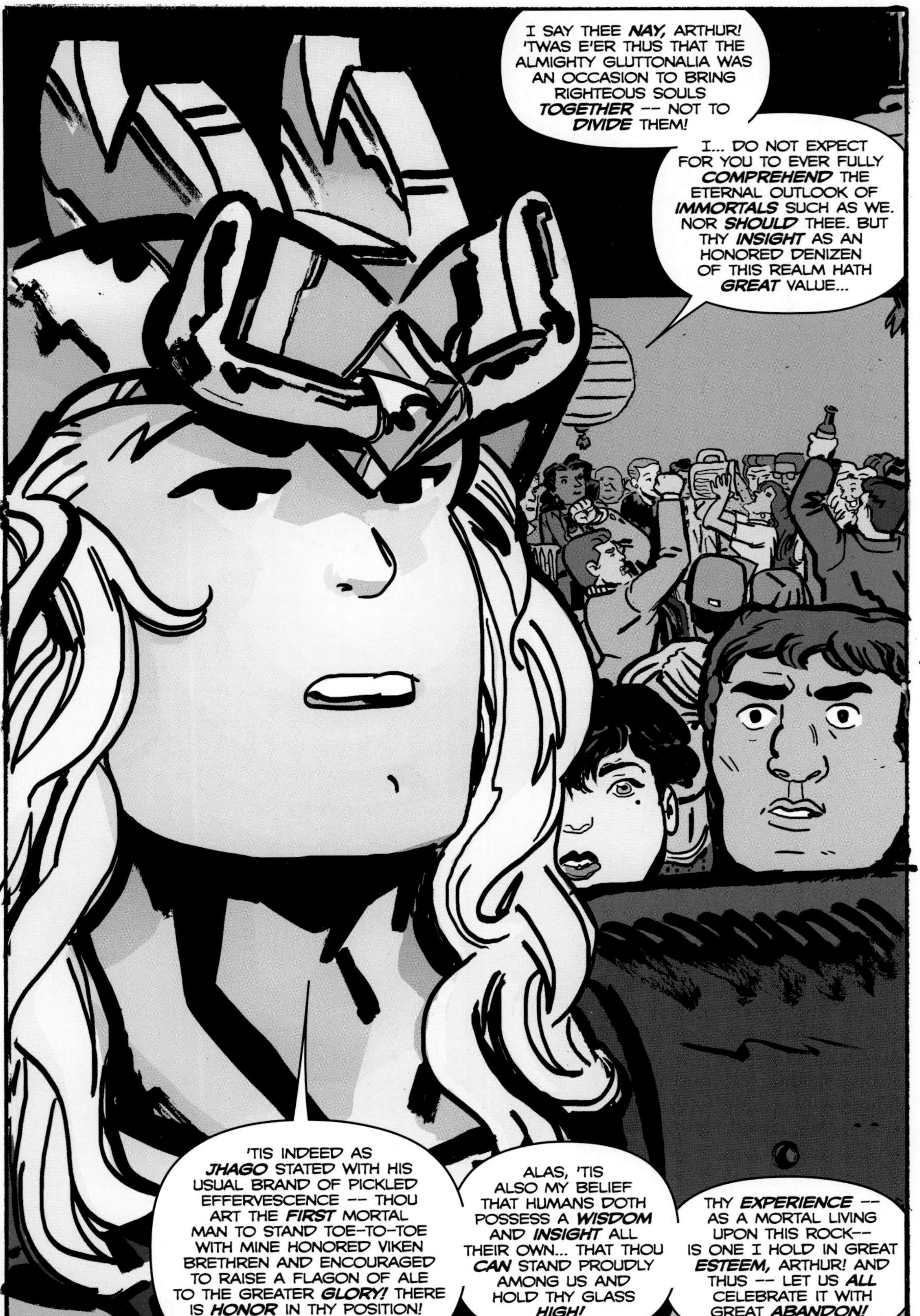
I SAY THEE NAY, ARTHUR! 'TWAS E'ER THUS THAT THE ALMIGHTY GLUTTONALIA WAS AN OCCASION TO BRING RIGHTEOUS SOULS TOGETHER -- NOT TO DIVIDE THEM!
I... DO NOT EXPECT FOR YOU TO EVER FULLY COMPREHEND THE ETERNAL OUTLOOK OF IMMORTALS SUCH AS WE. NOR SHOULD THEE. BUT THY INSIGHT AS AN HONORED DENIZEN OF THIS REALM HATH GREAT VALUE...
'TIS INDEED AS JHAGO STATED WITH HIS USUAL BRAND OF PICKLED EFFERVESCENCE -- THOU ART THE FIRST MORTAL MAN TO STAND TOE-TO-TOE WITH MINE HONORED VIKEN BRETHREN AND ENCOURAGED TO RAISE A FLAGON OF ALE TO THE GREATER GLORY! THERE IS HONOR IN THY POSITION!
ALAS, 'TIS ALSO MY BELIEF THAT HUMANS DOTH POSSESS A WISDOM AND INSIGHT ALL THEIR OWN... THAT THOU CAN STAND PROUDLY AMONG US AND HOLD THY GLASS HIGH!
THY EXPERIENCE -- AS A MORTAL LIVING UPON THIS ROCK-- IS ONE I HOLD IN GREAT ESTEEM, ARTHUR! AND THUS -- LET US ALL CELEBRATE IT WITH GREAT ABANDON!

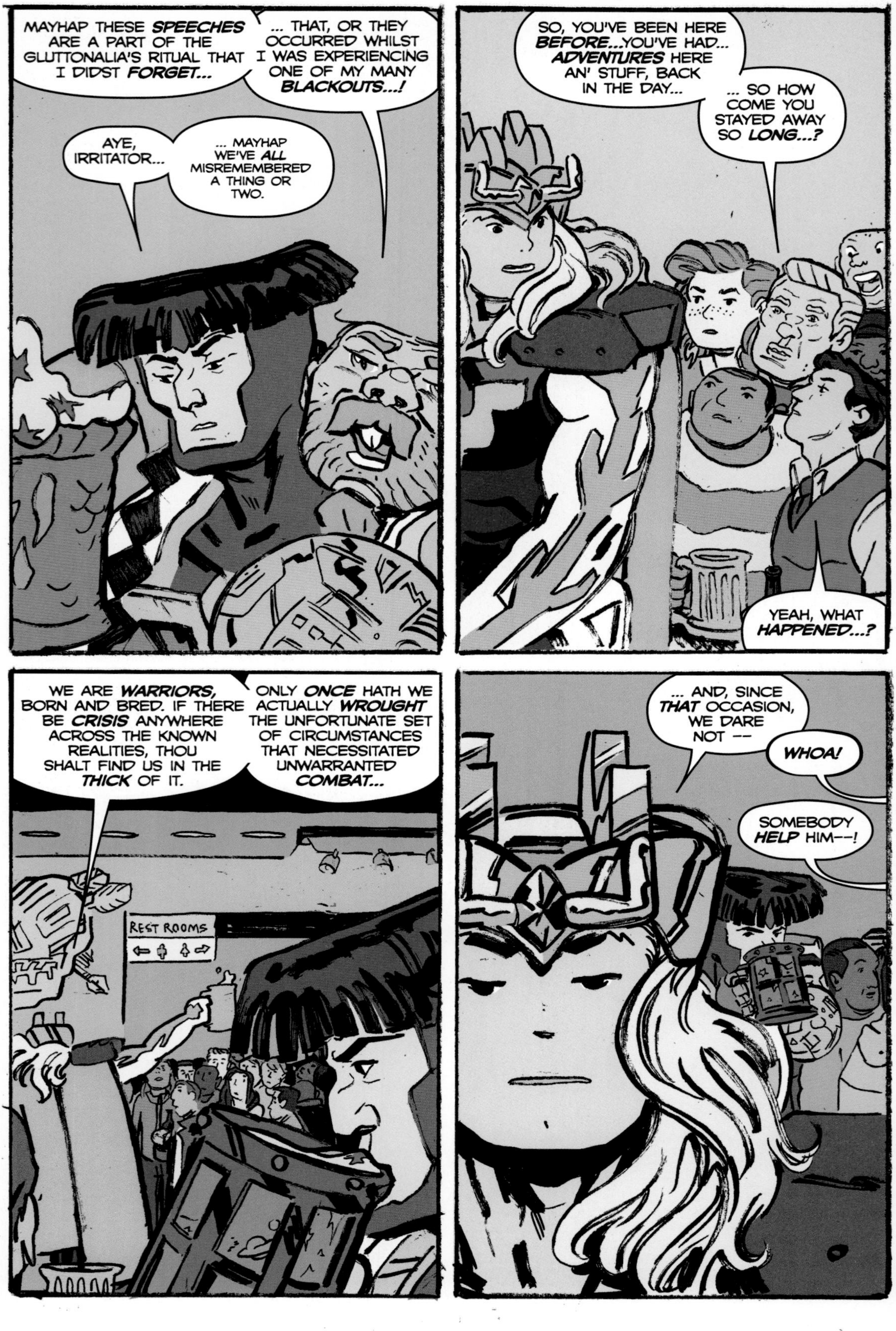
MAYHAP THESE SPEECHES ARE A PART OF THE GLUTTONALIA'S RITUAL THAT I DIDST FORGET...
... THAT, OR THEY OCCURRED WHILST I WAS EXPERIENCING ONE OF MY MANY BLACKOUTS...!
AYE, IRRITATOR...
... MAYHAP WE'VE ALL MISREMEMBERED A THING OR TWO.
SO, YOU'VE BEEN HERE BEFORE...YOU'VE HAD... ADVENTURES HERE AN' STUFF, BACK IN THE DAY...
... SO HOW COME YOU STAYED AWAY SO LONG...?
YEAH, WHAT HAPPENED...?
WE ARE WARRIORS, BORN AND BRED. IF THERE BE CRISIS ANYWHERE ACROSS THE KNOWN REALITIES, THOU SHALT FIND US IN THE THICK OF IT.
ONLY ONCE HATH WE ACTUALLY WROUGHT THE UNFORTUNATE SET OF CIRCUMSTANCES THAT NECESSITATED UNWARRANTED COMBAT...
REST ROOMS
... AND, SINCE THAT OCCASION, WE DARE NOT --
WHOA!
SOMEBODY HELP HIM--!

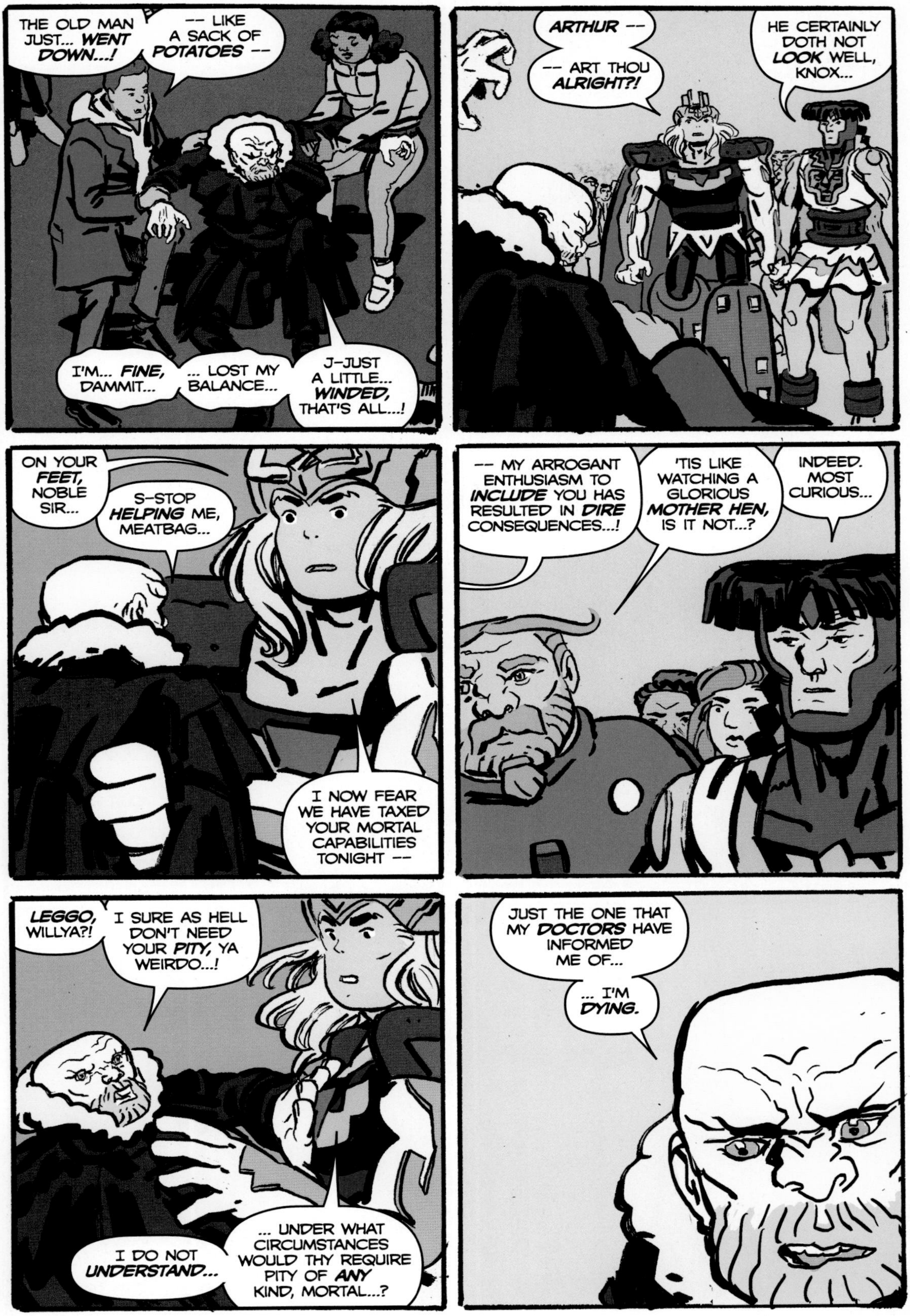
THE OLD MAN JUST... WENT DOWN...!
-- LIKE A SACK OF POTATOES --
I'M... FINE, DAMMIT...
... LOST MY BALANCE...
J-JUST A LITTLE... WINDED, THAT'S ALL...!
ARTHUR --
-- ART THOU ALRIGHT?!
HE CERTAINLY DOTH NOT LOOK WELL, KNOX...
ON YOUR FEET, NOBLE SIR...
S-STOP HELPING ME, MEATBAG...
I NOW FEAR WE HAVE TAXED YOUR MORTAL CAPABILITIES TONIGHT --
-- MY ARROGANT ENTHUSIASM TO INCLUDE YOU HAS RESULTED IN DIRE CONSEQUENCES...!
'TIS LIKE WATCHING A GLORIOUS MOTHER HEN, IS IT NOT...?
INDEED. MOST CURIOUS...
LEGGO, WILLYA?!
I SURE AS HELL DON'T NEED YOUR PITY, YA WEIRDO...!
I DO NOT UNDERSTAND...
... UNDER WHAT CIRCUMSTANCES WOULD THY REQUIRE PITY OF ANY KIND, MORTAL...?
JUST THE ONE THAT MY DOCTORS HAVE INFORMED ME OF...
... I'M DYING.

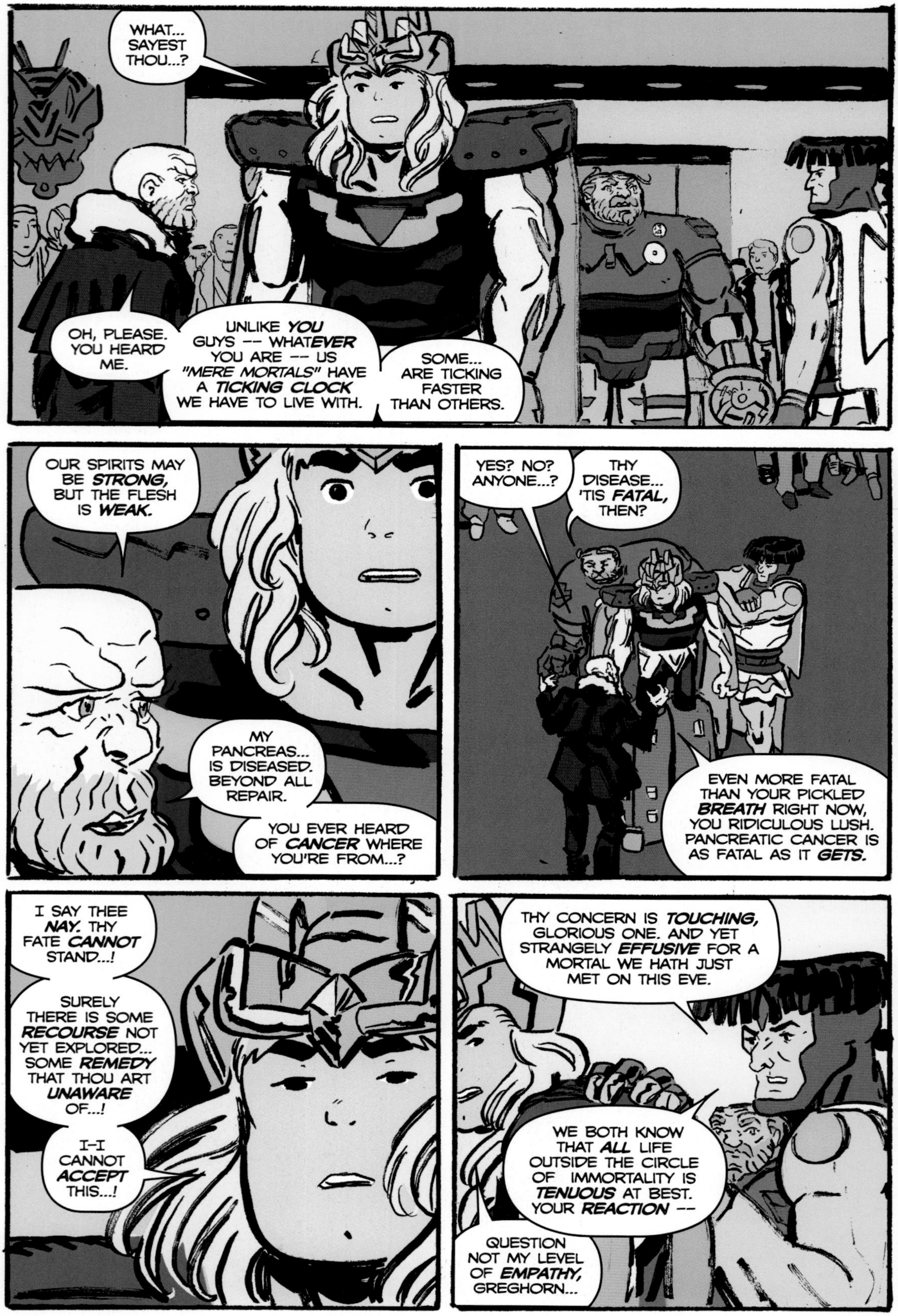
WHAT... SAYEST THOU...?
OH, PLEASE. YOU HEARD ME.
UNLIKE YOU GUYS -- WHATEVER YOU ARE -- US "MERE MORTALS" HAVE A TICKING CLOCK WE HAVE TO LIVE WITH.
SOME... ARE TICKING FASTER THAN OTHERS.
OUR SPIRITS MAY BE STRONG, BUT THE FLESH IS WEAK.
MY PANCREAS... IS DISEASED. BEYOND ALL REPAIR.
YOU EVER HEARD OF CANCER WHERE YOU'RE FROM...?
YES? NO? ANYONE...?
THY DISEASE... 'TIS FATAL, THEN?
EVEN MORE FATAL THAN YOUR PICKLED BREATH RIGHT NOW, YOU RIDICULOUS LUSH. PANCREATIC CANCER IS AS FATAL AS IT GETS.
I SAY THEE NAY. THY FATE CANNOT STAND...!
SURELY THERE IS SOME RECOURSE NOT YET EXPLORED... SOME REMEDY THAT THOU ART UNAWARE OF...!
I-I CANNOT ACCEPT THIS...!
THY CONCERN IS TOUCHING, GLORIOUS ONE. AND YET STRANGELY EFFUSIVE FOR A MORTAL WE HATH JUST MET ON THIS EVE.
WE BOTH KNOW THAT ALL LIFE OUTSIDE THE CIRCLE OF IMMORTALITY IS TENUOUS AT BEST. YOUR REACTION --
QUESTION NOT MY LEVEL OF EMPATHY, GREGHORN...

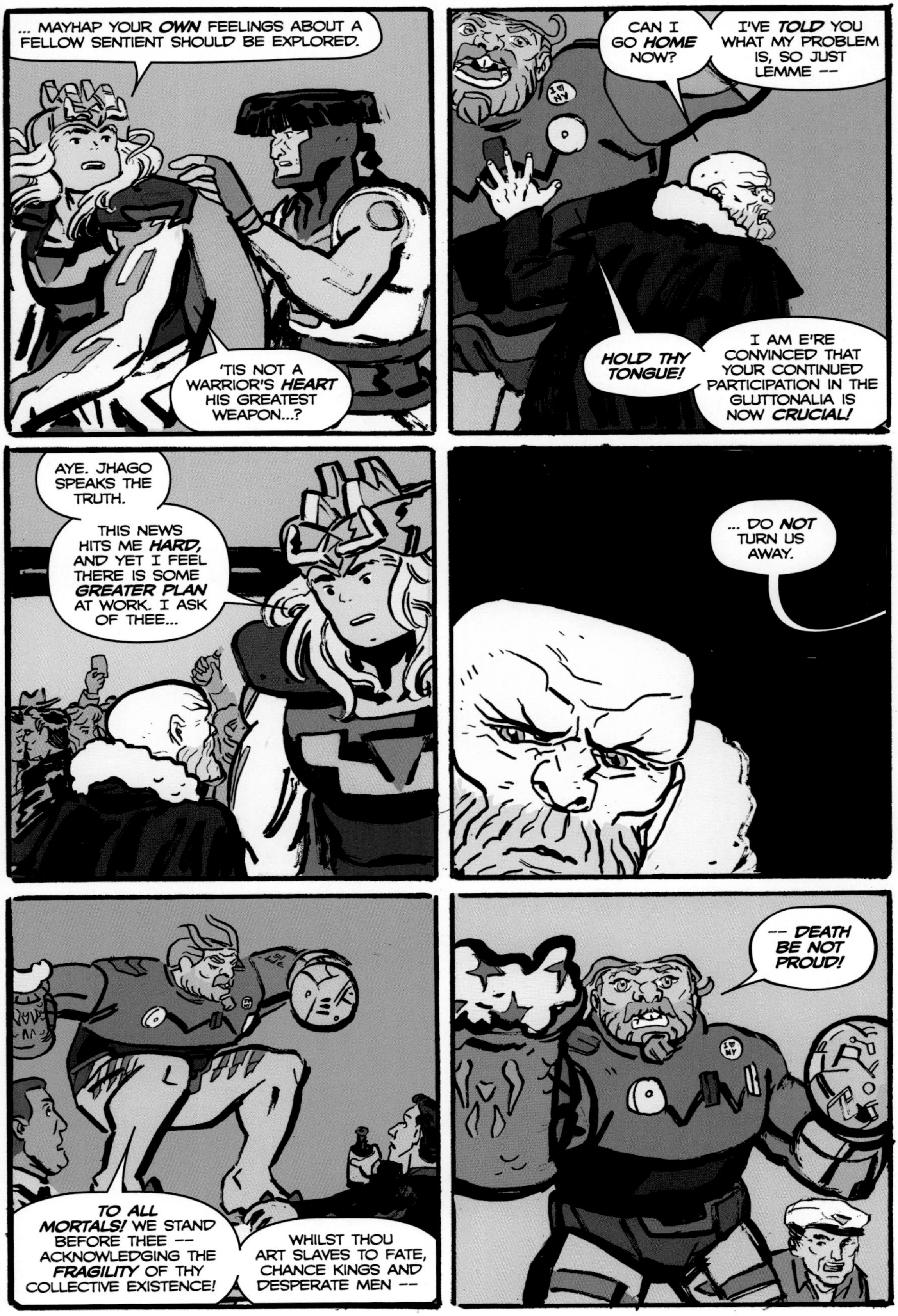
... MAYHAP YOUR OWN FEELINGS ABOUT A FELLOW SENTIENT SHOULD BE EXPLORED.
'TIS NOT A WARRIOR'S HEART HIS GREATEST WEAPON...?
CAN I GO HOME NOW?
I'VE TOLD YOU WHAT MY PROBLEM IS, SO JUST LEMME --
HOLD THY TONGUE!
I AM E'RE CONVINCED THAT YOUR CONTINUED PARTICIPATION IN THE GLUTTONALIA IS NOW CRUCIAL!
AYE. JHAGO SPEAKS THE TRUTH.
THIS NEWS HITS ME HARD, AND YET I FEEL THERE IS SOME GREATER PLAN AT WORK. I ASK OF THEE...
... DO NOT TURN US AWAY.
TO ALL MORTALS! WE STAND BEFORE THEE -- ACKNOWLEDGING THE FRAGILITY OF THY COLLECTIVE EXISTENCE!
WHILST THOU ART SLAVES TO FATE, CHANCE KINGS AND DESPERATE MEN --
-- DEATH BE NOT PROUD!

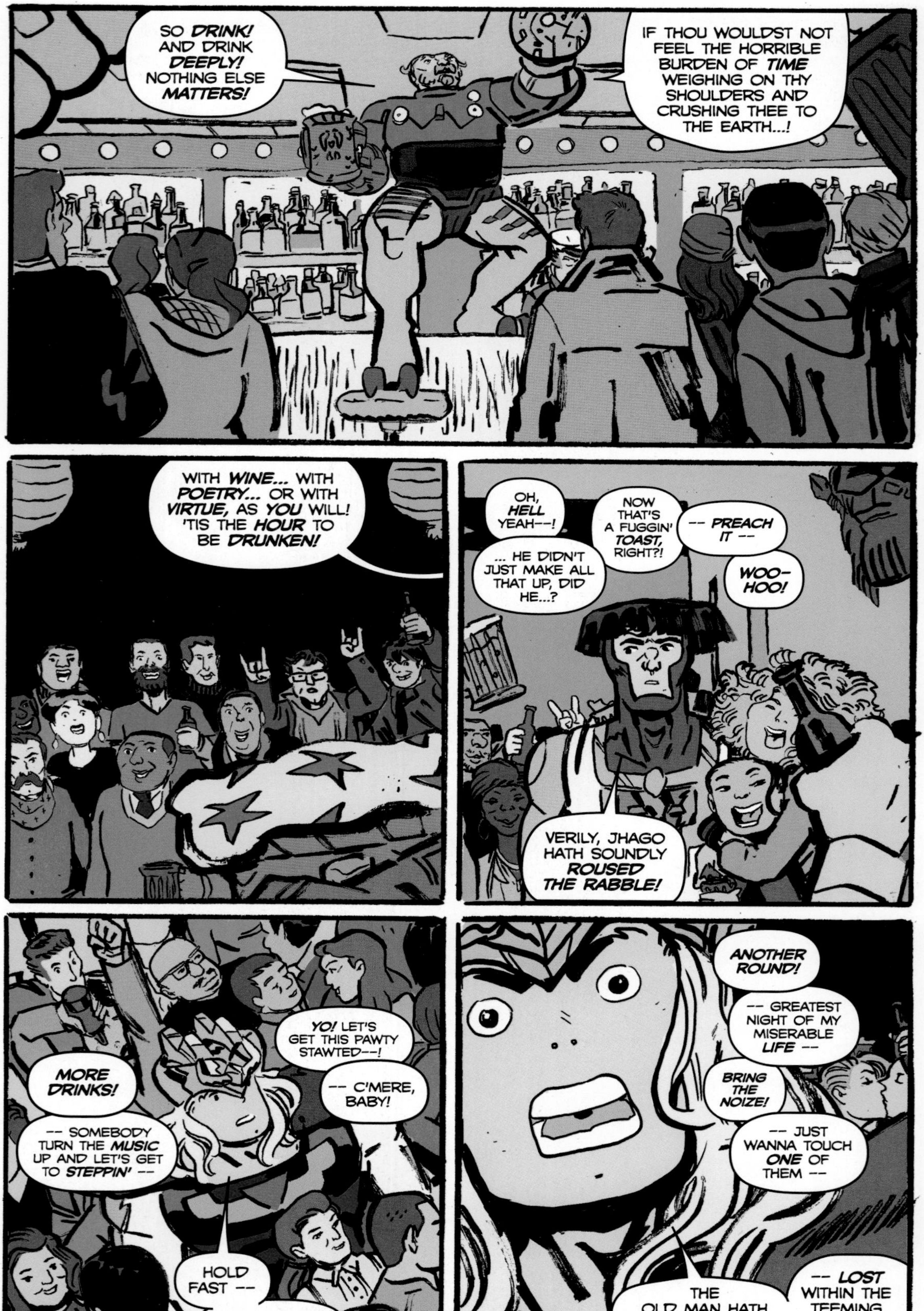
SO DRINK! AND DRINK DEEPLY! NOTHING ELSE MATTERS!
IF THOU WOULDST NOT FEEL THE HORRIBLE BURDEN OF TIME WEIGHING ON THY SHOULDERS AND CRUSHING THEE TO THE EARTH...!
WITH WINE... WITH POETRY... OR WITH VIRTUE, AS YOU WILL! 'TIS THE HOUR TO BE DRUNKEN!
OH, HELL YEAH--!
NOW THAT'S A FUGGIN' TOAST, RIGHT?!
-- PREACH IT --
... HE DIDN'T JUST MAKE ALL THAT UP, DID HE...?
WOO-HOO!
VERILY, JHAGO HATH SOUNDLY ROUSED THE RABBLE!
YO! LET'S GET THIS PAWTY STAWTED--!
MORE DRINKS!
-- C'MERE, BABY!
-- SOMEBODY TURN THE MUSIC UP AND LET'S GET TO STEPPIN' --
HOLD FAST --
-- ARTHUR?!
ANOTHER ROUND!
-- GREATEST NIGHT OF MY MISERABLE LIFE --
BRING THE NOIZE!
-- JUST WANNA TOUCH ONE OF THEM --
THE OLD MAN HATH DISAPPEARED --
-- LOST WITHIN THE TEEMING CROWD!

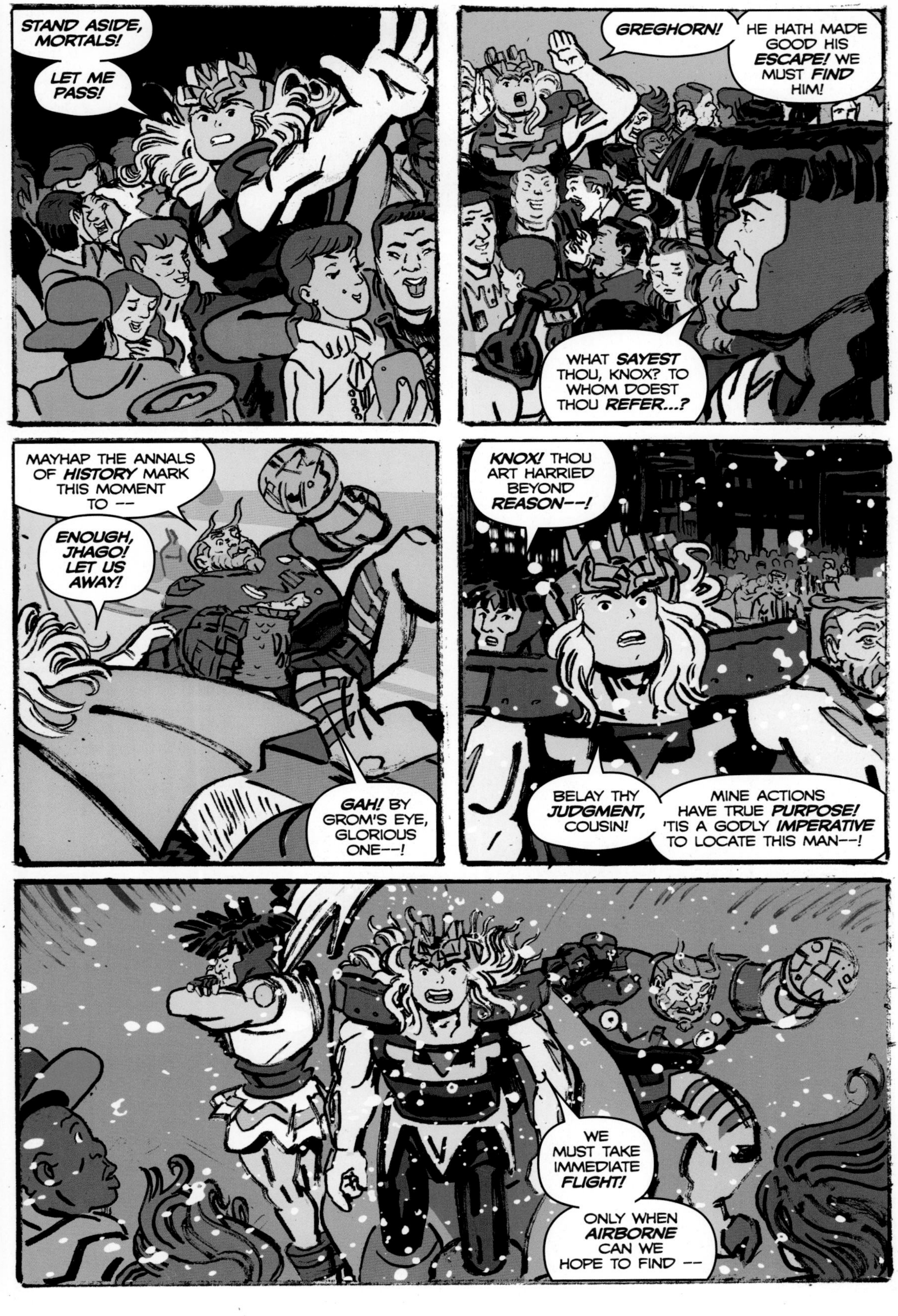
STAND ASIDE, MORTALS!
LET ME PASS!
GREGHORN!
HE HATH MADE GOOD HIS ESCAPE! WE MUST FIND HIM!
WHAT SAYEST THOU, KNOX? TO WHOM DOEST THOU REFER...?
MAYHAP THE ANNALS OF HISTORY MARK THIS MOMENT TO --
ENOUGH, JHAGO! LET US AWAY!
GAH! BY GROM'S EYE, GLORIOUS ONE--!
KNOX! THOU ART HARRIED BEYOND REASON--!
BELAY THY JUDGMENT, COUSIN!
MINE ACTIONS HAVE TRUE PURPOSE! 'TIS A GODLY IMPERATIVE TO LOCATE THIS MAN--!
WE MUST TAKE IMMEDIATE FLIGHT!
ONLY WHEN AIRBORNE CAN WE HOPE TO FIND --

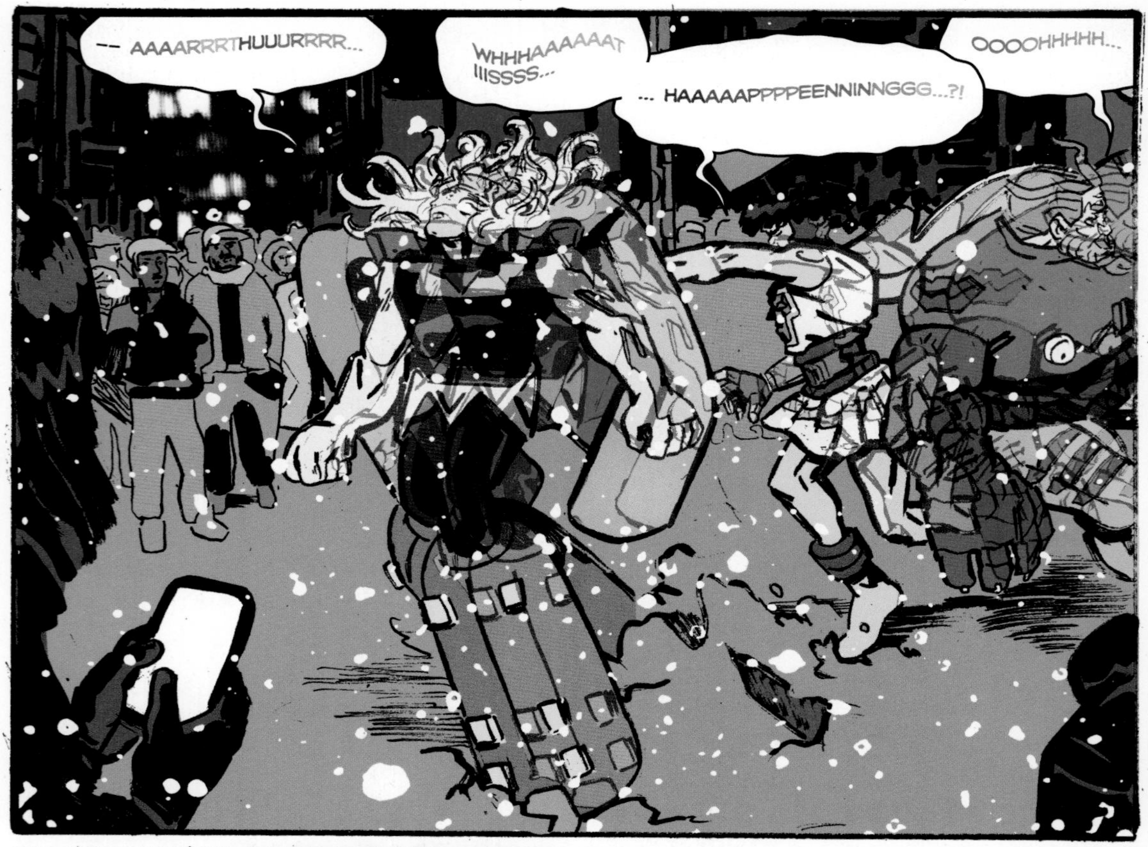
-- AAAARRRTHUUURRRR...
WHHHAAAAAAT IIISSSS...
... HAAAAAPPPPEENNINNGGG...?!
OOOOHHHHH...

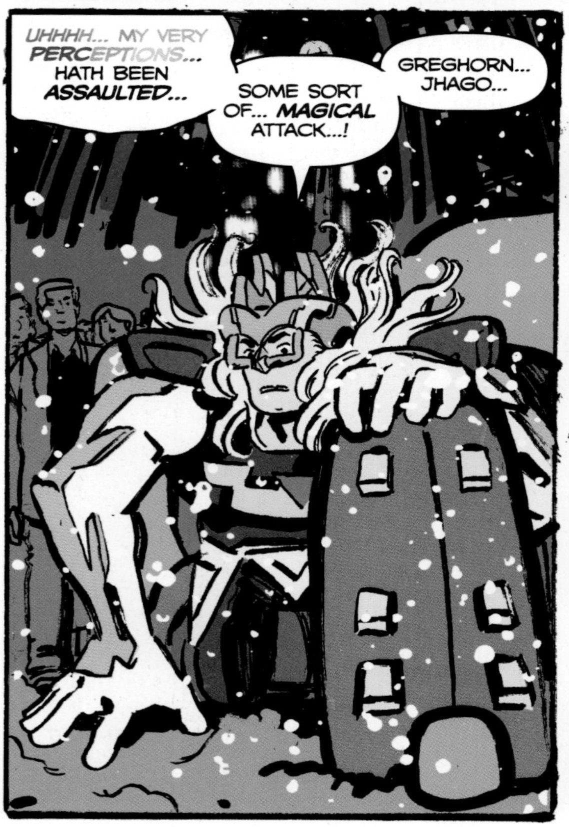
UHHHH... MY VERY PERCEPTIONS... HATH BEEN ASSAULTED...
SOME SORT OF... MAGICAL ATTACK...!
GREGHORN... JHAGO...

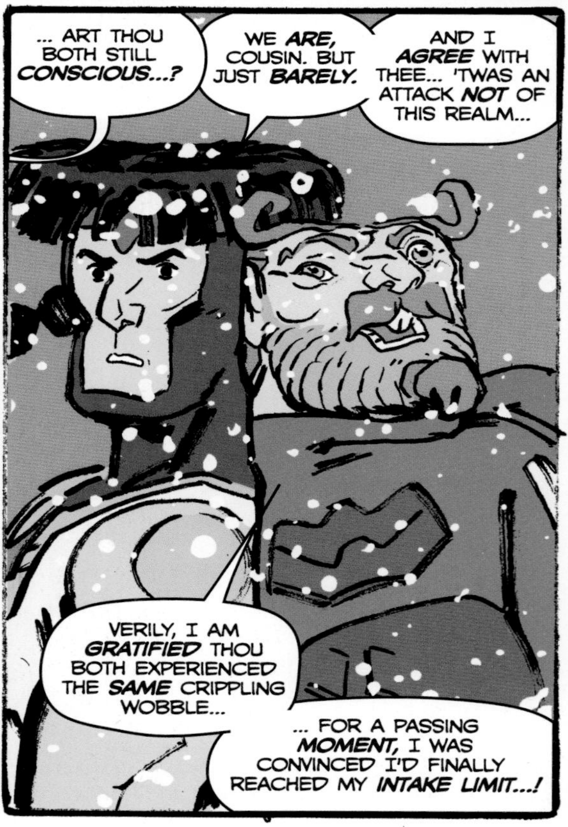
... ART THOU BOTH STILL CONSCIOUS...?
WE ARE, COUSIN. BUT JUST BARELY.
AND I AGREE WITH THEE... 'TWAS AN ATTACK NOT OF THIS REALM...
VERILY, I AM GRATIFIED THOU BOTH EXPERIENCED THE SAME CRIPPLING WOBBLE...
... FOR A PASSING MOMENT, I WAS CONVINCED I'D FINALLY REACHED MY INTAKE LIMIT...!

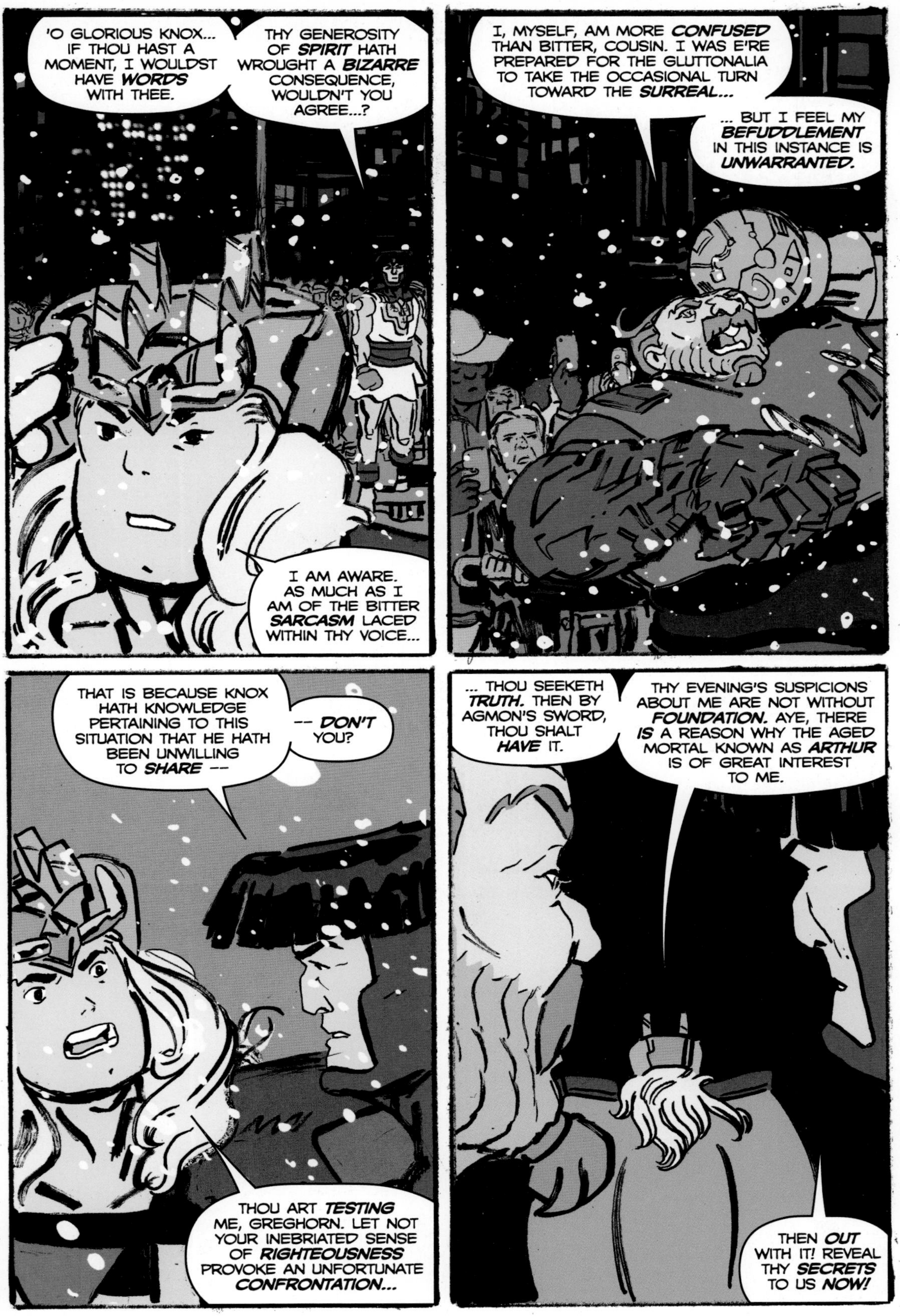
'O GLORIOUS KNOX... IF THOU HAST A MOMENT, I WOULDST HAVE WORDS WITH THEE.
THY GENEROSITY OF SPIRIT HATH WROUGHT A BIZARRE CONSEQUENCE, WOULDN'T YOU AGREE...?
I AM AWARE. AS MUCH AS I AM OF THE BITTER SARCASM LACED WITHIN THY VOICE...
I, MYSELF, AM MORE CONFUSED THAN BITTER, COUSIN. I WAS E'RE PREPARED FOR THE GLUTTONALIA TO TAKE THE OCCASIONAL TURN TOWARD THE SURREAL...
... BUT I FEEL MY BEFUDDLEMENT IN THIS INSTANCE IS UNWARRANTED.
THAT IS BECAUSE KNOX HATH KNOWLEDGE PERTAINING TO THIS SITUATION THAT HE HATH BEEN UNWILLING TO SHARE --
-- DON'T YOU?
THOU ART TESTING ME, GREGHORN. LET NOT YOUR INEBRIATED SENSE OF RIGHTEOUSNESS PROVOKE AN UNFORTUNATE CONFRONTATION...
... THOU SEEKETH TRUTH. THEN BY AGMON'S SWORD, THOU SHALT HAVE IT.
THY EVENING'S SUSPICIONS ABOUT ME ARE NOT WITHOUT FOUNDATION. AYE, THERE IS A REASON WHY THE AGED MORTAL KNOWN AS ARTHUR IS OF GREAT INTEREST TO ME.
THEN OUT WITH IT! REVEAL THY SECRETS TO US NOW!

ARTHUR IS BUT A MORTAL *SHELL* —— A MAGICAL *CONSTRUCT* MEANT TO FOREVER SUPPLANT HIS *TRUE* IDENTITY...

... THAT OF THE DREADED *AKUMO.*

AKUMO... THE *JACK-IN-IRONS?!*

SO THOU ART SAYING... OUR MOST *DREADED ENEMY* HATH BEEN HERE *ALL ALONG?!*

BUT... 'TWAS MY IMPRESSION THAT WE'D *DESTROYED* THAT WRETCHED VILLAIN AFTER A PAN-DIMENSIONAL *WAR* THAT INCLUDED THIS VERY *REALM!*

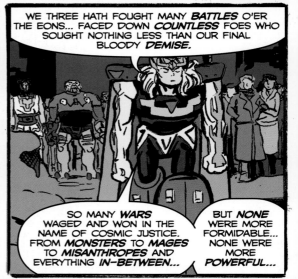

WE THREE HATH FOUGHT MANY *BATTLES* O'ER THE EONS... FACED DOWN *COUNTLESS* FOES WHO SOUGHT NOTHING LESS THAN OUR FINAL BLOODY *DEMISE.*

SO MANY *WARS* WAGED AND WON IN THE NAME OF COSMIC JUSTICE. FROM *MONSTERS* TO *MAGES* TO *MISANTHROPES* AND EVERYTHING *IN-BETWEEN...*

BUT *NONE* WERE MORE FORMIDABLE... NONE WERE MORE *POWERFUL...*

"... THAN THE ONE CALLED *AKUMO!*

"HIS *WAR RANKING* —— BESTOWED UPON HIM BY THE ANCIENT DEMON HORDES OF *KATHUNDRAL* —— WAS INDEED *'THE JACK-IN-IRONS'!* THE UNHOLY BRINGER OF ETERNAL NIHILISM! THE APOCALYPSE ON TWO LEGS!

"*AKUMO* WAS *BEYOND* IMMORTAL... HIS WAS A TERROR THAT WAS *UNKILLABLE!*"

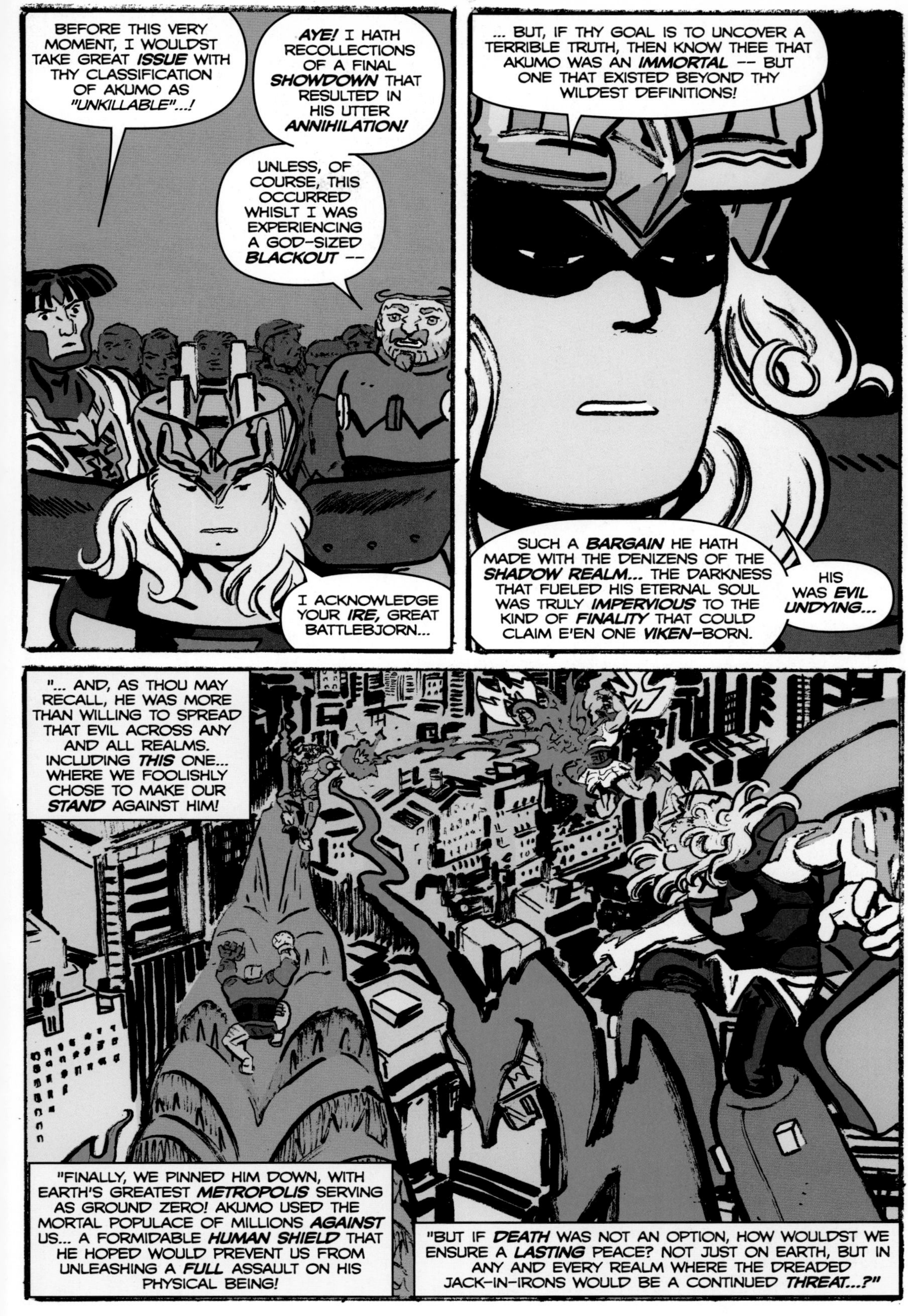
BEFORE THIS VERY MOMENT, I WOULDST TAKE GREAT *ISSUE* WITH THY CLASSIFICATION OF AKUMO AS "UNKILLABLE"...!
AYE! I HATH RECOLLECTIONS OF A FINAL *SHOWDOWN* THAT RESULTED IN HIS UTTER *ANNIHILATION!*
UNLESS, OF COURSE, THIS OCCURRED WHISLT I WAS EXPERIENCING A GOD-SIZED *BLACKOUT* --
I ACKNOWLEDGE YOUR *IRE,* GREAT BATTLEBJORN...
... BUT, IF THY GOAL IS TO UNCOVER A TERRIBLE TRUTH, THEN KNOW THEE THAT AKUMO WAS AN *IMMORTAL* -- BUT ONE THAT EXISTED BEYOND THY WILDEST DEFINITIONS!
SUCH A *BARGAIN* HE HATH MADE WITH THE DENIZENS OF THE *SHADOW REALM...* THE DARKNESS THAT FUELED HIS ETERNAL SOUL WAS TRULY *IMPERVIOUS* TO THE KIND OF *FINALITY* THAT COULD CLAIM E'EN ONE *VIKEN*-BORN.
HIS WAS *EVIL UNDYING...*
"... AND, AS THOU MAY RECALL, HE WAS MORE THAN WILLING TO SPREAD THAT EVIL ACROSS ANY AND ALL REALMS. INCLUDING *THIS* ONE... WHERE WE FOOLISHLY CHOSE TO MAKE OUR *STAND* AGAINST HIM!
"FINALLY, WE PINNED HIM DOWN, WITH EARTH'S GREATEST *METROPOLIS* SERVING AS GROUND ZERO! AKUMO USED THE MORTAL POPULACE OF MILLIONS *AGAINST* US... A FORMIDABLE *HUMAN SHIELD* THAT HE HOPED WOULD PREVENT US FROM UNLEASHING A *FULL* ASSAULT ON HIS PHYSICAL BEING!
"BUT IF *DEATH* WAS NOT AN OPTION, HOW WOULDST WE ENSURE A *LASTING* PEACE? NOT JUST ON EARTH, BUT IN ANY AND EVERY REALM WHERE THE DREADED JACK-IN-IRONS WOULD BE A CONTINUED *THREAT...?"*

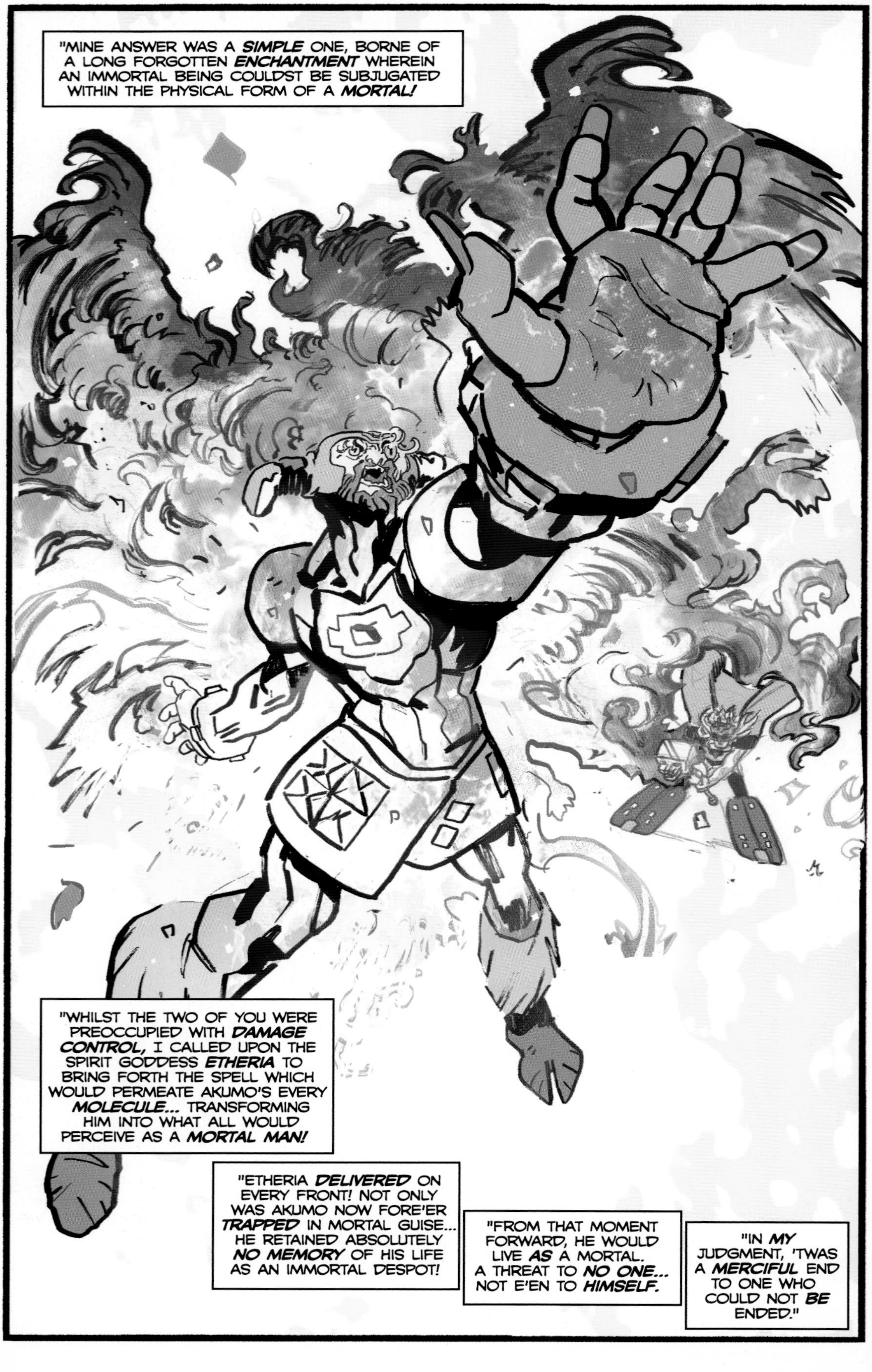
"MINE ANSWER WAS A SIMPLE ONE, BORNE OF A LONG FORGOTTEN ENCHANTMENT WHEREIN AN IMMORTAL BEING COULDST BE SUBJUGATED WITHIN THE PHYSICAL FORM OF A MORTAL!
"WHILST THE TWO OF YOU WERE PREOCCUPIED WITH DAMAGE CONTROL, I CALLED UPON THE SPIRIT GODDESS ETHERIA TO BRING FORTH THE SPELL WHICH WOULD PERMEATE AKUMO'S EVERY MOLECULE... TRANSFORMING HIM INTO WHAT ALL WOULD PERCEIVE AS A MORTAL MAN!
"ETHERIA DELIVERED ON EVERY FRONT! NOT ONLY WAS AKUMO NOW FORE'ER TRAPPED IN MORTAL GUISE... HE RETAINED ABSOLUTELY NO MEMORY OF HIS LIFE AS AN IMMORTAL DESPOT!
"FROM THAT MOMENT FORWARD, HE WOULD LIVE AS A MORTAL. A THREAT TO NO ONE... NOT E'EN TO HIMSELF.
"IN MY JUDGMENT, 'TWAS A MERCIFUL END TO ONE WHO COULD NOT BE ENDED."

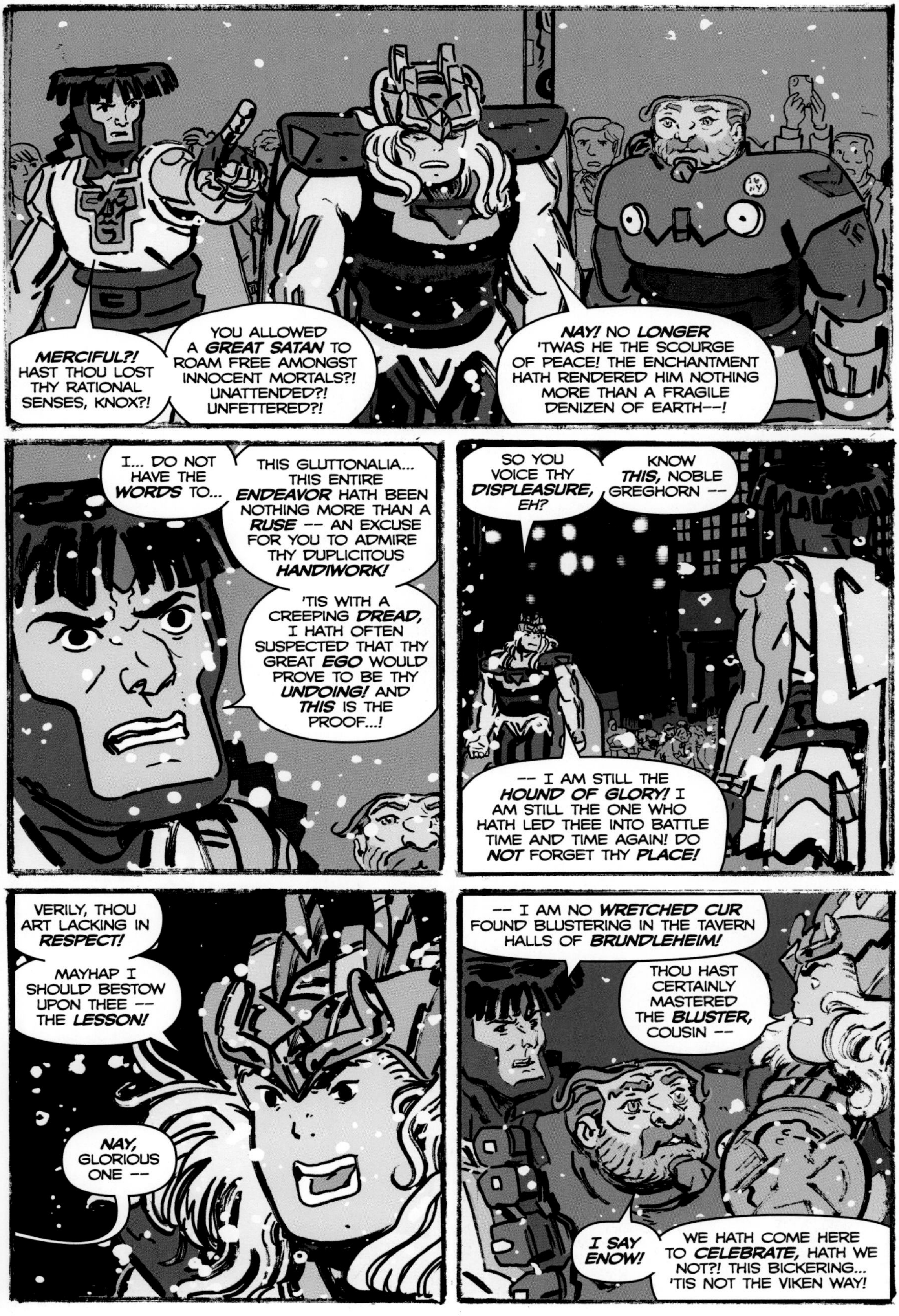

MERCIFUL?! HAST THOU LOST THY RATIONAL SENSES, KNOX?!
YOU ALLOWED A GREAT SATAN TO ROAM FREE AMONGST INNOCENT MORTALS?! UNATTENDED?! UNFETTERED?!
NAY! NO LONGER 'TWAS HE THE SCOURGE OF PEACE! THE ENCHANTMENT HATH RENDERED HIM NOTHING MORE THAN A FRAGILE DENIZEN OF EARTH--!
I... DO NOT HAVE THE WORDS TO...
THIS GLUTTONALIA... THIS ENTIRE ENDEAVOR HATH BEEN NOTHING MORE THAN A RUSE -- AN EXCUSE FOR YOU TO ADMIRE THY DUPLICITOUS HANDIWORK!
'TIS WITH A CREEPING DREAD, I HATH OFTEN SUSPECTED THAT THY GREAT EGO WOULD PROVE TO BE THY UNDOING! AND THIS IS THE PROOF...!
SO YOU VOICE THY DISPLEASURE, EH?
KNOW THIS, NOBLE GREGHORN --
-- I AM STILL THE HOUND OF GLORY! I AM STILL THE ONE WHO HATH LED THEE INTO BATTLE TIME AND TIME AGAIN! DO NOT FORGET THY PLACE!
VERILY, THOU ART LACKING IN RESPECT!
MAYHAP I SHOULD BESTOW UPON THEE -- THE LESSON!
NAY, GLORIOUS ONE --
-- I AM NO WRETCHED CUR FOUND BLUSTERING IN THE TAVERN HALLS OF BRUNDLEHEIM!
THOU HAST CERTAINLY MASTERED THE BLUSTER, COUSIN --
I SAY ENOW!
WE HATH COME HERE TO CELEBRATE, HATH WE NOT?! THIS BICKERING... 'TIS NOT THE VIKEN WAY!

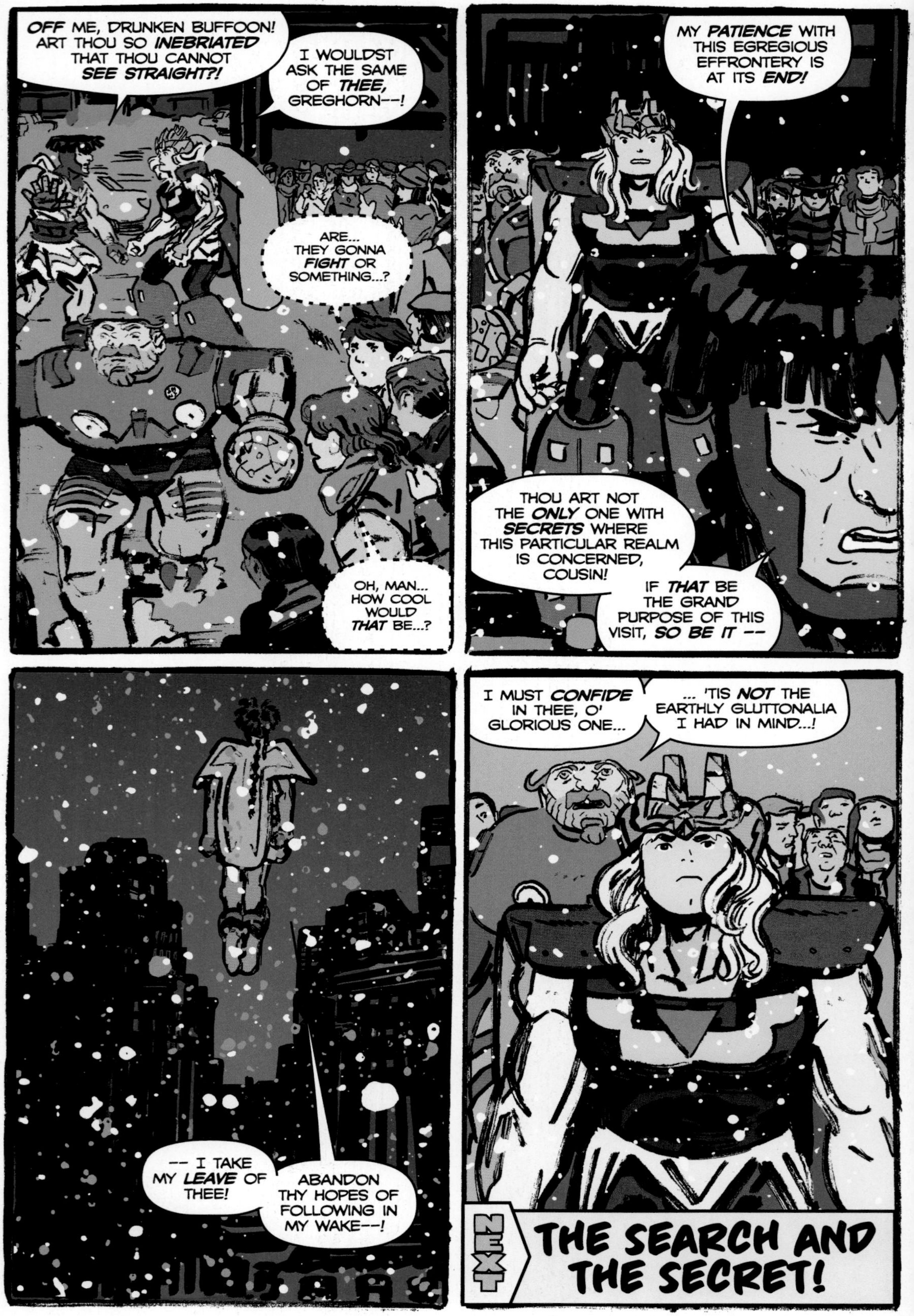
OFF ME, DRUNKEN BUFFOON! ART THOU SO INEBRIATED THAT THOU CANNOT SEE STRAIGHT?!
I WOULDST ASK THE SAME OF THEE, GREGHORN--!
ARE... THEY GONNA FIGHT OR SOMETHING...?
OH, MAN... HOW COOL WOULD THAT BE...?
MY PATIENCE WITH THIS EGREGIOUS EFFRONTERY IS AT ITS END!
THOU ART NOT THE ONLY ONE WITH SECRETS WHERE THIS PARTICULAR REALM IS CONCERNED, COUSIN!
IF THAT BE THE GRAND PURPOSE OF THIS VISIT, SO BE IT --
-- I TAKE MY LEAVE OF THEE!
ABANDON THY HOPES OF FOLLOWING IN MY WAKE--!
I MUST CONFIDE IN THEE, O' GLORIOUS ONE...
... 'TIS NOT THE EARTHLY GLUTTONALIA I HAD IN MIND...!
NEXT
THE SEARCH AND THE SECRET!

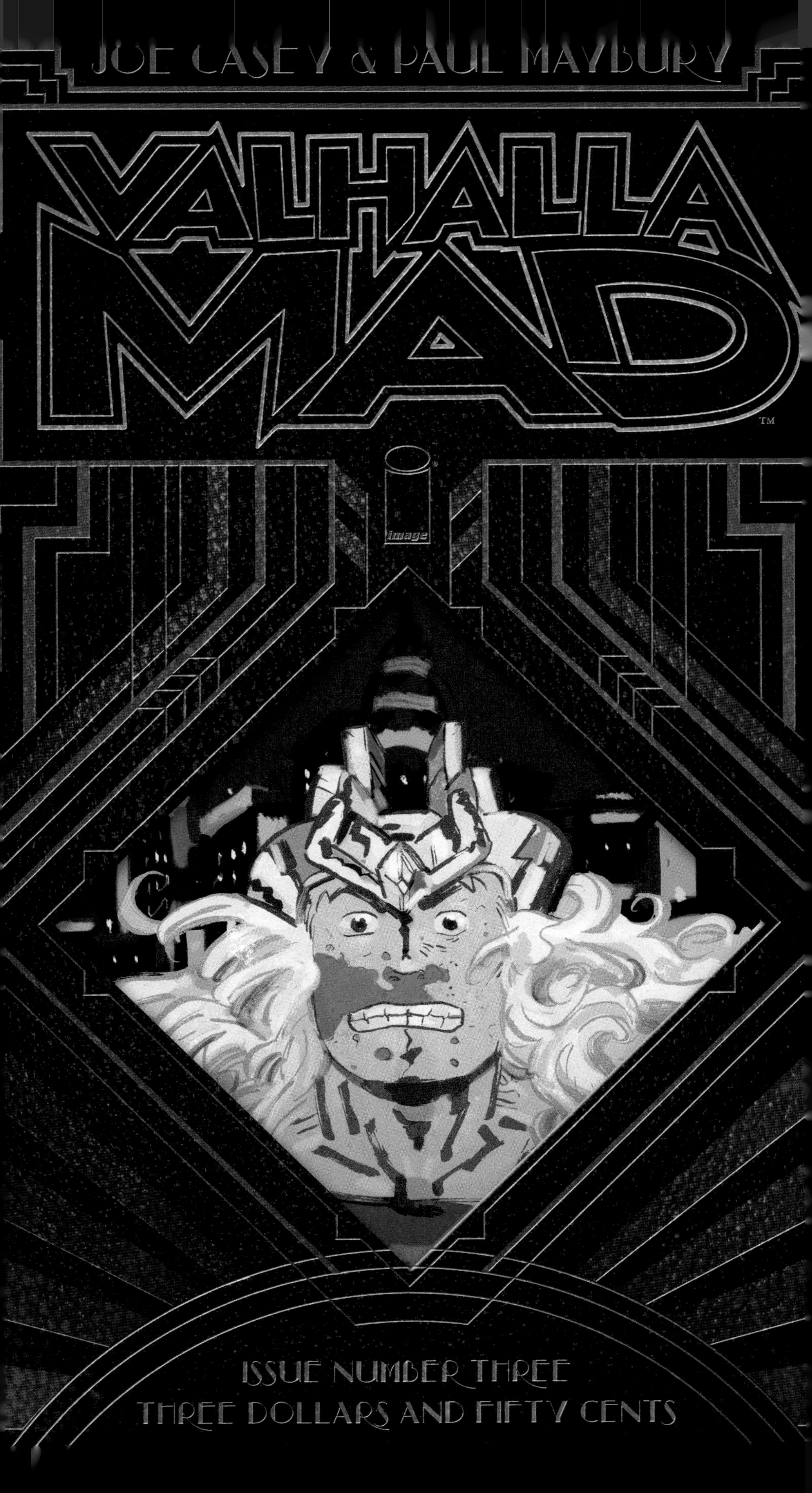
JOE CASEY & PAUL MAYBURY
VALHALLA MAD
ISSUE NUMBER THREE
THREE DOLLARS AND FIFTY CENTS

CHAPTER

3

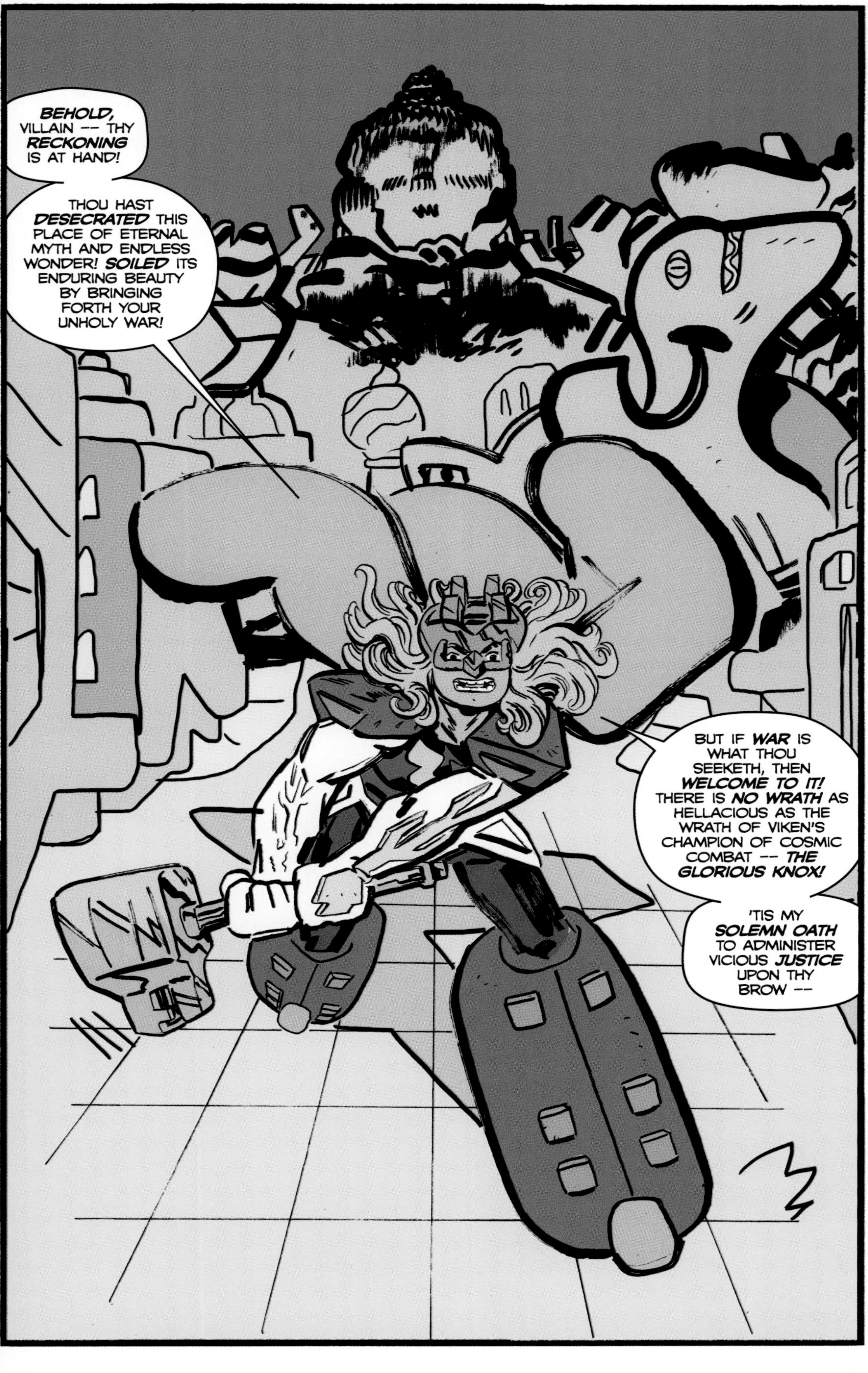
BEHOLD, VILLAIN -- THY RECKONING IS AT HAND!
THOU HAST DESECRATED THIS PLACE OF ETERNAL MYTH AND ENDLESS WONDER! SOILED ITS ENDURING BEAUTY BY BRINGING FORTH YOUR UNHOLY WAR!
BUT IF WAR IS WHAT THOU SEEKETH, THEN WELCOME TO IT! THERE IS NO WRATH AS HELLACIOUS AS THE WRATH OF VIKEN'S CHAMPION OF COSMIC COMBAT -- THE GLORIOUS KNOX!
'TIS MY SOLEMN OATH TO ADMINISTER VICIOUS JUSTICE UPON THY BROW --

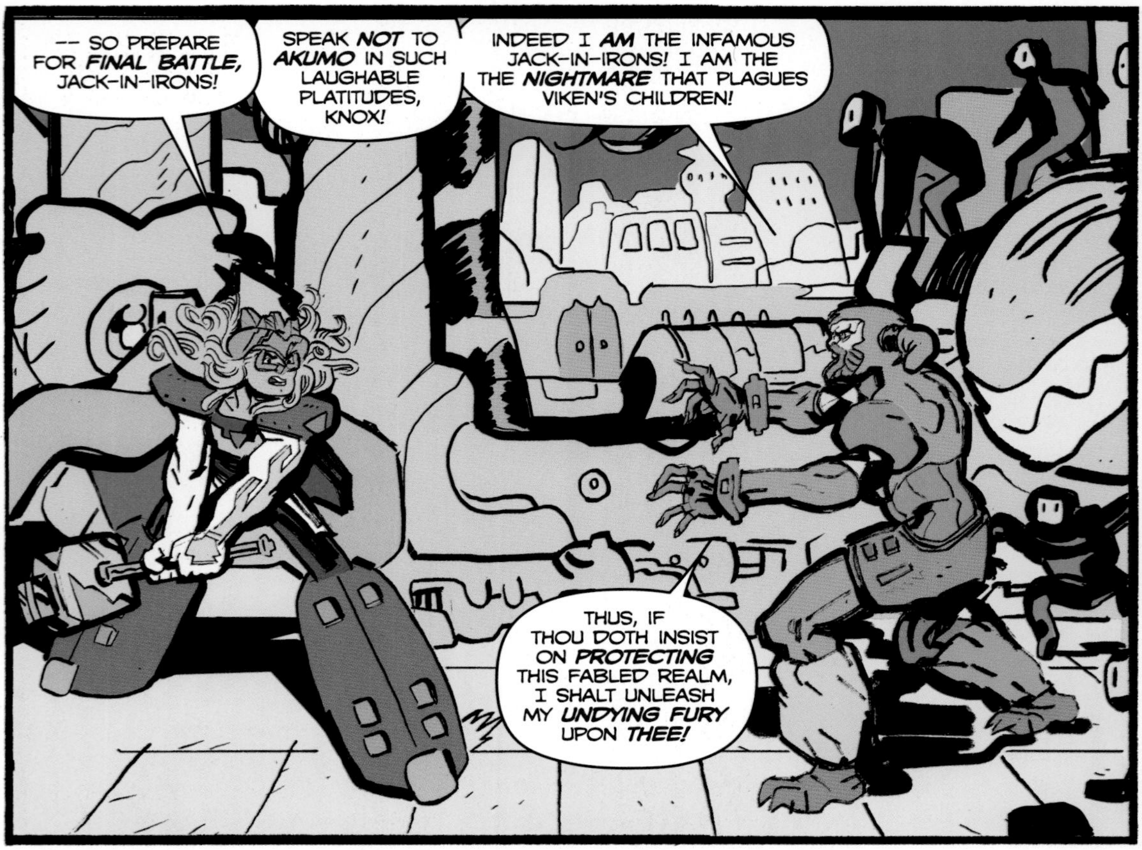
-- SO PREPARE FOR FINAL BATTLE, JACK-IN-IRONS!
SPEAK NOT TO AKUMO IN SUCH LAUGHABLE PLATITUDES, KNOX!
INDEED I AM THE INFAMOUS JACK-IN-IRONS! I AM THE THE NIGHTMARE THAT PLAGUES VIKEN'S CHILDREN!
THUS, IF THOU DOTH INSIST ON PROTECTING THIS FABLED REALM, I SHALT UNLEASH MY UNDYING FURY UPON THEE!

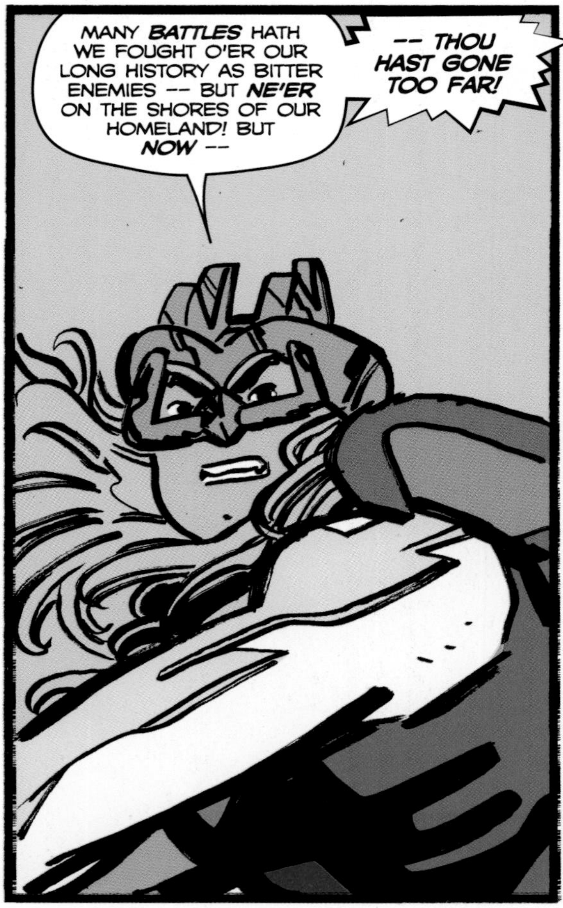
MANY BATTLES HATH WE FOUGHT O'ER OUR LONG HISTORY AS BITTER ENEMIES -- BUT NE'ER ON THE SHORES OF OUR HOMELAND! BUT NOW --
-- THOU HAST GONE TOO FAR!

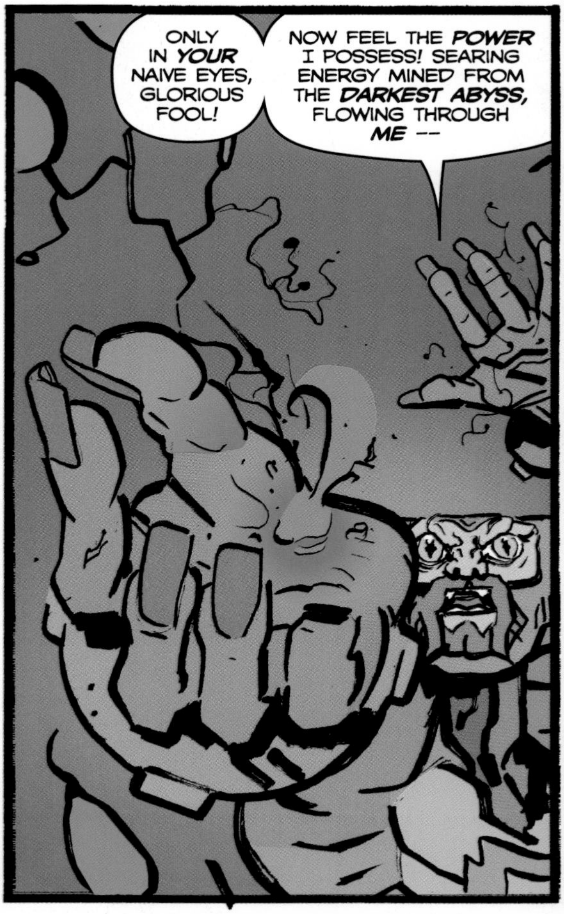
ONLY IN YOUR NAIVE EYES, GLORIOUS FOOL!
NOW FEEL THE POWER I POSSESS! SEARING ENERGY MINED FROM THE DARKEST ABYSS, FLOWING THROUGH ME --

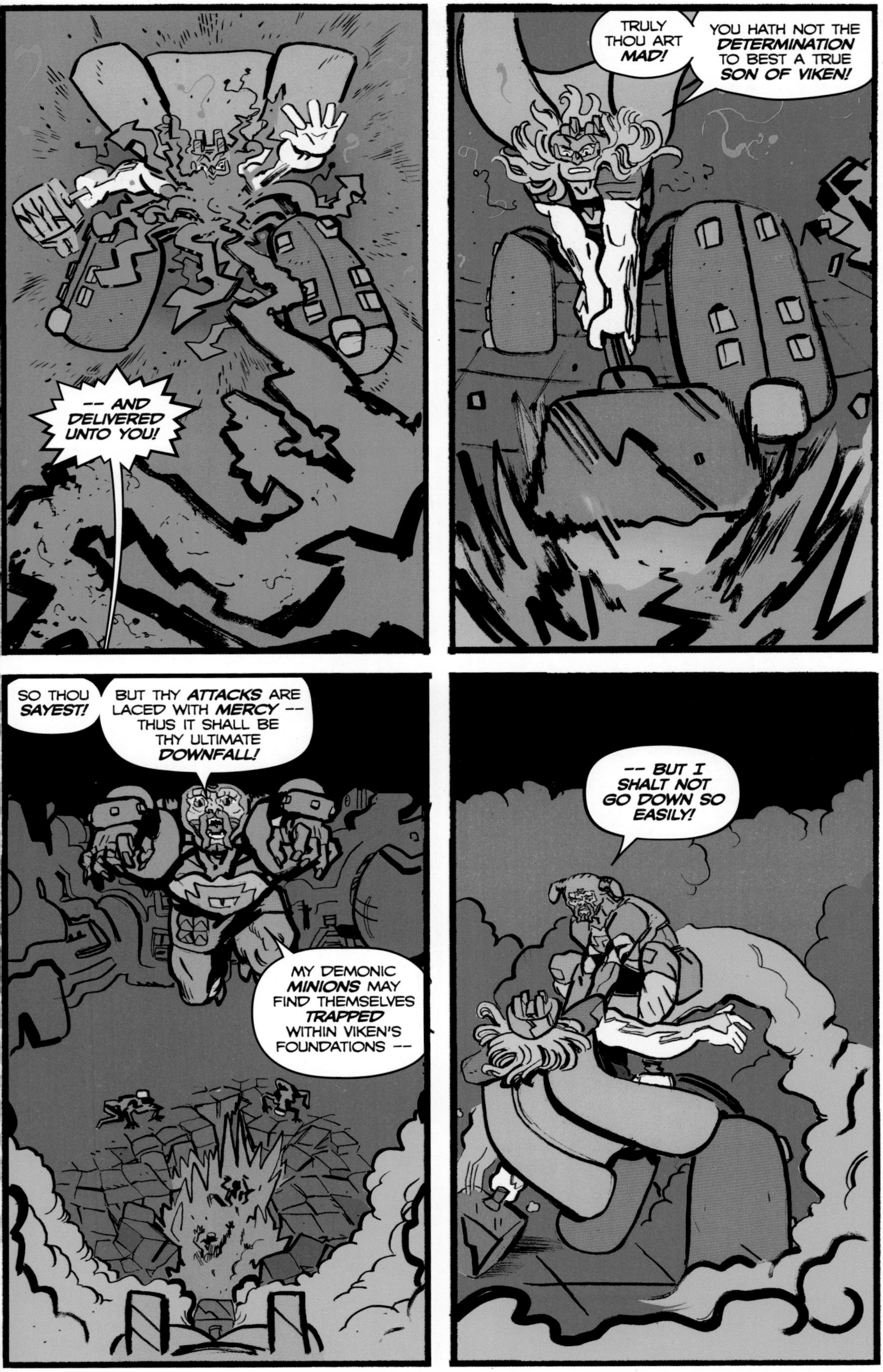
-- AND DELIVERED UNTO YOU!
TRULY THOU ART MAD!
YOU HATH NOT THE DETERMINATION TO BEST A TRUE SON OF VIKEN!
SO THOU SAYEST!
BUT THY ATTACKS ARE LACED WITH MERCY -- THUS IT SHALL BE THY ULTIMATE DOWNFALL!
MY DEMONIC MINIONS MAY FIND THEMSELVES TRAPPED WITHIN VIKEN'S FOUNDATIONS --
-- BUT I SHALT NOT GO DOWN SO EASILY!

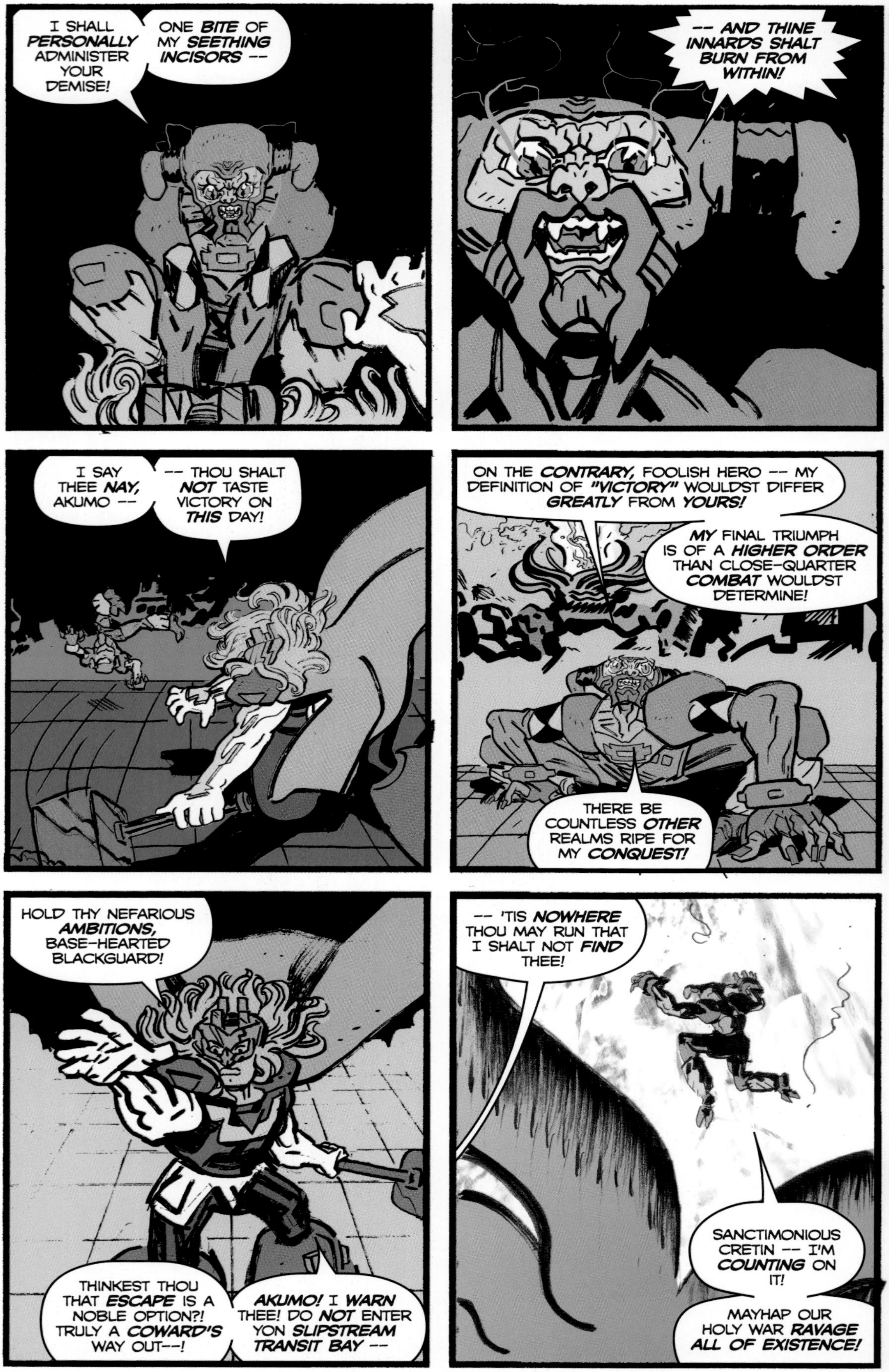
I SHALL PERSONALLY ADMINISTER YOUR DEMISE!
ONE BITE OF MY SEETHING INCISORS --
-- AND THINE INNARDS SHALT BURN FROM WITHIN!
I SAY THEE NAY, AKUMO --
-- THOU SHALT NOT TASTE VICTORY ON THIS DAY!
ON THE CONTRARY, FOOLISH HERO -- MY DEFINITION OF "VICTORY" WOULDST DIFFER GREATLY FROM YOURS!
MY FINAL TRIUMPH IS OF A HIGHER ORDER THAN CLOSE-QUARTER COMBAT WOULDST DETERMINE!
THERE BE COUNTLESS OTHER REALMS RIPE FOR MY CONQUEST!
HOLD THY NEFARIOUS AMBITIONS, BASE-HEARTED BLACKGUARD!
THINKEST THOU THAT ESCAPE IS A NOBLE OPTION?! TRULY A COWARD'S WAY OUT--!
AKUMO! I WARN THEE! DO NOT ENTER YON SLIPSTREAM TRANSIT BAY --
-- 'TIS NOWHERE THOU MAY RUN THAT I SHALT NOT FIND THEE!
SANCTIMONIOUS CRETIN -- I'M COUNTING ON IT!
MAYHAP OUR HOLY WAR RAVAGE ALL OF EXISTENCE!

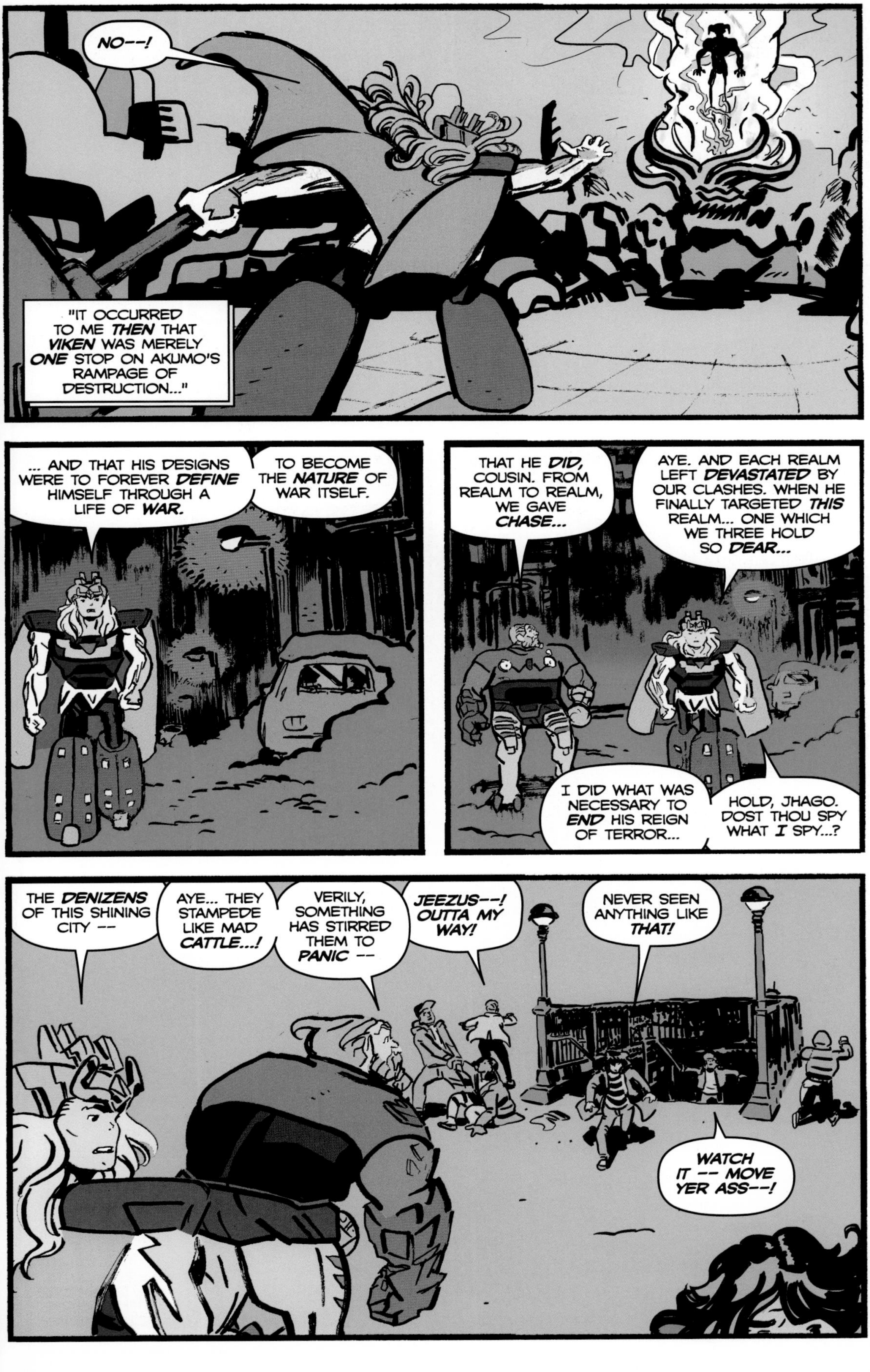
NO--!
"IT OCCURRED TO ME THEN THAT VIKEN WAS MERELY ONE STOP ON AKUMO'S RAMPAGE OF DESTRUCTION..."
... AND THAT HIS DESIGNS WERE TO FOREVER DEFINE HIMSELF THROUGH A LIFE OF WAR.
TO BECOME THE NATURE OF WAR ITSELF.
THAT HE DID, COUSIN. FROM REALM TO REALM, WE GAVE CHASE...
AYE. AND EACH REALM LEFT DEVASTATED BY OUR CLASHES. WHEN HE FINALLY TARGETED THIS REALM... ONE WHICH WE THREE HOLD SO DEAR...
I DID WHAT WAS NECESSARY TO END HIS REIGN OF TERROR...
HOLD, JHAGO. DOST THOU SPY WHAT I SPY...?
THE DENIZENS OF THIS SHINING CITY --
AYE... THEY STAMPEDE LIKE MAD CATTLE...!
VERILY, SOMETHING HAS STIRRED THEM TO PANIC --
JEEZUS--! OUTTA MY WAY!
NEVER SEEN ANYTHING LIKE THAT!
WATCH IT -- MOVE YER ASS--!

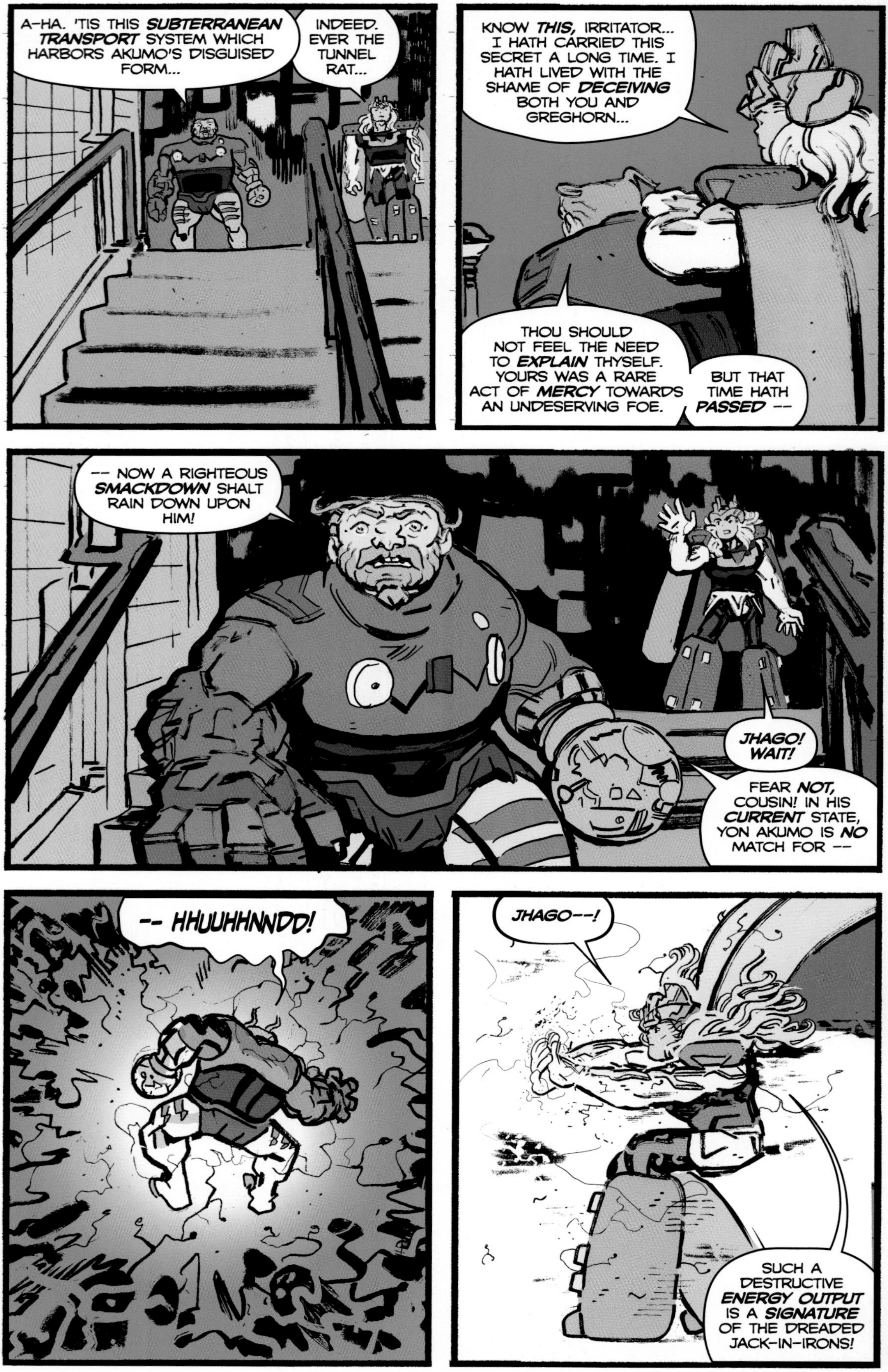
A-HA. 'TIS THIS SUBTERRANEAN TRANSPORT SYSTEM WHICH HARBORS AKUMO'S DISGUISED FORM...
INDEED. EVER THE TUNNEL RAT...
KNOW THIS, IRRITATOR... I HATH CARRIED THIS SECRET A LONG TIME. I HATH LIVED WITH THE SHAME OF DECEIVING BOTH YOU AND GREGHORN...
THOU SHOULD NOT FEEL THE NEED TO EXPLAIN THYSELF. YOURS WAS A RARE ACT OF MERCY TOWARDS AN UNDESERVING FOE.
BUT THAT TIME HATH PASSED --
-- NOW A RIGHTEOUS SMACKDOWN SHALT RAIN DOWN UPON HIM!
JHAGO! WAIT!
FEAR NOT, COUSIN! IN HIS CURRENT STATE, YON AKUMO IS NO MATCH FOR --
-- HHUUHHNNDD!
JHAGO--!
SUCH A DESTRUCTIVE ENERGY OUTPUT IS A SIGNATURE OF THE DREADED JACK-IN-IRONS!

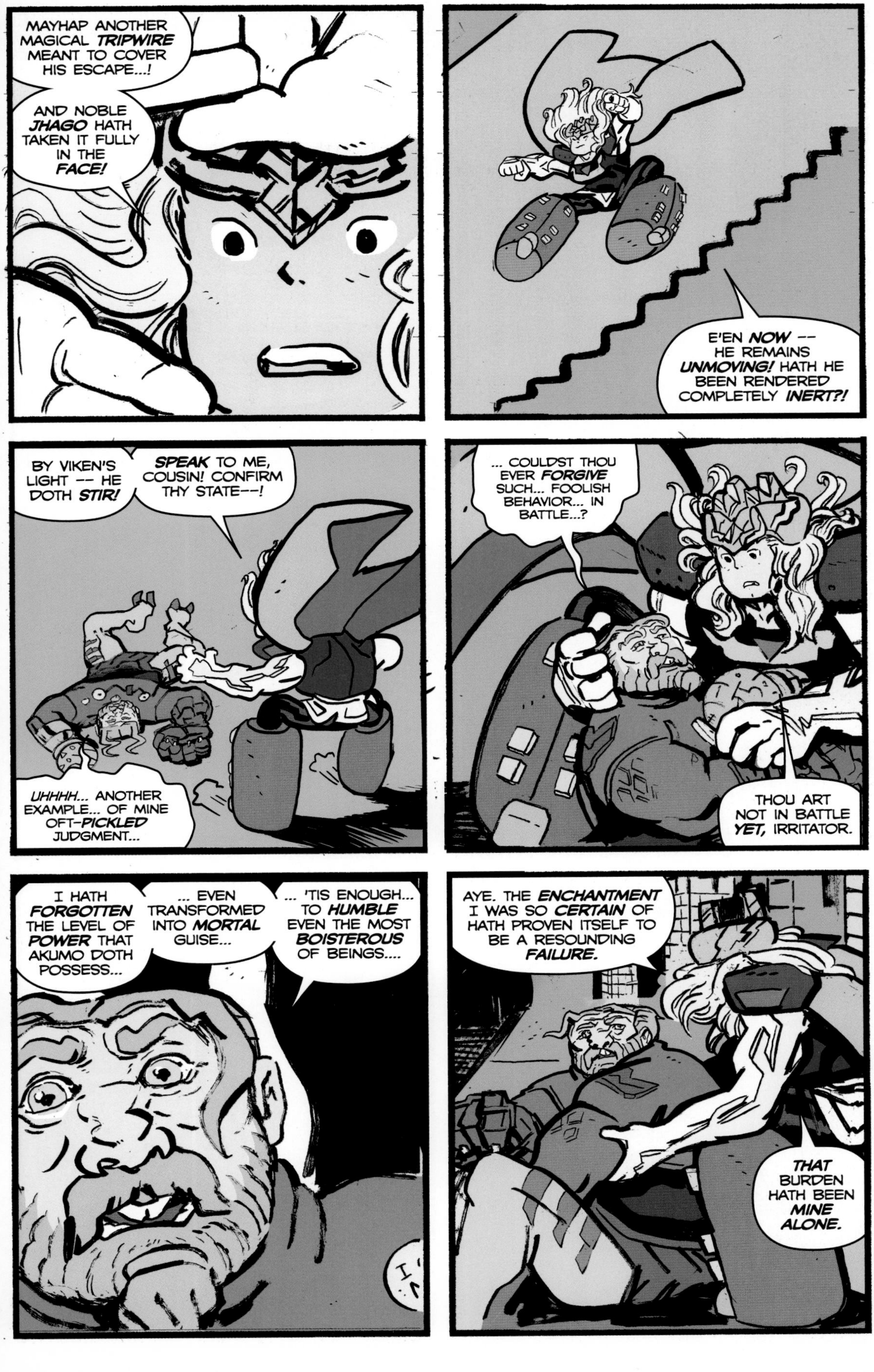
MAYHAP ANOTHER MAGICAL TRIPWIRE MEANT TO COVER HIS ESCAPE...!
AND NOBLE JHAGO HATH TAKEN IT FULLY IN THE FACE!
E'EN NOW -- HE REMAINS UNMOVING! HATH HE BEEN RENDERED COMPLETELY INERT?!
BY VIKEN'S LIGHT -- HE DOTH STIR!
SPEAK TO ME, COUSIN! CONFIRM THY STATE--!
UHHHH... ANOTHER EXAMPLE... OF MINE OFT-PICKLED JUDGMENT...
... COULDST THOU EVER FORGIVE SUCH... FOOLISH BEHAVIOR... IN BATTLE...?
THOU ART NOT IN BATTLE YET, IRRITATOR.
I HATH FORGOTTEN THE LEVEL OF POWER THAT AKUMO DOTH POSSESS...
... EVEN TRANSFORMED INTO MORTAL GUISE...
... 'TIS ENOUGH... TO HUMBLE EVEN THE MOST BOISTEROUS OF BEINGS....
AYE. THE ENCHANTMENT I WAS SO CERTAIN OF HATH PROVEN ITSELF TO BE A RESOUNDING FAILURE.
THAT BURDEN HATH BEEN MINE ALONE.

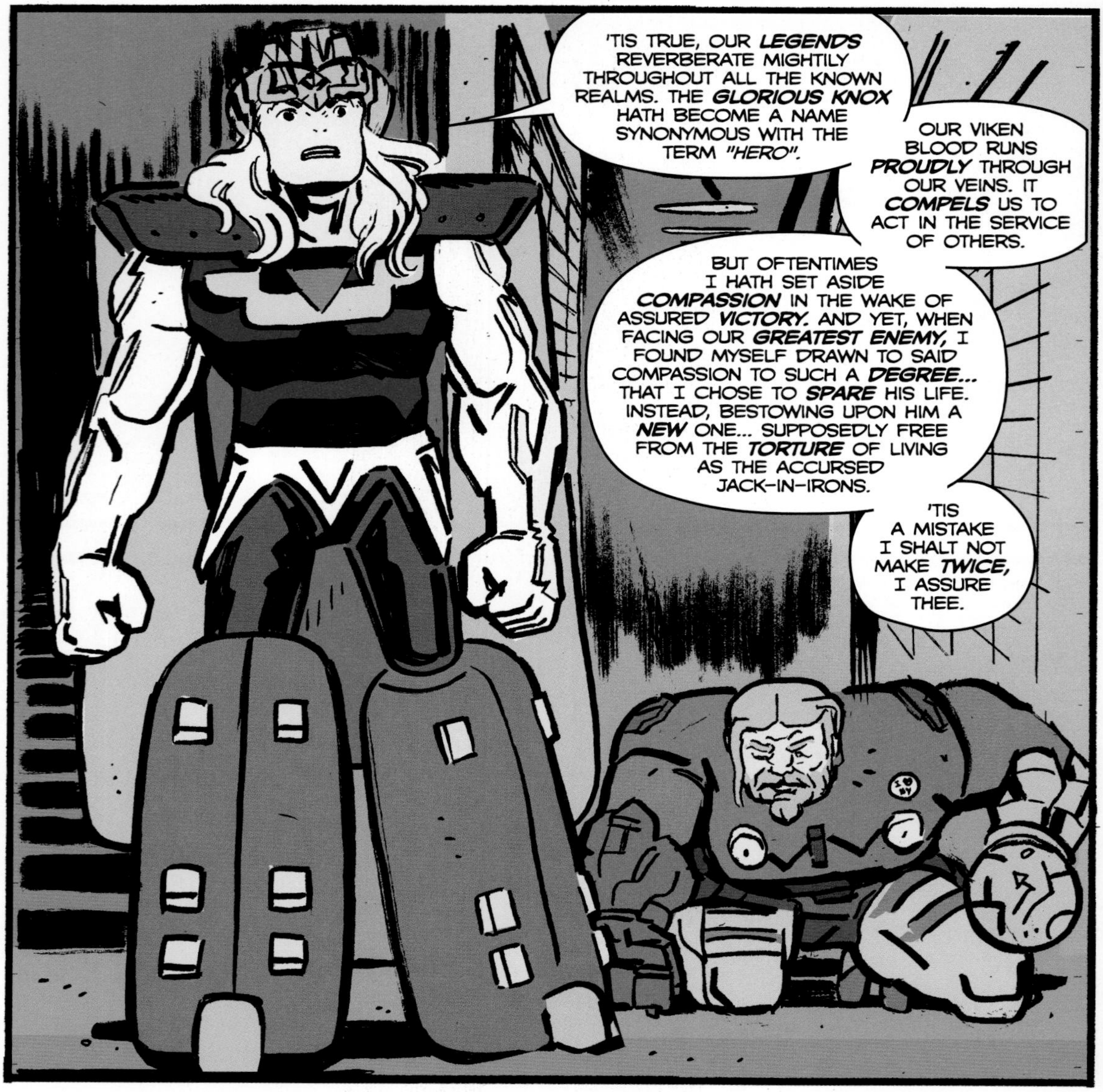
'TIS TRUE, OUR LEGENDS REVERBERATE MIGHTILY THROUGHOUT ALL THE KNOWN REALMS. THE GLORIOUS KNOX HATH BECOME A NAME SYNONYMOUS WITH THE TERM "HERO".
OUR VIKEN BLOOD RUNS PROUDLY THROUGH OUR VEINS. IT COMPELS US TO ACT IN THE SERVICE OF OTHERS.
BUT OFTENTIMES I HATH SET ASIDE COMPASSION IN THE WAKE OF ASSURED VICTORY. AND YET, WHEN FACING OUR GREATEST ENEMY, I FOUND MYSELF DRAWN TO SAID COMPASSION TO SUCH A DEGREE... THAT I CHOSE TO SPARE HIS LIFE. INSTEAD, BESTOWING UPON HIM A NEW ONE... SUPPOSEDLY FREE FROM THE TORTURE OF LIVING AS THE ACCURSED JACK-IN-IRONS.
'TIS A MISTAKE I SHALT NOT MAKE TWICE, I ASSURE THEE.
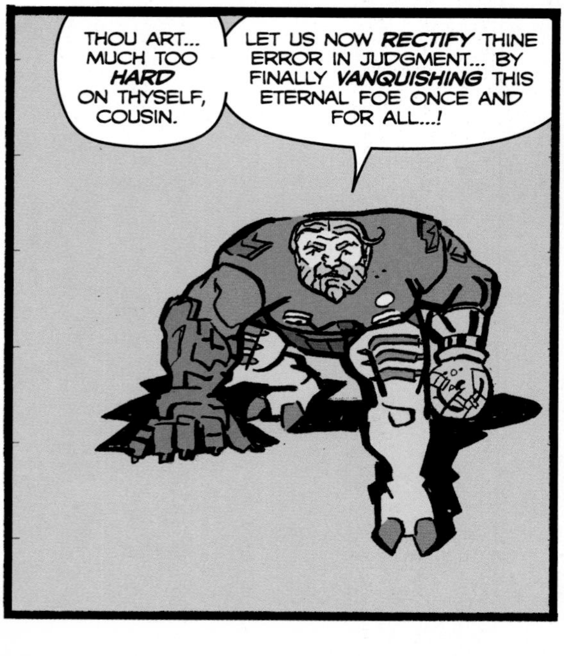
THOU ART... MUCH TOO HARD ON THYSELF, COUSIN.
LET US NOW RECTIFY THINE ERROR IN JUDGMENT... BY FINALLY VANQUISHING THIS ETERNAL FOE ONCE AND FOR ALL...!
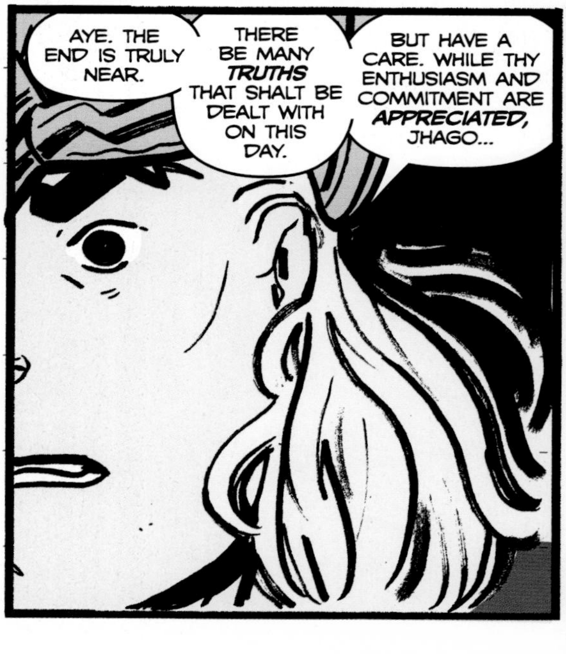
AYE. THE END IS TRULY NEAR.
THERE BE MANY TRUTHS THAT SHALT BE DEALT WITH ON THIS DAY.
BUT HAVE A CARE. WHILE THY ENTHUSIASM AND COMMITMENT ARE APPRECIATED, JHAGO...

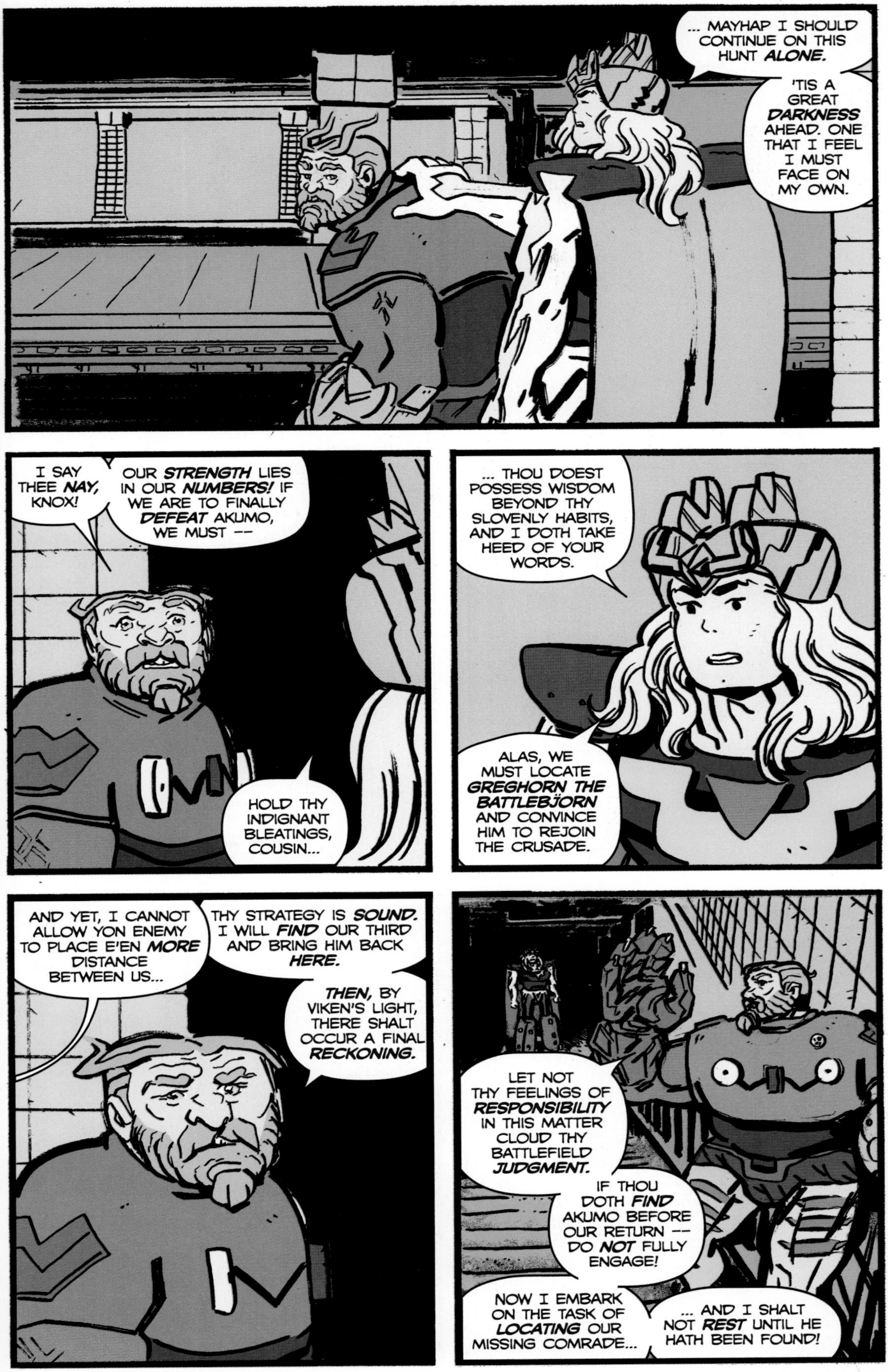
... MAYHAP I SHOULD CONTINUE ON THIS HUNT ALONE.
'TIS A GREAT DARKNESS AHEAD. ONE THAT I FEEL I MUST FACE ON MY OWN.
I SAY THEE NAY, KNOX!
OUR STRENGTH LIES IN OUR NUMBERS! IF WE ARE TO FINALLY DEFEAT AKUMO, WE MUST --
HOLD THY INDIGNANT BLEATINGS, COUSIN...
... THOU DOEST POSSESS WISDOM BEYOND THY SLOVENLY HABITS, AND I DOTH TAKE HEED OF YOUR WORDS.
ALAS, WE MUST LOCATE GREGHORN THE BATTLEBJÖRN AND CONVINCE HIM TO REJOIN THE CRUSADE.
AND YET, I CANNOT ALLOW YON ENEMY TO PLACE E'EN MORE DISTANCE BETWEEN US...
THY STRATEGY IS SOUND. I WILL FIND OUR THIRD AND BRING HIM BACK HERE.
THEN, BY VIKEN'S LIGHT, THERE SHALT OCCUR A FINAL RECKONING.
LET NOT THY FEELINGS OF RESPONSIBILITY IN THIS MATTER CLOUD THY BATTLEFIELD JUDGMENT.
IF THOU DOTH FIND AKUMO BEFORE OUR RETURN -- DO NOT FULLY ENGAGE!
NOW I EMBARK ON THE TASK OF LOCATING OUR MISSING COMRADE...
... AND I SHALT NOT REST UNTIL HE HATH BEEN FOUND!

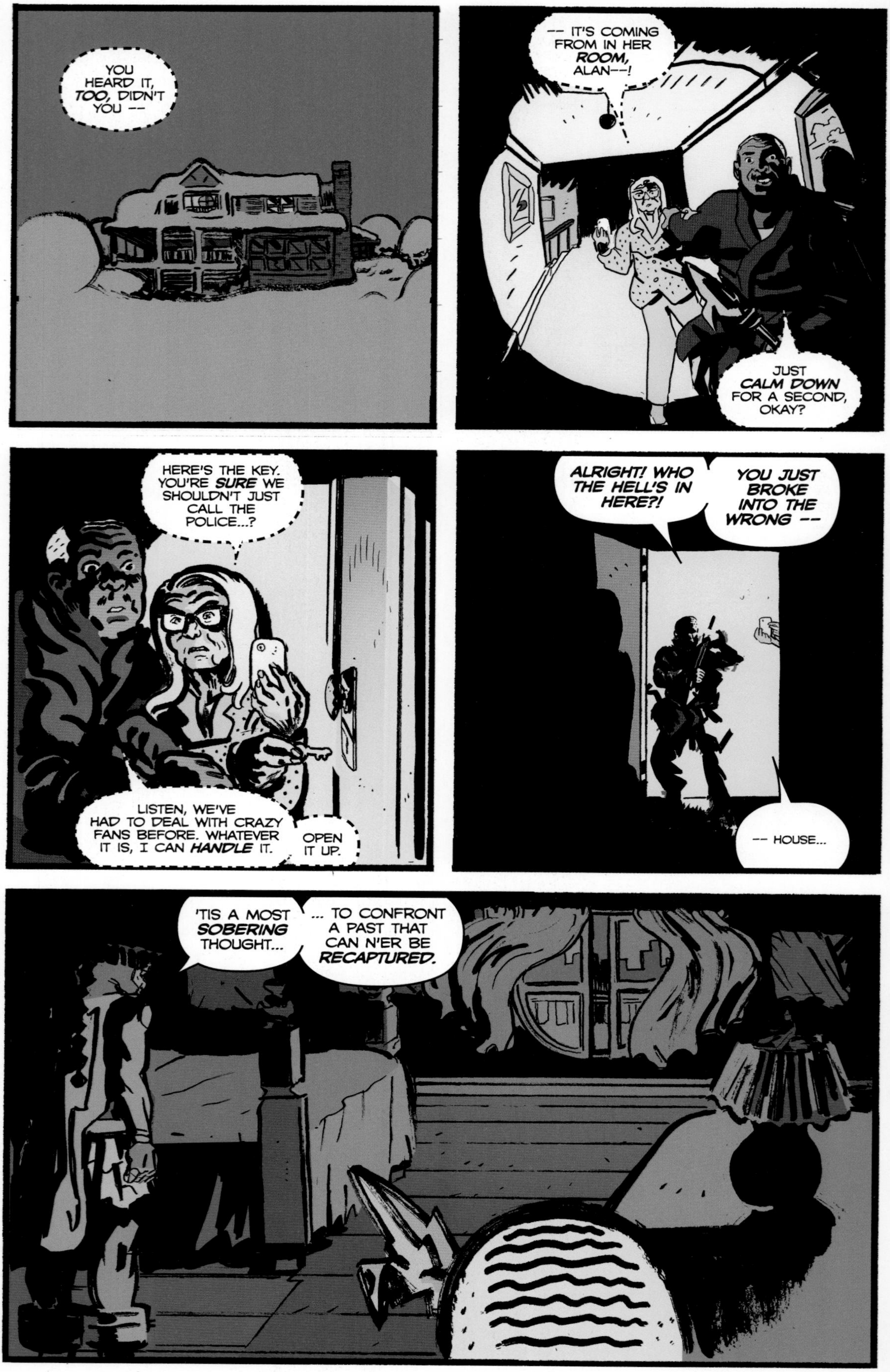
YOU HEARD IT, TOO, DIDN'T YOU --
-- IT'S COMING FROM IN HER ROOM, ALAN--!
JUST CALM DOWN FOR A SECOND, OKAY?
HERE'S THE KEY. YOU'RE SURE WE SHOULDN'T JUST CALL THE POLICE...?
LISTEN, WE'VE HAD TO DEAL WITH CRAZY FANS BEFORE. WHATEVER IT IS, I CAN HANDLE IT.
OPEN IT UP.
ALRIGHT! WHO THE HELL'S IN HERE?!
YOU JUST BROKE INTO THE WRONG --
-- HOUSE...
'TIS A MOST SOBERING THOUGHT...
... TO CONFRONT A PAST THAT CAN N'ER BE RECAPTURED.

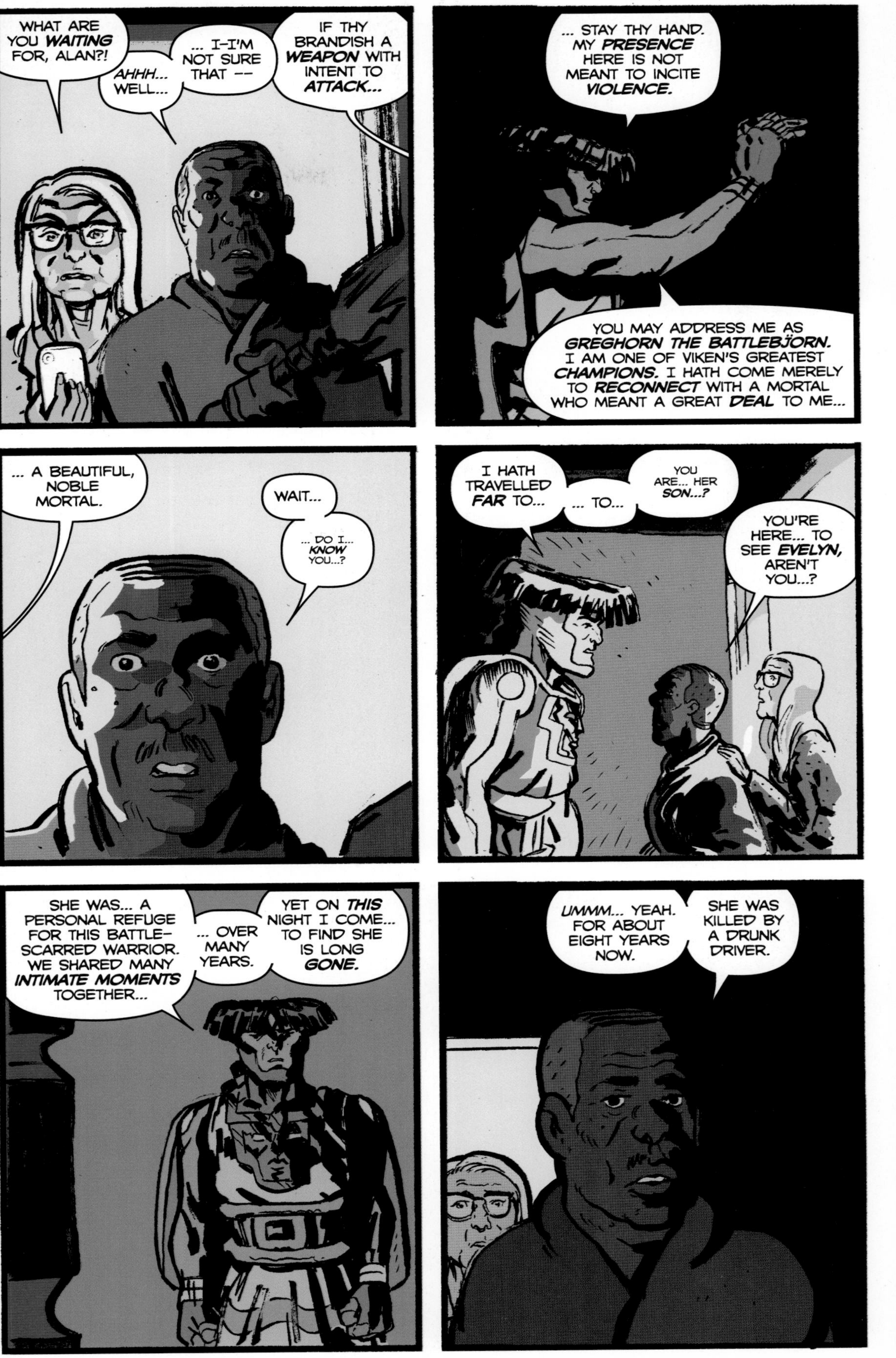
WHAT ARE YOU WAITING FOR, ALAN?!
AHHH... WELL...
... I-I'M NOT SURE THAT --
IF THY BRANDISH A WEAPON WITH INTENT TO ATTACK...
... STAY THY HAND. MY PRESENCE HERE IS NOT MEANT TO INCITE VIOLENCE.
YOU MAY ADDRESS ME AS GREGHORN THE BATTLEBJÖRN. I AM ONE OF VIKEN'S GREATEST CHAMPIONS. I HATH COME MERELY TO RECONNECT WITH A MORTAL WHO MEANT A GREAT DEAL TO ME...
... A BEAUTIFUL, NOBLE MORTAL.
WAIT...
... DO I... KNOW YOU...?
I HATH TRAVELLED FAR TO...
... TO...
YOU ARE... HER SON...?
YOU'RE HERE... TO SEE EVELYN, AREN'T YOU...?
SHE WAS... A PERSONAL REFUGE FOR THIS BATTLE-SCARRED WARRIOR. WE SHARED MANY INTIMATE MOMENTS TOGETHER...
... OVER MANY YEARS.
YET ON THIS NIGHT I COME... TO FIND SHE IS LONG GONE.
UMMM... YEAH. FOR ABOUT EIGHT YEARS NOW.
SHE WAS KILLED BY A DRUNK DRIVER.

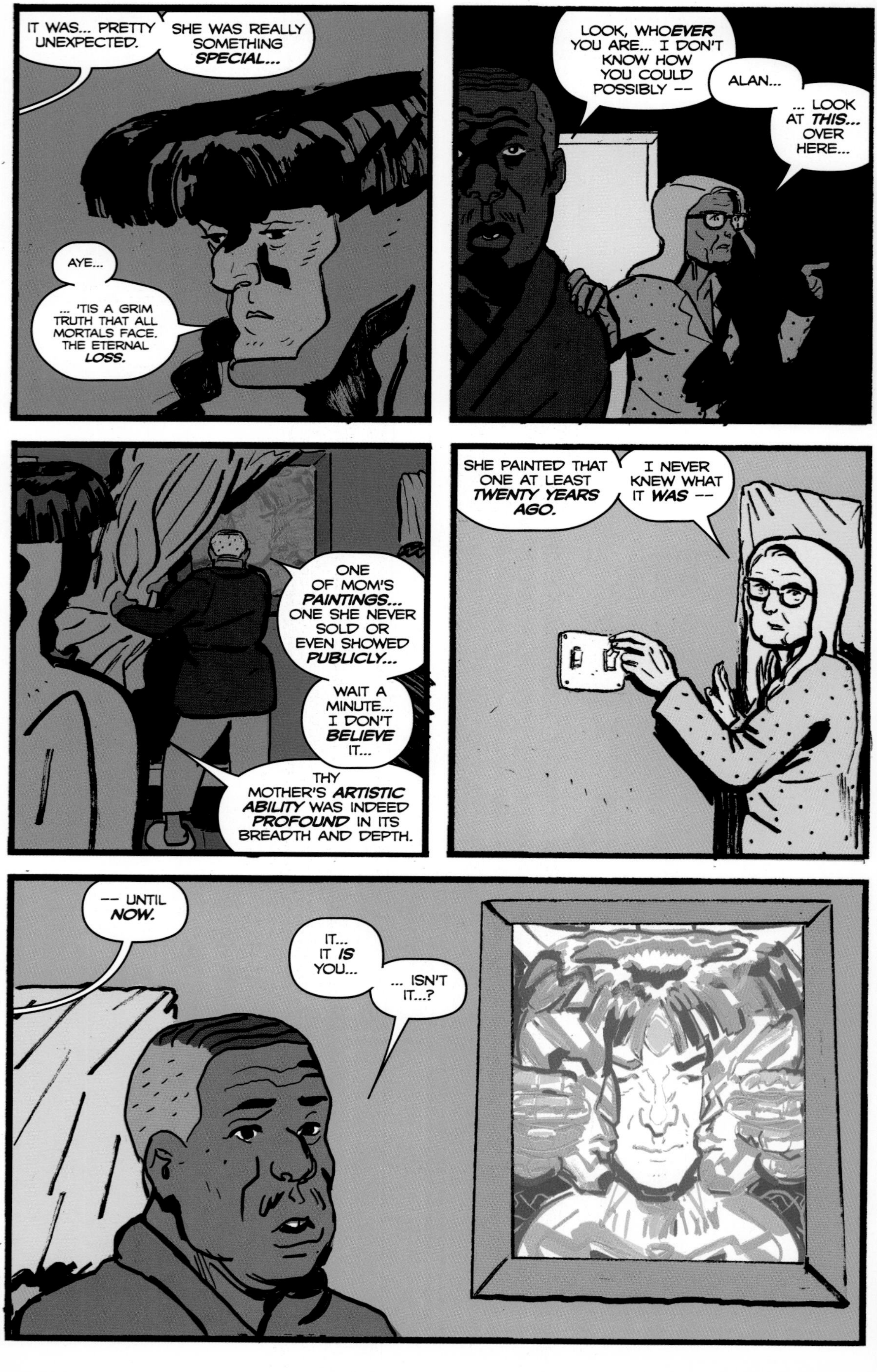
IT WAS... PRETTY UNEXPECTED.
SHE WAS REALLY SOMETHING SPECIAL...
AYE...
... 'TIS A GRIM TRUTH THAT ALL MORTALS FACE. THE ETERNAL LOSS.
LOOK, WHOEVER YOU ARE... I DON'T KNOW HOW YOU COULD POSSIBLY --
ALAN...
... LOOK AT THIS... OVER HERE...
ONE OF MOM'S PAINTINGS... ONE SHE NEVER SOLD OR EVEN SHOWED PUBLICLY...
WAIT A MINUTE... I DON'T BELIEVE IT...
THY MOTHER'S ARTISTIC ABILITY WAS INDEED PROFOUND IN ITS BREADTH AND DEPTH.
SHE PAINTED THAT ONE AT LEAST TWENTY YEARS AGO.
I NEVER KNEW WHAT IT WAS --
-- UNTIL NOW.
IT... IT IS YOU...
... ISN'T IT...?

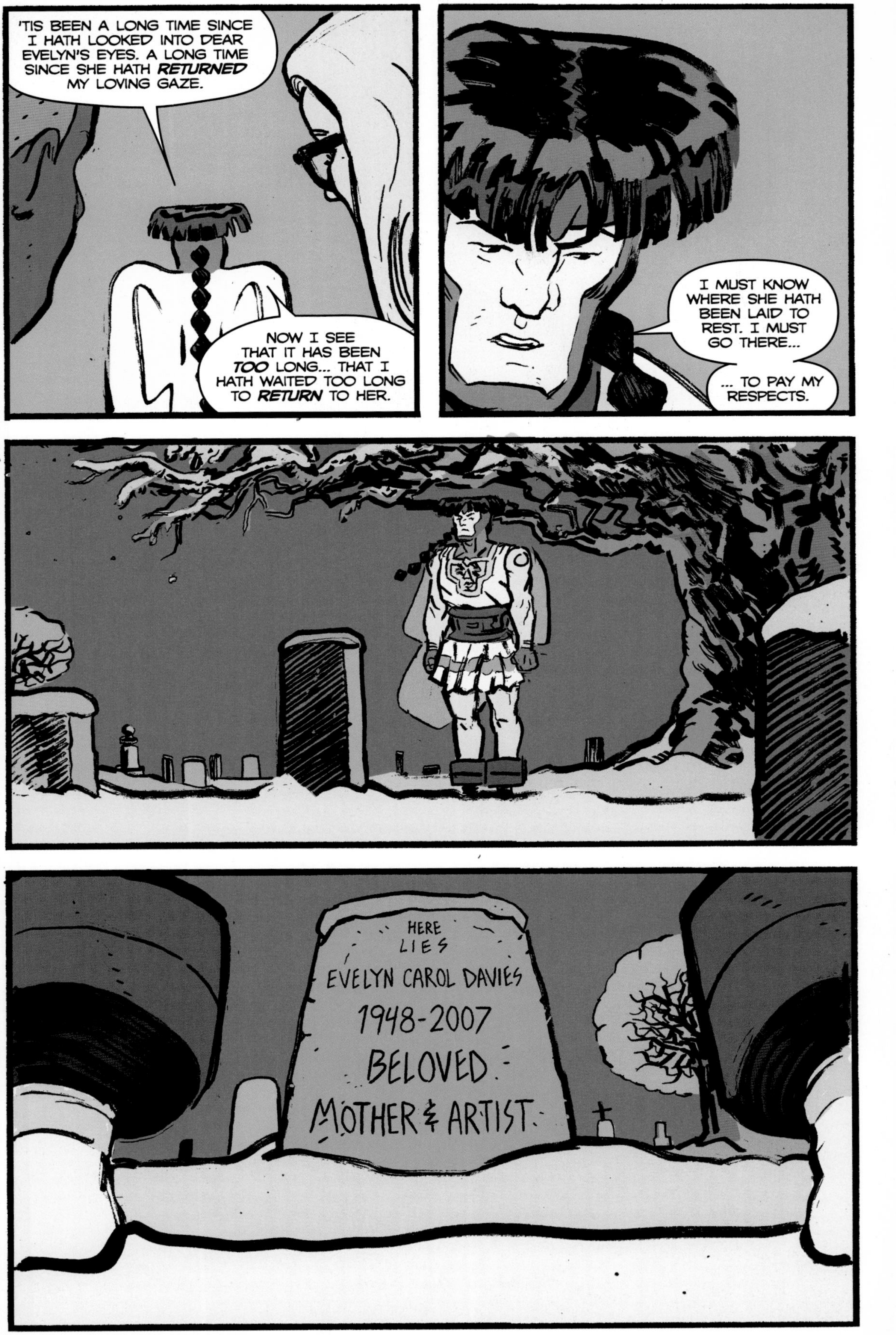
'TIS BEEN A LONG TIME SINCE I HATH LOOKED INTO DEAR EVELYN'S EYES. A LONG TIME SINCE SHE HATH *RETURNED* MY LOVING GAZE.
NOW I SEE THAT IT HAS BEEN *TOO* LONG... THAT I HATH WAITED TOO LONG TO *RETURN* TO HER.
I MUST KNOW WHERE SHE HATH BEEN LAID TO REST. I MUST GO THERE...
... TO PAY MY RESPECTS.
HERE LIES
EVELYN CAROL DAVIES
1948-2007
BELOVED
MOTHER & ARTIST

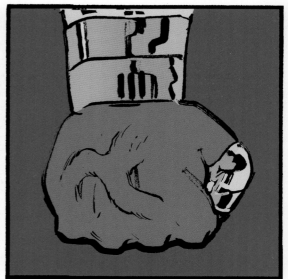

'TIS NOT FAIR, MORTAL REALM --

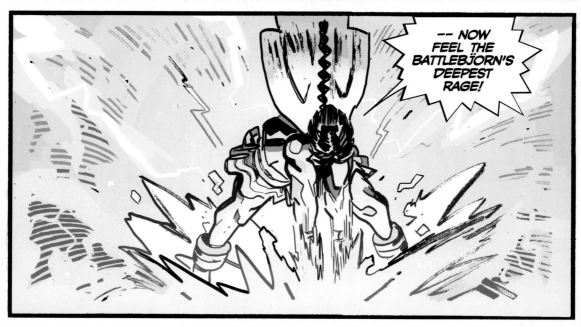

-- NOW FEEL THE BATTLEBJÖRN'S DEEPEST RAGE!

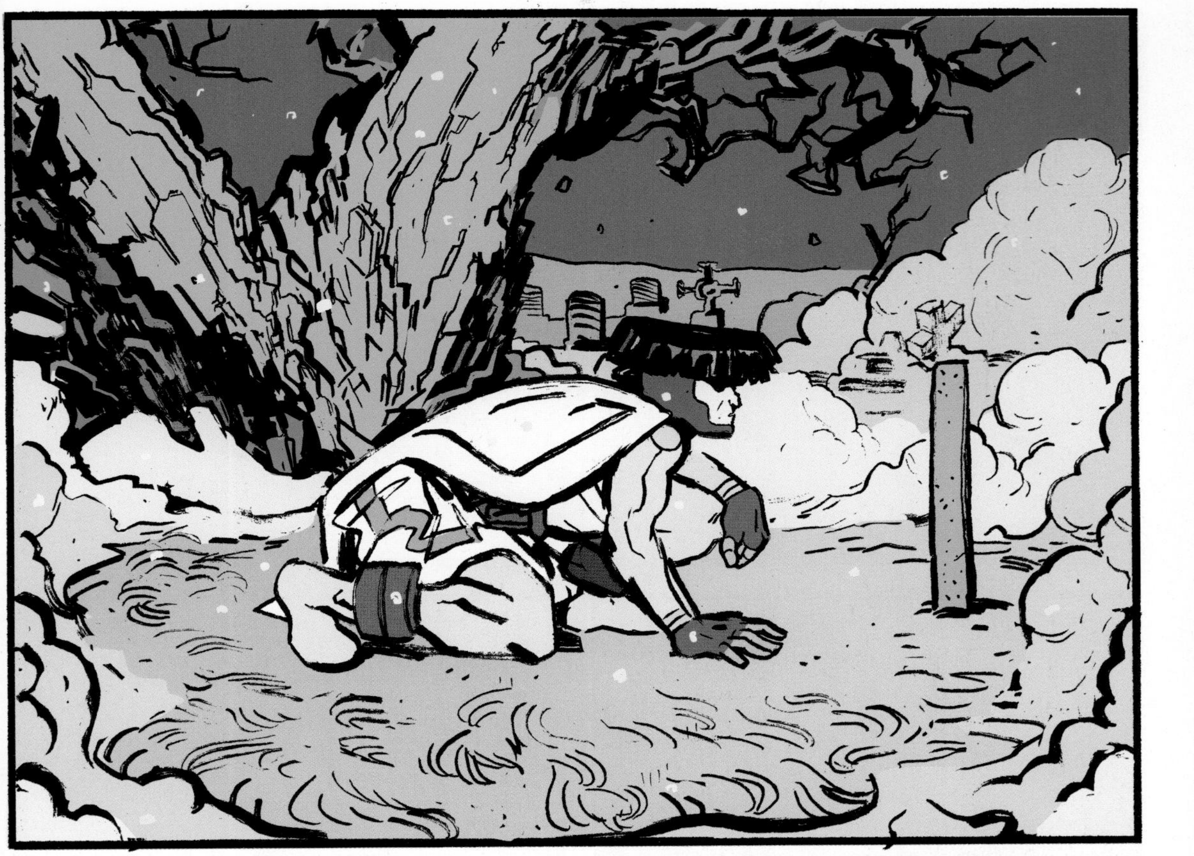

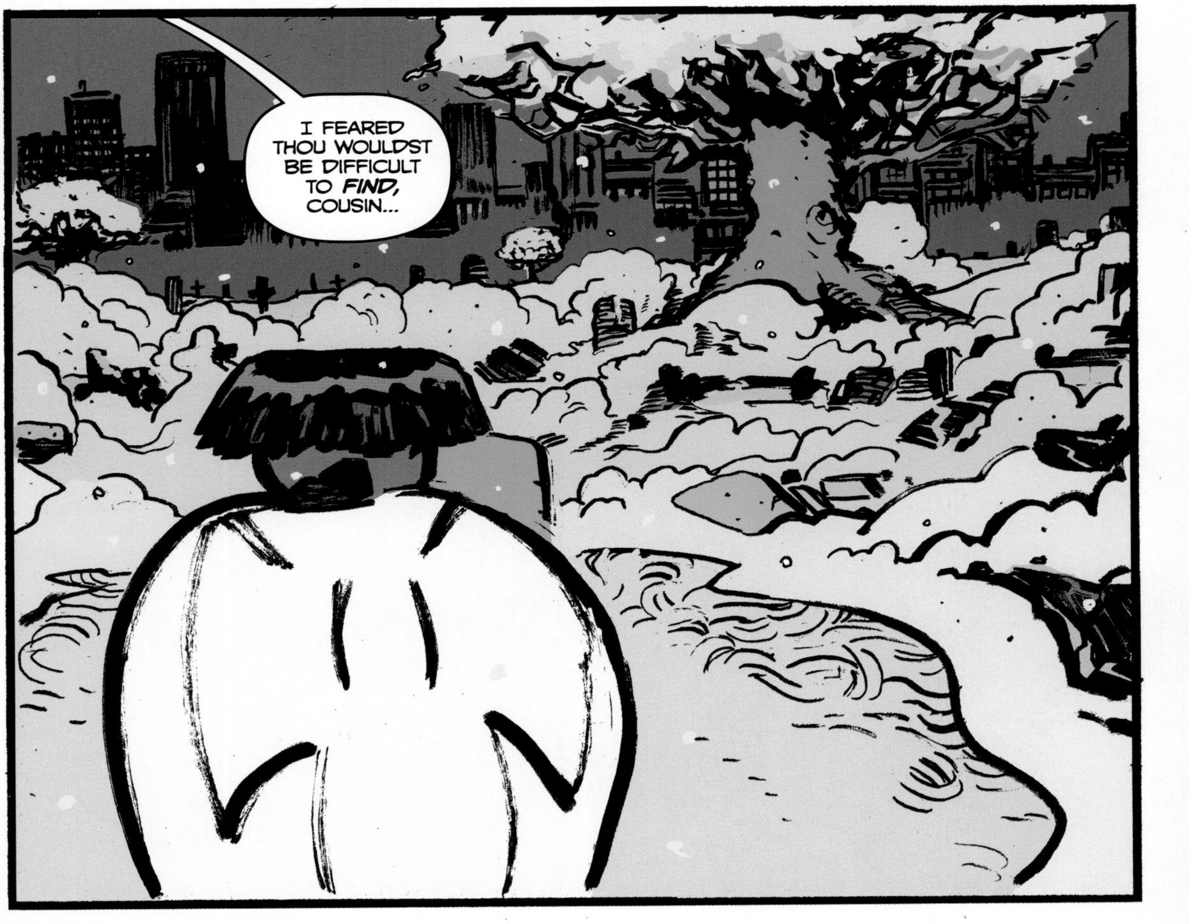
I FEARED THOU WOULDST BE DIFFICULT TO *FIND*, COUSIN...

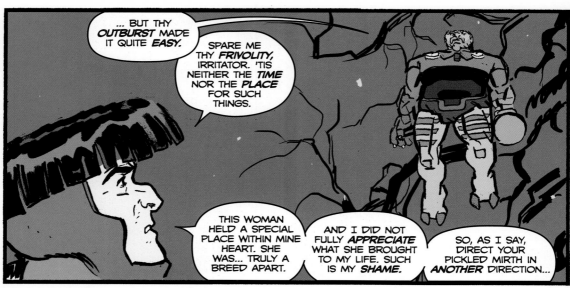

... BUT THY *OUTBURST* MADE IT QUITE *EASY.*

SPARE ME THY *FRIVOLITY,* IRRITATOR. 'TIS NEITHER THE *TIME* NOR THE *PLACE* FOR SUCH THINGS.

THIS WOMAN HELD A SPECIAL PLACE WITHIN MINE HEART. SHE WAS... TRULY A BREED APART.

AND I DID NOT FULLY *APPRECIATE* WHAT SHE BROUGHT TO MY LIFE. SUCH IS MY *SHAME.*

SO, AS I SAY, DIRECT YOUR PICKLED MIRTH IN *ANOTHER* DIRECTION...

NAY, GREGHORN -- THOU MISUNDERSTAND MY *INTENT.* I HATH COME TO *JOIN* YOU IN THY VIGIL FOR A FALLEN LOVED ONE.

IF THOU TRULY BELIEVE YOUR *MORTAL PARAMOUR* WAS SOME SORT OF *SECRET...* THOU ART GRAVELY *MISTAKEN.*

BOTH MYSELF *AND* THE GLORIOUS KNOX WERE WELL AWARE. DESPITE OUR *CONCERNS,* 'TWAS NE'ER A QUESTION OF *DISSUADING* THEE FROM SUCH MATTERS OF THE HEART.

ALTHOUGH MAYHAP, IN THY FIT OF ANGER, THOU HATH DONE MORE *DAMAGE* THAN THOU *MEANT* TO...

AYE... 'TWAS THE ONLY THING I COULD *THINK* TO DO. A COMPLETELY *IMPOTENT* GESTURE, I GRANT THEE...

SHE DESERVES *BETTER* THAN MORE OF THE CHAOS *WE* HATH BROUGHT TO THIS REALM...

OUR LEGENDARY STATUS AS DIMENSION-HOPPING WARMAKERS CARRIES WITH IT AN UNSPOKEN *BURDEN...*

... AND WE ALL HATH LEARNED TO *CARRY* IT IN DIFFERENT WAYS.

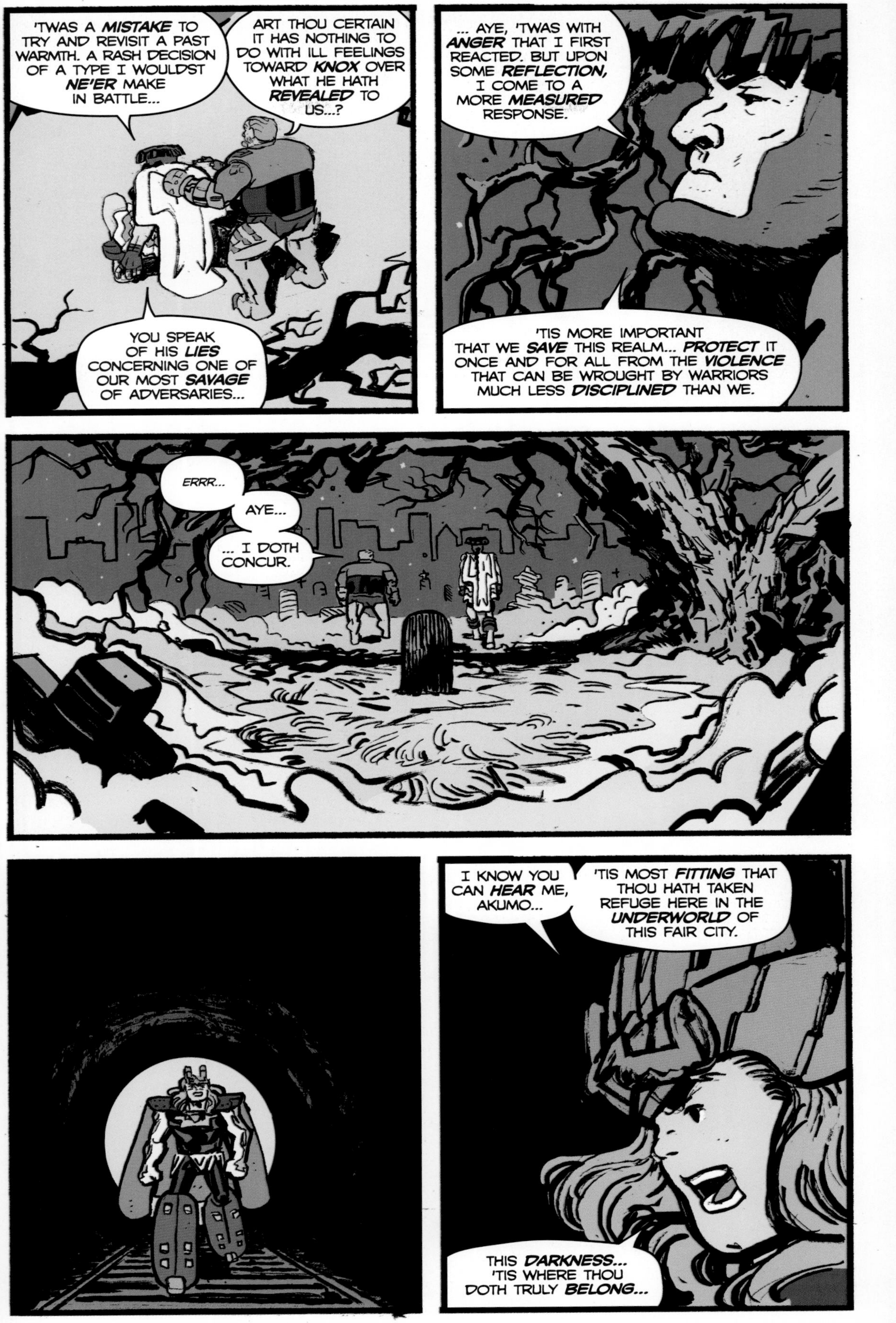
'TWAS A MISTAKE TO TRY AND REVISIT A PAST WARMTH. A RASH DECISION OF A TYPE I WOULDST NE'ER MAKE IN BATTLE...
ART THOU CERTAIN IT HAS NOTHING TO DO WITH ILL FEELINGS TOWARD KNOX OVER WHAT HE HATH REVEALED TO US...?
YOU SPEAK OF HIS LIES CONCERNING ONE OF OUR MOST SAVAGE OF ADVERSARIES...
... AYE, 'TWAS WITH ANGER THAT I FIRST REACTED. BUT UPON SOME REFLECTION, I COME TO A MORE MEASURED RESPONSE.
'TIS MORE IMPORTANT THAT WE SAVE THIS REALM... PROTECT IT ONCE AND FOR ALL FROM THE VIOLENCE THAT CAN BE WROUGHT BY WARRIORS MUCH LESS DISCIPLINED THAN WE.
ERRR...
AYE...
... I DOTH CONCUR.
I KNOW YOU CAN HEAR ME, AKUMO...
'TIS MOST FITTING THAT THOU HATH TAKEN REFUGE HERE IN THE UNDERWORLD OF THIS FAIR CITY.
THIS DARKNESS... 'TIS WHERE THOU DOTH TRULY BELONG...

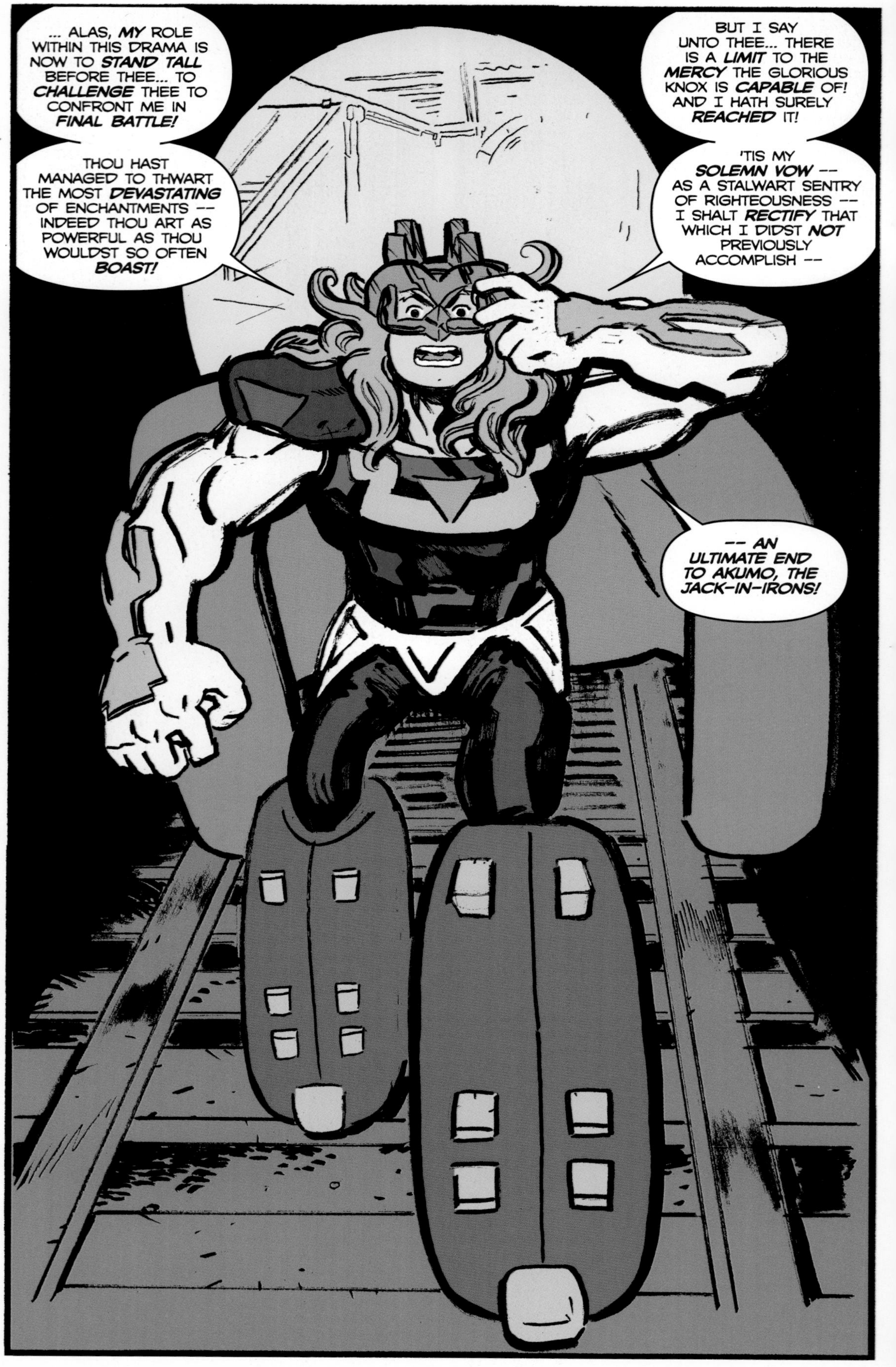
... ALAS, MY ROLE WITHIN THIS DRAMA IS NOW TO STAND TALL BEFORE THEE... TO CHALLENGE THEE TO CONFRONT ME IN FINAL BATTLE!
THOU HAST MANAGED TO THWART THE MOST DEVASTATING OF ENCHANTMENTS -- INDEED THOU ART AS POWERFUL AS THOU WOULDST SO OFTEN BOAST!
BUT I SAY UNTO THEE... THERE IS A LIMIT TO THE MERCY THE GLORIOUS KNOX IS CAPABLE OF! AND I HATH SURELY REACHED IT!
'TIS MY SOLEMN VOW -- AS A STALWART SENTRY OF RIGHTEOUSNESS -- I SHALT RECTIFY THAT WHICH I DIDST NOT PREVIOUSLY ACCOMPLISH --
-- AN ULTIMATE END TO AKUMO, THE JACK-IN-IRONS!

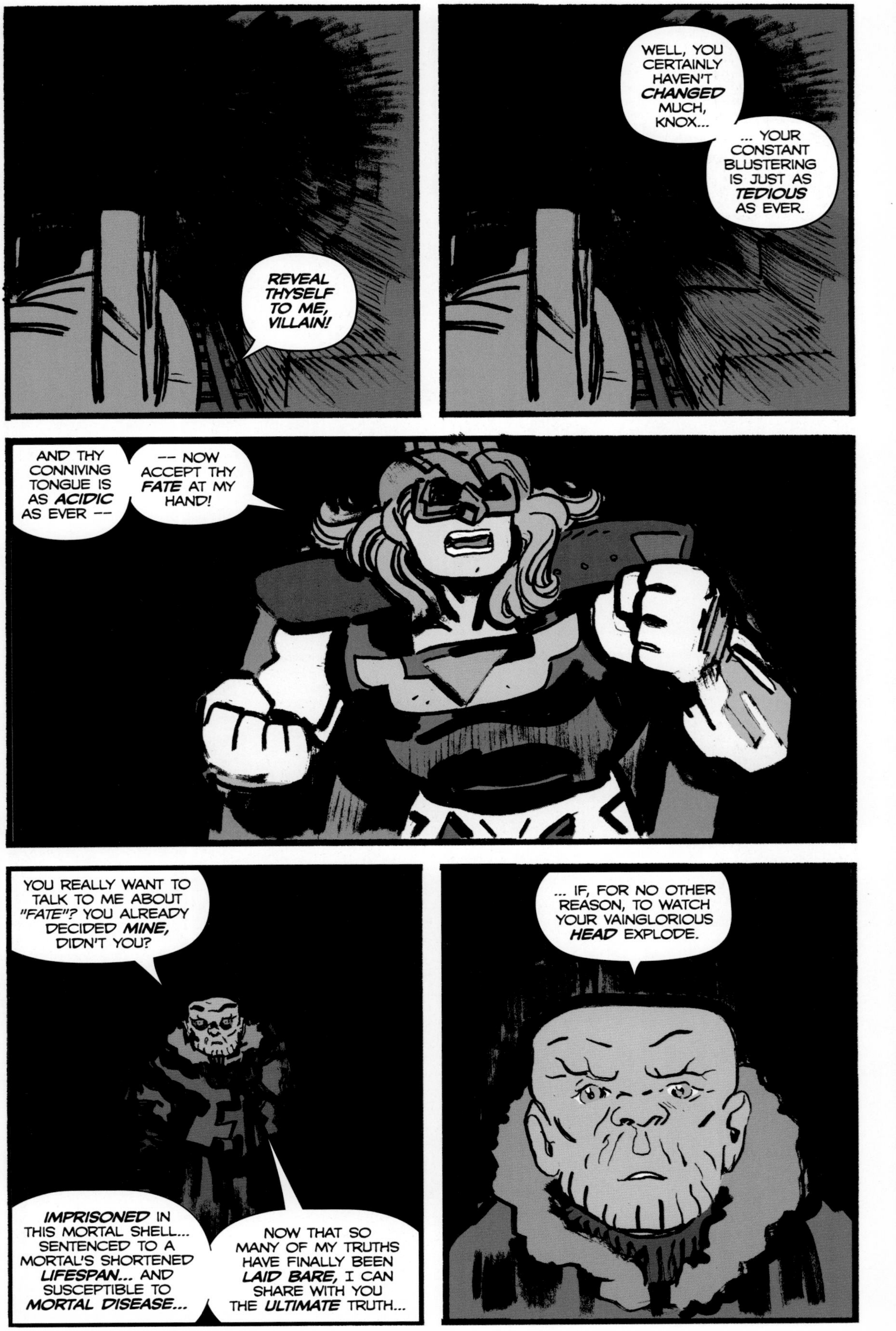
REVEAL THYSELF TO ME, VILLAIN!
WELL, YOU CERTAINLY HAVEN'T CHANGED MUCH, KNOX...
... YOUR CONSTANT BLUSTERING IS JUST AS TEDIOUS AS EVER.
AND THY CONNIVING TONGUE IS AS ACIDIC AS EVER --
-- NOW ACCEPT THY FATE AT MY HAND!
YOU REALLY WANT TO TALK TO ME ABOUT "FATE"? YOU ALREADY DECIDED MINE, DIDN'T YOU?
IMPRISONED IN THIS MORTAL SHELL... SENTENCED TO A MORTAL'S SHORTENED LIFESPAN... AND SUSCEPTIBLE TO MORTAL DISEASE...
NOW THAT SO MANY OF MY TRUTHS HAVE FINALLY BEEN LAID BARE, I CAN SHARE WITH YOU THE ULTIMATE TRUTH...
... IF, FOR NO OTHER REASON, TO WATCH YOUR VAINGLORIOUS HEAD EXPLODE.

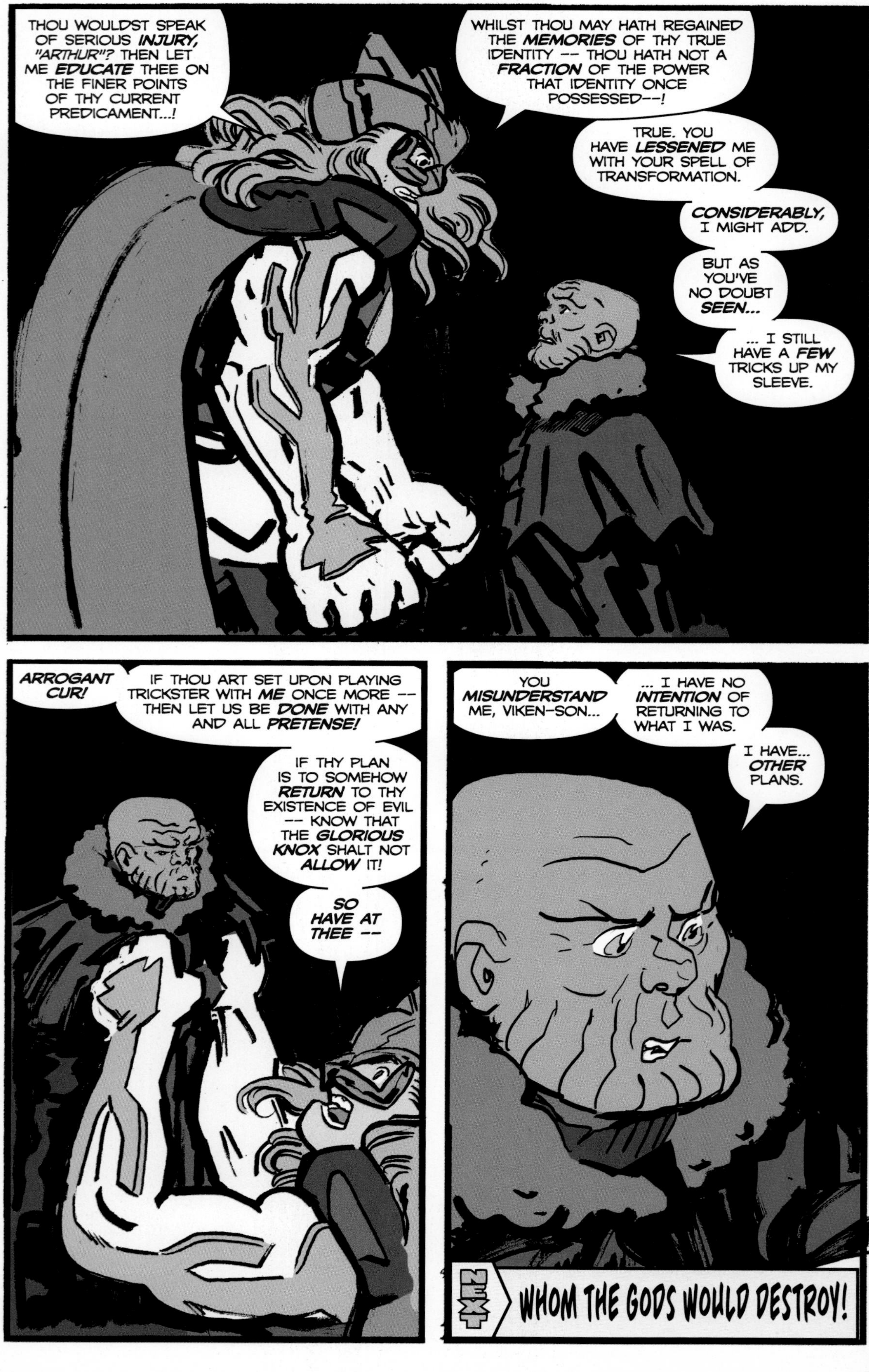
THOU WOULDST SPEAK OF SERIOUS INJURY, "ARTHUR"? THEN LET ME EDUCATE THEE ON THE FINER POINTS OF THY CURRENT PREDICAMENT...!
WHILST THOU MAY HATH REGAINED THE MEMORIES OF THY TRUE IDENTITY -- THOU HATH NOT A FRACTION OF THE POWER THAT IDENTITY ONCE POSSESSED--!
TRUE. YOU HAVE LESSENED ME WITH YOUR SPELL OF TRANSFORMATION.
CONSIDERABLY, I MIGHT ADD.
BUT AS YOU'VE NO DOUBT SEEN...
... I STILL HAVE A FEW TRICKS UP MY SLEEVE.
ARROGANT CUR!
IF THOU ART SET UPON PLAYING TRICKSTER WITH ME ONCE MORE -- THEN LET US BE DONE WITH ANY AND ALL PRETENSE!
IF THY PLAN IS TO SOMEHOW RETURN TO THY EXISTENCE OF EVIL -- KNOW THAT THE GLORIOUS KNOX SHALT NOT ALLOW IT!
SO HAVE AT THEE --
YOU MISUNDERSTAND ME, VIKEN-SON...
... I HAVE NO INTENTION OF RETURNING TO WHAT I WAS.
I HAVE... OTHER PLANS.
NEXT
WHOM THE GODS WOULD DESTROY!

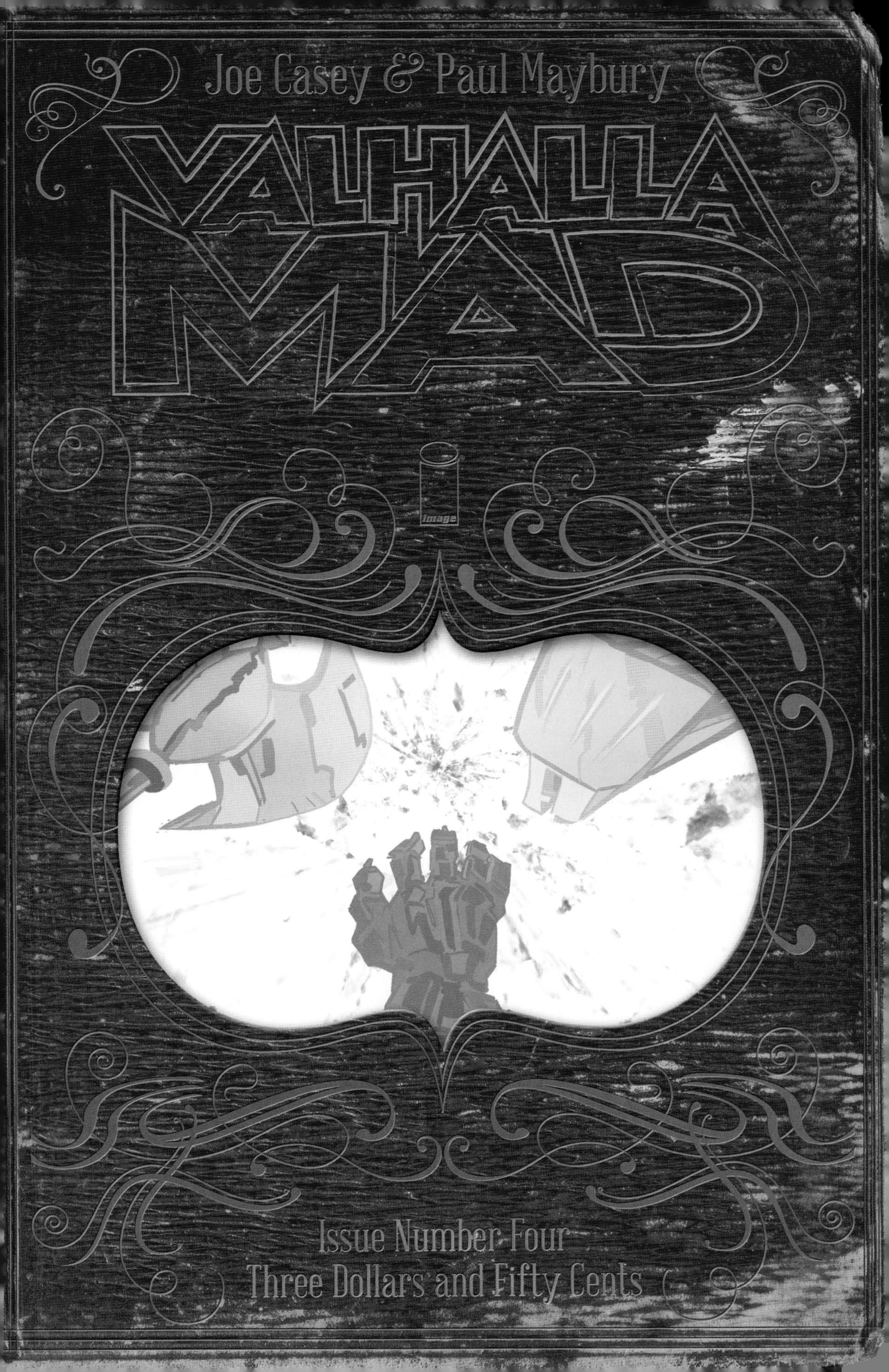
Joe Casey & Paul Maybury
VALHALLA MAD
Issue Number Four
Three Dollars and Fifty Cents

CHAPTER

4

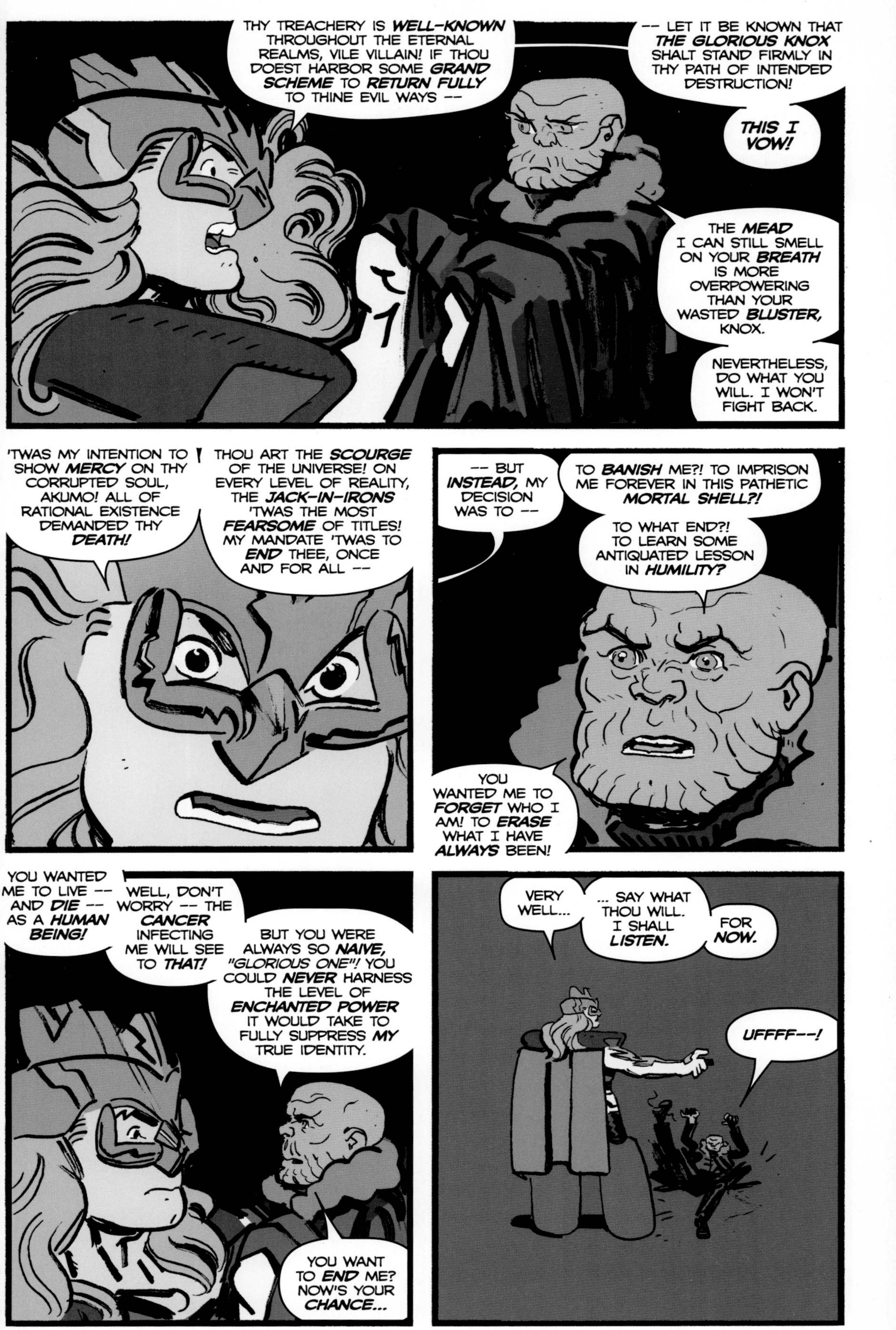
THY TREACHERY IS WELL-KNOWN THROUGHOUT THE ETERNAL REALMS, VILE VILLAIN! IF THOU DOEST HARBOR SOME GRAND SCHEME TO RETURN FULLY TO THINE EVIL WAYS --
-- LET IT BE KNOWN THAT THE GLORIOUS KNOX SHALT STAND FIRMLY IN THY PATH OF INTENDED DESTRUCTION!
THIS I VOW!
THE MEAD I CAN STILL SMELL ON YOUR BREATH IS MORE OVERPOWERING THAN YOUR WASTED BLUSTER, KNOX.
NEVERTHELESS, DO WHAT YOU WILL. I WON'T FIGHT BACK.
'TWAS MY INTENTION TO SHOW MERCY ON THY CORRUPTED SOUL, AKUMO! ALL OF RATIONAL EXISTENCE DEMANDED THY DEATH!
THOU ART THE SCOURGE OF THE UNIVERSE! ON EVERY LEVEL OF REALITY, THE JACK-IN-IRONS 'TWAS THE MOST FEARSOME OF TITLES! MY MANDATE 'TWAS TO END THEE, ONCE AND FOR ALL --
-- BUT INSTEAD, MY DECISION WAS TO --
TO BANISH ME?! TO IMPRISON ME FOREVER IN THIS PATHETIC MORTAL SHELL?!
TO WHAT END?! TO LEARN SOME ANTIQUATED LESSON IN HUMILITY?
YOU WANTED ME TO FORGET WHO I AM! TO ERASE WHAT I HAVE ALWAYS BEEN!
YOU WANTED ME TO LIVE -- AND DIE -- AS A HUMAN BEING!
WELL, DON'T WORRY -- THE CANCER INFECTING ME WILL SEE TO THAT!
BUT YOU WERE ALWAYS SO NAIVE, "GLORIOUS ONE"! YOU COULD NEVER HARNESS THE LEVEL OF ENCHANTED POWER IT WOULD TAKE TO FULLY SUPPRESS MY TRUE IDENTITY.
YOU WANT TO END ME? NOW'S YOUR CHANCE...
VERY WELL...
... SAY WHAT THOU WILL. I SHALL LISTEN.
FOR NOW.
UFFFF--!

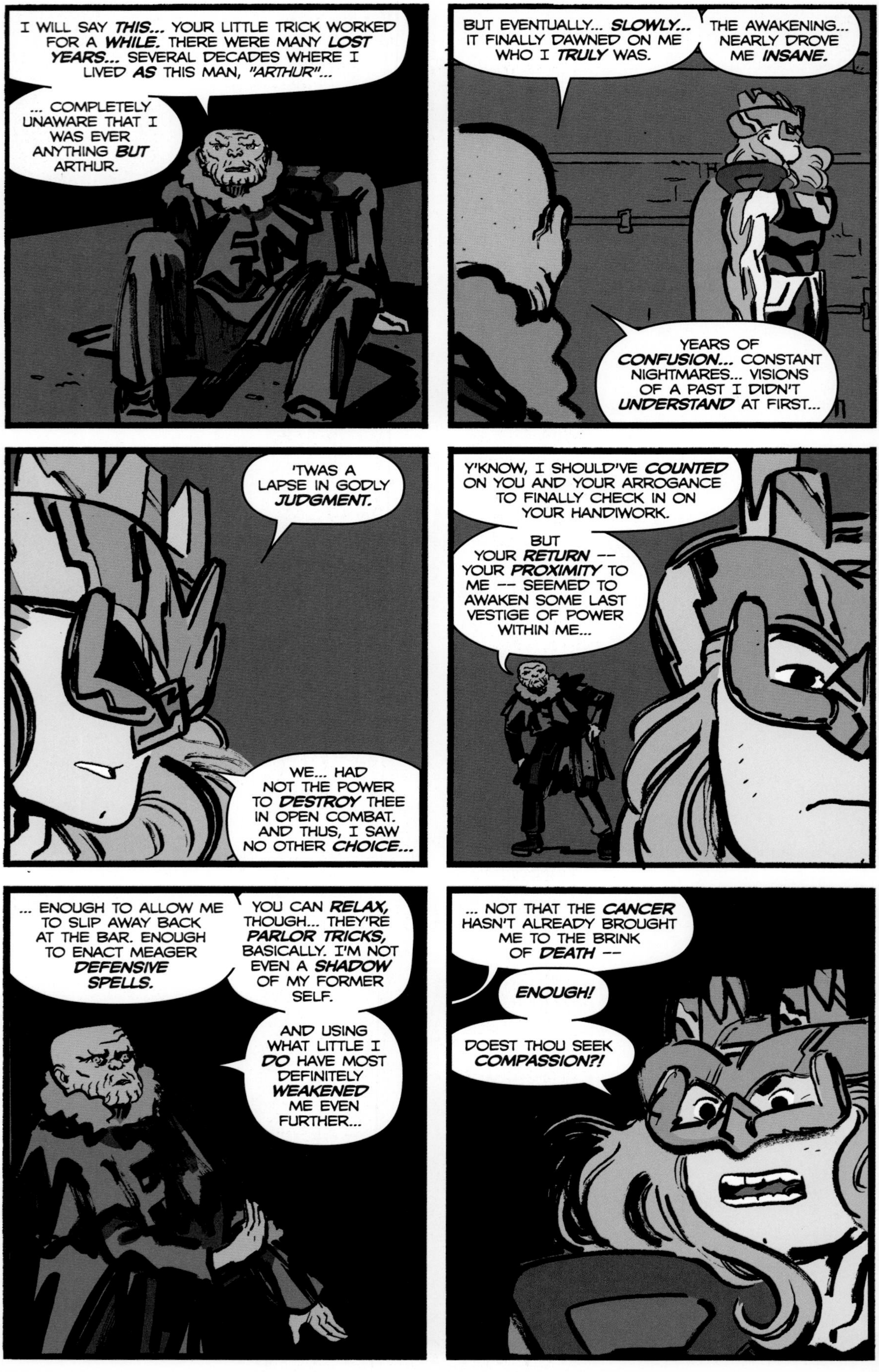
I WILL SAY THIS... YOUR LITTLE TRICK WORKED FOR A WHILE. THERE WERE MANY LOST YEARS... SEVERAL DECADES WHERE I LIVED AS THIS MAN, "ARTHUR"...
... COMPLETELY UNAWARE THAT I WAS EVER ANYTHING BUT ARTHUR.
BUT EVENTUALLY... SLOWLY... IT FINALLY DAWNED ON ME WHO I TRULY WAS.
THE AWAKENING... NEARLY DROVE ME INSANE.
YEARS OF CONFUSION... CONSTANT NIGHTMARES... VISIONS OF A PAST I DIDN'T UNDERSTAND AT FIRST...
'TWAS A LAPSE IN GODLY JUDGMENT.
WE... HAD NOT THE POWER TO DESTROY THEE IN OPEN COMBAT. AND THUS, I SAW NO OTHER CHOICE...
Y'KNOW, I SHOULD'VE COUNTED ON YOU AND YOUR ARROGANCE TO FINALLY CHECK IN ON YOUR HANDIWORK.
BUT YOUR RETURN -- YOUR PROXIMITY TO ME -- SEEMED TO AWAKEN SOME LAST VESTIGE OF POWER WITHIN ME...
... ENOUGH TO ALLOW ME TO SLIP AWAY BACK AT THE BAR. ENOUGH TO ENACT MEAGER DEFENSIVE SPELLS.
YOU CAN RELAX, THOUGH... THEY'RE PARLOR TRICKS, BASICALLY. I'M NOT EVEN A SHADOW OF MY FORMER SELF.
AND USING WHAT LITTLE I DO HAVE MOST DEFINITELY WEAKENED ME EVEN FURTHER...
... NOT THAT THE CANCER HASN'T ALREADY BROUGHT ME TO THE BRINK OF DEATH --
ENOUGH!
DOEST THOU SEEK COMPASSION?!

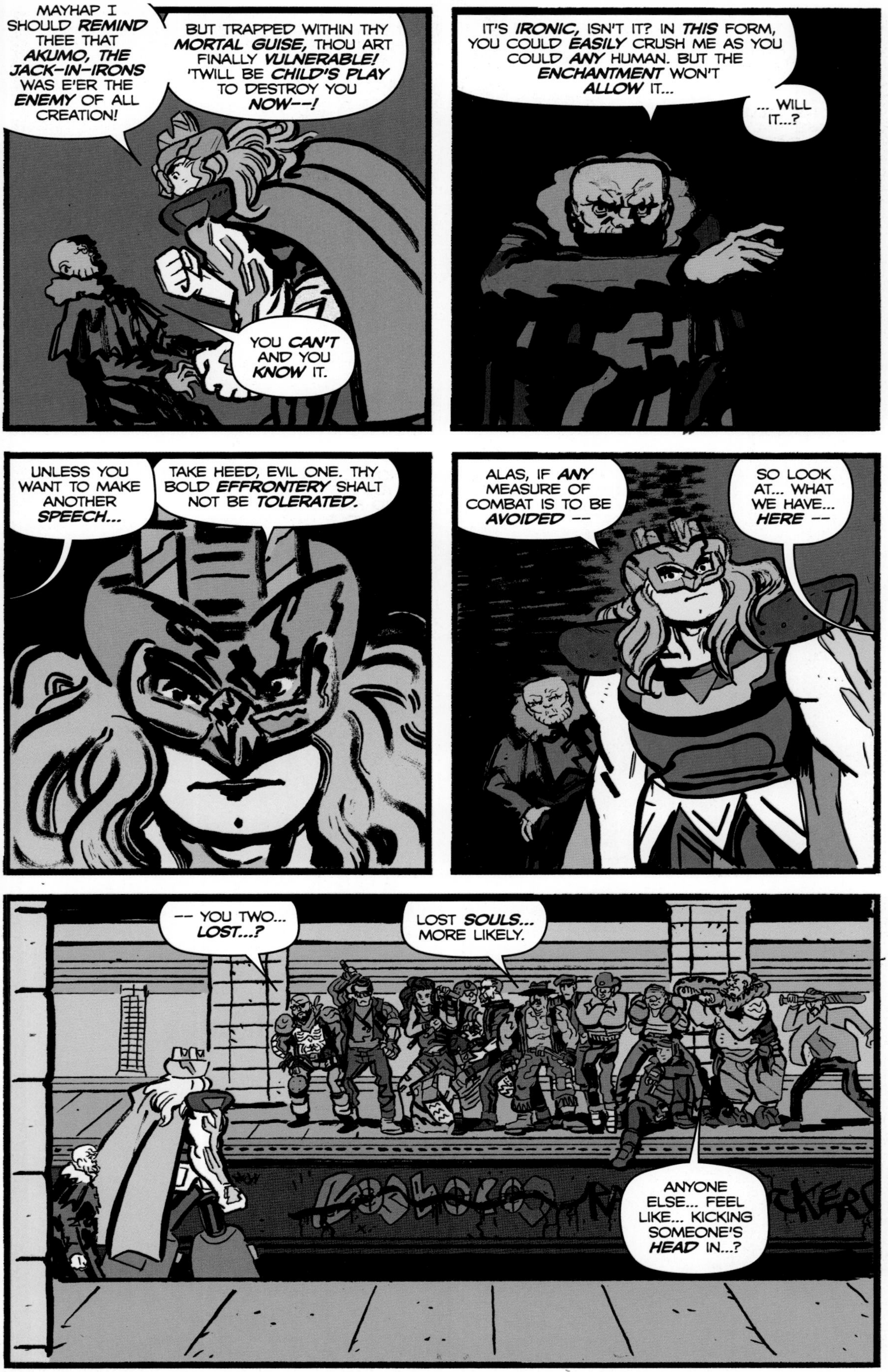
MAYHAP I SHOULD REMIND THEE THAT AKUMO, THE JACK-IN-IRONS WAS E'ER THE ENEMY OF ALL CREATION!
BUT TRAPPED WITHIN THY MORTAL GUISE, THOU ART FINALLY VULNERABLE! 'TWILL BE CHILD'S PLAY TO DESTROY YOU NOW--!
YOU CAN'T AND YOU KNOW IT.
IT'S IRONIC, ISN'T IT? IN THIS FORM, YOU COULD EASILY CRUSH ME AS YOU COULD ANY HUMAN. BUT THE ENCHANTMENT WON'T ALLOW IT...
... WILL IT...?
UNLESS YOU WANT TO MAKE ANOTHER SPEECH...
TAKE HEED, EVIL ONE. THY BOLD EFFRONTERY SHALT NOT BE TOLERATED.
ALAS, IF ANY MEASURE OF COMBAT IS TO BE AVOIDED --
SO LOOK AT... WHAT WE HAVE... HERE --
-- YOU TWO... LOST...?
LOST SOULS... MORE LIKELY.
ANYONE ELSE... FEEL LIKE... KICKING SOMEONE'S HEAD IN...?

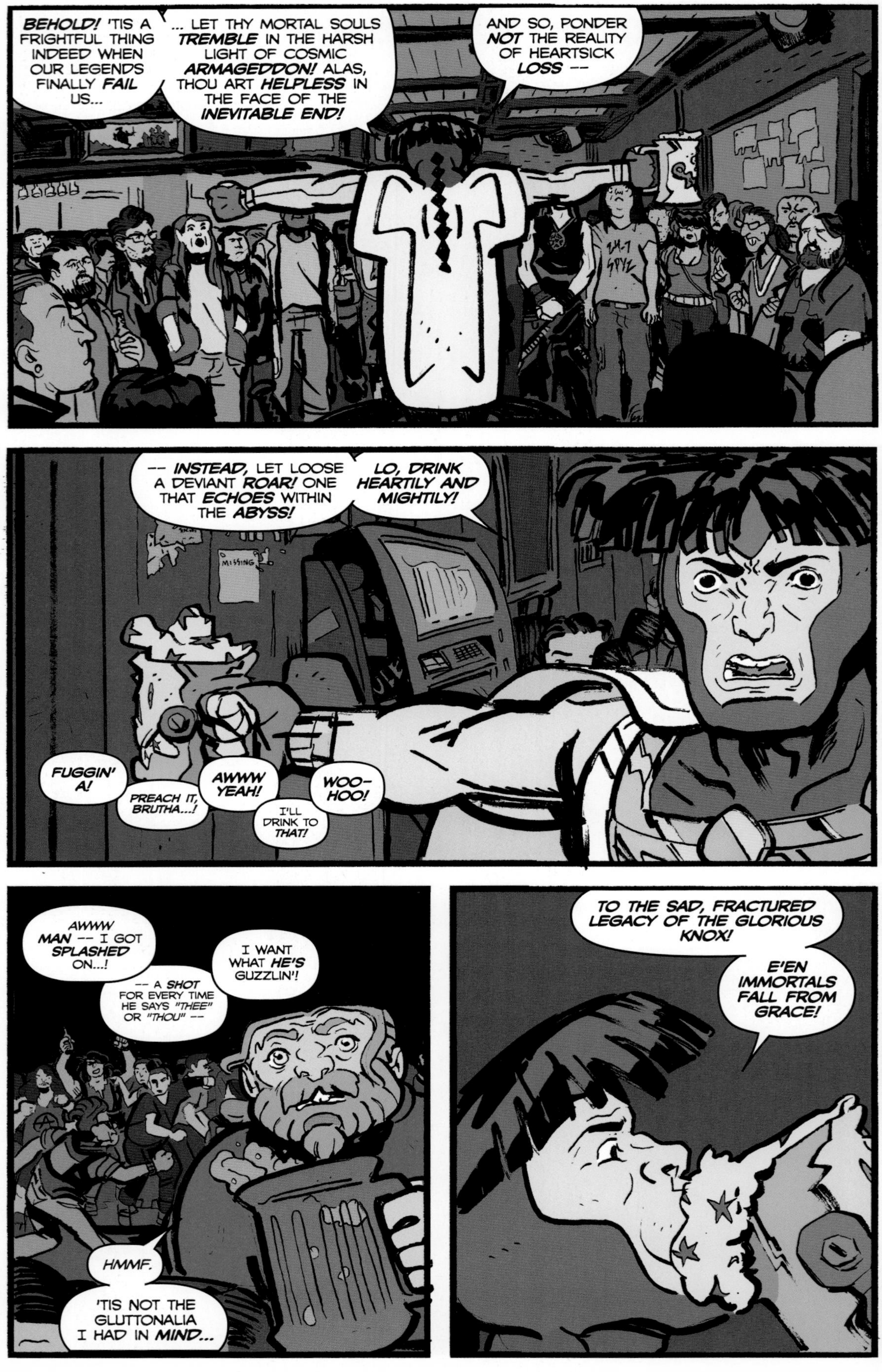
BEHOLD! 'TIS A FRIGHTFUL THING INDEED WHEN OUR LEGENDS FINALLY FAIL US...
... LET THY MORTAL SOULS TREMBLE IN THE HARSH LIGHT OF COSMIC ARMAGEDDON! ALAS, THOU ART HELPLESS IN THE FACE OF THE INEVITABLE END!
AND SO, PONDER NOT THE REALITY OF HEARTSICK LOSS --
-- INSTEAD, LET LOOSE A DEVIANT ROAR! ONE THAT ECHOES WITHIN THE ABYSS!
LO, DRINK HEARTILY AND MIGHTILY!
MISSING
FUGGIN' A!
PREACH IT, BRUTHA...!
AWWW YEAH!
I'LL DRINK TO THAT!
WOO-HOO!
AWWW MAN -- I GOT SPLASHED ON...!
-- A SHOT FOR EVERY TIME HE SAYS "THEE" OR "THOU" --
I WANT WHAT HE'S GUZZLIN'!
HMMF.
'TIS NOT THE GLUTTONALIA I HAD IN MIND...
TO THE SAD, FRACTURED LEGACY OF THE GLORIOUS KNOX!
E'EN IMMORTALS FALL FROM GRACE!

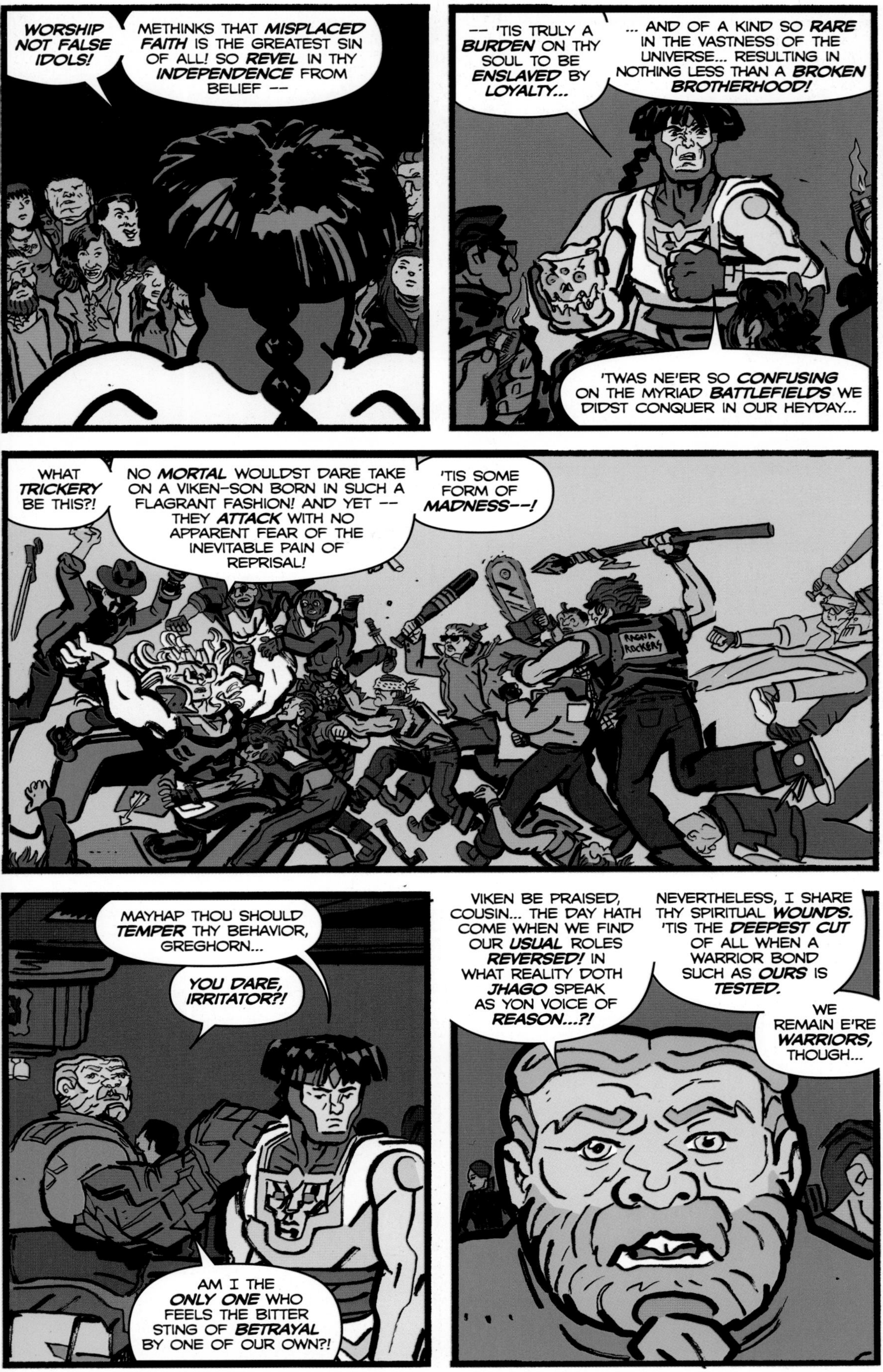
WORSHIP NOT FALSE IDOLS!
METHINKS THAT MISPLACED FAITH IS THE GREATEST SIN OF ALL! SO REVEL IN THY INDEPENDENCE FROM BELIEF --
-- 'TIS TRULY A BURDEN ON THY SOUL TO BE ENSLAVED BY LOYALTY...
... AND OF A KIND SO RARE IN THE VASTNESS OF THE UNIVERSE... RESULTING IN NOTHING LESS THAN A BROKEN BROTHERHOOD!
'TWAS NE'ER SO CONFUSING ON THE MYRIAD BATTLEFIELDS WE DIDST CONQUER IN OUR HEYDAY...
WHAT TRICKERY BE THIS?!
NO MORTAL WOULDST DARE TAKE ON A VIKEN-SON BORN IN SUCH A FLAGRANT FASHION! AND YET -- THEY ATTACK WITH NO APPARENT FEAR OF THE INEVITABLE PAIN OF REPRISAL!
'TIS SOME FORM OF MADNESS--!
RAGNA ROCKERS
MAYHAP THOU SHOULD TEMPER THY BEHAVIOR, GREGHORN...
YOU DARE, IRRITATOR?!
AM I THE ONLY ONE WHO FEELS THE BITTER STING OF BETRAYAL BY ONE OF OUR OWN?!
VIKEN BE PRAISED, COUSIN... THE DAY HATH COME WHEN WE FIND OUR USUAL ROLES REVERSED! IN WHAT REALITY DOTH JHAGO SPEAK AS YON VOICE OF REASON...?!
NEVERTHELESS, I SHARE THY SPIRITUAL WOUNDS. 'TIS THE DEEPEST CUT OF ALL WHEN A WARRIOR BOND SUCH AS OURS IS TESTED.
WE REMAIN E'RE WARRIORS, THOUGH...

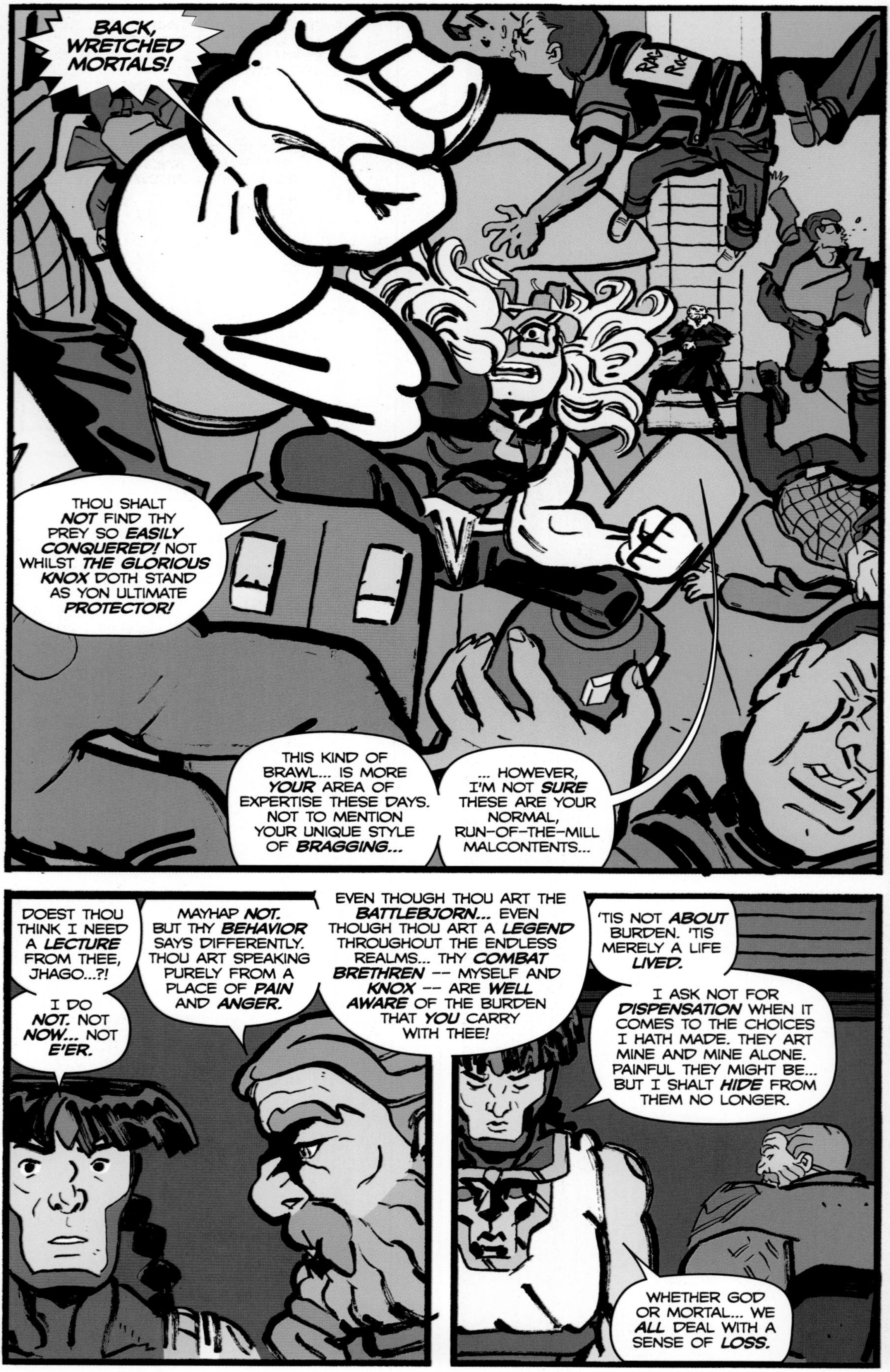
BACK, WRETCHED MORTALS!
THOU SHALT NOT FIND THY PREY SO EASILY CONQUERED! NOT WHILST THE GLORIOUS KNOX DOTH STAND AS YON ULTIMATE PROTECTOR!
THIS KIND OF BRAWL... IS MORE YOUR AREA OF EXPERTISE THESE DAYS. NOT TO MENTION YOUR UNIQUE STYLE OF BRAGGING...
... HOWEVER, I'M NOT SURE THESE ARE YOUR NORMAL, RUN-OF-THE-MILL MALCONTENTS...
DOEST THOU THINK I NEED A LECTURE FROM THEE, JHAGO...?!
I DO NOT. NOT NOW... NOT E'ER.
MAYHAP NOT. BUT THY BEHAVIOR SAYS DIFFERENTLY. THOU ART SPEAKING PURELY FROM A PLACE OF PAIN AND ANGER.
EVEN THOUGH THOU ART THE BATTLEBJORN... EVEN THOUGH THOU ART A LEGEND THROUGHOUT THE ENDLESS REALMS... THY COMBAT BRETHREN -- MYSELF AND KNOX -- ARE WELL AWARE OF THE BURDEN THAT YOU CARRY WITH THEE!
'TIS NOT ABOUT BURDEN. 'TIS MERELY A LIFE LIVED.
I ASK NOT FOR DISPENSATION WHEN IT COMES TO THE CHOICES I HATH MADE. THEY ART MINE AND MINE ALONE. PAINFUL THEY MIGHT BE... BUT I SHALT HIDE FROM THEM NO LONGER.
WHETHER GOD OR MORTAL... WE ALL DEAL WITH A SENSE OF LOSS.

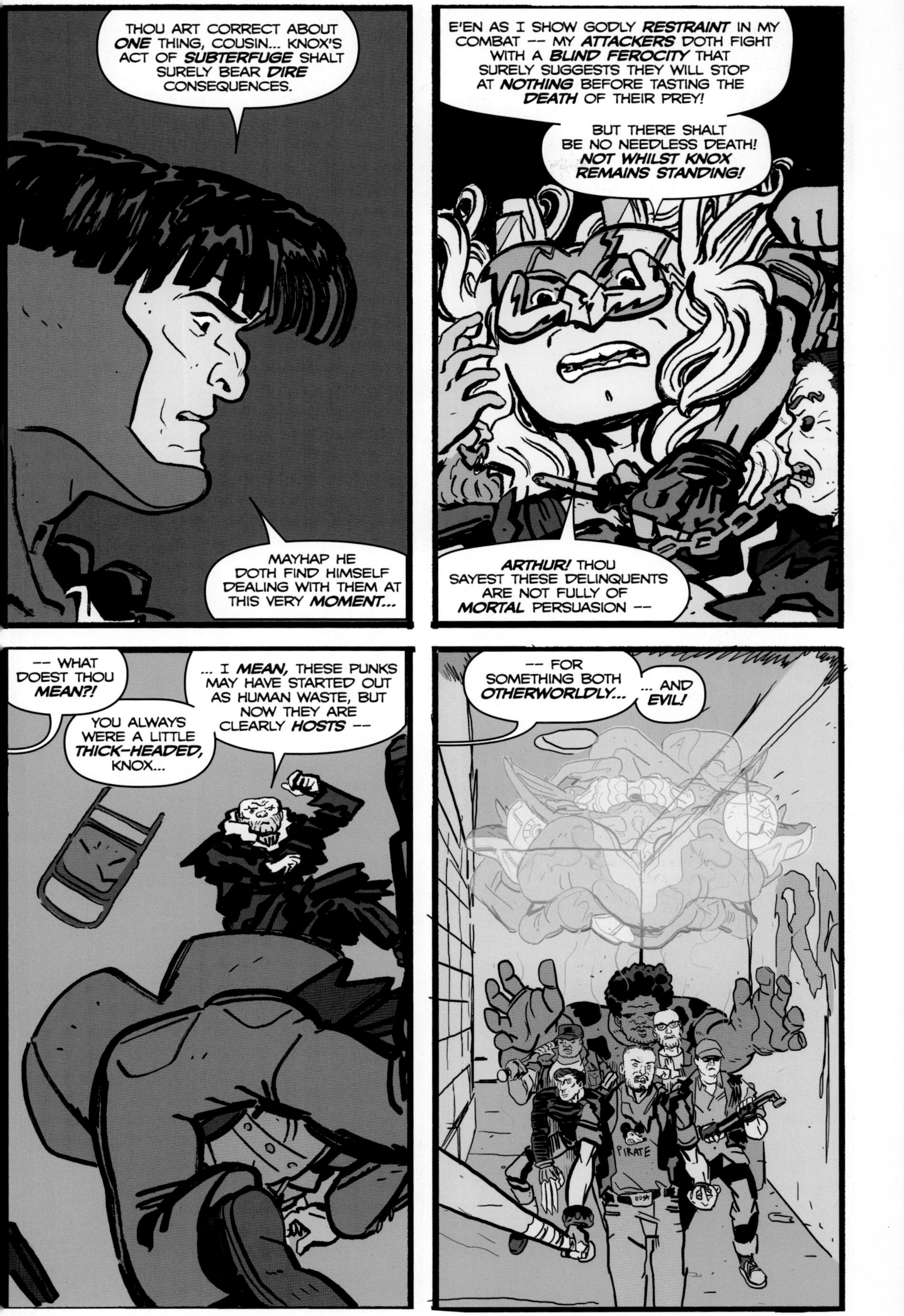
THOU ART CORRECT ABOUT ONE THING, COUSIN... KNOX'S ACT OF SUBTERFUGE SHALT SURELY BEAR DIRE CONSEQUENCES.
MAYHAP HE DOTH FIND HIMSELF DEALING WITH THEM AT THIS VERY MOMENT...
E'EN AS I SHOW GODLY RESTRAINT IN MY COMBAT -- MY ATTACKERS DOTH FIGHT WITH A BLIND FEROCITY THAT SURELY SUGGESTS THEY WILL STOP AT NOTHING BEFORE TASTING THE DEATH OF THEIR PREY!
BUT THERE SHALT BE NO NEEDLESS DEATH! NOT WHILST KNOX REMAINS STANDING!
ARTHUR! THOU SAYEST THESE DELINQUENTS ARE NOT FULLY OF MORTAL PERSUASION --
-- WHAT DOEST THOU MEAN?!
YOU ALWAYS WERE A LITTLE THICK-HEADED, KNOX...
... I MEAN, THESE PUNKS MAY HAVE STARTED OUT AS HUMAN WASTE, BUT NOW THEY ARE CLEARLY HOSTS --
-- FOR SOMETHING BOTH OTHERWORLDLY...
... AND EVIL!
PIRATE

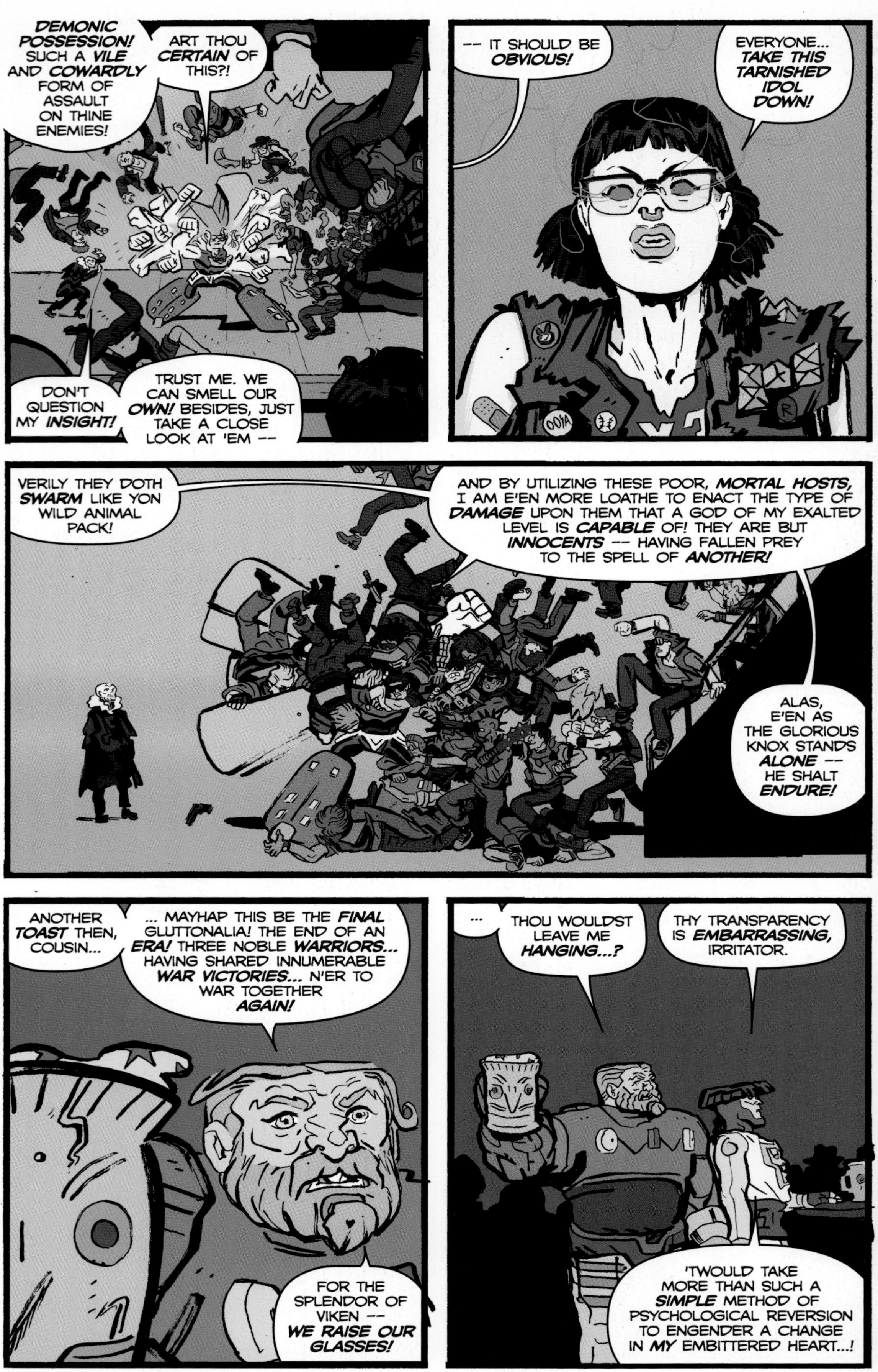
DEMONIC POSSESSION! SUCH A VILE AND COWARDLY FORM OF ASSAULT ON THINE ENEMIES!
ART THOU CERTAIN OF THIS?!
DON'T QUESTION MY INSIGHT!
TRUST ME. WE CAN SMELL OUR OWN! BESIDES, JUST TAKE A CLOSE LOOK AT 'EM --
-- IT SHOULD BE OBVIOUS!
EVERYONE... TAKE THIS TARNISHED IDOL DOWN!
VERILY THEY DOTH SWARM LIKE YON WILD ANIMAL PACK!
AND BY UTILIZING THESE POOR, MORTAL HOSTS, I AM E'EN MORE LOATHE TO ENACT THE TYPE OF DAMAGE UPON THEM THAT A GOD OF MY EXALTED LEVEL IS CAPABLE OF! THEY ARE BUT INNOCENTS -- HAVING FALLEN PREY TO THE SPELL OF ANOTHER!
ALAS, E'EN AS THE GLORIOUS KNOX STANDS ALONE -- HE SHALT ENDURE!
ANOTHER TOAST THEN, COUSIN...
... MAYHAP THIS BE THE FINAL GLUTTONALIA! THE END OF AN ERA! THREE NOBLE WARRIORS... HAVING SHARED INNUMERABLE WAR VICTORIES... N'ER TO WAR TOGETHER AGAIN!
FOR THE SPLENDOR OF VIKEN -- WE RAISE OUR GLASSES!
...
THOU WOULDST LEAVE ME HANGING...?
THY TRANSPARENCY IS EMBARRASSING, IRRITATOR.
'TWOULD TAKE MORE THAN SUCH A SIMPLE METHOD OF PSYCHOLOGICAL REVERSION TO ENGENDER A CHANGE IN MY EMBITTERED HEART...!

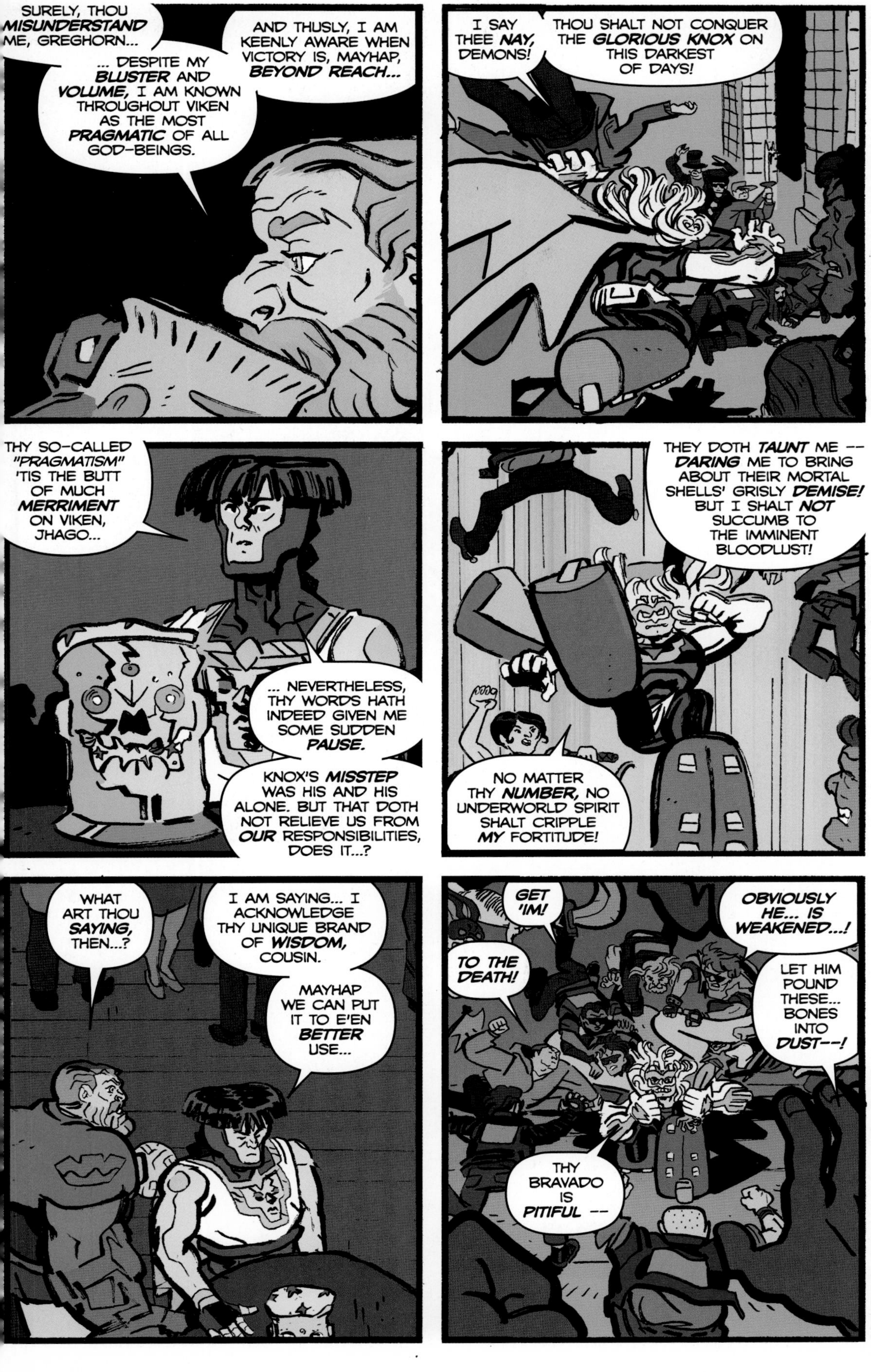
SURELY, THOU MISUNDERSTAND ME, GREGHORN...
... DESPITE MY BLUSTER AND VOLUME, I AM KNOWN THROUGHOUT VIKEN AS THE MOST PRAGMATIC OF ALL GOD-BEINGS.
AND THUSLY, I AM KEENLY AWARE WHEN VICTORY IS, MAYHAP, BEYOND REACH...
I SAY THEE NAY, DEMONS!
THOU SHALT NOT CONQUER THE GLORIOUS KNOX ON THIS DARKEST OF DAYS!
THY SO-CALLED "PRAGMATISM" 'TIS THE BUTT OF MUCH MERRIMENT ON VIKEN, JHAGO...
... NEVERTHELESS, THY WORDS HATH INDEED GIVEN ME SOME SUDDEN PAUSE.
KNOX'S MISSTEP WAS HIS AND HIS ALONE. BUT THAT DOTH NOT RELIEVE US FROM OUR RESPONSIBILITIES, DOES IT...?
THEY DOTH TAUNT ME -- DARING ME TO BRING ABOUT THEIR MORTAL SHELLS' GRISLY DEMISE! BUT I SHALT NOT SUCCUMB TO THE IMMINENT BLOODLUST!
NO MATTER THY NUMBER, NO UNDERWORLD SPIRIT SHALT CRIPPLE MY FORTITUDE!
WHAT ART THOU SAYING, THEN...?
I AM SAYING... I ACKNOWLEDGE THY UNIQUE BRAND OF WISDOM, COUSIN.
MAYHAP WE CAN PUT IT TO E'EN BETTER USE...
GET 'IM!
TO THE DEATH!
OBVIOUSLY HE... IS WEAKENED...!
LET HIM POUND THESE... BONES INTO DUST--!
THY BRAVADO IS PITIFUL --

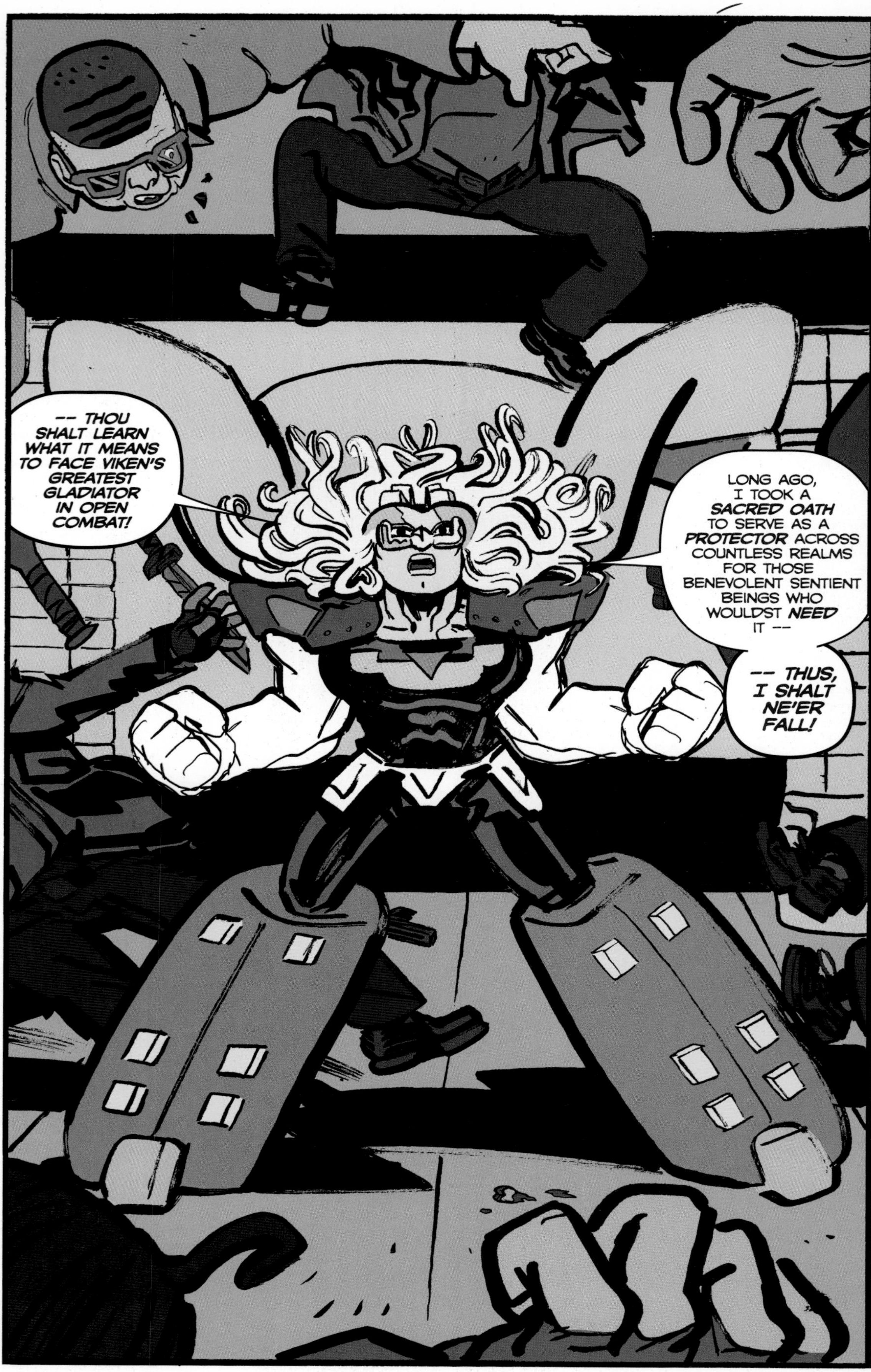

-- THOU SHALT LEARN WHAT IT MEANS TO FACE VIKEN'S GREATEST GLADIATOR IN OPEN COMBAT!
LONG AGO, I TOOK A SACRED OATH TO SERVE AS A PROTECTOR ACROSS COUNTLESS REALMS FOR THOSE BENEVOLENT SENTIENT BEINGS WHO WOULDST NEED IT --
-- THUS, I SHALT NE'ER FALL!

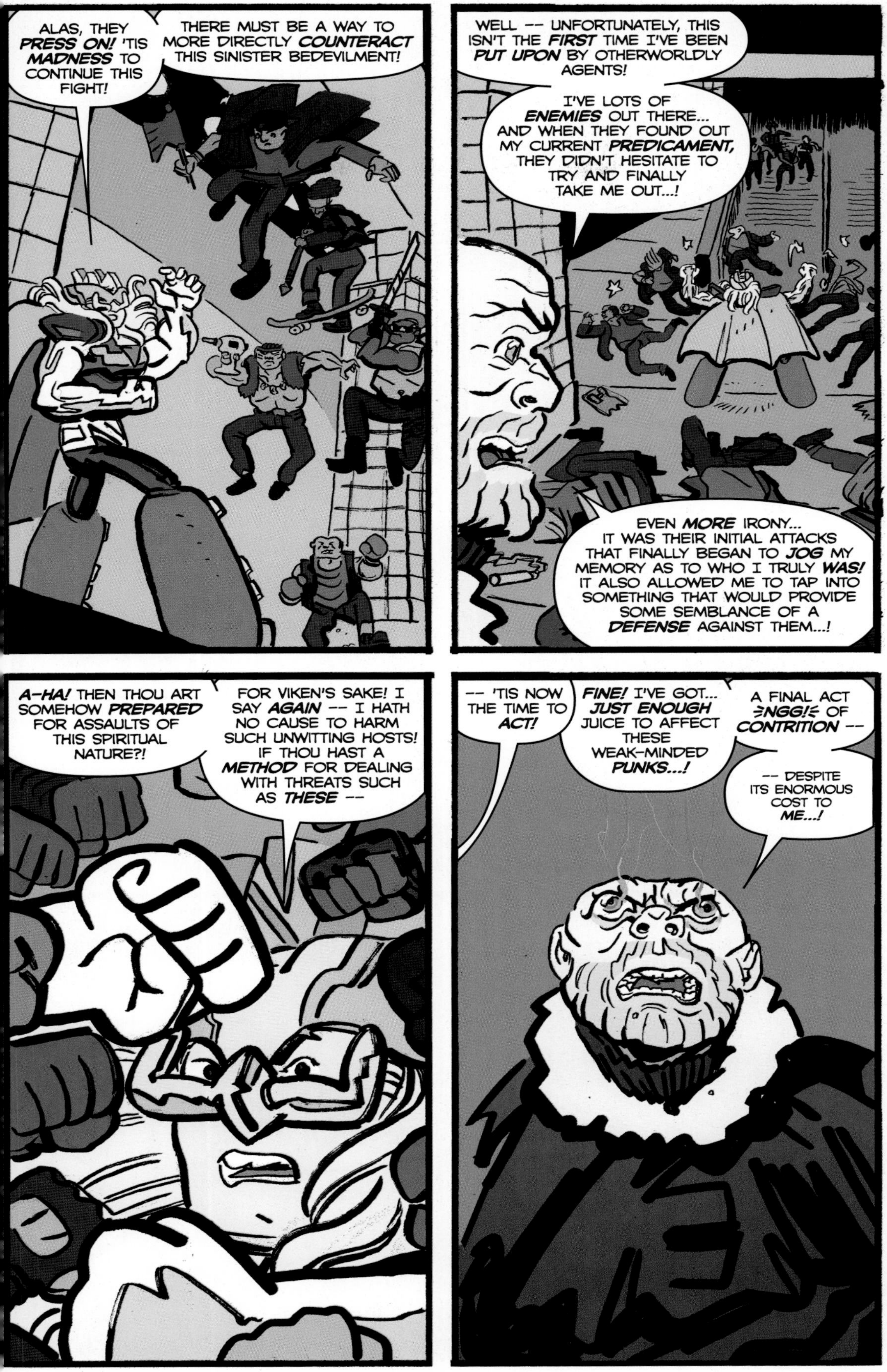

ALAS, THEY PRESS ON! 'TIS MADNESS TO CONTINUE THIS FIGHT!
THERE MUST BE A WAY TO MORE DIRECTLY COUNTERACT THIS SINISTER BEDEVILMENT!
WELL -- UNFORTUNATELY, THIS ISN'T THE FIRST TIME I'VE BEEN PUT UPON BY OTHERWORLDLY AGENTS!
I'VE LOTS OF ENEMIES OUT THERE... AND WHEN THEY FOUND OUT MY CURRENT PREDICAMENT, THEY DIDN'T HESITATE TO TRY AND FINALLY TAKE ME OUT...!
EVEN MORE IRONY... IT WAS THEIR INITIAL ATTACKS THAT FINALLY BEGAN TO JOG MY MEMORY AS TO WHO I TRULY WAS! IT ALSO ALLOWED ME TO TAP INTO SOMETHING THAT WOULD PROVIDE SOME SEMBLANCE OF A DEFENSE AGAINST THEM...!
A-HA! THEN THOU ART SOMEHOW PREPARED FOR ASSAULTS OF THIS SPIRITUAL NATURE?!
FOR VIKEN'S SAKE! I SAY AGAIN -- I HATH NO CAUSE TO HARM SUCH UNWITTING HOSTS! IF THOU HAST A METHOD FOR DEALING WITH THREATS SUCH AS THESE --
-- 'TIS NOW THE TIME TO ACT!
FINE! I'VE GOT... JUST ENOUGH JUICE TO AFFECT THESE WEAK-MINDED PUNKS...!
A FINAL ACT *NGG!* OF CONTRITION --
-- DESPITE ITS ENORMOUS COST TO ME...!

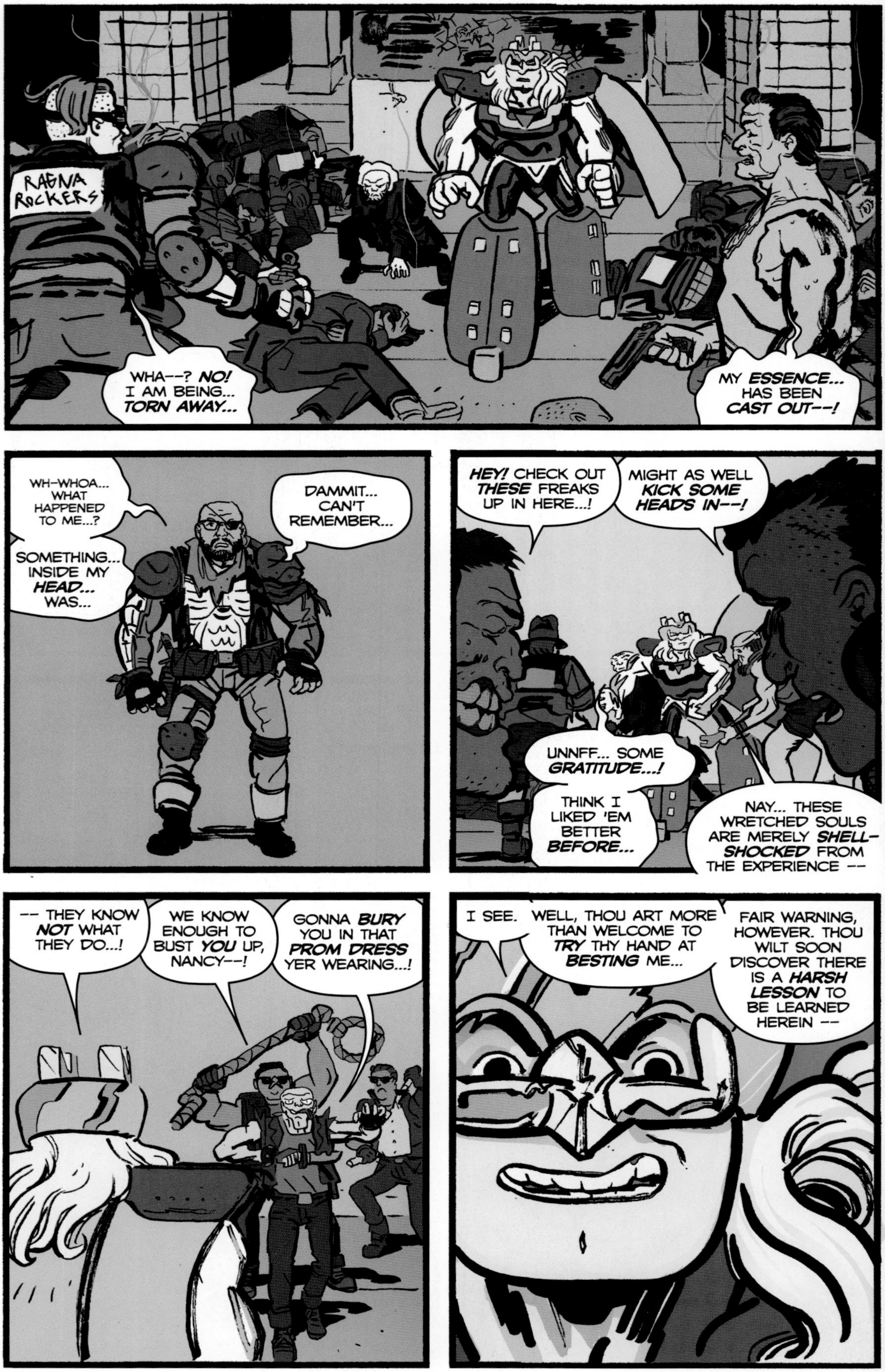
RAGNA ROCKERS
WHA--? NO! I AM BEING... TORN AWAY...
MY ESSENCE... HAS BEEN CAST OUT--!
WH-WHOA... WHAT HAPPENED TO ME...?
SOMETHING... INSIDE MY HEAD... WAS...
DAMMIT... CAN'T REMEMBER...
HEY! CHECK OUT THESE FREAKS UP IN HERE...!
MIGHT AS WELL KICK SOME HEADS IN--!
UNNFF... SOME GRATITUDE...!
THINK I LIKED 'EM BETTER BEFORE...
NAY... THESE WRETCHED SOULS ARE MERELY SHELL-SHOCKED FROM THE EXPERIENCE --
-- THEY KNOW NOT WHAT THEY DO...!
WE KNOW ENOUGH TO BUST YOU UP, NANCY--!
GONNA BURY YOU IN THAT PROM DRESS YER WEARING...!
I SEE.
WELL, THOU ART MORE THAN WELCOME TO TRY THY HAND AT BESTING ME...
FAIR WARNING, HOWEVER. THOU WILT SOON DISCOVER THERE IS A HARSH LESSON TO BE LEARNED HEREIN --

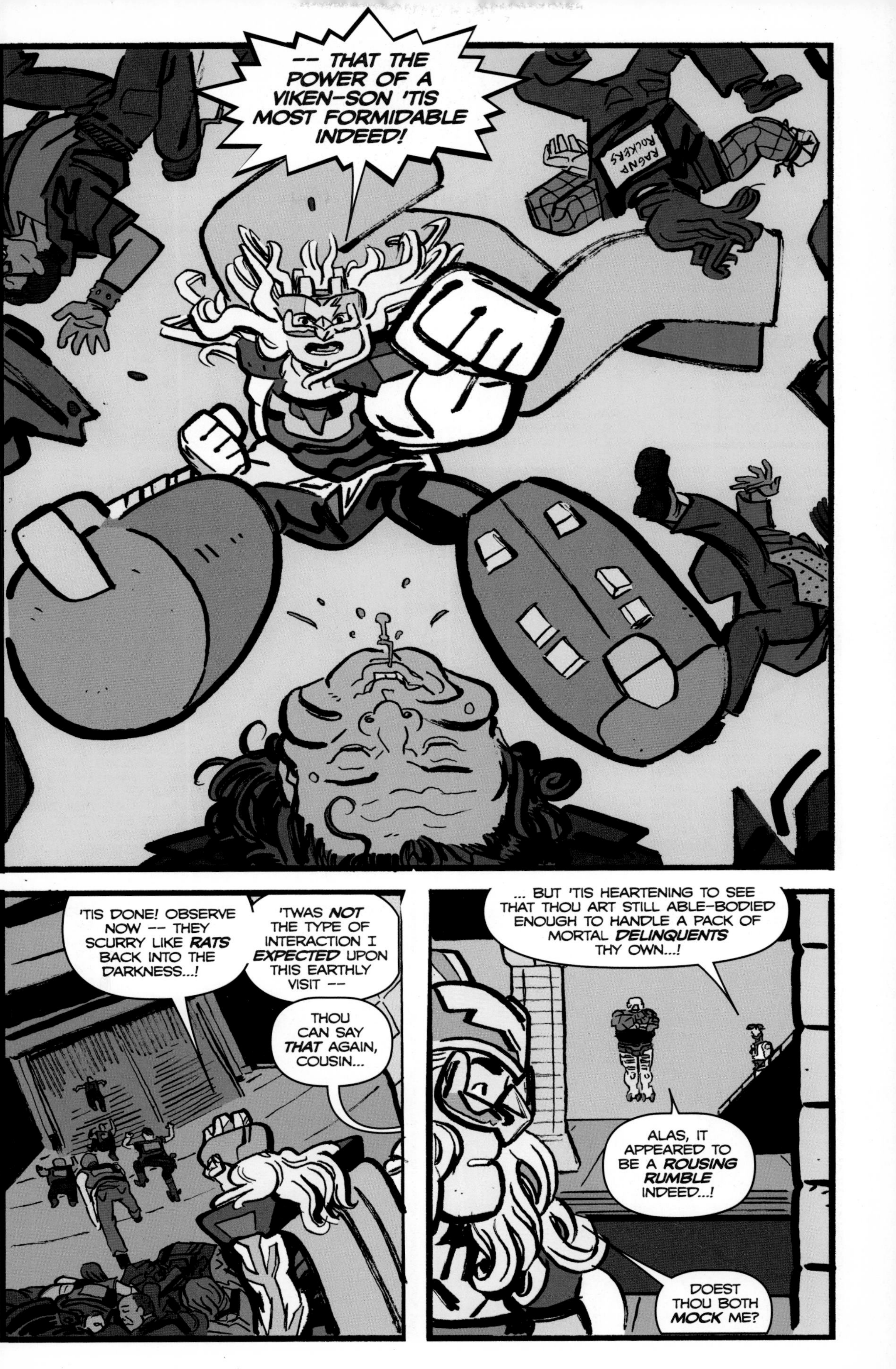
-- THAT THE POWER OF A VIKEN-SON 'TIS MOST FORMIDABLE INDEED!
'TIS DONE! OBSERVE NOW -- THEY SCURRY LIKE RATS BACK INTO THE DARKNESS...!
'TWAS NOT THE TYPE OF INTERACTION I EXPECTED UPON THIS EARTHLY VISIT --
THOU CAN SAY THAT AGAIN, COUSIN...
... BUT 'TIS HEARTENING TO SEE THAT THOU ART STILL ABLE-BODIED ENOUGH TO HANDLE A PACK OF MORTAL DELINQUENTS THY OWN...!
ALAS, IT APPEARED TO BE A ROUSING RUMBLE INDEED...!
DOEST THOU BOTH MOCK ME?

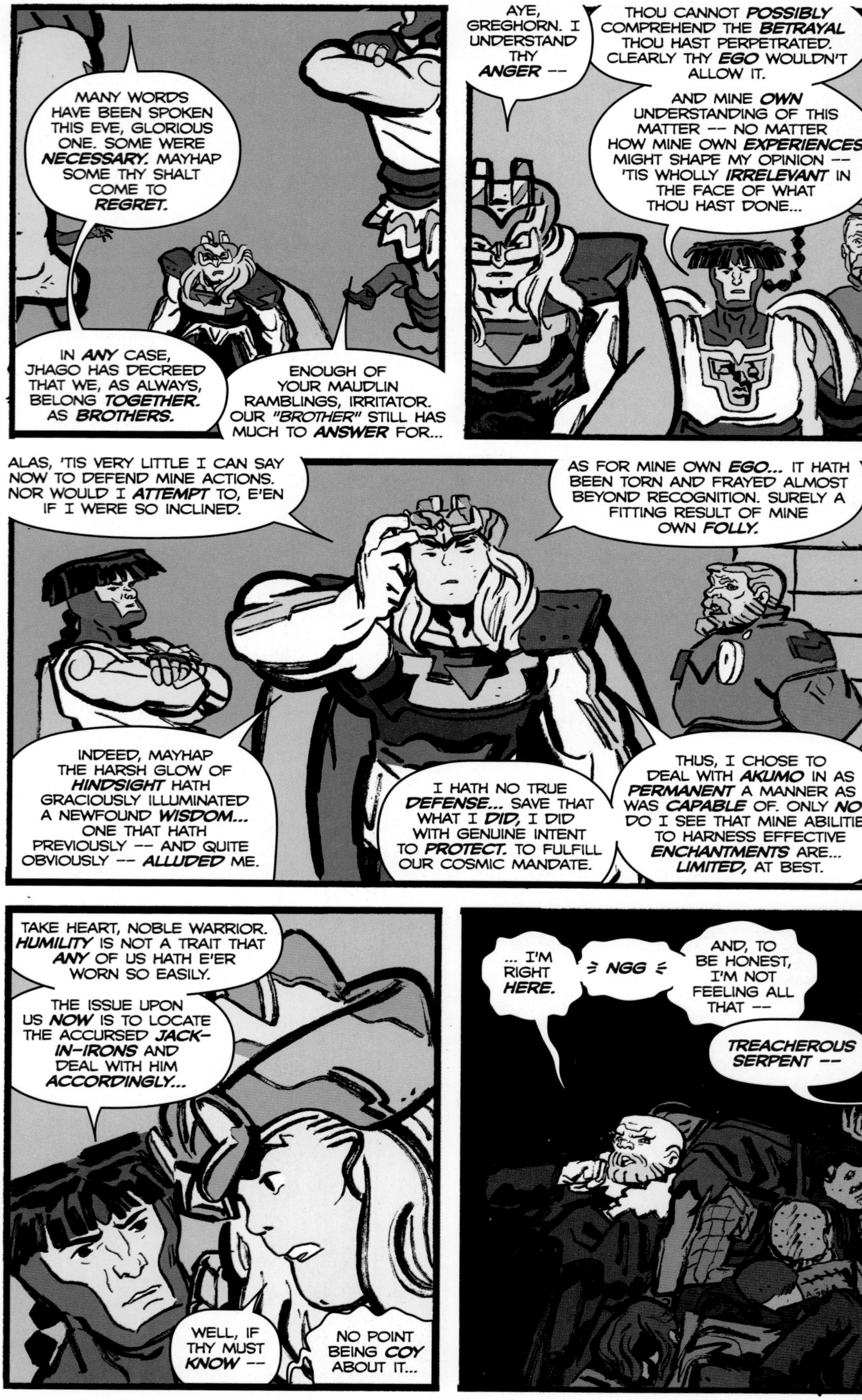
MANY WORDS HAVE BEEN SPOKEN THIS EVE, GLORIOUS ONE. SOME WERE NECESSARY. MAYHAP SOME THY SHALT COME TO REGRET.
IN ANY CASE, JHAGO HAS DECREED THAT WE, AS ALWAYS, BELONG TOGETHER. AS BROTHERS.
ENOUGH OF YOUR MAUDLIN RAMBLINGS, IRRITATOR. OUR "BROTHER" STILL HAS MUCH TO ANSWER FOR...
AYE, GREGHORN. I UNDERSTAND THY ANGER --
THOU CANNOT POSSIBLY COMPREHEND THE BETRAYAL THOU HAST PERPETRATED. CLEARLY THY EGO WOULDN'T ALLOW IT.
AND MINE OWN UNDERSTANDING OF THIS MATTER -- NO MATTER HOW MINE OWN EXPERIENCES MIGHT SHAPE MY OPINION -- 'TIS WHOLLY IRRELEVANT IN THE FACE OF WHAT THOU HAST DONE...
ALAS, 'TIS VERY LITTLE I CAN SAY NOW TO DEFEND MINE ACTIONS. NOR WOULD I ATTEMPT TO, E'EN IF I WERE SO INCLINED.
AS FOR MINE OWN EGO... IT HATH BEEN TORN AND FRAYED ALMOST BEYOND RECOGNITION. SURELY A FITTING RESULT OF MINE OWN FOLLY.
INDEED, MAYHAP THE HARSH GLOW OF HINDSIGHT HATH GRACIOUSLY ILLUMINATED A NEWFOUND WISDOM... ONE THAT HATH PREVIOUSLY -- AND QUITE OBVIOUSLY -- ALLUDED ME.
I HATH NO TRUE DEFENSE... SAVE THAT WHAT I DID, I DID WITH GENUINE INTENT TO PROTECT. TO FULFILL OUR COSMIC MANDATE.
THUS, I CHOSE TO DEAL WITH AKUMO IN AS PERMANENT A MANNER AS I WAS CAPABLE OF. ONLY NOW DO I SEE THAT MINE ABILITIES TO HARNESS EFFECTIVE ENCHANTMENTS ARE... LIMITED, AT BEST.
TAKE HEART, NOBLE WARRIOR. HUMILITY IS NOT A TRAIT THAT ANY OF US HATH E'ER WORN SO EASILY.
THE ISSUE UPON US NOW IS TO LOCATE THE ACCURSED JACK-IN-IRONS AND DEAL WITH HIM ACCORDINGLY...
WELL, IF THY MUST KNOW --
NO POINT BEING COY ABOUT IT...
... I'M RIGHT HERE.
NGG
AND, TO BE HONEST, I'M NOT FEELING ALL THAT --
TREACHEROUS SERPENT --

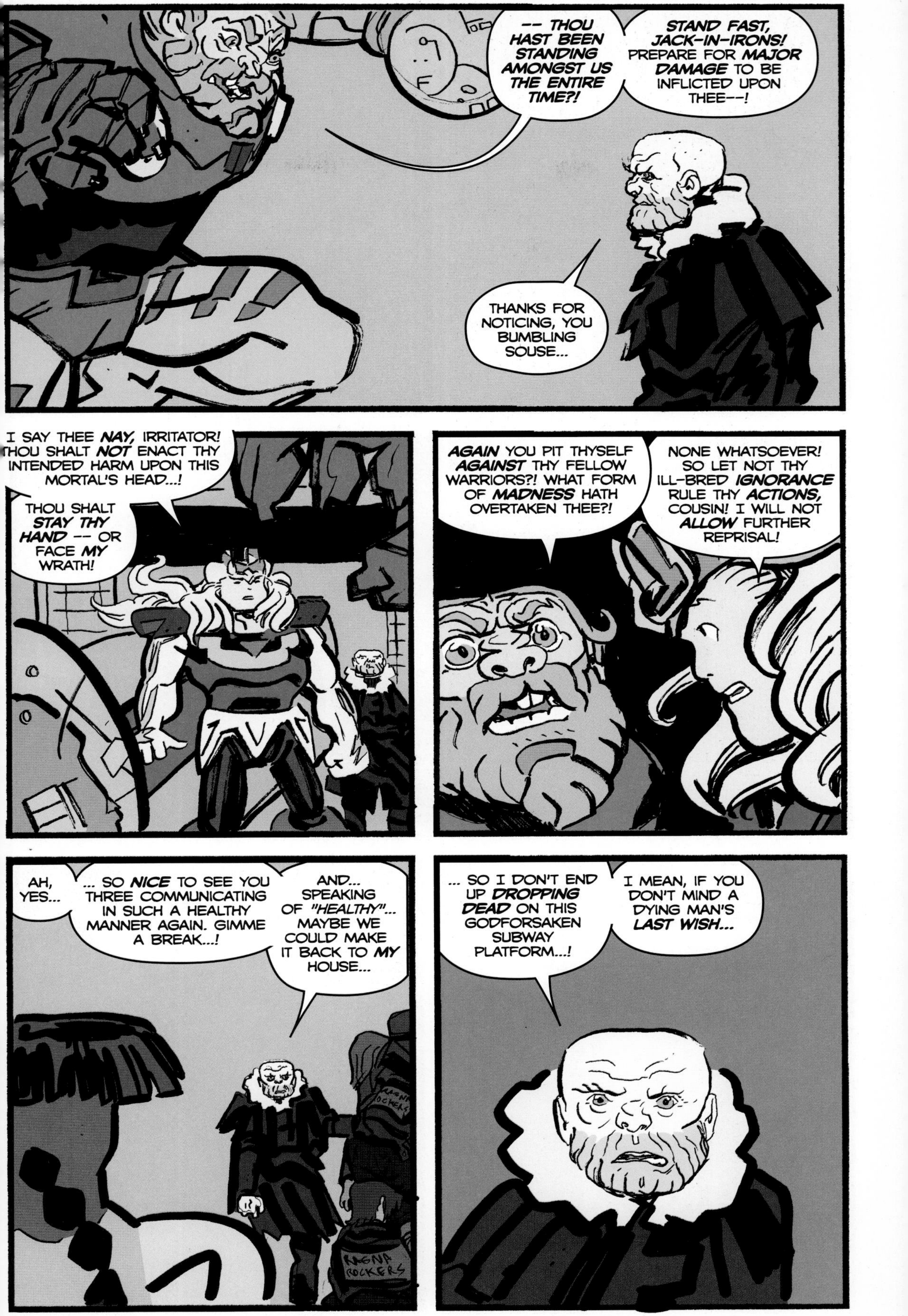
STAND FAST, JACK-IN-IRONS! PREPARE FOR MAJOR DAMAGE TO BE INFLICTED UPON THEE--!
-- THOU HAST BEEN STANDING AMONGST US THE ENTIRE TIME?!
THANKS FOR NOTICING, YOU BUMBLING SOUSE...
I SAY THEE NAY, IRRITATOR! THOU SHALT NOT ENACT THY INTENDED HARM UPON THIS MORTAL'S HEAD...!
THOU SHALT STAY THY HAND -- OR FACE MY WRATH!
AGAIN YOU PIT THYSELF AGAINST THY FELLOW WARRIORS?! WHAT FORM OF MADNESS HATH OVERTAKEN THEE?!
NONE WHATSOEVER! SO LET NOT THY ILL-BRED IGNORANCE RULE THY ACTIONS, COUSIN! I WILL NOT ALLOW FURTHER REPRISAL!
AH, YES...
... SO NICE TO SEE YOU THREE COMMUNICATING IN SUCH A HEALTHY MANNER AGAIN. GIMME A BREAK...!
AND... SPEAKING OF "HEALTHY"... MAYBE WE COULD MAKE IT BACK TO MY HOUSE...
RAGNA ROCKERS
... SO I DON'T END UP DROPPING DEAD ON THIS GODFORSAKEN SUBWAY PLATFORM...!
I MEAN, IF YOU DON'T MIND A DYING MAN'S LAST WISH...

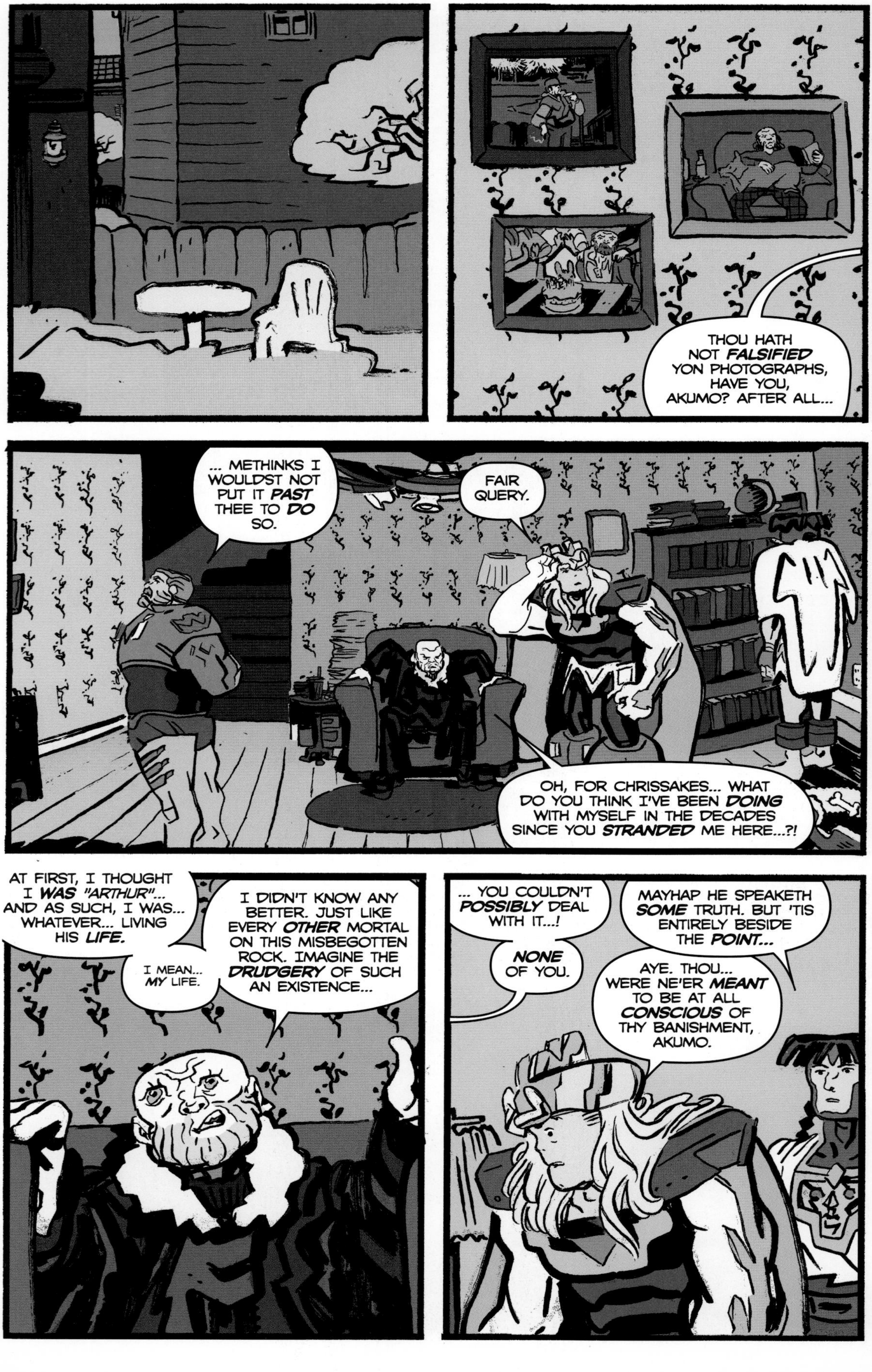
THOU HATH NOT FALSIFIED YON PHOTOGRAPHS, HAVE YOU, AKUMO? AFTER ALL...
... METHINKS I WOULDST NOT PUT IT PAST THEE TO DO SO.
FAIR QUERY.
OH, FOR CHRISSAKES... WHAT DO YOU THINK I'VE BEEN DOING WITH MYSELF IN THE DECADES SINCE YOU STRANDED ME HERE...?!
AT FIRST, I THOUGHT I WAS "ARTHUR"... AND AS SUCH, I WAS... WHATEVER... LIVING HIS LIFE.
I MEAN... MY LIFE.
I DIDN'T KNOW ANY BETTER. JUST LIKE EVERY OTHER MORTAL ON THIS MISBEGOTTEN ROCK. IMAGINE THE DRUDGERY OF SUCH AN EXISTENCE...
... YOU COULDN'T POSSIBLY DEAL WITH IT...!
NONE OF YOU.
MAYHAP HE SPEAKETH SOME TRUTH. BUT 'TIS ENTIRELY BESIDE THE POINT...
AYE. THOU... WERE NE'ER MEANT TO BE AT ALL CONSCIOUS OF THY BANISHMENT, AKUMO.

WELL, I *WASN'T*, AT FIRST. BUT YOU DON'T *GET* IT, KNOX. WHAT YOU *DID* TO ME...

LOOK, NOW I *KNOW* WHAT I WAS BEFORE. I WAS A FORCE OF NATURE. I WAS PATRON SAINT OF THE *MORALLY CORRUPT.* I WAS...

... WELL, I WAS *EVIL PERSONIFIED,* WASN'T I...?

ONCE I BEGAN TO *REMEMBER* THAT... IT WAS ALMOST TOO MUCH TO BEAR...

BECAUSE THE UNIVERSE IS A *COLD* AND *UNFORGIVING* PLACE... FILLED WITH ENDLESS, DARK *NOTHINGNESS* THAT -- NO MATTER WHAT YOU MAY BELIEVE TO THE *CONTRARY* -- IS UTTERLY *INESCAPABLE.*

NO MERCY... NO HOPE... NO *JUDGMENT*...

I WAS *BORN* FROM THAT NOTHINGNESS. I WAS THE *ENTROPY* THAT HAUNTS OUR COLLECTIVE NIGHTMARES... THE PRIMAL *FURY* OF THE UNIVERSE *UNLEASHED*...

... I LIVED AND I ACTED COMPLETELY WITHOUT *CONSCIENCE*... IT WAS PURE AND IT WAS *REAL* AND IT TOOK NO *EFFORT* ON MY PART. AS YOU WELL KNOW, THE GAMES OF WAR NEVER DO...

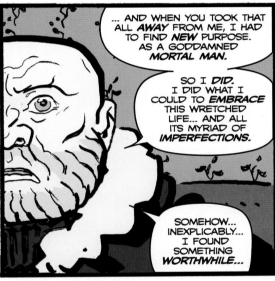

... AND WHEN YOU TOOK THAT ALL *AWAY* FROM ME, I HAD TO FIND *NEW* PURPOSE. AS A GODDAMNED *MORTAL MAN.*

SO I *DID.* I DID WHAT I COULD TO *EMBRACE* THIS WRETCHED LIFE... AND ALL ITS MYRIAD OF *IMPERFECTIONS.*

SOMEHOW... INEXPLICABLY... I FOUND SOMETHING *WORTHWHILE*...

... THE *STRUGGLE* OF DAY-TO-DAY LIFE HERE. IN HINDSIGHT, THE GREATEST CHALLENGE I EVER FACED.

YOU THREE... WITH YOUR IMMORTAL BLOOD AND ENDLESS LIFESPAN... YOUR *PERCEPTIONS* ARE NOWHERE *NEAR* MINE WHEN IT COMES TO THE GREAT *MYSTERIES* ILLUMINATED BY THE *QUIET DETERMINATION* OF THIS TYPE OF EXISTENCE.

AND HERE WE ARE... I'M FACING MY OWN *MORTALITY.* I'M FACING *DEATH ITSELF.*

THINK ABOUT IT. WHAT GREATER CHALLENGE *IS* THERE...?

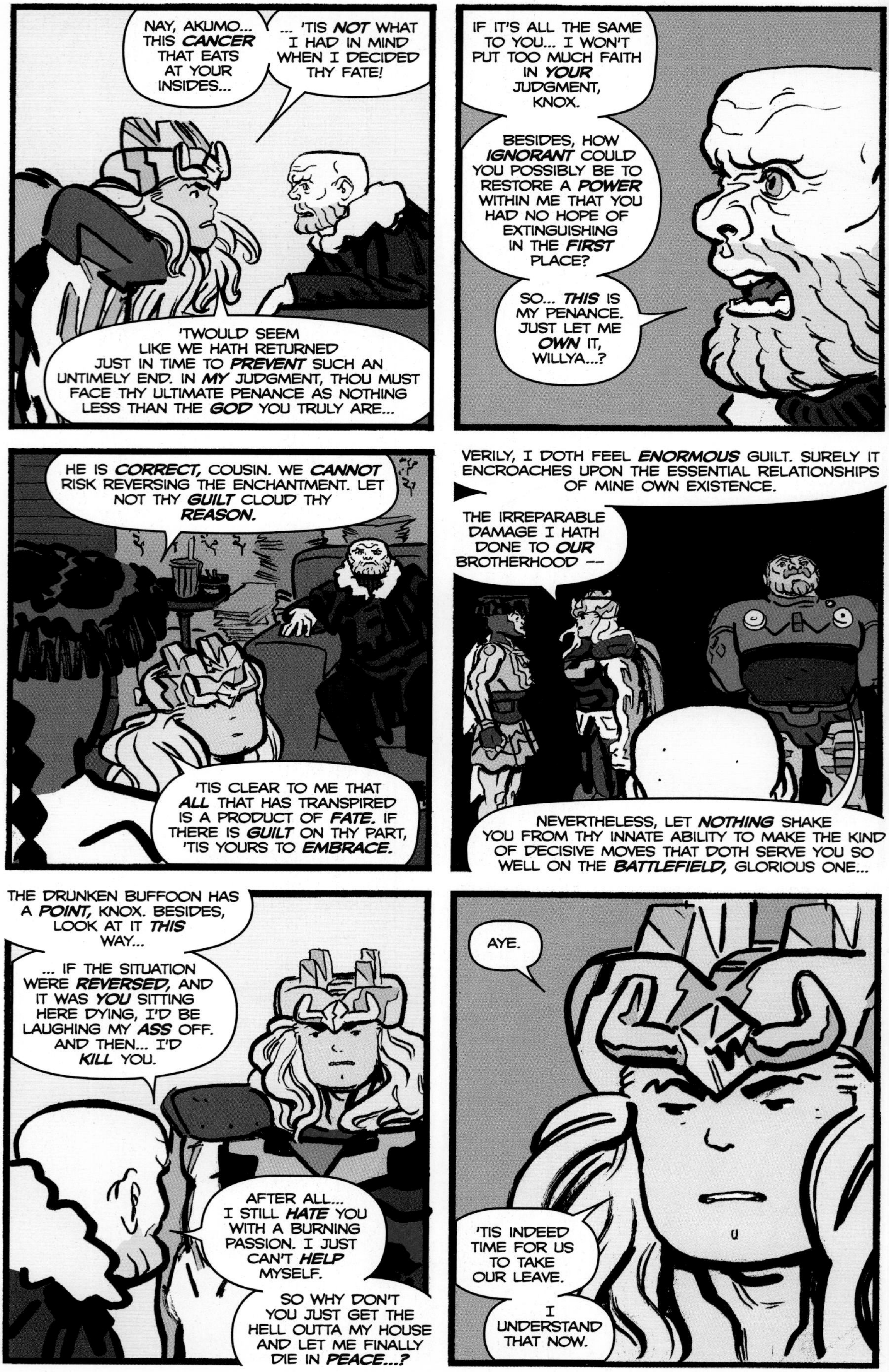
NAY, AKUMO... THIS CANCER THAT EATS AT YOUR INSIDES...
... 'TIS NOT WHAT I HAD IN MIND WHEN I DECIDED THY FATE!
'TWOULD SEEM LIKE WE HATH RETURNED JUST IN TIME TO PREVENT SUCH AN UNTIMELY END. IN MY JUDGMENT, THOU MUST FACE THY ULTIMATE PENANCE AS NOTHING LESS THAN THE GOD YOU TRULY ARE...
IF IT'S ALL THE SAME TO YOU... I WON'T PUT TOO MUCH FAITH IN YOUR JUDGMENT, KNOX.
BESIDES, HOW IGNORANT COULD YOU POSSIBLY BE TO RESTORE A POWER WITHIN ME THAT YOU HAD NO HOPE OF EXTINGUISHING IN THE FIRST PLACE?
SO... THIS IS MY PENANCE. JUST LET ME OWN IT, WILLYA...?
HE IS CORRECT, COUSIN. WE CANNOT RISK REVERSING THE ENCHANTMENT. LET NOT THY GUILT CLOUD THY REASON.
'TIS CLEAR TO ME THAT ALL THAT HAS TRANSPIRED IS A PRODUCT OF FATE. IF THERE IS GUILT ON THY PART, 'TIS YOURS TO EMBRACE.
VERILY, I DOTH FEEL ENORMOUS GUILT. SURELY IT ENCROACHES UPON THE ESSENTIAL RELATIONSHIPS OF MINE OWN EXISTENCE.
THE IRREPARABLE DAMAGE I HATH DONE TO OUR BROTHERHOOD --
NEVERTHELESS, LET NOTHING SHAKE YOU FROM THY INNATE ABILITY TO MAKE THE KIND OF DECISIVE MOVES THAT DOTH SERVE YOU SO WELL ON THE BATTLEFIELD, GLORIOUS ONE...
THE DRUNKEN BUFFOON HAS A POINT, KNOX. BESIDES, LOOK AT IT THIS WAY...
... IF THE SITUATION WERE REVERSED, AND IT WAS YOU SITTING HERE DYING, I'D BE LAUGHING MY ASS OFF. AND THEN... I'D KILL YOU.
AFTER ALL... I STILL HATE YOU WITH A BURNING PASSION. I JUST CAN'T HELP MYSELF.
SO WHY DON'T YOU JUST GET THE HELL OUTTA MY HOUSE AND LET ME FINALLY DIE IN PEACE...?
AYE.
'TIS INDEED TIME FOR US TO TAKE OUR LEAVE.
I UNDERSTAND THAT NOW.

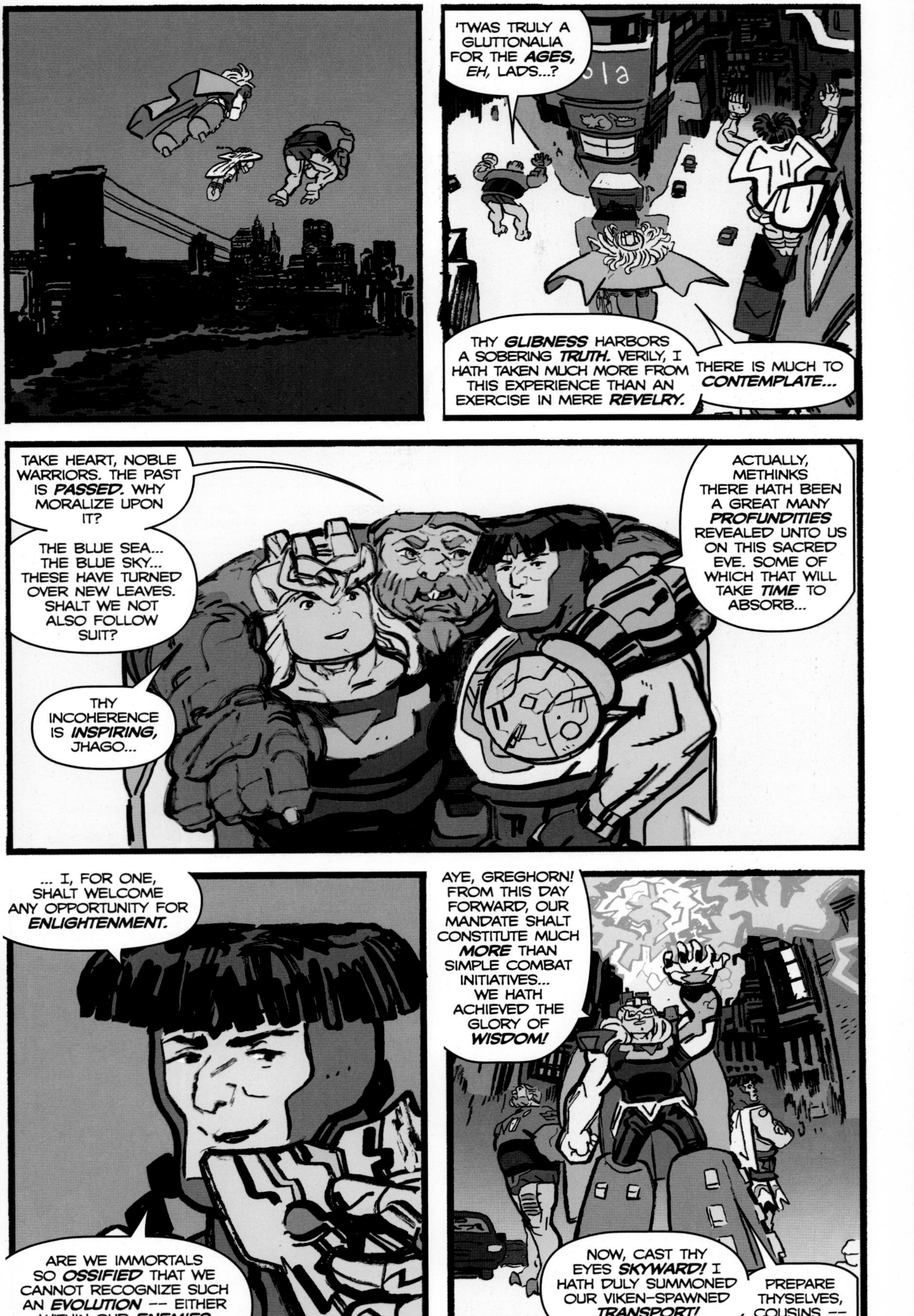
'TWAS TRULY A GLUTTONALIA FOR THE AGES, EH, LADS...?
THY GLIBNESS HARBORS A SOBERING TRUTH. VERILY, I HATH TAKEN MUCH MORE FROM THIS EXPERIENCE THAN AN EXERCISE IN MERE REVELRY.
THERE IS MUCH TO CONTEMPLATE...
TAKE HEART, NOBLE WARRIORS. THE PAST IS PASSED. WHY MORALIZE UPON IT?
THE BLUE SEA... THE BLUE SKY... THESE HAVE TURNED OVER NEW LEAVES. SHALT WE NOT ALSO FOLLOW SUIT?
THY INCOHERENCE IS INSPIRING, JHAGO...
ACTUALLY, METHINKS THERE HATH BEEN A GREAT MANY PROFUNDITIES REVEALED UNTO US ON THIS SACRED EVE. SOME OF WHICH THAT WILL TAKE TIME TO ABSORB...
... I, FOR ONE, SHALT WELCOME ANY OPPORTUNITY FOR ENLIGHTENMENT.
ARE WE IMMORTALS SO OSSIFIED THAT WE CANNOT RECOGNIZE SUCH AN EVOLUTION -- EITHER WITHIN OUR ENEMIES OR E'EN WITHIN OURSELVES?
AYE, GREGHORN! FROM THIS DAY FORWARD, OUR MANDATE SHALT CONSTITUTE MUCH MORE THAN SIMPLE COMBAT INITIATIVES... WE HATH ACHIEVED THE GLORY OF WISDOM!
NOW, CAST THY EYES SKYWARD! I HATH DULY SUMMONED OUR VIKEN-SPAWNED TRANSPORT!
PREPARE THYSELVES, COUSINS --

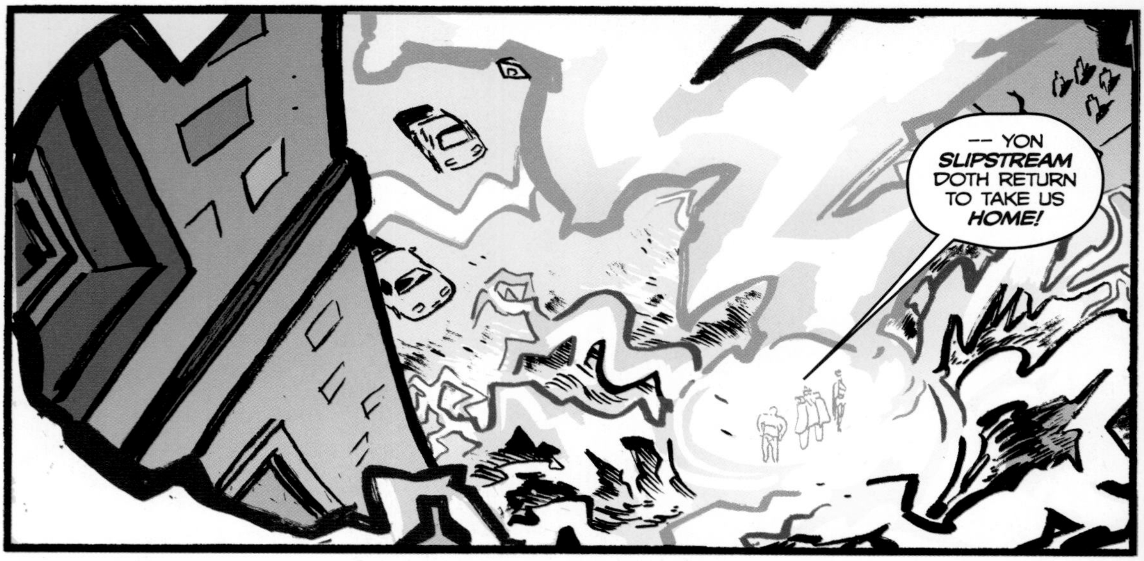
-- YON SLIPSTREAM DOTH RETURN TO TAKE US HOME!

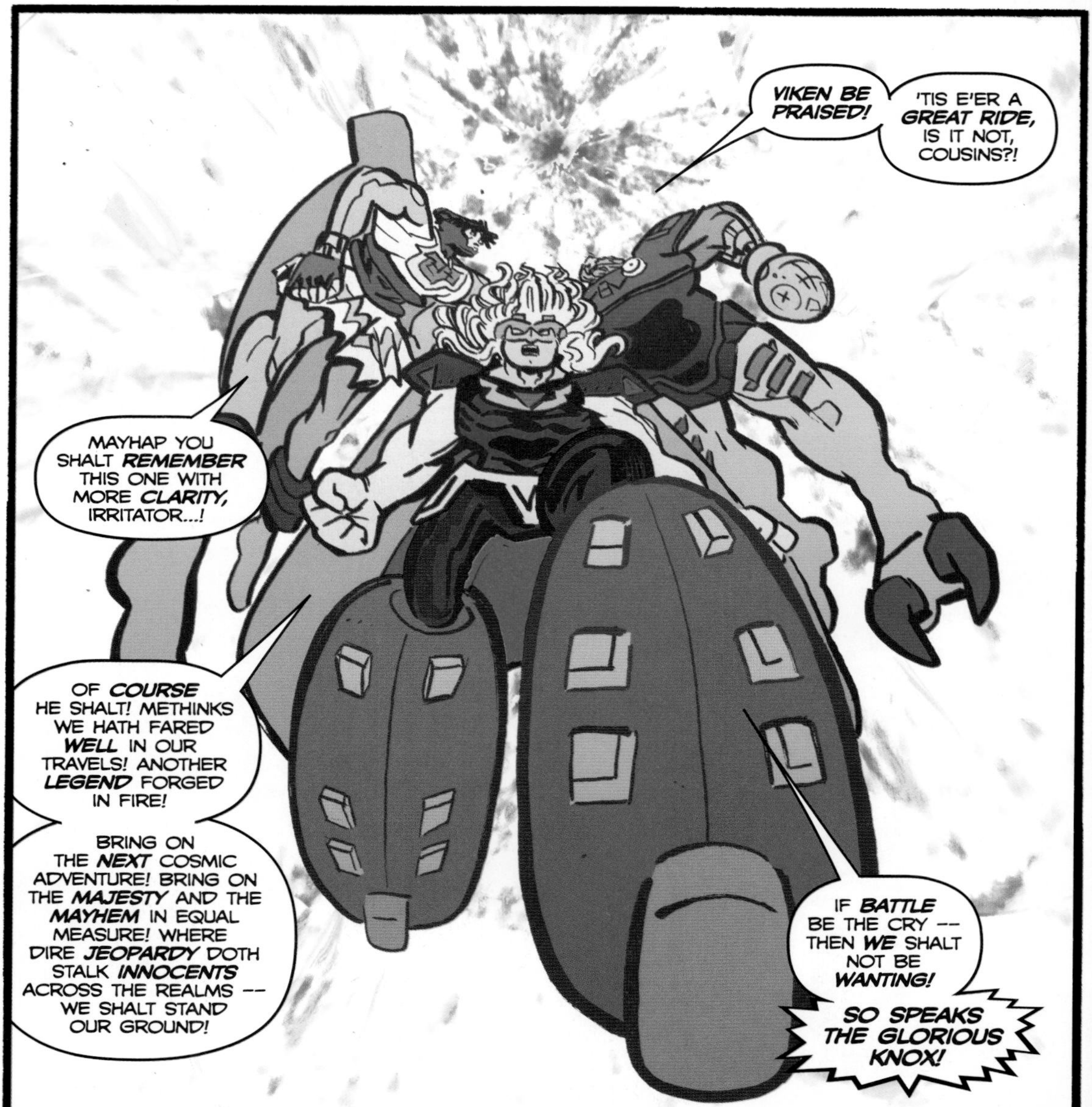
VIKEN BE PRAISED!
'TIS E'ER A GREAT RIDE, IS IT NOT, COUSINS?!
MAYHAP YOU SHALT REMEMBER THIS ONE WITH MORE CLARITY, IRRITATOR...!
OF COURSE HE SHALT! METHINKS WE HATH FARED WELL IN OUR TRAVELS! ANOTHER LEGEND FORGED IN FIRE!
BRING ON THE NEXT COSMIC ADVENTURE! BRING ON THE MAJESTY AND THE MAYHEM IN EQUAL MEASURE! WHERE DIRE JEOPARDY DOTH STALK INNOCENTS ACROSS THE REALMS -- WE SHALT STAND OUR GROUND!
IF BATTLE BE THE CRY -- THEN WE SHALT NOT BE WANTING!
SO SPEAKS THE GLORIOUS KNOX!

The End

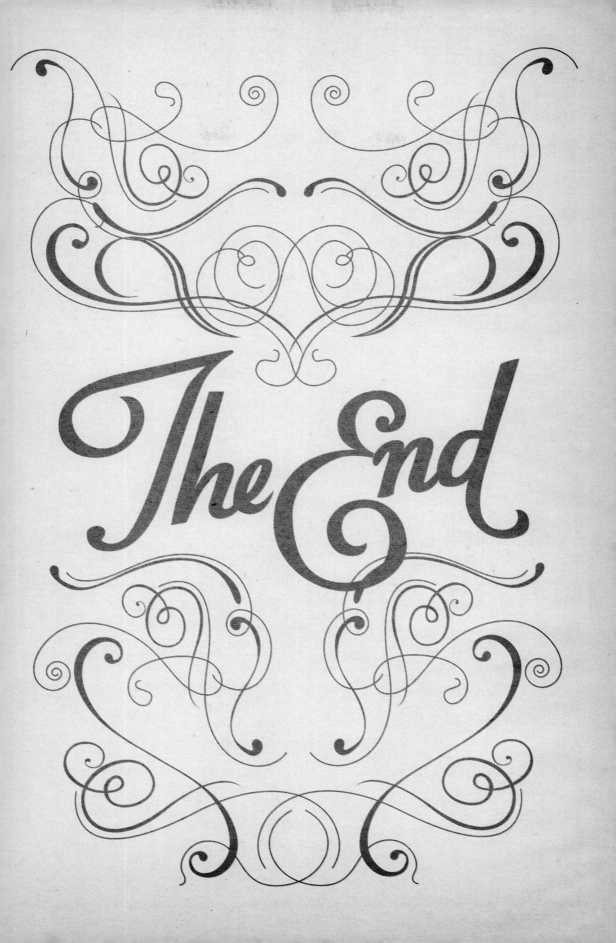

VALHALLA MAD

PINUPS

DEVIN FINCH
ALEXIS ZIRITT
BRIAN FLINT
NICK PITARRA
ANDREW MACLEAN
ANAS AWAD
DEREK M. BALLARD

CONCEPT SKETCHES

PAUL MAYBURY

PAUL MAYBURY 2014

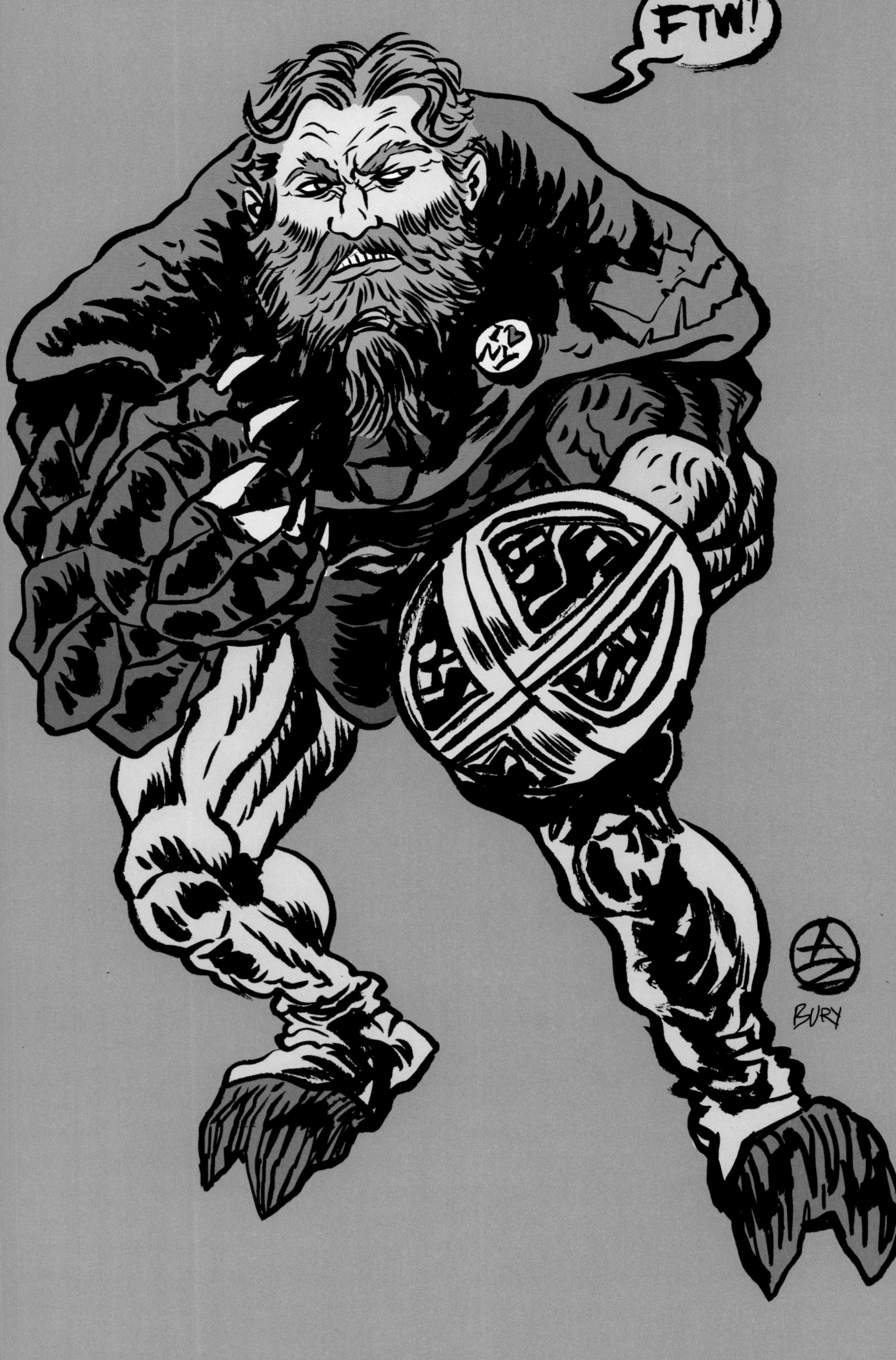
FTW!
I ♥ NY
BURY

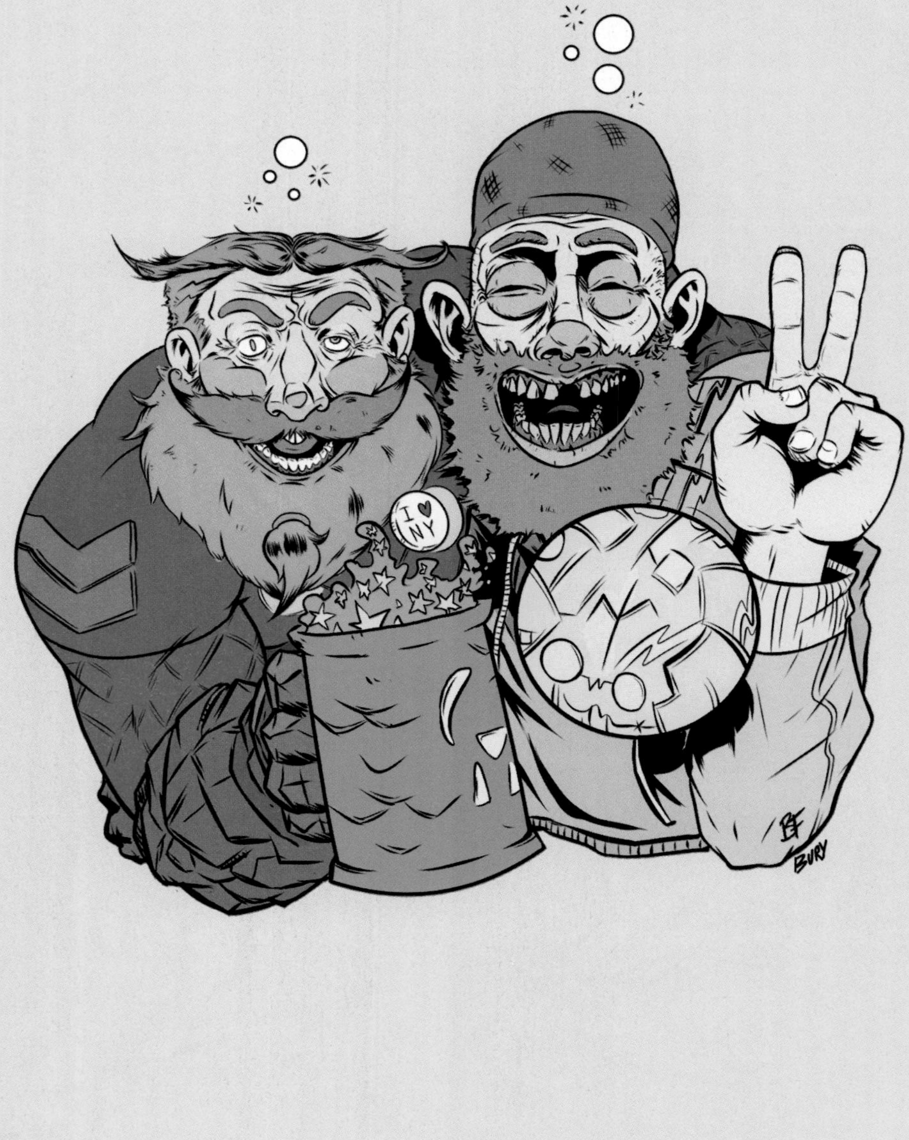
I ♥ NY
BURY

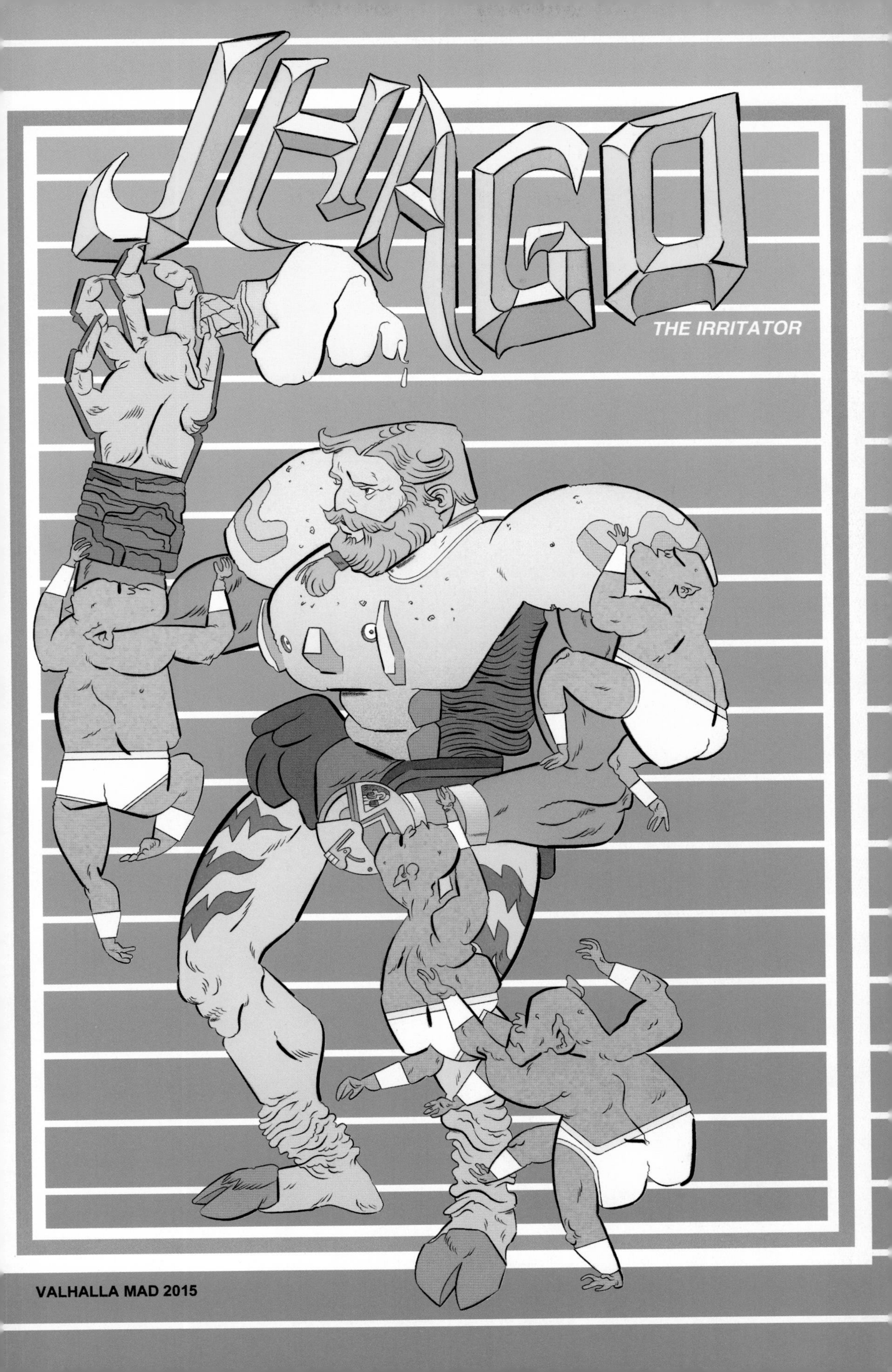
JHAGO
THE IRRITATOR
VALHALLA MAD 2015

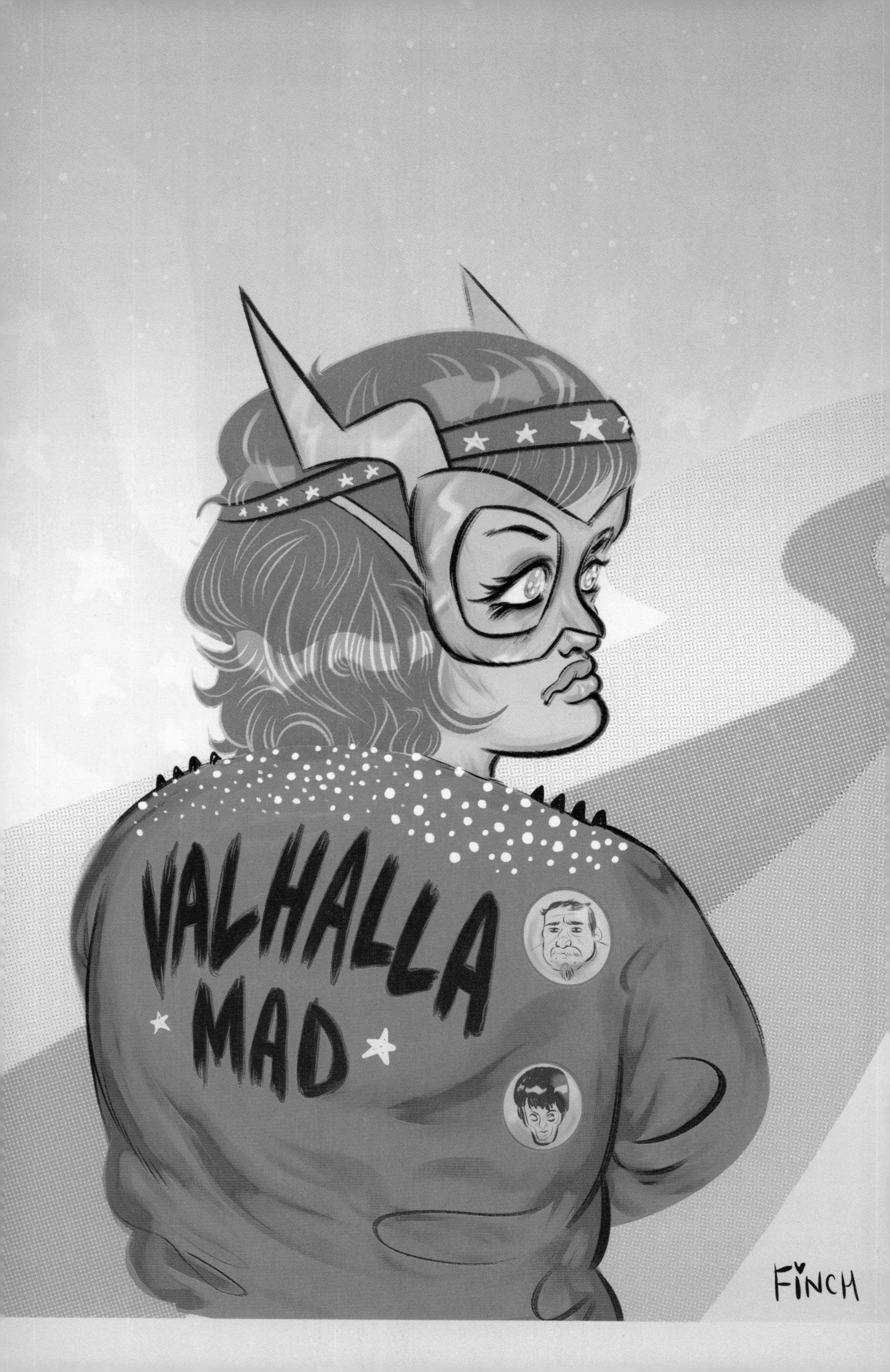
VALHALLA
MAD
FINCH

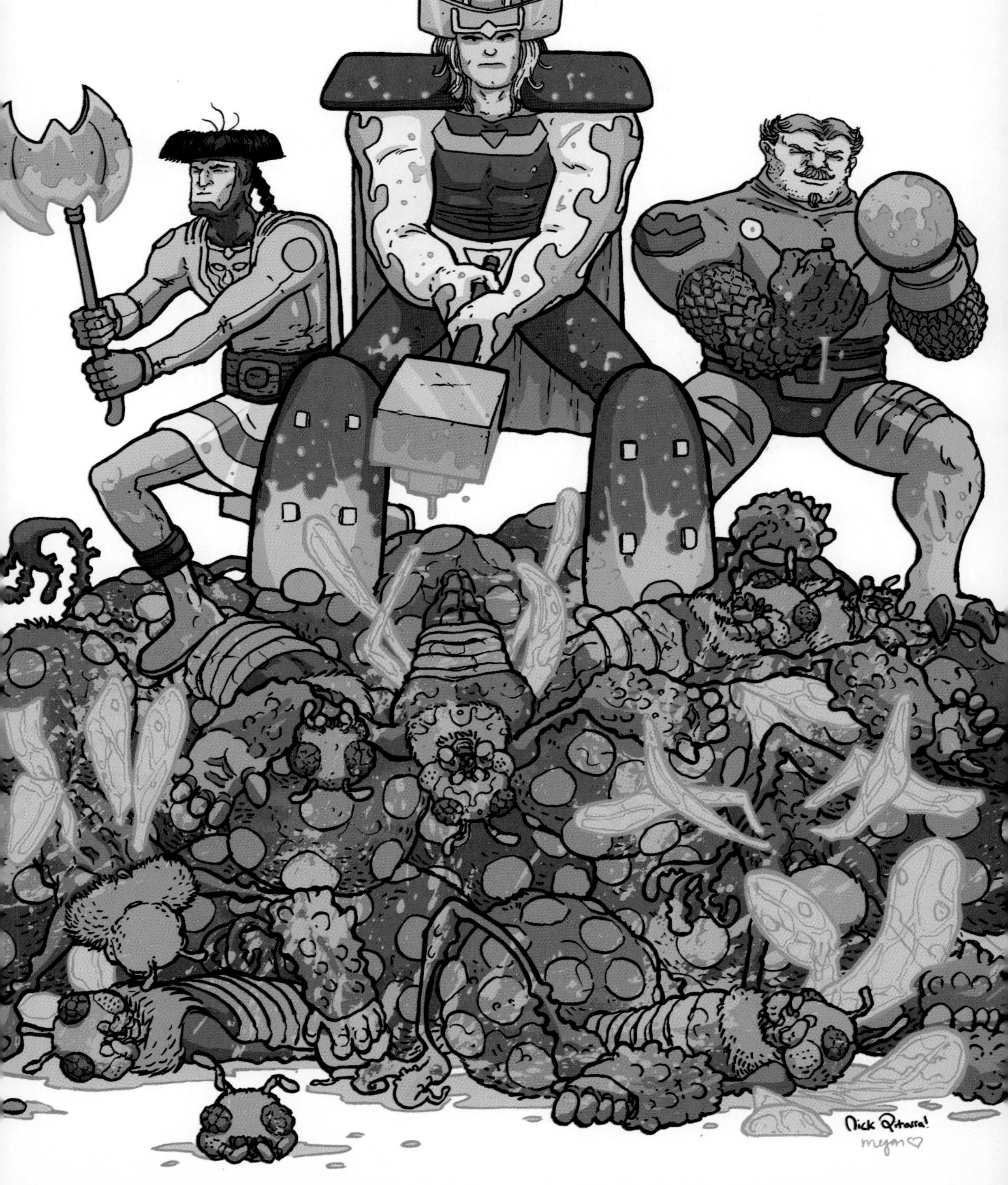
Nick Pitarra!
megan♡

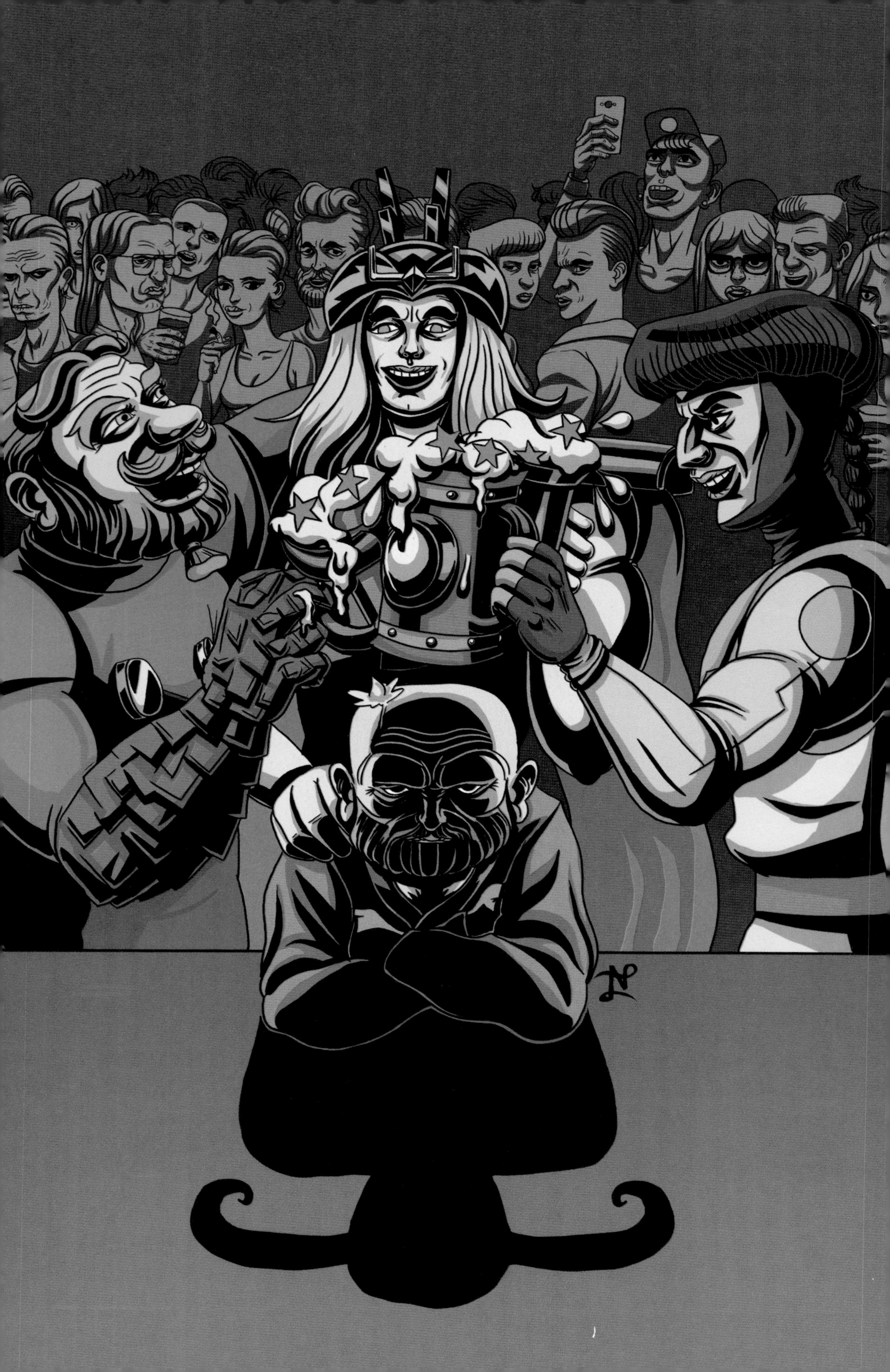

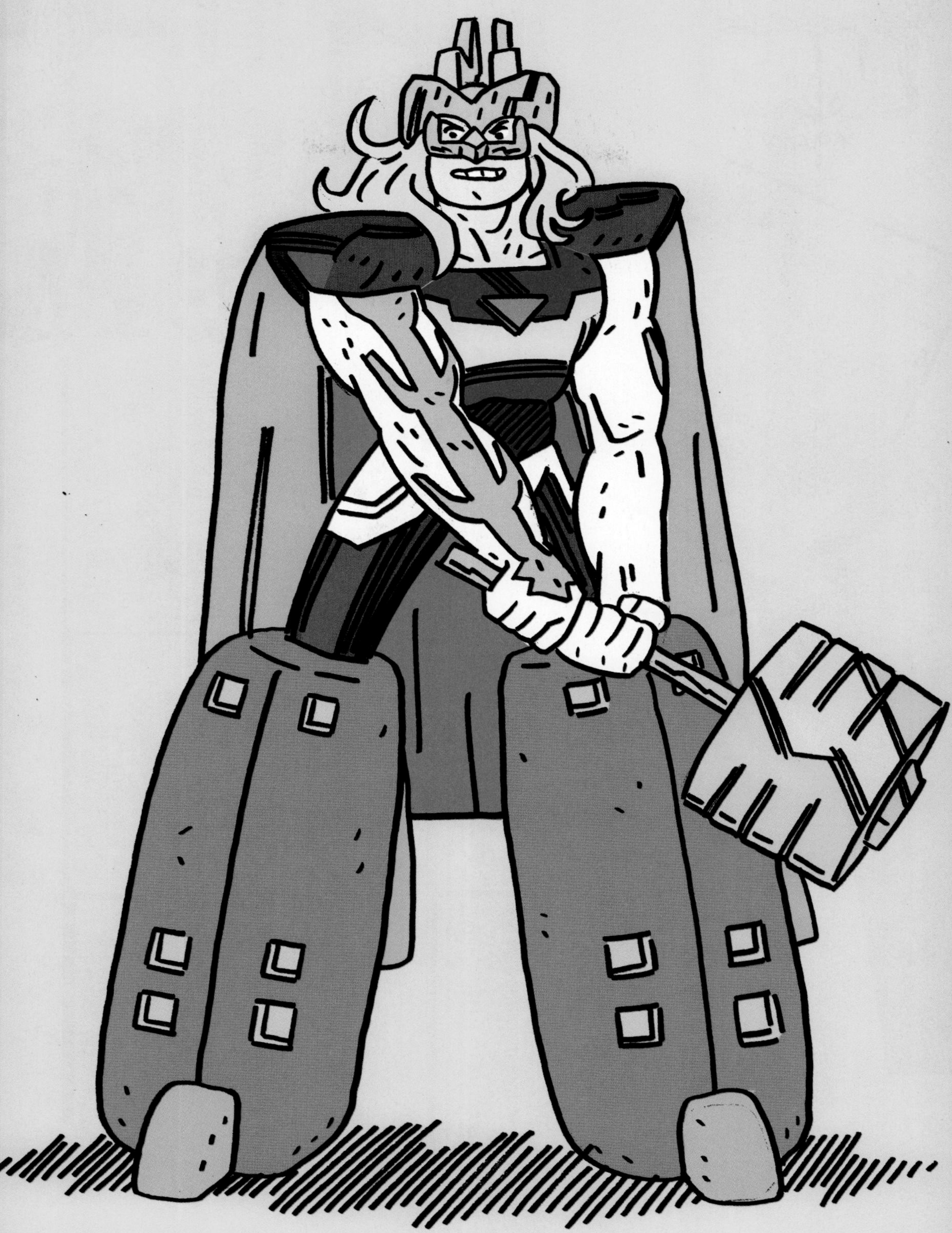

MACLEAN

PAUL MAYBURY 2015

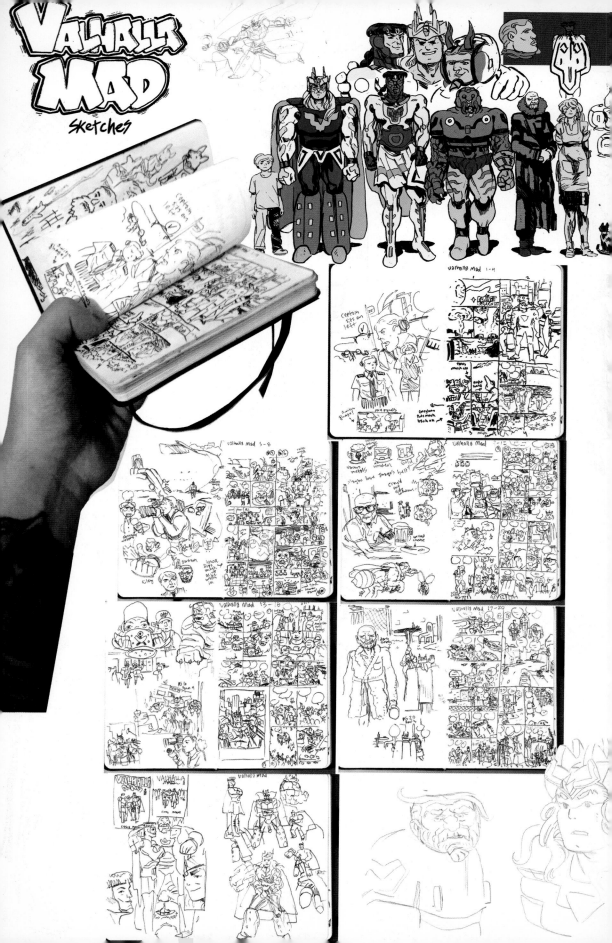

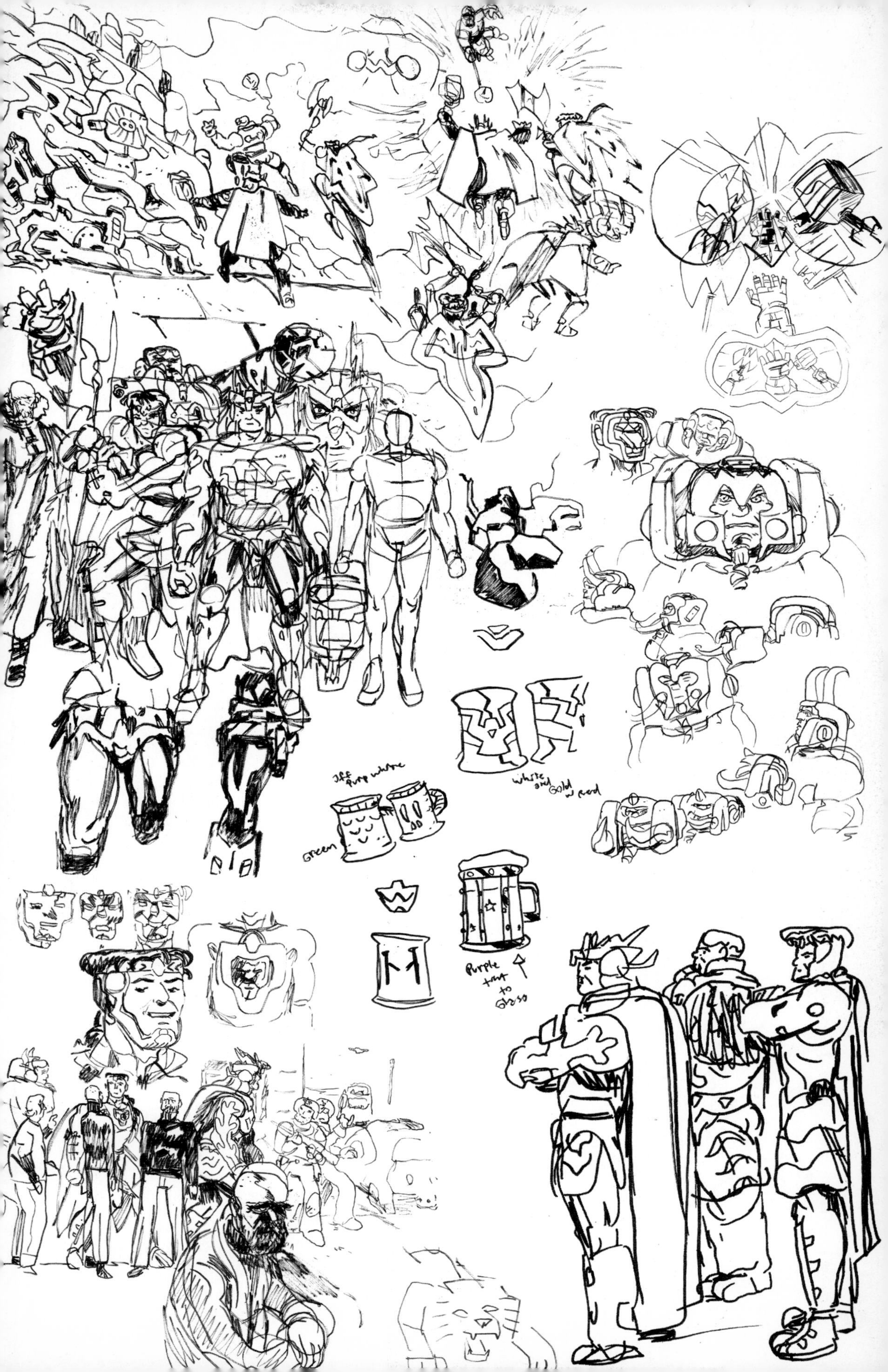
white and Gold w red
Green
Purple

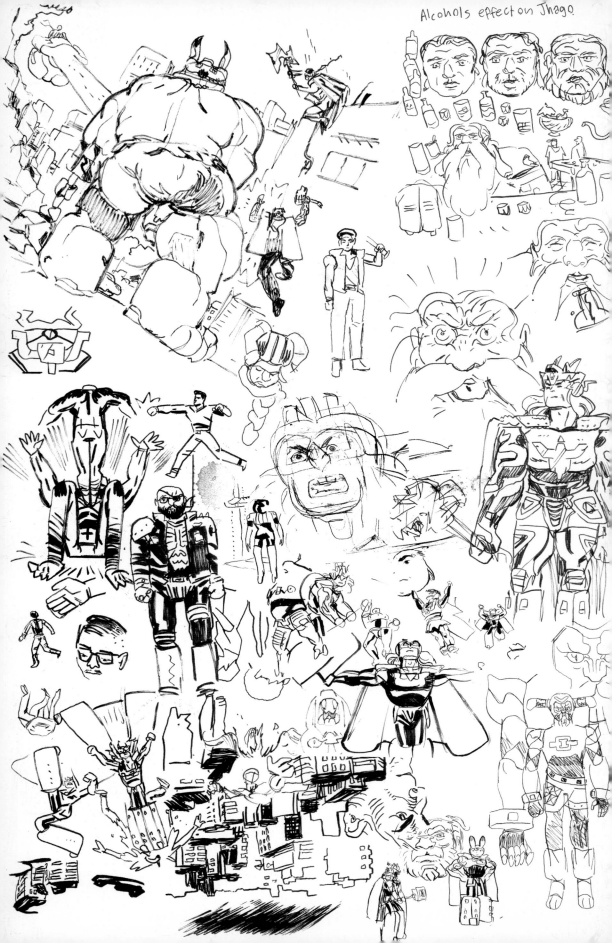

Alcohols effect on Jhago.

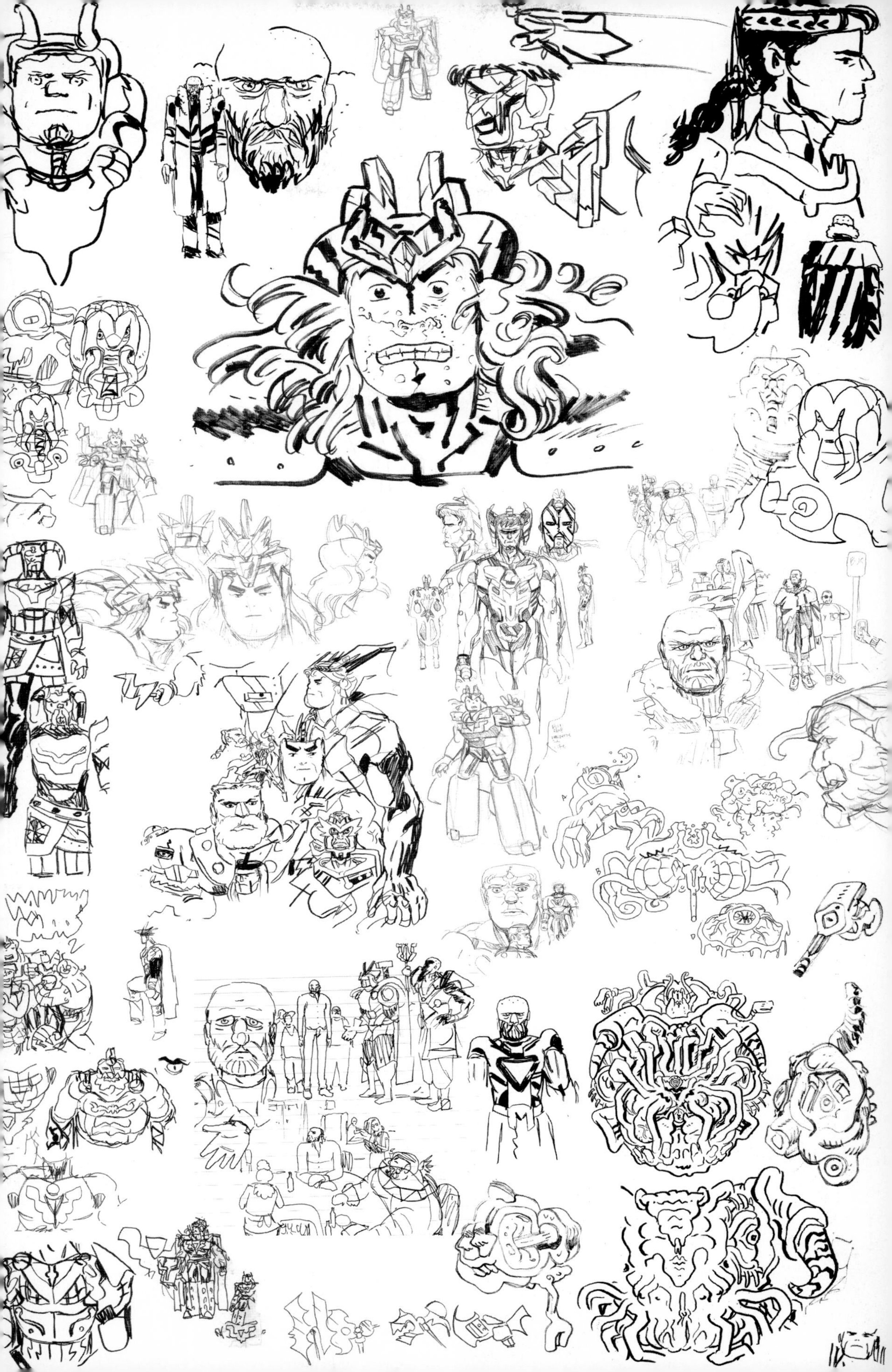

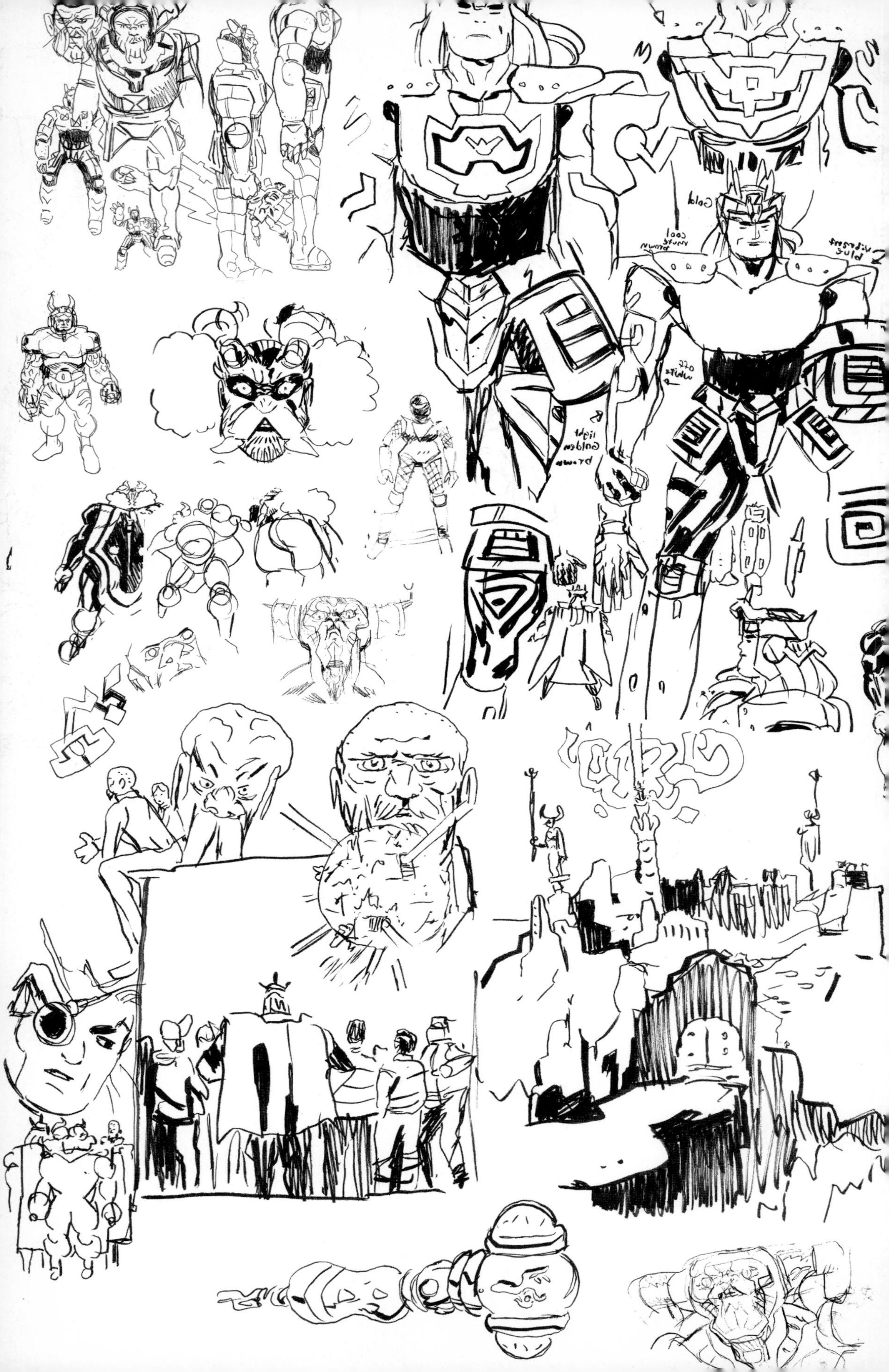

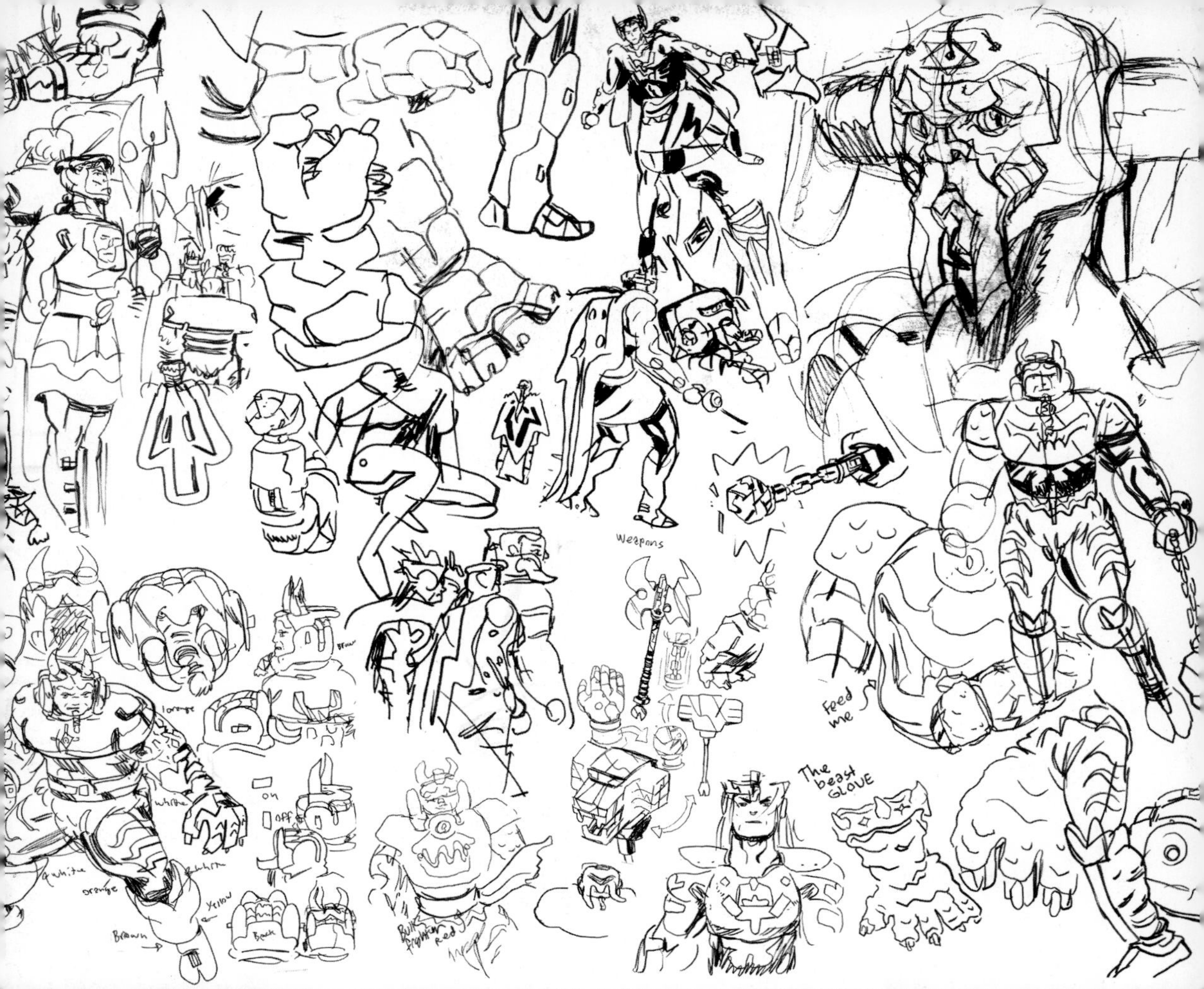
orange
white
white
orange
Yellow
Brown
on
off
Back
Weapons
Feed me
The beast GLOVE

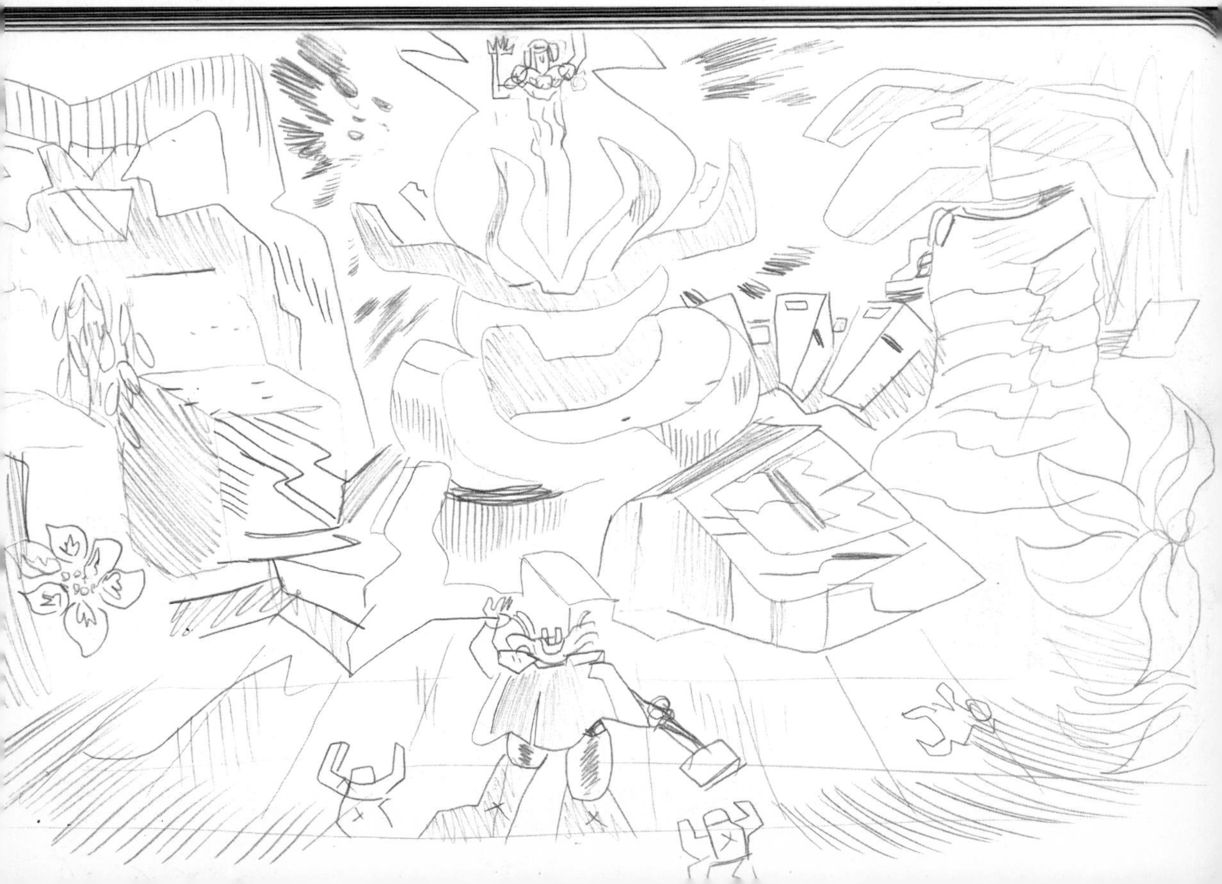

Other Works by Joe Casey

GØDLAND
VOLUME ONE
"HELLO, COSMIC!"
JOE CASEY • TOM SCIOLI

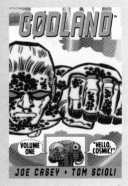

Gødland
(with Tom Scioli)

THE BOUNCE

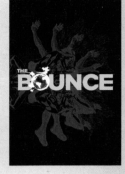

The Bounce
(with David Messina/
Sonia Harris)

SEX
JOE CASEY BOOK ONE PIOTR KOWALSKI
THE SUMMER OF HARD

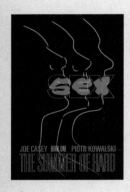

Sex
(with Piotr Kowalski)

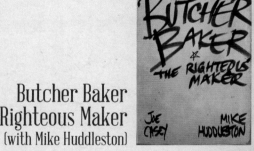

BUTCHER BAKER
THE RIGHTEOUS MAKER
JOE CASEY
MIKE HUDDLESTON

Butcher Baker
The Righteous Maker
(with Mike Huddleston)

FULL MOON FEVER
CASEY
GERARD
COUCEIRO

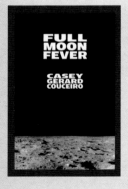

Full Moon Fever
(with Caleb Gerard/
Damian Couceiro)

THE MILKMAN MURDERS
JOE CASEY
STEVE PARKHOUSE

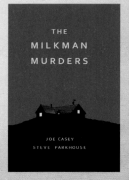

The Milkman Murders
(with Steve Parkhouse)

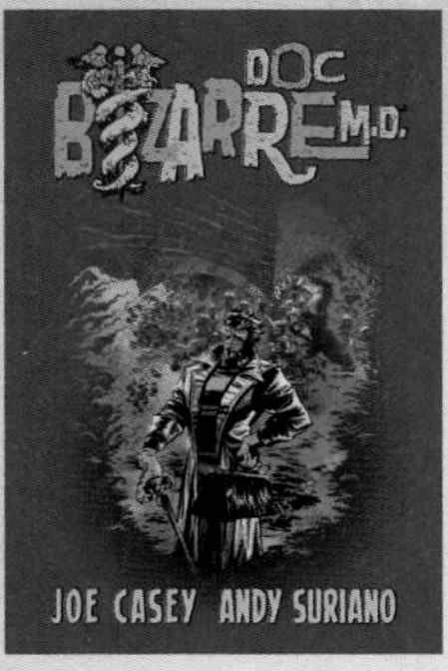
DOC BIZARRE M.D.
JOE CASEY ANDY SURIANO

Doc Bizarre, M.D.
(with Andy Suriano)

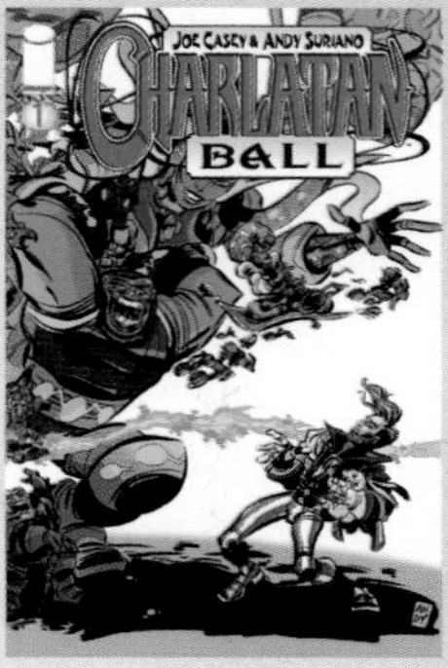
JOE CASEY & ANDY SURIANO
CHARLATAN
BALL

Charlatan Ball
(with Andy Suriano)

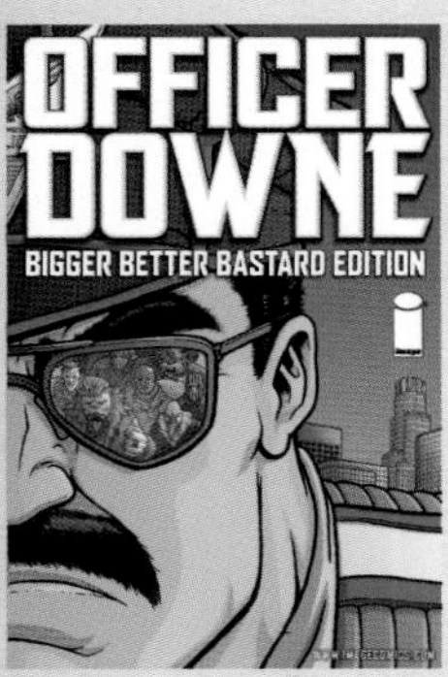
OFFICER
DOWNE
BIGGER BETTER BASTARD EDITION

Officer Downe
(with Chris Burnham)

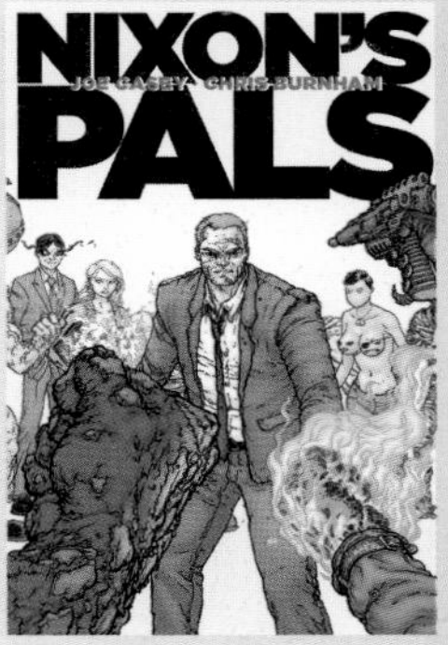
NIXON'S
JOE CASEY CHRIS BURNHAM
PALS

Nixon's Pals
(with Chris Burnham)

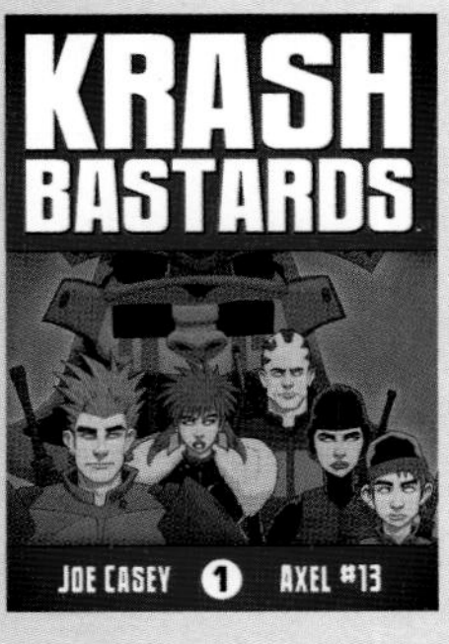
KRASH
BASTARDS
JOE CASEY 1 AXEL #13

Krash Bastards
(with Axel 13)

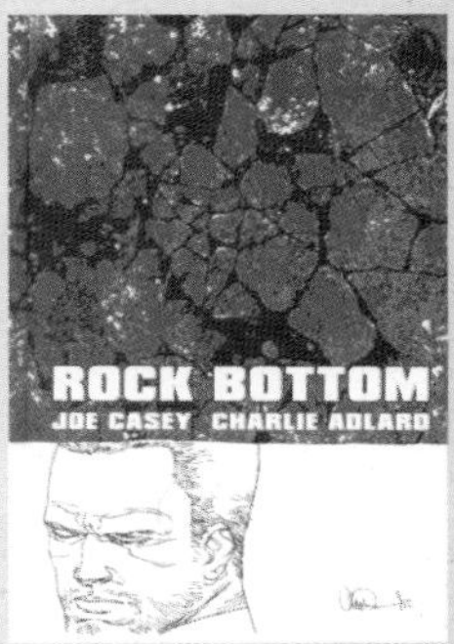
ROCK BOTTOM
JOE CASEY CHARLIE ADLARD

Rock Bottom
(with Charlie Adlard)

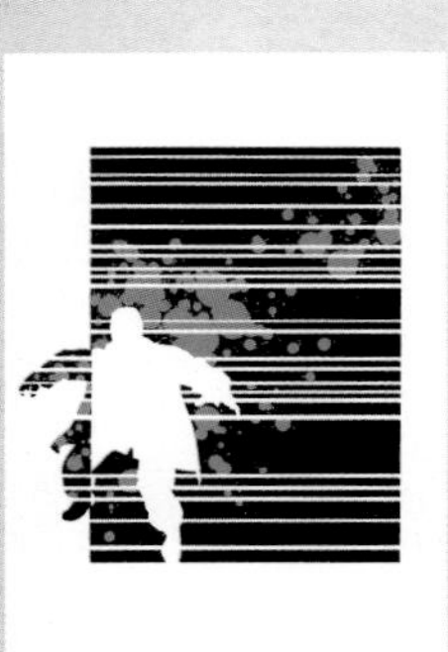

Codeflesh
(with Charlie Adlard)

VARIANT COVER FOR ISSUE #1 BY NICK PITARRA

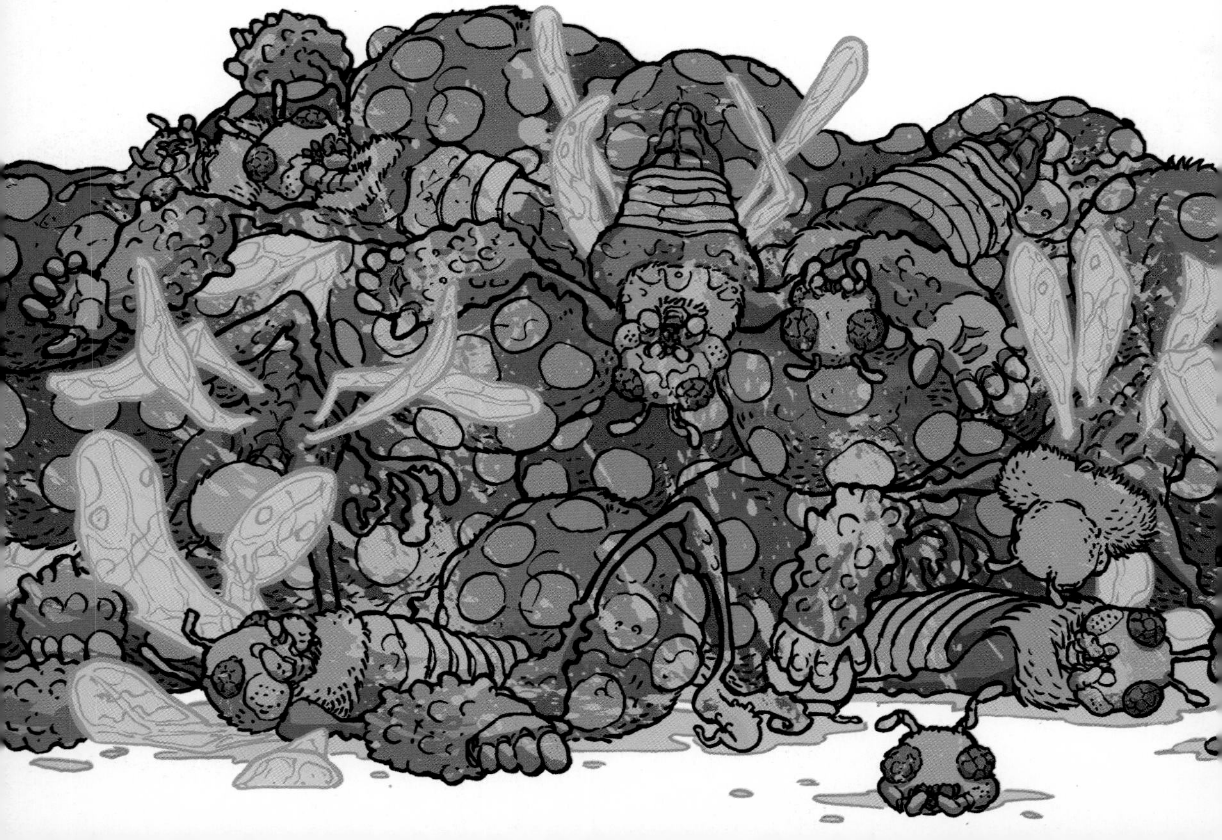

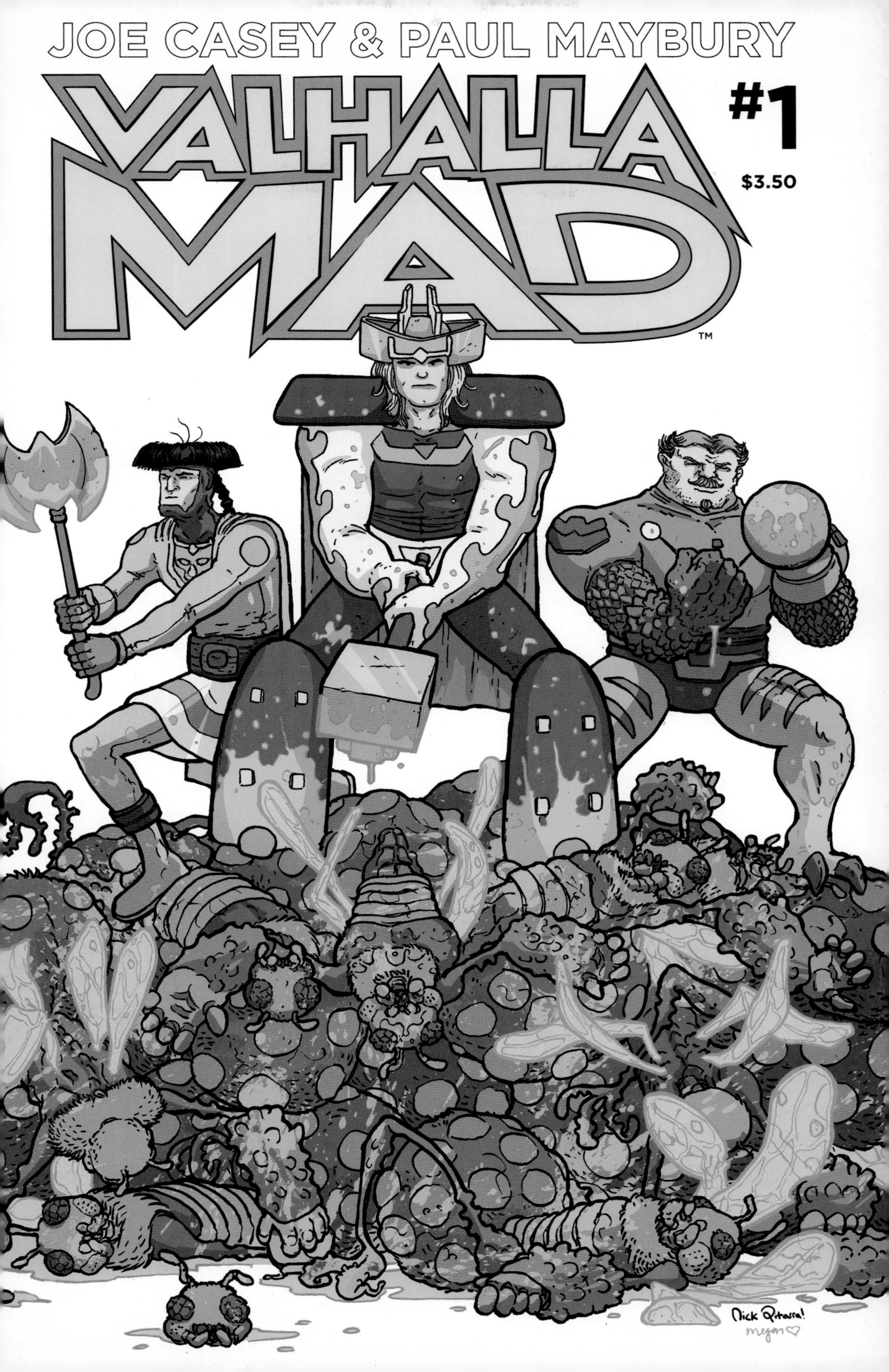
JOE CASEY & PAUL MAYBURY
VALHALLA MAD
#1
$3.50
™
Nick Pitarra!
megan

IMAGE COMICS, INC.
Robert Kirkman - Chief Operating Officer
Erik Larsen - Chief Financial Officer
Todd McFarlane - President
Marc Silvestri - Chief Executive Officer
Jim Valentino - Vice-President

Eric Stephenson - Publisher
Corey Murphy - Director of Sales
Jeff Boison - Director of Publishing Planning & Book Trade Sales
Jeremy Sullivan - Director of Digital Sales
Kat Salazar - Director of PR & Marketing
Emily Miller - Director of Operations
Branwyn Bigglestone - Senior Accounts Manager
Sarah Mello - Accounts Manager
Drew Gill - Art Director
Jonathan Chan - Production Manager
Meredith Wallace - Print Manager
Briah Skelly - Publicity Assistant
Randy Okamura - Marketing Production Designer
David Brothers - Branding Manager
Ally Power - Content Manager
Addison Duke - Production Artist
Vincent Kukua - Production Artist
Sasha Head - Production Artist
Tricia Ramos - Production Artist
Jeff Stang - Direct Market Sales Representative
Emilio Bautista - Digital Sales Associate
Chloe Ramos-Peterson - Administrative Assistant
IMAGECOMICS.COM